DANCING BETWEEN T

Based on actual events I can still remember

from the 1980s in New York City

By Nelson Aspen

A RED SKY PRESENTS BOOK

This is a work of fiction. Names, characters, businesses, places, events and incidents are either the products of the author's imagination or used in a fictitious manner. Any resemblance to actual persons, living or dead, or to actual events, is purely coincidental.

Book and Cover Design by Jerry Todd

ISBN: 978-1-941015-78-0

Published by Red Sky Presents
A Division of Red Sky Entertainment

To my dad, the first Nelson Aspen,
who always remarked that my knack for survival
was like dancing between the raindrops.
And to New York City.

INTRODUCTION

Heading for the Nineties

A light, freezing drizzle should have made it miserable for the assembled throngs gathered in Times Square to ring out the 1980s. The decade that kicked off with Jimmy Carter in the White House and John Lennon murdered outside his lavish apartment building, the Dakota, was finally coming to a close and almost everyone seemed excited about the prospect of the Nineties, so what if it was bone-chilling? Standing shoulder to shoulder, underneath umbrellas, revelers excitedly awaited midnight while millions of Americans were at home watching Dick Clark's traditional countdown on ABC's New Year's Rockin' Eve.

In downtown Manhattan, high atop the North Tower on the 107th floor of the World Trade Center, the Windows on the World restaurant was at full capacity, even if the usually spectacular view was non-existent due to the outside elements of windswept sleet. The atmosphere was energetic and festive, with diners already well lubricated by 10p.m., their party hats and tiaras askew on their heads and intermittent blares from noisemakers reverberating around the complex, even with two hours still to go. Most people had finished their Jacques Pepin and James Beard conceived dinners of Whole Lobster in Star Anise Broth and Vegetables with Garlic Croutons, Sautéed Fresh Venison with Wild Mushrooms and Ginger Potatoes, or Roast Breast of Mallard Duck with Grapes, and had moved on to the serious task of keeping the party going until the midnight hour. A line was forming outside both the Men's and Ladies rooms, more likely for patrons to recharge themselves with cocaine bumps than to actually use the toilets.

At a banquet closest to the southeastern expanse that would ordinarily have offered a spectacular view of the Statue of Liberty, four friends mulled over their dessert choices with a distinct lack of enthusiasm. For them, the new decade upon them promised important changes. While much of it looked significantly brighter than the weather, the mere fact that their unified world was poised to fracture made them disquieted.

The two young men at the table, T.J. and Leo, aged twenty-six and twenty-seven respectively, had switched back to their preferred cocktail, screwdrivers, after polishing off a bottle of the least expensive Chardonnay. They were very particular about how these were to be prepared: in the style of Leo's Aunt Jenny, an alcoholic bartender who had passed away of liver disease in her early forties. "Boys, they're no good unless you can see through them," she'd exclaim as she'd add a splash of orange juice to the vodka, just for color.

The two women who sat across from them, Bella and Carolyn Lee, were not imbibing. The former had just turned the big 3-0 while in her latest stint in rehab and the latter was six months into a surprise pregnancy at age thirty-four. However, cigarettes were in constant rotation for almost everyone in the room except for Leo, who had somehow never picked up the habit. The tobacco haze inside the dining room was nearly as thick as the fog that would roll in on New Year's Day.

“We have nearly two hours to go, guys,” Leo said, lifting his glass after checking the time on his latest new Rolex. “What’ll we drink to now?”

“No one says we have to stay here ‘til Midnight,” Bella said.

“Well, you know we can’t go back to my place,” Carolyn Lee commented with a tinge of sadness.

“Who says we have to go anywhere?” Bella countered. “We can make it an early night.”

T.J. took a gulp of his drink, big enough to feel the vodka sting the back of his throat. “No one is going anywhere until 1990,” he declared.

“Some of us are going further away than others,” said Leo, casting his eyes away from T.J.

So there it was. The unspoken topic that was dragging them down. T.J. knew he had to address it, but he was determined to do it in the most upbeat way. “It will only be for a year or two until I find the great gig. And if nothing comes up, I’ll come back and enroll at NYU.”

There was a moment of uncomfortable silence which T.J. determinedly pushed through by brightly adding, “Besides, Leo, you’re moving up to Citibank and Carolyn Lee is going to be busy changing diapers. Or at least supervising the nanny to change diapers.”

“Don’t worry,” Bella offered in a comical monotone, “I won’t be going anywhere at all.”

“At least we’re not leaving New York,” Leo said.

T.J. wasn’t used to dissent, especially from his best friend, so he shot back defensively, “I’m sorry, Mr. Moneybags, that I don't earn almost six figures like you do. Besides, since you moved in with Don, we hardly see you anymore."

" That's not fair, T.J. When does Don ever stop us from going out?

T.J. polished off the last of his drink and immediately pulled a fresh cigarette out of the sterling silver case that was always in his breast pocket. Bella heaved a heavy sigh and cut the tension with, "God, I wish I had some coke." T.J. reflexively patted his other pocket and she quickly added, "No, no...I wasn't asking. I've been good so far, I don't want to blow it again. No pun intended."

"Change will be good for all of us," Carolyn Lee suddenly sang out, offering up her club soda in a toast. "But thank God for all the blessings of the Eighties."

"Or we wouldn't all be sitting here right now," Leo added.

"Holy fuck, how did we survive?" Bella asked in wonderment.

T.J. knew the answer. "It's like my dad always tells me: we have been dancing between the raindrops."

CHAPTER ONE

Welcome to the City

Thomas John Porter, Jr. had turned seventeen just over a month before he arrived in New York City in September of 1980. Everyone called him "T.J.," since his father back in Connecticut was the one-and-only Thomas John Porter, Esq. and his were big, if not impossible, shoes to fill. Nonetheless, T.J. was the apple of his parents' eyes: an only child, excellent student and "squeaky clean" in both behavior and appearance. That was the only reason he was driving into Manhattan with a rented U-Haul truck full of his belongings instead of being dropped off at a college dormitory which had, until recently, been the assumed plan. The Porters couldn't say No to their son when he skillfully argued his case to deviate from a traditional transition from high school to college in lieu of pursuing a professional acting career.

T.J. reasoned that since he had graduated a year ahead of schedule (having precociously been able to skip the second grade) and as class Valedictorian, to boot ("I'm not smarter than anybody else," he told his classmates, "I'm just really excellent at taking tests!"), he could afford to take a gap year to try his hand at acting and get a jump start on the competition. He had been bitten by the acting bug early and encouraged by his doting mother, Janice, not to settle for the leads in all the school plays but to pursue local community theater and even some local TV commercials.

While other kids' extracurricular activities were usually related to sports, T.J. spent long hours outside of class learning lines, rehearsing and taking voice and movement classes. He definitely had talent, but more importantly he had humor and confidence. Not many kids could hold their own with the adults in social situations, but he always made eye contact and held up his end of the conversation with wit and style. His handshake was firm and his manners always impeccable. While some of his school mates may have found that prissy or irritating, most people genuinely found him winning. So his proposition to forego college seemed perfectly reasonable, even to his Navy veteran dad, who was now a successful lawyer specializing in medical malpractice.

That didn't mean there wasn't pressure. The senior Porter negotiated a generous deal with his namesake, having calculated what each month would cost for T.J.'s tuition, room and board. That figure would be his monthly allowance for exactly twelve months and, if he wasn't supporting himself with a job in the Arts by the following September, it would be off to freshman year with the other 18 year olds.

There was just enough in the budget for T.J. to rent a decent sized one bedroom apartment right in the heart of the theater district on West 45th Street, directly across the street from the Martin Beck Theater. T.J.'s new home was on the top floor of the six-story building built in 1914 and obviously hadn't been updated since. It did have an elevator, which worked sporadically, and it had roaches. Lots of roaches. And even though the entire Times Square neighborhood had at least one XXX movie theater, Go-Go bar, peep show or sex shoppe for every legitimate Broadway theater, rehearsal space or dance studio, to a stage-struck boy who grew up inside a colonial farmhouse with manicured lawn and white picket fence . . . it was Heaven!

After T.J. unpacked his meager kitchen wares, including a brand new Mr. Coffee coffeemaker, an electric hot plate and an old set of dishes and utensils Janice was happy to replace for herself, he hung up his calendar next to the refrigerator. He crossed out the days every morning, keenly aware that the clock was ticking and he had a big To-Do List. Get an answering service, pound the pavement with the brand new headshots he'd had taken over the summer and sign up for a reputable acting class.

There weren't many preppy teenagers walking the mean streets of Times Square who weren't tourists, but T.J. didn't notice. He was too mesmerized with the sights, sounds and smells exploding all around him, day and night. Many of them were unpleasant, but all of them added to the symphony of excitement as he feasted on delectable NYC pizza slices and bottles of Budweiser. The drinking age was eighteen and no one ever asked for I.D. He regularly purchased Back Stage, the weekly Arts industry trade publication with casting news, career advice, theater listings and ads for all the various services an aspiring actor could want or need. He would sit hunched over it at his little kitchen table, pretending not to notice scurrying cockroaches, as he circled items of interest with his red marking pen while the light of the famous Coca-Cola sign bathed the room in a red glow. No set designer could have conceived a more stereotypical depiction of a "struggling actor's flat."

One characteristic T.J. did not possess was patience. He was privileged and accustomed to things coming easily for him, scholastically and socially, so he didn't like to sit still. By the end of the first week in his new pad, he had not only set up his home, he had appointments all around town to meet with various acting coaches and agents.

He had read about "Second Act'ing" Broadway shows, which was the colloquialism for slipping into a theater during its Intermission to enjoy the second half of a performance without having to buy a ticket. Ordinarily a stickler for playing by the rules, T.J.'s budget wouldn't allow for frequent patronage so he quickly became an expert at Second Act'ing—and why not!? Not only was he smack dab in the center of the theatrical universe, he was certain that all working actors would want their performances seen by as large an audience as possible.

Loving the musical theater genre, his long wish list included revivals of Brigadoon and The Music Man as well as 42nd Street at the Majestic Theater and the drama, Charlie and Algernon, at the Helen Hayes Theater. T.J. had played Young Charlie in a Connecticut production while in high school and was eager to see this version.

He was enchanted by all the Broadway houses and had a special fondness for Shubert's Music Box, built in 1920 and only a block away from his apartment. His parents had taken him to his first Broadway show there a few years earlier—Side by Side by Sondheim—and that was followed by a memorable school trip with his high school drama club to see Deathtrap. Another show he had already done was the classic, The Fantasticks, so he paid full price and braved an unnerving subway ride to Greenwich Village to attend a performance. It was Off-Broadway's longest running production, having opened in 1960, but T.J. thought his company had done a better job back at the Connecticut Yankees Playhouse.

Returning home from the Village via the Number 2 subway line, T.J. emerged from the 42 Street/Times Square station and navigated his way toward Eighth Avenue with all the vigor and alertness of a native New Yorker, dodging the panhandlers and prostitutes that lined the littered sidewalks. A block before getting home, he passed the old Milford Plaza Hotel, which was undergoing a much needed renovation, having been mostly neglected since it was built in 1961. Tucked adjacent, barely noticeable beneath all the graffiti-covered scaffolding was a tiny establishment named Tom Kats. The "S' was burned out on the neon sign of this seedy bar but something about it piqued T.J.'s curiosity, beyond the fact that they shared a first name.

It was still early and he wasn't tired. In fact, he was eager to get The Fantasticks' theme song, Try to Remember, out of his head, so he pushed open the door and walked right in. His first thought was that the electricity had to be out: that's how dark it was. Once his eyes adjusted to the dim lighting, he was able to see just how derelict this place was, even though it was impressively busy. An assortment of barflies who looked like they were part of the furniture, and older men of all shapes and sizes were visible through the fog of cigarette smoke. The few women there looked not to be women at all. Even a country bumpkin, T.J. thought, could spot that these were transvestites and as eager for paying customers as the hookers he'd just passed on his walk from the subway. Queen's new hit song, Another One Bites the Dust, was playing on the ancient jukebox, but T.J.'s entrance seemed to stop everything going on except for the music.

"Come on in, baby," one of the ladies said, scratching herself.

T.J. didn't hesitate. From his years in community theater, he was used to being around grownups, especially those who drank and smoked. Two guys on barstools managed to shift their considerable girths to allow him to go right up to the bar. The bartender, a 40-ish bald guy with mascara on his eyelashes and a few missing teeth in his mouth, asked, "What'll you have?"

Knowing he wouldn't want to put his lips on any of the glassware there, T.J. asked for a bottle of Budweiser.

"Where you visiting from?" one of the men beside him inquired.

"I'm not visiting. I just moved here," T.J. answered matter of factly, taking the bottle from the bartender.

"Welcome to the neighborhood, kid. First one's on the house." He smiled, showing that the missing teeth were preferable to the crooked and discolored ones that remained.

As the next song began, Diana Ross' Upside Down, T.J. remembered how he dealt with the annoyance of being surrounded by chronic cigarette smoke on the advice of his father: "If you can't beat 'em, join 'em. Then it won't bother you." So he asked the bartender if they sold cigarettes and was pointed to the vending machine in the corner by a pinball machine with a sign that read, Out of Order.

T.J. walked over to it, fishing quarters out of the pockets of his khakis, and one of the skinny ladies gyrated alongside him as if to encourage him to dance. He smiled politely, genuinely amused. He noticed two guys in the corner, who looked to be not much older than he. They were dancing close together, sleepily, as if they were drunk or stoned. Instinctively, T.J. knew it was a sexual encounter.

T.J. had never danced with a man, but at that moment he decided he definitely wanted to.

To distract himself, T.J. forced his thoughts to the acting class he'd just enrolled in. It would be taught by a popular guru of the Circle-In-The-Square theater company, Sarah Saperstein. Her methods were well reviewed (at least according to the quarter page ads that ran in every issue of Back Stage) and class size was limited to only twenty students, so when Sarah herself answered the phone and said she had one available slot left for the next six month session, T.J. grabbed it. He prepared two monologues, one comic and one dramatic, and excitedly walked across town to the world famous Carnegie Hall where the classes were conducted in one of a windowless rehearsal studio.

T.J.'s classmates were a mixture of other aspiring actors in their twenties and a few older people who looked like they'd been around the showbiz block more than a few times. One lady, Veronica, had been a nun in the chorus of the original Broadway cast of The Sound of Music and was trying to resuscitate her career now that her kids were grown. T.J. was a bit star struck by the thought that he was studying alongside someone who'd been in such a hit show, with Mary Martin no less. When it came time to team up with a scene partner, he unhesitatingly offered himself up to Veronica, who was flattered and suggested they work on something from Tea and Sympathy, the famous coming-of-age play about a young man and an older woman.

Saperstein's teaching style was Stanislavsky meets Method with a dash of Uta Hagen thrown in for good measure. In other words, it was like combining therapy sessions with script reading. One young woman, Randi, was working on a monologue from the Greek play Antigone, but Saperstein first managed to reduce her to tears by getting her to admit that she hated the size of her ample bosoms.

"Put your hands on your breasts," she commanded to her trembling student, "and fill in the blank. Say, My ____ Breasts."

Haltingly, Randi started with "My Big Breasts."

"Keep going!" Saperstein yelled. "Give me more!"

"My giant, annoying breasts—"

"What do you feel about those giant breasts, Randi?" Saperstein interrupted. "Hold on to them and tell me!"

T.J. and everyone else in the room was mesmerized by what they were watching as poor Randi clutched her breasts.

"My Agonizing Breasts! My Hateful Breasts!"

"What else? What else!"

Randi's eyes began to spill out tears as she shook violently and said more loudly, "My Father Doesn't Love Me Breasts!"

Saperstein leapt from her seat with a thrill in her voice saying, "Yes! Now go from there!"

While Randi sobbed and held on to her big tits, she then

launched into her Antigone monologue. When she finished, Saperstein led the room in applause for Randi's job well done.

T.J. was in no rush for whatever treatment the teacher had in store for him, especially as he didn't consider himself as having any inner torments sufficient to such a task.

The following week, when it was time for T.J. and Veronica to perform their scene for the first time, Saperstein had some praise for Veronica but wasn't as kind to T.J. "You're just phoning it in," she told him. "You're merely performing the lines. You're not feeling their intention."

His character, Tom Lee, is accused by school mates of being effeminate and is seduced by the older woman who wants to help him assert his true masculinity. Saperstein was blunt and asked T.J. if he'd ever been teased at school about being homosexual.

T.J. was immediately self conscious, being asked something so personal in a room full of new people. "Yeah," he admitted. "You know how it is in school. Especially 'cause I was doing plays."

"And are you a homosexual, T.J.?"

He swallowed hard. He'd never been so directly confronted about anything. There was a pregnant pause while everyone in the class looked expectantly at T.J. for his answer. To T.J., it felt like an eternity.

Used to being a teacher's pet, he wasn't sure what the correct answer should be. Was there even a correct answer? His mind raced. Of course he was attracted to men, but he'd only ever kissed and petted with girls. If you're still a virgin, can you even know what your sexuality is?

"I think," he stumbled, searching for the word, "I think I am bisexual."

Saperstein sat back, studying him for a moment before she replied, "You think? Well, your assignment is to figure it out before you can really do this scene any kind of justice. You work on that."

As she called up the next scene partners, T.J. took his seat. He felt flushed. How was he going to figure it out?

It weighed on him the whole walk home. He'd never worried about sexuality before and thought about both genders whenever he thought of sex. Accustomed to being around adults of all persuasions, he was easily and equally titillated by the nude models in a Playboy magazine as he was by heartthrobs like David Cassidy and Andy Gibb. By the time he made his way westward to Broadway, dusk was setting in and he was looking around at people, searching for one who would arouse him.

Passing by a deserted schoolyard playground, he noticed someone climbing on the jungle gym. He stopped to observe through the chain link fence and watched a fit young man doing a series of acrobatics on the bars. It wasn't just horse play—this person actually had serious gymnastic skills. It was like a private show by Olympian Kurt Thomas!

The man swung around and, in doing so, faced T.J. and noticed him watching. He smiled and did a few more moves, obviously enjoying the feeling of having an audience. He finished off with an impressive cartwheel and round off, purposely landing within a few feet of his admiring fan. They were separated only by the fence wire.

"That was amazing," T.J. told him.

"Thank you," the well-built man answered in a French accent. "It is a living."

"You're a gymnast?"

"Yes. I am working for the Big Apple Circus. We performed at this school today."

The man smiled and his handsome face crinkled with laugh lines. He moved right up to the fence and T.J. could see that his eyes were green.

"Do you live close?" he asked T.J.

Smiling back, T.J. said. "Two blocks."

The French circus performer walked around the fence to join T.J. and together they walked to the little apartment on West 45th Street. The man stayed for hours, showing off more skills than he had displayed on the playground. They never asked each other's names; in fact they barely spoke at all. But T.J. had his answer now for Sarah Saperstein.

It was T.J.'s first taste, literally, of what it was like to be physical with another man—and he wanted more. Since he couldn't count on running into another handsome French acrobat while walking down the block, he decided to visit one of the city's many gay bars or clubs listed in the Village Voice. New Wave music was beginning to get a lot of play on mainstream radio and The Saint over on Second Avenue was known as the place to hear it and to dance and drink with other horny young men. He dug through his closet looking for anything that could be considered Manhattan fashion and was disappointed with his predominantly preppy wardrobe. Christmas would be coming soon and he would have to remember to ask his mother for the gift of a trip to Bloomingdales.

Settling on a black turtleneck and his favorite Jordache jeans, T.J. bumped his way over to the East side on a cross town bus and treated himself to a big bowl of spaghetti and meatballs at a little Trattoria around the corner from the club. He tried his first glass of Chianti, which he thought was overrated, and switched to a Coke. He was excited to see what kind of guys he would discover that night.

Once inside, however, the most mesmerizing encounter was the club itself. The gigantic circular dance floor was topped by a planetarium dome, and five hundred speakers blasted out the pulsating music in something called surround sound. Above and beyond that dome was a balcony from where you could look down on the packed dance floor. After fighting his way through the crowd to the bar for a beer, T.J. hiked up there to take in the view. It seemed like there were hundreds of men appearing and disappearing in the strobe lights, gyrating and swaying so closely together that they seemed to be attached to each other. T.J. could barely distinguish any one in particular and assumed there must have been a lot of drug use fueling them on. It really wasn't as much fun as he'd expected it to be, but it was interesting. He made his way back home shortly after midnight and was more motivated to get back to acting class the next afternoon. He definitely didn't see himself as a club kid.

The next take on the Tea & Sympathy scene was much improved, T.J. thought, and Saperstein was more encouraging.

Randi was conspicuously absent so he assumed she and her agonized breasts had dropped out. If he wasn't against losing the prepaid tuition fee, he might have done the same. Besides, he liked the way going to Carnegie Hall made him feel: like a true New York City actor. He may not have found an agent to represent him yet, but T.J. was proud of himself: in less than two months he had moved into the heart of Hell's Kitchen, enrolled in a reputable acting class and figured out that he was gay. What next?

Sarah Saperstein, he thought, may be of help to him as he prepared for a career on the stage, but T.J. was also drawn to the idea of working in television. He had grown up in the era of classic TV sitcoms like The Brady Bunch, M*A*S*H and All in the Family and, thanks to his grandmother, also enjoyed afternoon soap operas whenever he had a day off from school. Dark Shadows was his favorite because it combined horror movie themes with the daytime drama formula. A Back Stage ad for the Gotham TV Academy of Acting offered pay-as-you-go workshops with a roster of TV casting directors, so T.J. chose one affiliated with his Nana's favorite serial, Tomorrow's Promise.

He immediately took to the fast-paced style of acting. The casting director, a middle-aged bald man named Harry Cohn, was assisted by the show's Production Coordinator, a pretty olive-skinned girl, Isabella Black, who handed students Xeroxed copies of actual soap scripts. They were expected to learn on the spot and then perform in front of the video camera she operated. Harry would play back the scenes and critique them. T.J. loved seeing himself on the TV screen and, being so experienced at learning lines, was able to almost instantly memorize the dialogue. Harry seemed to have nothing but praise for him and only advised him to slow down his delivery and make everything half as big. "Television," Harry said, "is not a proscenium stage. The camera and microphones pick up the smallest of gestures and sounds, so it's a more intimate way of performing." T.J. got it, and instantly adjusted to the medium.

At the end of class, everyone inundated Harry and Isabella with their headshots and resumes, hoping to eventually be called in for actual work on Tomorrow's Promise. As T.J. turned his in, Isabella said, "Really nice job tonight." He smiled proudly and admitted, "It was fun." Harry looked up from his pile of 8x10 black-and-white glossies and added, "You should come back again next week."

So he did, and Harry gave T.J. a more complicated scene to perform alongside another student, an older actor. It was between a father and son, with T.J.'s character having to explain that he was going to give up his dream of going to medical school to marry the town tramp who had tricked him into getting her pregnant. Classic soap stuff. It would have been easy to camp it up, maybe even play it for laughs, but T.J. understood the assignment and treated it with all the earnest intent he gave to the drama of Tea and Sympathy.

Harry had no critique other than to caution T.J. against upstaging himself by turning his head away from the camera. "The greatest acting in the world doesn't count if the folks at home can't see it!"

That night, as the students were filtering out of the classroom, Isabella made a point of introducing herself (she was simply

"Bella" to friends) and telling T.J. that he should stay in touch with them via the occasional picture postcard and to let them know if he would be performing in any showcases around the City. "You're definitely soap material," she added. T.J. went home on a cloud and immediately addressed and stamped postcards to both Harry and Bella, thanking them for the classes and encouragement.

Starting the following day, T.J. added at least an hour of soap opera viewing to his schedule, determined to study the actors and be prepared in case he got the chance for a TV break. He found himself really enjoying As the World Turns and The Guiding Light, in addition to Tomorrow's Promise. When the final scene played for the day, he would then call his answering service to check for messages. He continued to scour Back Stage for auditions and performing opportunities (some of which actors had to pay for), believing Bella was sincere about coming to see him if he was on stage somewhere. As much as he disliked the idea of having to fork over money for the chance to be seen, he knew it was a means to an end, especially when faced with endless open calls to audition against a zillion other aspiring actors.

That opportunity, T.J. decided, would be in the form of a showcase dubbed Dottie O'Hara's Next Broadway Stars. A sixty-something Grande Dame, Dottie O'Hara was a veteran star of many Broadway musicals and TV comedies as well as a sought after guest panelist on game and talk shows. She was riding high on her most recent Tony Award and was a beloved pillar of the showbiz community. This showcase, for which T.J. had to audition and pay for, would highlight a dozen young talents, directed by the distinguished Ross Woodhouse and coached personally by Ms. O'Hara. T.J. tried out with the ballad, Soon It's Gonna Rain, from The Fantasticks and Dottie O'Hara decided he would perform that along with the up tempo novelty song by Irving Berlin, I Love a Piano.

Dottie was larger than life in every possible way her many fans would expect: brash, loud, and engagingly hammy. There was nothing subtle about her. Even rolling in an hour late for the noon rehearsals, obviously foggy with hangovers, was a stage-worthy performance.

"Good morning, my little ones," she'd say. "Somebody get Dottie a black coffee with extra Sweet 'n Low—and make it a double!" Inevitably, after her second or third cup from the bodega next to the rehearsal hall, she would pull the silver flask out of her purse and start liberally spiking them.

By then, any attempts at her giving any serious coaching or criticism went out the window and she would take over the taped-off area representing the stage. "No, no, no!" And she would wave at whichever of the young artists was giving it their all. "Do it like this!" She would then turn to the accompanist at the piano and say, "Hit it!" And she would launch into her own rendition of the number, wildly gesticulating with her over-the-top mannerisms, often slurring the lyrics. T.J. and the others would look at each other uncomfortably, but no one would dare interrupt her once she got started. At least it was a front row seat to an original performance by the lady herself.

Dottie was also in the unfortunate habit of making late night calls to her prodigies, always after imbibing too many drinks. When T.J.'s phone would ring and wake him around midnight, he knew exactly what to expect: rambling stories about her late husband who died unexpectedly of a massive heart attack only a year after they married, and after she had waited decades for him to be free from his first wife. For all her comedic skills and the joy she brought to her audiences, she was obviously a very sad and lonely lady. T.J. felt badly for her but wished she were less of a night owl.

The showcase performances went off without a hitch, T.J. wisely pulling back from Dottie's advice for broad comedy as she draped herself over the piano like a cat in heat and belted out, "I love me a P-I-A-N-O, Oh Oh Oh!" Unfortunately, however, in spite of T.J. mailing them several postcard reminders, neither Harry nor Bella made an appearance.

December of 1980 arrived and T.J. enjoyed his first Christmas season in New York City by taking in all the famous, traditional sights. The tree at Rockefeller Center, Macy's Santa Land and all the decorated window displays in the department stores along Fifth Avenue. Now that the Dottie O'Hara showcase was over and it hadn't resulted in the job opportunities he'd hoped for, T.J. was back on the open-call audition circuit.

He took the subway down to Greenwich Village to audition for a way Off-Broadway adult spin of the Snow White story called Someday My Prince Will Come, a bawdy fractured fairy tale that had absolutely nothing in common with the Walt Disney version. "Sir Duncelot" was the male lead and T.J. sang his usual ballad with appropriate schmaltz, ably accompanied by the musical director. The limited run would be an Equity Approved

Showcase, which meant no pay but the cast would be eligible to join the Actors Equity union of stage artists, so T.J. was hopeful. The producer, who would also be casting, sat in the darkened house of the tiny theater, several rows back from the stage. All T.J. could see was the small red glow of his cigarette.

"Thank you, Mr. Porter, that was very nice," said the producer, sounding almost as if he was suppressing a chuckle. Someone else was sitting beside him and they were whispering to each other. T.J. waited to see if he should clear the stage for the next actor or if they wanted more from him. Finally the producer said, "Instead of a monologue, we'd like you to tell us a joke."

"A joke," T.J. repeated, stalling for time. That was something he hadn't prepared. His mind raced to try and think of one.

"Any joke," the producer prodded.

He thought of all the off color jokes his dad used to tell to his pals at the Country Club, usually prompting a swat from his mother. "I'm afraid the only ones I know are . . . dirty."

"Even better," the voice in the dark enthused.

T.J. cleared his throat, took a deep breath and went for it with a delivery that would have made his father proud. He was determined to get that Actor's Equity Association union card, whatever it took.

"Tony and Angela were Italian newlyweds who spent the first night of their marriage in the home of her widowed mother, as was the tradition of their village," he began. "Mama was in the kitchen and told Angela—" and here he put on a very exaggerated, funny Italian accent—"You go uppa stairs and do your duty, I stay here and stir da sauce. In the bedroom, Tony took off his shirt and Angela comes running down crying, 'Mama, mama, Tony got the hair all over his back!' Mama says, 'Your papa had hair all over his back, he was a good husband, you go uppa stairs and do your duty, I stay here and stir da sauce.' In the bedroom, Tony took off his pants and Angela comes running down crying, 'Mama, mama, Tony got the hair all over his butt!' Mama says, "Your papa had hair all over his butt, he was a good husband, you go uppa stairs and do your duty, I stay here and stir da sauce.' In the bedroom, Tony took off his socks. One foot was normal, but the other was actually cut in half. Angela comes running down crying, 'Mama, mama, Tony got a foot-and-a-half!' Mama says, 'You stay here and stir da sauce, I'm a goin' uppa stairs!"

And on the punch line, T.J. got a big laugh from everyone in the theater.

"Thank you, Mr. Porter," the producer told him, standing up so he could be seen a little better. "We'll be in touch."

T.J. looked at the thirty-something producer, who was heavy-set and prematurely balding but masculine and attractive, and still smiling at him. T.J. was hopeful for a callback.

That night, even though there was still no message about the audition, T.J. was in a good mood. He decided to stroll over to Tom Kats for a beer, but when he walked in the place was strangely quiet and most of the lights were on. The jukebox wasn't playing.

"You guys open?" he asked, looking over at the bartender.

"We just heard. John Lennon was shot and killed outside his apartment building tonight."

T.J. was speechless. Finally, someone over by the jukebox said, "Here—I found one." He deposited a few quarters and Imagine began to play. Lennon's voice filled the room in a way that was both eerie and tragic. The bartender, unprompted, handed T.J. a bottle of Budweiser.

The song played all the way through before being followed by All You Need is Love. The bartender switched on a small television set behind the bar and the news was showing the crowds gathering outside of the Dakota apartment house on West 72nd Street where Lennon had been murdered.

T.J. was startled from the somber moment when a stranger sidled up beside him and suggested, "Let's get out of here."

Whoever this young man was, he didn't seem like one of the usual patrons. He looked more like a tourist, fresh-faced and friendly. What was he proposing? But given the surreal nature of the moment, T.J. simply threw a few dollars down on the bar and walked out with the guy, who said his name was Jay.

It turned out that Jay was, in fact, a tourist. A wealthy one, from Atlanta, who was visiting friends in nearby New Jersey. They were a gay couple celebrating their anniversary and were outside waiting for Jay, who'd been on a mission to find himself a date for the night. One of the friends was an Air Force veteran and licensed helicopter pilot and they had rented a chopper for two hours to take in the sights.

"You wanna go for a ride?" Jay asked enthusiastically.

The proposal was so out of left field that it seemed unbelievable, like everything else about the evening. After a fleeting moment of thinking, "My mother would be absolutely furious about this," T.J. just nodded and soon found himself running through Times Square to the West 30th Street heliport.

An hour earlier, T.J. had been walking into his neighborhood dive bar and now he was soaring over Manhattan, its glittering skyscrapers twinkling like crown jewels so close he felt could touch them. His first chopper ride, zooming around the Statue of Liberty and then northward up the Hudson River toward the George Washington Bridge gave him, quite literally, a bird's eye view of the magnificent Big Apple. T.J. had ventured into the heavens with these merry, happily "out" strangers who seemed not to have a care or a fear in the world while just below mourners were gathering together because of the loss of an icon. T.J. appreciated the sad irony that this was the night John Lennon's life ended while his own was actually just beginning.

It was after one a.m. by the time he returned to his apartment. He had left Jay and his friends at the heliport when they finished their ride and there had been no pressure for anything further to develop between them. Jay had been earnestly looking for a companion on his NYC adventure and T.J. felt lucky that he'd been in the right place at the right time to be that person. The breathtaking experience of flying above his beloved new home city was unforgettable and, T.J. felt, a good omen of things to come.

That would prove true when he woke the next morning and called in to his answering service. There was a message from the producer, Andy Kelly, offering him the role of Sir Duncelot. Rehearsals would begin right after New Year's Day.

Even though acting classes and auditions generally went on hiatus as Christmas approached, T.J. was happy to putter around the City and enjoy the seasonal festivities like ice skating in Central Park, second act'ing as many Broadway shows as possible and cruising guys in various bars and clubs. It seemed like gay men were everywhere and all it took was some eye contact and a grin to find someone willing to mess around. T.J. was rapidly becoming an expert at this sport. In fact, it led to some hot and heavy encounters with a visiting Canadian and a closeted, older character actor T.J. recognized from TV commercials. There was also a memorable night with an Ivy League grad student, sneaking into his room at the venerable old Harvard Club. It felt like a drag to T.J. that he would have to pause the fun to go back to Connecticut for a few days of Yuletide with his family.

But the weekend before he was set to leave Manhattan for the first time since he'd made the move, he received one more midnight call from Dottie O'Hara. She was sloshed and belligerent.

"Kid, I'm having a Christmas party tomorrow night and you'll be there at eight."

He had no other plans and she was certain to have a well stocked bar. Besides, it was more of a command than an invitation. "I can't wait," he told her, still half asleep.

"It's 67 Central Park West, Penthouse A." Then she hung up.

The next night was cold and clear, pleasant for a walk up Broadway to Columbus Circle and along Central Park to Dottie's building. T.J. donned his forest green, goose down puffer coat and paired it with the new black wool gloves he'd bought from a street vendor on Eighth Avenue. He'd learned to blow dry his air upside down (a trick he'd seen on a Vidal Sassoon commercial), straightening out his natural brown curls and locking in the style with Aqua Net hair spray once he'd achieved maximum height and volume. Along the way, he stopped at a Christmas stand at Grand Army Plaza and bought an inexpensive Cinnamon scented candle wrapped in red paper, as a hostess gift.

He arrived at Dottie's majestic looking building, across the street from the world famous Tavern on the Green restaurant, and nervously gave his name to the uniformed doorman on duty. What kind of mood would she be in tonight? T.J. wondered. The doorman scanned the guest list and checked off T.J.' name, then pointed to an ornate lobby elevator. "Go right up, sir. Top floor."

After a long, slow climb of fourteen stories, the elevator jolted to a stop and slowly opened to the small vestibule outside her front door. A rack with hangers had been placed there and there seemed to be a dozen or so coats and jackets so T.J. added his alongside them. He could hear piano music and the murmur of voices coming from inside the apartment, but above it all was the omnipresent, never ceasing sound of one of Dottie's distinctive, loud and sing-songy monologues. He took a deep breath and entered, putting on the biggest smile he could muster, remembering how his mom had taught him to do it without looking fake. "This is how I've won so many invisible Oscars," she always quipped.

The massive old place looked like something out of Rosemary's Baby, with dark, wood paneled walls covered with Broadway show posters and oil paintings. Built-in shelves were crammed with books and bric-a-brac while antique furniture hid almost all of the thick, shag carpeting. There were probably two dozen guests milling around, most of whom T.J. recognized from the showcase. No big stars other than the hostess herself, who was in an adjacent dining room, holding court beside a table set wih a rather basic buffet of crudités and the kind of cocktail foods you could find at any corner bodega or deli. The piano music wasn't coming from the beautiful black Steinway in the corner—it was from a record player at which she had enlisted someone to play her pre-selected collection of albums.

Dottie took notice of the new arrival, even if she couldn't immediately place who it was. She kept on talking to whoever was standing beside her, without missing a beat, and waved T.J. to come in. He indicated the gift wrapped candle in his hand and left it on a side table where some other offerings had been set.

"You could use a drink," a deep, familiar voice said to him. It was Ross Woodhouse, the older gent who had directed the showcase.

"Hey, Ross, how are you doing?" T.J. said, relieved for the social interaction, and offered his hand to shake. Instead, Ross surprised him by greeting him with a kiss on the cheek. T.J. could feel the whiskers on his face and smell the whiskey on his breath.

"Trying to fortify myself before our hostess gets too much further in the bag," Ross replied. "What can I get you?"

"How about a gin and tonic?"

"I'll meet you behind the potted palm," Ross added, nodding toward a large plant over by a corner window. T.J. wasn't expecting a proposition, but Ross clarified, "I find that as these nights with Dottie go on, it's best to find a spot where you can avoid direct fire."

He'd seen her lose her cool before, so he thought this was probably good advice.

When Ross came back with their drinks (he was already pretty tipsy), T.J. told him about the new role he'd just landed as Sir Duncelot, thanks to the off-color joke he had told. "I can always use an extra dirty joke," Ross responded. "You'll have to tell me."

The murmur of conversation in the room came to an abrupt halt when Dottie suddenly bellowed from the dining room, "Go fuck yourself!"

Her hapless victim was someone T.J. didn't recognize but the fellow was doing his best to defend himself against whatever perceived sleight had set her off. He was stammering something like, "Dottie, I'm just giving my opinion. I thought the score was wonderful."

"It was absolute horse shit," she drawled back derisively, enunciating the expletive for added effect. "Which just goes to show that your taste is up your ass."

T.J. shrank back further behind the palm and Ross squatted down onto the leather ottoman beside it, patting the seat for T.J. to join him. "Now she's warmed up."

At that point, the guest in charge of the music wisely turned up the volume and put on the original cast recording of one of Dottie's Broadway triumphs. That seemed to quell any further conflict for the moment. A couple of other featured performers from their showcase drifted by to say hello, but T.J. noticed that some people were already slipping quietly out of the party, without any goodbyes or thank-yous.

Ross noticed too and suggested, "How about one for the road and we share a cab back downtown?" T.J. nodded.

However, when he stood up from their hideout, Dottie spotted them. She strode into the center of the living room, a freshly drained crystal snifter still clutched in her hand.

"Come on, Ross, isn't he a little young—even for you?"

Everyone turned to look at Ross, holding their empty glasses, and T.J., red faced on the ottoman.

"We were just about to say our goodnights and share a taxi, Dottie. It's been a lovely—"

Dottie cut Ross off with a theatrical snort. "Share a taxi? Is that the euphemism your group is using these days?"

Knowing there was no use tangling with her, Ross cast a directorial glance at T.J. who stood up and tried to bring back that smile his mother had taught him. "Thank you for the party, Miss O'Hara." T.J. couldn't bring himself to address this drunken bitch by her first name.

"See how they are?" Dottie said. "Daddy calls and Baby follows."

Ross set the glasses down on a coffee table and wordlessly walked to the door, T.J. a few steps behind with his head down.

"Merry Fucking Christmas, girls," she bellowed from behind them.

By the time they'd collected their coats and made it down to the lobby, T.J. was shaking. He couldn't ever recall being so unkindly bullied by an adult before. Ross noticed and as he started looking for a cab to hail, advised, "Don't let her get to you. She's just an unhappy old drunk. She only gets away with it because she's so damned talented."

They climbed into the back of a big, checkered Yellow cab.

"Where are you?" Ross asked him.

"45th and 8th."

"First stop, 45th and 8th please. Then down to Manhattan Plaza," he told the driver. Then, shimmying closer to T.J., he added, "Unless you want to come up to my place for a nightcap?"

"Thanks, but I'm heading to Connecticut early in the morning," T.J. countered. Was Dottie right about Ross?

It wasn't long before they were heading down Broadway and passing by Lincoln Center, exquisitely decked out for the holidays. T.J. was drinking it all in and didn't even realize his thoughts were coming out of his mouth when he said, "So beautiful."

That is when Ross echoed, "So beautiful," and lunged right for T.J. with a powerful embrace and pulled him in for a wet kiss, right on the mouth.

T.J. was as disgusted as he was surprised, pulling back but trying to be polite to the man he still considered a director and authority figure. "Oh, that's nice of you to say, but—"

Undeterred, Ross kept his arms wrapped right where they were and pulled him back for another lip lock. T.J. moved his head to the side to avoid further contact. Ross was like a hungry dog and his eyes were wide and wild.

"Come on, honey, give me a kiss."

T.J.'s puffer coat was the only insulation between them and he managed to pull his hands up to push Ross off him. Perhaps thinking the third try would be a charm, Ross surged forward again, lips parted. T.J. could think of nothing more repulsive than that tongue touching his face, and he wondered why the cabbie didn't intervene.

Hair pulling might be playing dirty, but T.J. was not about to give in to this advance. He grabbed at the short curls on Ross' head and what followed was probably the biggest surprise T.J. had ever known. Simultaneously, with a sound like ripping Velcro, he was suddenly holding Ross Woodhouse's entire head of hair in his hands. T.J. managed to look away from Ross's leering expression to see the mane of light brown locks entwined in his fingers.

T.J.'s eyes went back to Ross, now as completely bald as Yul Brynner but still waiting to pounce again, smiling strangely as he proposed, "I bet you had no idea it wasn't real."

"No. No idea," T.J. said, dropping it between them onto the vinyl seat of the taxi.

Ross gathered it up, explaining, "It cost me two thousand. Made by the same guy who does Burt Reynolds."

They rode the rest of the way in silence to 45th Street and T.J. got out and scurried into his building, oddly appreciating the unique madness of "just another night out in New York City."

CHAPTER TWO

Folding Sweaters

T.J.'s brief holiday at home was pleasant enough and gave him the chance to spend time with his parents, some aunts and uncles, and take a temporary carbohydrate break from Manhattan pizza, bagels and knishes. They were pleased to hear about his acting classes and the musical showcase with Dottie O'Hara, but were dubious about the "adult" fairy tale production on which he'd soon be embarking. His favorite gift was, not surprisingly, a $150 gift certificate to Bloomingdales which he could really stretch for value with the after-Christmas sales.

Watching Dick Clark's Rockin' New Year's Eve from their living room couch, however, was unbearable for him. Hosts Erin Moran of Happy Days and John Schneider from The Dukes of Hazzard introduced musical guests that included Barry Manilow, Blondie and the Village People, all lip-synching for their lives before throngs of people partying in a packed Times Square. It was all happening just around the corner from T.J.'s apartment and he was frustrated at not being able to be there. Did being homesick mean that Manhattan was now officially his home?

The next morning, he decided to kick off 1981 by packing up his suitcase and heading back to the city two days ahead of schedule. So as not to hurt their feelings, he told his parents he needed to prepare for his first day of rehearsal with the New York company of Someday My Prince Will Come. How could they argue with that? Metro North whizzed him back to Grand Central Station and he was back in time for Happy Hour at Tom Kats.

Monday, the 5th of January, was the first read-through for the play and T.J. had treated himself to a trim at a local barber shop—not too much as he was working valiantly to grow his mane into a proper Bowie-esque mullet. He broke in some of his wardrobe purchases that were of the au currant Yuppie variety: Ralph Lauren V-neck sweater and khakis with Jakob Hetzer penny loafers. He rode the subway downtown to Houston Street but opted to stand the whole way to avoid the risk of soiling his pristine new duds on the dirty train seats. A couple of good looking men cruised him during the commute, so he emerged above ground feeling pretty confident about how he looked. Why shouldn't he? He was playing the handsome albeit vacuous lead in a new play Off-Off Broadway.

Joining Andy Kelly, the musical director and the five other cast members (one of whom was Andy's co-producer) around a long table set up on the tiny stage, T.J. was disappointed at how small and run down the entire theater looked, illuminated by the house lights. He'd shaken hands with everyone during introductions, but was surprised that burly Andy welcomed him with a big bear hug. It might have been the tightest hug he'd ever received. Andy was certainly not a handsome man, but there was something virile and attractive about him.

Scripts were stacked on the table and glasses of water and ashtrays were there for the taking. Andy had a cigarette clenched between his teeth while he addressed his company.

"Okay, kids, let's just have a cold read through. No performances necessary," he said, very much in command. He was taller and broader than T.J. expected, now that he could see him up close. Andy pulled a pack of Marlboro reds out of his shirt pocket and tossed them onto the table top, followed by a pack of matches from The Duplex Cabaret & Piano Bar. "Help yourselves." The top two buttons of his shirt were open and T.J. noticed the thick thatch of reddish brown hair on his chest. He might as well have tossed a Frisbee, he seemed so cool and casual.

There was absolutely nothing about Andy that seemed gay to T.J., aside from the matchbook and maybe that was an assumption he shouldn't make. A smoker will need a light no matter where it comes from. However, the speculation made it even more titillating.

It quickly became evident, as they read through dialogue with the musical director stepping in to perform the songs, that everyone there were friends. T.J. was the only newcomer. Taking a ten-minute coffee break between Acts One and Two, T.J. casually asked the co-producer, David, how they all knew each other.

"We all went to school together. The American Academy of Dramatic Arts," David replied. "We've been auditioning around town for a couple years and can't seem to land the jobs we need to join Actors Equity, so we figured we'd write and produce our own show."

The Academy was a distinguished institution on Madison Avenue that turned out some equally distinguished alumni like Anne Bancroft, Charles Durning and Judd Hirsch. T.J. was impressed: these were talented and enterprising people.

Andy, having heard David speaking to T.J., stubbed out his latest smoke and sauntered over to join them. "The one part we couldn't fill on our own was yours," he told T.J. "But as soon as you told that joke, I knew I'd found the right guy. Handsome and funny."

T.J. wasn't the blushing type but he immediately felt himself go red. He managed to say, "Equity rules state you have to hold open auditions, anyway."

Andy let out a gravelly chuckle and pulled out a fresh cigarette to put between his teeth. "Touché," he said with a smile, offering a smoke to T.J., who accepted. As T.J. stepped back to the table to retrieve the matchbook, Andy swooped his large hand to quickly intercept it, then struck a match.

"Have you ever been to the Duplex?" he asked, holding out the match. T.J. shook his head as he leaned in to take the light. Andy's hand touched his and guided him to it seductively. "We'll have to go sometime."

All throughout the reading of the second act, T.J. had an erection he thought he managed to hide in spite of periodically looking up from the script and making eye contact with Andy.

The next day, there was a rehearsal to begin learning the score and the cast, as directed, brought their tape recorders. Rhonda, an attractive woman around the same age as Andy, was playing the Evil Queen and she was dressed in what looked to be a brand new exercise outfit: dance-inspired leg warmers, cropped t-shirt, tights and a braided headband. Considering there was no dancing in this show, T.J. thought she was just being overzealous, but Rhonda quite obviously enjoyed showing off her curves and eagerly sidled up to him for the scenes in which her character attempts to seduce the clueless Sir Duncelot. (Changed to "Duncelot" for consistency)

During a smoke and coffee break, Andy sauntered up from the house seat where he was observing. With a cocky tilt of his head at T.J., he beckoned him to the foot of the stage. T.J. complied, unsure if it was a personal or professional summons.

"When we finish on Friday," Andy suggested softly but assuredly, "dinner and the Duplex?"

T.J. smiled broadly and nodded before the musical director called out, "Back in five minutes, people."

David, the co-producer, handed T.J. a hobby-horse stick toy. T.J. shrugged, puzzled. "What's this for?" he asked.

"It's your horse," David replied. "That's how you make your first entrance."

Of course, T.J. realized. His opening number was entitled Straddle My Steed.

By Friday, it seemed everyone had learned their lines, songs and blocking. The biggest challenges were making the burlesque and bawdy script actually funny. As written, it was simply silly and everyone recognized the need to improvise and improve it. Andy and David, as actors themselves, were more open to the process than the musical director who'd written it and wanted to keep everything locked in as he'd originally intended. T.J. didn't have high hopes for the show, but was looking forward to being able to join Actors Equity. Besides, he was having the time of his life fielding the flirtations he was receiving from Rhonda and Andy. He also sensed that David seemed interested in him.

For dinner, Andy took T.J. to the Minetta Tavern, the charming stalwart of Greenwich Village. It felt like an actual date, something T.J. had never had with a man, and Andy was laying it on thick: holding the door open for him, pulling out his chair, ordering the wine and lighting his next cigarette. It made T.J. think of his own lovely mother, who seemed to always have attention from any men around her. He had realized from an early age that she was winsome, but now he was starting to think she may have used her looks and personality as an actual superpower.

After a good meal, Andy retrieved their heavy winter wear from Coat Check and they huddled closely together during the hike over to the Duplex. At one point, when they were scurrying to cross a street against the traffic light, Andy slung his arm around T.J.'s shoulder. T.J. loved the feeling of this big, older man being so protective of him. He was momentarily sidetracked by this and a gypsy cab zoomed by them, honking its horn. Andy pulled T.J. close to him at the curbside. They were both breathless for a moment.

"I can't have anything happen to my star," Andy whispered.

T.J. never thought of himself as a sap, but that was a swoon-worthy moment and he felt himself melting. Andy's grab suddenly became an embrace and he leaned down to put his mouth on T.J.'s. Right there on the curb at the corner of MacDougall and West 3rd, underneath a frigid and starless sky, they kissed openly and hungrily.

When they finally moved apart, Andy said, "You know the Duplex will be packed now. Standing room only. Want to save it for another night?"

"Does that mean you're sending me home?" T.J. asked, realizing he had the ability to flirt back.

Andy responded exactly as T.J. had hoped: "I thought we could go back to my home."

A twenty-minute cab ride later, they emerged onto West 73rd Street and entered Andy's impressive first floor, one-bedroom apartment in an old Upper West Side brownstone. It even had a backyard, a rare commodity in the city. There was no real decor to see when he flipped on the lights, just the basics: a dining table and chairs, L-shaped sofa and coffee table in front of the television and a loft bed accessed by a ladder with a work station and desk underneath. A Soloflex bench and exercise machine dominated one side of the living room and had clothes draped over it. Empty wine glasses and overflowing ashtrays were peppered around the apartment. This guy was not a housekeeper.

He took their coats and tossed them atop the pile on the Soloflex.

"Glass of wine?" he offered T.J.

"I'm good, thanks. Give me the tour."

Smiling, he was able to oblige by merely pointing across the apartment. "Kitchen, living, dining, bedroom, office. Bathroom back there."

An overweight orange and white tabby cat suddenly sauntered out from somewhere, yawning. T.J. thought it had the same walk as its owner.

"That's Romeo," Andy told him. "Juliet died last year."

As Romeo rubbed his head against Andy's leg, T.J. looked up at the loft bed. "Show me the bedroom."

"I call it upstairs," Andy said with a little laugh, and he took T.J.'s hand and walked him over to the ladder.

Except for bathroom breaks and to retrieve food deliveries from the local Chinese restaurant and the deli next door or to feed the cat, they didn't go downstairs for the next two days.

The weekend was a revelation to T.J. He had never slept beside another man before (even though Andy's snoring didn't really allow for much slumber) let alone experience the kind of physical intimacies they were enjoying. The queen-sized loft bed rapidly became a tangle of sheets and blankets, decimated by lubricants and body fluids. The built-in shelf along its headboard quickly filled up with coffee cups and cardboard food containers next to the ubiquitous packs of cigarettes and bottles of amyl nitrate labeled Rush that Andy liked to sniff as he reached orgasm. T.J. tried it but found the sexual acts heady enough without chemical enhancement.

By the time Sunday arrived, Andy climbed down at midday, buck naked, to retrieve the jumbo-sized New York Times that was delivered to his doorstep. "Maybe a shower and brunch somewhere?" he asked.

"Sounds great. My treat, you've been paying for everything all weekend."

"Eggrolls, bagels and a six pack of Tab won't break the bank," Andy replied, pulling out the Arts section and heading back up to join T.J.

"After brunch, I'll go back to my apartment," T.J. told him. "Rehearsal's at ten tomorrow, right?"

"T.J., you don't have to go home just because there's rehearsal tomorrow," was Andy's answer as he rolled his full body weight on top of T.J. "Just don't wear any clothes when you're here."

As their limbs intertwined again and Andy thrust against him, T.J. wondered if this meant he now had an actual boyfriend. He guessed he'd be finding out the next day.

Monday morning, T.J. managed to extricate himself from beneath Andy's sleeping, snoring hulk and climb down from the loft to head back to 45th Street and get ready for the day's rehearsal. Feeling happy and light headed, he paid a little extra attention to his grooming routine and made sure to get a close shave and a splash of Gray Flannel before proceeding downtown to the theater. Rehearsal began shortly after ten a.m. but Andy wasn't there. Silently, T.J. worried that maybe he'd misinterpreted the dynamics of what he'd considered an amazing weekend of passion and romance.

Andy finally appeared a little after eleven, looking a bit worse for wear. Coffee and cigarette in hand, he plopped himself down in a front row seat. David noticed his co-producer's bleary eyes and asked, sarcastically, "Rough night?"

Shooting back a sly grin as T.J. looked on expectantly and clutched the stick horse, Andy corrected David. "Big night. Big weekend, in fact."

T.J. felt himself blushing again even though nothing further was said.

"Back to work, kids, the musical director called out. "Top of Act One."

The company took a lunch break at one, falling into their ritual of getting soup or sandwiches from the bodega down the block and taking their meals back to the theater. As the actors were on their way out, Andy called out to T.J.

"Can you hang back a minute?"

T.J. moved down to the front row of seats where Andy was still sitting. Unsure if it was unseemly to display affection in the theater, he waited for Andy to take the lead. He was the producer, after all.

"I want to apologize."

T.J.'s stomach flipped. Was whatever this was about to be over as quickly as it had begun?

"Apologize for what?"

"We never got to the Duplex. I want to make it up to you."

Relieved, T.J. laughed, "You can make it up to me by losing the stick horse."

"The horse stays. It's the title of the song, for fuck's sake."

"Okay, then how?"

"Duplex, Friday. And for Saturday . . ."

Andy pulled an envelope out of his pocket and handed it to him. T.J. was enjoying every moment of this exchange and even more so when he saw the contents of the envelope. It contained two orchestra seat tickets to preview performances of Jacques Brel is Alive and Well and Living in Paris. The revival was playing at Town Hall.

"Love it," he said. "Let me bring you back some lunch?"

"Hot roast beef and Swiss on a roll, thanks."

Before he walked out of the theater, T.J. turned back to Andy. "Your cat's not the only Romeo, you know."

Andy winked at him.

T.J. was the last one back from the bodega because, after getting Andy's sandwich, he'd wanted to get some cold cans of Tab, which were getting harder and harder to find after the recent and well publicized cancer-scare involving Saccharine. He finally found some at a corner deli but everyone was already midway through their meals when he got back to the theater. He noticed Rhonda sitting two seats away from Andy, picking at a salad with a flimsy plastic fork. They were smiling and chatting conspiratorially, but he couldn't hear what they were saying.

As he was unpacking the bags of food items, he saw Andy pull another envelope out of his pocket. Was Rhonda getting theater tickets, too? She accepted it happily and tucked it into the purse beside her.

At day's end, as everyone was packing up, T.J. asked Andy what his plans were for the night. "There's a dinner meeting with the crew to go over the final proofs for posters and programs. "But we're on for Friday," Andy assured him. "And Saturday."

Considering for a moment, T.J. ventured with his best attempt at seduction, "What if I can't last until Friday?"

"Good things come to those who wait."

The thought of whatever was in that envelope Andy handed to Rhonda weighed on T.J. all that night and the next day. He tried to distract himself by drilling song lyrics for the show and by reading new monologues for when he'd return to Saperstein's class, but curiosity and jealousy were slowly getting the better of him.

At the next rehearsal, T.J. asked the musical director if they could run the trio number he sang with the Princess and the

Evil Queen. It would give him a chance to size up Rhonda and maybe get some more information. She was not her usually flirtatious self, even though the song called for it, with Sir Duncelot caught in a love triangle between the step-mother and daughter. On the next coffee break, T.J. made a point of thanking her for taking the extra time to go over it with him.

"Sure, anytime."

"Hey, I saw Andy giving you something yesterday," he ventured, trying unsuccessfully to sound off the cuff. "Theater tickets?"

Looking like the proverbial cat that ate the canary, her voice dropped a full register and she purred, "No, honey. You're the one getting orchestra seats. I just won a little wager, that's all."

"Oh," he said and nodded as if he understood—which he didn't.

"Andy and me, we're both from Jersey. We're always gambling."

T.J. said nothing more about it for the rest of the week and by Friday he'd pretty much forgotten about it, until they were at the Duplex piano bar and Andy mentioned how much he was looking forward to seeing Jacques Brel the next night.

"Me, too," T.J. said, seeing an opening. "After you gave me the tickets, I saw you giving Rhonda an envelope and I thought maybe she was coming, too."

Laughing, Andy commented, "I see enough of Rhonda at rehearsals."

"She said you owed her, for a bet."

Andy paused and gave him a hard look. "Are you jealous, T.J.?"

"Would you blame me if I were?"

"She was telling you the truth. I lost a bet."

As someone at the piano launched loudly into The Man That Got Away in an off-key impersonation of Judy Garland, Andy continued, "If you must know, it was a bet about you. I wasn't sure if you were gay but she was certain you were."

T.J. didn't know if he should be offended or flattered. Either way, he was surprised by having been the centerpiece of a wager.

Under the table, Andy picked his foot up off the floor and wedged it in between T.J.'s legs. "You were worth every buck, baby."

It was another great weekend full of fun, food and especially sex. T.J. felt like he was quickly becoming skilled in the ways of carnal pleasure thanks to plenty of practice and being an enthusiastic student. By the time he went back to his own apartment Monday morning, he'd even managed to exhaust Andy's seemingly endless stamina.

Andy made his appearance at the theater that day later than usual, after everyone had returned from lunch. He was obviously in a somber mood that didn't look to be a hangover or fatigue. As the musical director was about to call everyone back to rehearsal, Andy cleared his throat and announced, "I need a moment with you guys."

Andy stepped up on to the stage and dragged a folding chair into the center, lighting a cigarette and taking a big drag on it. The others gathered around him in a semi circle as if it were Story Hour.

"I've got some bad news and good news," he began. "The bad news is that the theater has raised its rental price and our two main backers have decided not to go forward." Everyone looked at David, the co-producer, and it was obvious he'd seen the writing on the wall.

"And that means what, exactly?" asked Rhonda, almost as an accusation.

Andy took a deep breath to fortify himself. "It means that the show isn't going to open. In fact, we need to be out of here by the end of the afternoon."

The musical director, teary eyed, broke the awkward silence that followed with, "You say there's good news?"

"Everyone is still eligible to join Actors Equity. So we achieved that, at least."

Although he wouldn't say it aloud, T.J. was thinking that, in addition to Equity membership, there was still more good news than bad: He would never have to don tights and gallop in on a hobby horse, and he was in the throes of first love.

When he awoke in the loft bed the next morning, and didn't have to scurry off to rehearsal, T.J. was the most hung over he'd ever been. The whole company had all commiserated over the demise of their production until the wee hours. Regardless, T.J.'s morning erection was seeking satisfaction and he nestled closely against Andy, sending Romeo flying off the mattress and landing on the sofa below with a solid thump.

Andy murmured a refusal and snored himself back to a deep slumber. Without rehearsals to rely on, T.J. needed to ensure he would still have frequent access to Andy beyond an occasional weekend romp. He came up with a plan and it was the first time since his move to New York that his usual laser-focus wasn't arts related.

He was still on the hunt for a job, but not one that would necessarily make him a star. Rather, he was determined to work somewhere near Andy's place on West 73rd Street so that meant hitting all the popular retail clothing stores up and down that stretch of Columbus Avenue.

He had plenty of work experience, especially for someone his age, but never in retail sales. As a performer and outgoing conversationalist, he was sure it would come naturally. Since he wasn't worried about the money as much as he was the proximity of the job, he assumed he would have his choice of offers. He started at his favorite store, Charivari, and worked his way down the avenue, filling out applications at every place that sold men's wear, including Tommy Hilfiger, Parachute, the Coca Cola store and The Gap. Not only was Charivari his favorite of them all, it had two locations close to each other so the odds were in his favor.

However, the only place that seemed encouraging was The Gap and T.J. had to admit his own preppy look was more suited to that than the New Wavy padded shoulders of Charivari, the high-waisted stone-washed denim at Hilfiger's, the nylon harem pants of Parachute or the riotous bubble-gum colors of Coca Cola. Sure enough, a day later, Armand (the androgynous French African manager from the Gap), left a message that T.J. could pick up as many shifts as he'd like whenever he was available.

Scrutinizing his kitchen calendar, T.J. decided he could start the very next day. After calling Armand to accept the offer, he called Andy to tell him that he'd picked up a survival job around the corner from his place. It turned out that Andy was doing something similar, but helping out his elderly father at the family lumber business in Rahway, New Jersey. T.J. figured if he worked at The Gap until six p.m., they would both be available at the same time. It meant giving up acting classes with Sarah Saperstein, but he reasoned that there would still be plenty of flexibility to go on casting calls.

Armand explained to T.J. that he would get an allowance of five hundred dollars worth of Gap clothing to wear on the job, so he came early his first day to pick out some wardrobe. Once he was decked out in a medium-size red, geometric cable knit sweater and a pair of their signature blue jeans, he would meet his fellow "fashion consultants" and get a lesson in working the cash register. The credit card and traveler's check options were kind of tricky for him. He hoped most sales would be cash.

There were a half dozen other employees in their early twenties and an assistant manager who was the "old man" of the group. T.J. assumed he was somewhere in his forties. The person closest to T.J.'s age was a cute Hunter Business College student named Leo Tucci, a tall puppy dog of a boy from a blue-collar Italian Catholic part of Staten Island. He was working part time to help subsidize his tuition costs and T.J. couldn't tell whether or not he was gay until he overheard him comment to Armand about a good looking customer, "Holy crap, he is gorgeous." Armand obviously agreed, batting his eyelashes coquettishly and whispering, "Oh yes, she is finer than fine."

Armand was the most flamboyant, effeminate man T.J. had ever seen. It would have seemed cartoonish on anyone else, but his theatrical qualities and exotic, dark black skin made him somehow other worldly. Everybody liked him.

It didn't take long to become abundantly clear that ninety-eight percent of T.J.'s job at The Gap was to fold. Fold shirts, sweaters, jeans. Stack and fold. Take clothes from the fitting rooms and refold and restack. The problem was that there were several household skills he'd never managed to master while living at home, especially since his mother had a full-time housekeeper. These included but were not limited to ironing, executing a well-made bed and, most especially, folding clothes. Leo, however, was a meticulous folder.

Astonished, T.J. had to ask, "How did you learn to fold so fast and so perfectly?"

"My dad was in the Navy. We learned to fold as soon as we were out of diapers."

"My father was Navy, too," said T.J. "Does he know you're gay?"

Leo's small, brown eyes narrowed, even though he didn't look up from his folding duties. "Are you kidding?" he replied. "He'd crucify me!" Then, looking up, he asked, "How about yours?"

T.J. hadn't ever considered discussing his sexuality with his parents. His family and life in Connecticut were an entirely different world from the one he was living in now. Aside from his repertoire of off-color jokes and giving him a box of condoms when he turned sixteen, the most his father ever said to him about sex was, "Before you marry a woman, check out her mother—because that's what you're going to end up with."

"We've never talked about it," T.J. admitted. "But I don't think he'd mind." To be honest with himself, T.J. believed that. His parents had always supported his choices. He wouldn't even be in New York, otherwise.

Leo saw what a mangled mess T.J. was making of a branded, hooded sweatshirt and pulled it away from him. "You have a boyfriend?"

"I'm seeing somebody. He lives around the corner, actually."

"Is he hot? I mean, because you're handsome."

"Oh, thanks," T.J. replied, surprised by the ease with which this guy was able to give a compliment. "He's older, almost thirty."

"Older men can be sexy."

"At our age, everybody's older than us," T.J. observed, and they laughed.

"That's true," Leo admitted. "I should find a boyfriend one of these days. You know anybody?"

The only person T.J. could think of was David, from the play—and he certainly wasn't right for someone as adorable as Leo. He shook his head.

"Then let's go out sometime and find me one. We'll go to Brandy's uptown. The piano bar. You been?"

"No. I know the Duplex though."

‘It’s fun. All the bartenders sing and some of them are gorgeous.”

Armand sashayed by them and cooed, “Ladies . . . back to work, please.”

Andy began spending more time in New Jersey, where he was working his lumber job, and he often stayed overnight at his father’s. When he did come back to the city, it was later in the evenings so T.J.’s plan wasn’t working out the way he’d hoped. Andy promised they’d spend the weekends together, so T.J. decided to take Leo up on the offer to hang out at Brandy’s.

T.J. loved the place, which was far less crowded than the Duplex and it was kind of quaint. Leo was right about the waiters. They were indeed gorgeous and one in particular, Luke, was outstanding in looks and talent. He had all the patrons, male and female, clamoring for barstools when he was working, flashing his blinding white smile and showing his muscular torso through tight white T-shirts. When he sang, it was doubly swoon-worthy. He had a pitch-perfect tenor voice and every hour or two he would treat the audience to a song from a Sondheim score. He big glass bowl on top of the piano was soon filled with dollar bills. It quickly became a regular after-work haunt for T.J. and Leo, who encouraged T.J. to croon a tune. T.J. opted for a sure-fire with Soon It’s Gonna Rain from The Fantasticks.

“You’re really good, T.J.,” Leo gushed when he finished to thunderous applause. “You should work here as a bartender, instead of at The Gap.”

“Don’t tell,” T.J. admitted, leaning in close, “but I won’t be eighteen until summer.”

"No wonder old man Andy likes you," Leo said with a laugh. "When do I get to meet him?"

"He should be around this weekend."

"I'll be working. Bring him into the store."

Andy resisted getting out of the apartment that weekend. He was tired from a long work week and told T.J. he really just wanted to watch TV, drink vodka cokes and fuck. So that was pretty much all they did from the time Andy got home Friday night until Sunday afternoon, which was a sunny and unseasonably warm day.

"We should get outside for a while," T.J. finally suggested. "It's so nice out. Want to get some dinner?"

"Okay," Andy acquiesced, flopping on the sofa with Romeo on his lap. "Let's have a drink at The Works." The Works was a neighborhood gay bar on Columbus Avenue, a few blocks north of The Gap. T.J. had been there once with Leo, who picked up a guy at the pool table almost as soon as they arrived, leaving T.J. to call it an early night.

"We can swing by the store so you can meet Leo."

"Leo, Leo, Leo. Do you realize how much you talk about him? You have a crush on him?"

The idea was ludicrous to T.J. who felt like Leo was the brother he'd never had—his first real friend around his own age. He climbed on top of Andy, sending the cat scurrying.

"I'm only interested in one guy, you know." They started making out and T.J. could feel Andy coming to attention through his sweatpants. The Works could wait.

Eventually, they did get out of the apartment and headed

up Columbus to The Gap. "If you see anything you want, I'll get you my employee discount," T.J. offered.

"Does that include your buddy, Leo?" Andy teased.

The store was busy on this sparkling Sunday, so the introductions were quick and polite and as they continued on toward the bar, Andy commented, "He isn't as hot as I expected. What's all the fuss about?"

"Not everything is about sex."

"Says who?" Andy grinned and gave T.J. a hard squeeze on his butt cheek.

The Works was packed with a festive crowd of young gay men, feeling feisty and loose after an afternoon of brunching. The music was loud and pulsating and the whole place smelled like beer and cigarettes, but everyone seemed to be in a great mood. T.J. and Andy found a cocktail table in the back to lean against and take in the atmosphere over drinks.

"Vodka coke?" Andy offered.

"A screwdriver please," T.J. answered. Leo had introduced him to them, saying that they were his Aunt Jenny's favorite, especially if they were so strong "you can see through them."

While they sipped their cocktails and puffed on cigarettes, T.J. noticed Andy's heavy lidded eyes focusing on another man—a trim guy in his early twenties wearing a tank top and running shorts. He didn't like how blatantly Andy was staring at him but said nothing. After they finished their drinks, T.J. suggested they move on to dinner.

"I'm not hungry yet."

The guy in the running shorts noticed Andy's gaze and

smiled. Then he turned and walked toward the exit, his firm, athletic rear end almost obscenely falling out of the tight shorts.

T.J. was glad to see him leaving until Andy, eyes still following the runner, said, "Okay. We can go."

They circled back to one of Andy's local favorites on 72nd Street, Il Buon Gusto, a small casual, family-run Italian place with excellent chicken parmigiana and spaghetti. They shared a carafe of Chianti, which T.J. was starting to like. It was dark by the time they came out and started to walk back to Andy's place. He suggested a nightcap.

"I don't think I can drink anymore," T.J. replied.

"It's going to be a bitch of a work week for me so I want one. You can go back to the apartment if you want."

"No way—I want to spend every minute I can with you this weekend." Besides, he didn't want to think of Andy going back to The Works in search of that runner.

They walked a couple blocks up Amsterdam Avenue to a tiny, almost hidden bar with a dilapidated sign identifying the place as the Candle Bar.

"Here," Andy said, opening the door with a familiarity that told T.J. he'd been there many times before.

As festive and fun as The Works was, Candle Bar was sleazy by comparison. It had the same pumping music, like The Human League and Duran Duran, but the vibe was sordid and sexual. The air smelled like intermingled smoke and sweat. The men, older than the clientele from the afternoon, also seemed intermingled with each other. The cruising was blatant and lascivious, and T.J. felt like it was Ross Woodhouse in the back of the taxi all over again with these guys leering at him.

Andy moved to the packed bar and ordered two vodka cokes, not asking T.J. what he wanted. When handed the glass, T.J. didn't argue; he just took an obligatory sip. Andy was swaying, but not to the music. He was drunk now and leaning on one hip, absorbing the atmosphere with obvious appreciation. Halfway through his drink, he jerked his head, beckoning T.J. to follow him and they went to the back of the bar where a set of rickety steps led down to a basement.

Is this a bar or a fucking haunted house? T.J. wondered.

The small underground area was just as crowded as the main floor but there was no music and the lights were pink, bathing everyone in a rose glow. Andy leaned against the wall, so T.J. did the same, his glass still almost full. He was completely unprepared for what he saw. The men in the room were in various states of undress and anyone who wasn't actively engaged in sexual activity was doing the same as Andy, leaning against the wall and watching.

T.J. didn't know where to look. Two men were on their knees taking turns having oral sex with a well-hung man in a cowboy hat. A small Asian guy was getting pounded from behind by a muscular bodybuilder type, with two more just like him lined up to take their turns. Guys were making out and groping each other. T.J. looked at Andy, who was sleepily mesmerized.

A Freddie Mercury lookalike (or was it actually Freddie Mercury?) came brazenly up to T.J. and put his hand on his crotch. T.J. actually gasped out loud, not that anyone could hear it over all the ambient moaning and groaning. Andy looked at the groper like a pit bull and said, "Back off," and he did.

T.J. would have bolted back upstairs and out the door, if it weren't for Andy who finally turned to him and asked with a distinctive slur, "Want to fuck?"

"Sure. In a bed," was T.J.'s answer and he said it with a venom he'd never felt before.

They walked back upstairs and went home, but there was no fucking. Andy passed out as soon as his head hit the pillow. T.J. was rattled and it took hours for him to shake off the images of what he'd seen and finally fall asleep.

The following week, still troubled by Andy's behavior and feeling insecure about their relationship, T.J. managed to go to two open calls for industrial films and a go-see for a print ad. They were good distractions and a nice break from folding clothes. It was mid March and the month had come in like the proverbial lion. The city was cold, wet and bleak like T.J.'s mood.

He took comfort in a giant club sandwich and French fries at the Malibu Diner on West 23rd Street. He and Leo had planned to meet there before hitting the bars, and T.J. regaled him with the story of what had happened at the Candle Bar.

"You should play the field," Leo counseled. "There's a city full of guys out there." Then, noticing the package on the young waiter walking by the table, he added, "God, I love men."

T.J. laughed. "You're a crotch watcher," he said.

"Is Andy hung?"

Shrugging, T.J. answered, "I don't have a lot to compare him to, but no. Not really, I guess."

"One more reason to move on."

"It was so great when we were doing the play. I don't know what happened after that. Maybe he's depressed."

"My Aunt Jenny says there's no cure for an old love like a new love. Let's go find you one."

T.J. didn't think his heart was in it, but had to admit it might be worth a try. Leo helped him finish his fries and they were off to Uncle he Charlie's, the popular video bar on Greenwich Avenue.

As usual, the place was packed. They pushed through the crowd to find a spot near the bar, with Leo leading the way because he was tall enough to see an opening.

"I have to pee," T.J. lamented. "But I hate the bathroom here." The dark and smelly lavatory had only one terrifying stall and an open, stainless steel urinal trough that ran the length of the wall.

"Just stare at the wall and do math in your head." Leo advised. It worked.

When T.J. returned he found Leo chatting with a curly-haired blond guy, drinking beer. Shouting over the Soft Cell video for Tainted Love that was blaring from the TV screens, Leo said, "T.J. this is Jason. He just invited us to a party at the Waldorf."

"Fancy. Can we go dressed like this?" T.J. asked, indicating his Gap attire.

Jason nodded shyly and Leo told him, "You won't believe the occasion. Peter Allen's birthday."

Peter Allen was the flamboyant, energetic entertainer and Broadway star divorced from Liza Minnelli.

"It started about an hour ago. Should be going strong by now," Jason explained. "One of his assistants invited me but I felt weird about showing up alone. He told me I could bring people. As long as they're gay."

"So what are we waiting for?" Leo said, polishing off the last of his beer. With a nod to T.J. he added, "The bathrooms are sure to be nicer."

That would prove to be an understatement. As soon as they got to the ornate Waldorf Astoria Hotel on Park Avenue, the Concierge directed them to a suite on the fortieth floor. They could hear the music and laughter coming from the party as soon as they stepped off the elevator.

The doors to the suite were propped open so they just walked in to see scores of people gathered together. It was packed with a hodgepodge of artsy types from the theater world. Young, old, male, female, straight, gay—all in high spirits and most of them high in general. Everyone was clutching champagne flutes and an attentive waiter handed them theirs within moments of arriving.

"Jason!" a man called in their direction, waving frantically. It was the assistant who'd invited him. At first they thought it was Peter Allen, himself (they looked so much alike and he obviously had a thing for Jason). He came over to them and gave Jason a kiss, right on the lips.

"Randall, these are my friends—"

Before Jason could complete the introductions, Randall took him by the hand and led him away to another part of the suite. "There's blow in the bathroom," he said over his shoulder to T.J. and Leo. "Help yourselves."

"Let's check it out," Leo suggested. T.J. had never tried cocaine but he was keen to see everything there was to see in that suite. It was the most beautiful place he'd ever been.

The lavish bathroom was beyond elegant, with a sunken marble tub and gold fixtures. Even the toilet was gold. There were more than a dozen people in there, all seeming to talk at the same time, putting their champagne glasses down only long enough to snort some cocaine from the lines laid out on the marble sink counter.

Someone handed Leo a rolled-up hundred dollar bill to use as a straw. Without hesitation, he took it and inhaled a long line of the white powder. He kept sniffing to make sure he got it full into his nostril and then pinched his nose with a little sniff. T.J. thought it looked like Leo had done this before.

Smiling, Leo said, "That's good stuff" and handed the makeshift straw to T.J.

Trying to seem casual about it, T.J. copied the way his friend had inhaled the drug, although it took him two sniffs to complete the line. He felt an immediate sensation in the back of his throat and a head rush that followed shortly after. A skinny woman with thinning hair pulled the bill out of his hand, eager to take her turn.

Suddenly, the voices all abruptly stopped when someone dropped a glass onto the mosaic tiled floor. It shattered and a few people jumped away from it.

Only a moment later, everyone laughed, including the person who dropped the glass, and the levity resumed. A redheaded man in black suit tilted his head back, downed the last drops from his glass, and then proceeded to toss it into the tub. It, too, shattered and everyone laughed.

One after another, the guests began throwing their glasses into the tub and the cacophony of smashed glass filled the bathroom. Now feeling the full effects of their cocaine bumps, T.J. and Leo finished their champagne and tossed their glasses in with the rest.

They went back into the living room to get another round and hopefully find Peter Allen. As a waiter handed him a new flute, Leo asked, "Is there a bathroom where we can actually pee?"

As the waiter pointed to the other end of the suite, T.J. told Leo, "Make sure to do math in your head."

"Be right back," Leo answered before disappearing.

Right back turned into twenty minutes, during which T.J. picked at some of the hors d'oeuvres that were being passed and took in the amazing views high above Park Avenue. The magnificent cathedral of St. Bartholomew's was below to the north and the ornate facade of Grand Central Station with the Pan Am building soaring over it was to the south. He realized he never ceased to be dazzled by this incredible metropolis he'd come to think of as home. The thought of ever leaving it to go to school or anywhere else was unimaginable. He renewed his resolve to forge his career and his relationship with Andy, or whoever Mr. Right turned out to be.

Leo found him there at the windows.

"Any sign of Peter Allen?" T.J. asked.

"No, but I just made out with Michael Feinstein in the bathroom!"

***

A flurry of assorted side jobs started coming to T.J., thanks to the Spring uptick in audition opportunities. Of course, some jobs were better than others. He landed a print ad for the new USA Today newspaper, which paid a respectable flat fee and promised nationwide exposure. Unfortunately, the image they decided to use showed his face only from the nose, up, reacting with wide-eyed amazement to something he was reading in the paper.

The famous FAO Schwarz toy store hired actors to launch a line of kids' scents, soaps and shampoos. For ten bucks an hour, he and his "co-stars" would stand on their feet all day asking privileged little menaces and their parents, "Would you care to try a fragrance for children?" while the famously mind-numbing store theme song (Welcome To Our World of Toys) played over and over and over. More maddening, T.J. found himself still humming it on the subway ride home at the end of the day.

One gig was a private event at the Helmsley Hotel. It was an Alice in Wonderland themed tea party and T.J. was dressed as the White Rabbit, ushering people into the dining room with an excited, "Don't be late! Hurry hurry! You don't want to be late for the party!" It was embarrassing but at least no one would recognize him in the bunny costume.

A similar but less mortifying event was a gig in Central Park sponsored by the popular game, Trivial Pursuit. Actors, portraying different historical figures from the question cards, were giant, life-sized playing pieces, and they had to move around a board that took up an entire softball field. T.J. portrayed Marc Antony and was paired with a vivacious young Cleopatra.

Not long after, he was back at the Waldorf Astoria (no cocaine or broken glasses this time) for a fundraising black-tie gala for the upcoming restoration of the Statue of Liberty. He was the offstage announcer for the evening and had auditioned using his best Casey Kasem voice, which landed him the booking. Even though he wasn't in front of the audience, he had to wear a rented tuxedo as he read from the script as cued by the stage manager. When he saw a line of very effeminate waiters getting their desserts ignited for presentation, he feared he'd flub the line, "And now, welcome your waiters with their flaming fruit extravaganza!"

Fortunately, the only mishap was the stage manager's fault when he gave T.J. the wrong cue, reading into the microphone, "Ladies and Gentlemen, the Ambassador of Jazz—Lionel Hampton!" and instead Donald Trump came walking onto the stage to make a speech. From backstage, T.J. had no idea it was the wrong line until he heard the laughter from the audience. Trump milked the moment for all it was worth. T.J. would get a laugh of his own when, after the speech, he delivered the line again with a slight modification, "And NOW, Ladies and Gentlemen, the Ambassador of Jazz—Lionel Hampton." The esteemed bandleader made his entrance to the proper intro, generating thunderous applause.

It was becoming clear that his days at The Gap were numbered, even though Armand was always accommodating when it came to T.J.'s unpredictable schedule. It was also a healthy change for his relationship with Andy. Since they couldn't see as much of each other in person, they managed with daily phone calls. T.J.'s funny spin on his experiences amused Andy and they started to miss each other's company.

By the time April rolled around, they were seeing each other a night or two during the week and almost all of each weekend. An occasional drink at The Works was fun, but to T.J.'s relief, there were no more detours to Candle Bar. He even managed to squeeze in the odd voice lesson between auditions and time with Andy, who was mulling over the idea of producing another play—one that might actually open, this time. T.J. was hopeful that there would be a future for them, as their early days together seemed to have foretold.

In private moments with his friend, Leo was more skeptical. "Why don't you just fuck around and have fun?"

T.J. couldn't explain it himself. He'd never had a serious romantic relationship before but every movie, TV show or play he'd ever seen seemed to point out that a monogamous, committed relationship was what Adulthood was all about. And being officially an adult was everything he'd wanted since his mother took him on his first audition.

As if responding to his thought of her, Janice called her son as he was getting a Snapple out of his refrigerator. She called often to check in, even though he was rarely home. She was happy to catch him.

"Your big birthday will be here before you know it," she enthused, "so do you want us to make plans? We could come in for a visit."

He looked at the calendar with all the red Xs working through April. Sure enough, his eighteenth birthday in July was on the horizon. He was less enthused for a celebration or gifts than he was for finally being of legal age. Besides, as much as he loved his parents, the thought of them visiting him in Manhattan seemed like more of a chore than a treat. Was he ready for them to see the roach infestation? To meet Andy? They certainly wouldn't appreciate drinks at Tom Kats or The Works.

"I'm pretty focused on auditions and classes, Mom," he explained. "Maybe I'll just come home for a weekend and we can have dinner at the Club?"

"Whatever you want, honey. Just let us know. Oh, hang on, your father wants to say hello."

T.J. sighed heavily. Chances are Dad wanted to talk about money or school, two subjects T.J. was keen to avoid as long as possible.

His father's deep voice greeted him and after a few perfunctory moments of small talk came the inevitable question. "How's the job hunt going there?"

Trying to feign optimism over irritability, T.J. answered, "Like I told you, I had to quit The Gap because I was getting so many small things here and there."

"You didn't leave university to work in a clothing store."

"I'm auditioning all the time, trying to find the big show. Lots of of cattle and chorus calls."

"Keep me posted," his father said, and while he may not have meant for it to sound like a command, that was how

T.J. interpreted it. "If we need to get you registered for the fall semester, we'll have to act soon."

"Okay, Dad, I understand," he said quickly, anxious to wrap up the conversation as quickly as possible. He made up an excuse. "I've got to get to a voice lesson now. Give Mom a hug for me. "

He hung up and looked at the calendar. For the first time since he'd come to New York City to embark on this adventure, he felt like he was running out of time.

Andy called on Friday afternoon to say he was stuck at work in New Jersey and didn't expect to be back until late that night, so they'd have to see each other the next day. Disappointed, T.J. tried not to be suspicious. He asked Leo to go out somewhere and give him a distraction. They arranged to meet at The Gap after his shift and find a place to grab a bite.

By eight, they were enjoying the warm spring night at an outdoor table at Pappardella on the corner of Columbus and 75th. T.J. was still fixated on Andy and his absence.

"Do you think he really had to work late?" he asked Leo. "I mean, it's the weekend."

"Forget about it," Leo advised, slurping up some linguini. T. J. couldn't help thinking how it paled in comparison to his Nona's. "Where shall we go after dinner?"

Mind racing, T.J. suggested, "The Works."

It wasn't far from Pappardella, and they walked the five blocks. "Looking for Andy?" Leo asked when they'd found a spot at the bar. "I think you wanted to come here to see if he's out and about without you." The place was unusually crowded and the atmosphere electric, thanks to everyone's Spring Fever.

"No—not true," T.J. quipped, trying to make it light. After they got their beers, he added, "Let's check out the talent."

Leo said nothing, even though T.J. knew that he knew he knew he was right. They wandered the circumference of the room, eventually winding up in the back by the pool tables. No sign of Andy.

"I guess he's actually working late," Leo teased.

"Let me check my service. In case he can meet us."

That was a prospect Leo didn't relish, but he nodded patiently while T.J. stepped outside to use a pay phone. There was certainly no way to hear or be heard over the music inside.

A quarter later, one of the nasal operators for the answering service told him him, "Andy called at nine p.m. saying he'd be leaving New Jersey shortly, and you can call him in the morning, but not too early."

Disappointed, T.J. went back inside the bar and offered to get them another round, but Leo suggested a change of scenery. "Let's stop by Brandy's."

T.J. had another idea.

"This place is gross," Leo said loudly, right into T.J.'s ear as they first walked into the Candle Bar.

"I know it is," T.J. shouted back over the music. "That's why I want to make sure he isn't here. Let me just check downstairs and then we can go."

"You're not leaving me alone here."

The two young men ventured to the back and down the

stairs to the back room that had so chilled T.J. during his previous visit. Leo's reaction to the room full of men engaged in assorted sexual activities was less of revulsion and more of surprise. "He actually gets off on this?"

Squinting to get a better look around, T.J. just shrugged. "He's not here. We might as well go."

They returned upstairs and Leo was heading for the door to the street when T.J. stopped at the bar and flagged down the busy bartender.

"Come on—let's not stay," Leo urged.

Undaunted, T.J. opened his wallet as if he were buying a drink but instead pulled out a photo of Andy he'd taken during the rehearsal for Someday My Prince Will Come. "I'm looking for my friend," he said to the bartender. "Have you seen him tonight?"

The busy bartender took a cursory look at the photo and shook his head.

"Like he'd tell you," Leo said quietly.

"Thanks, anyway," T.J. said.

As he started to move away, the bartender called to him, "Tell Andy I said hey."

Leo and T.J. looked at each other in surprise.

Using his best improvisation skills, T.J. said, "I need to let him know something. It's a family emergency."

The clientele at the bar were calling for service and the bartender was preoccupied. "Maybe you can find him at Les Hommes."

T.J.'s French wasn't very good but he knew that meant,

The Gentlemen.

"Merci," he told the bartender, with deliberate irony. Starting to shake, he walked outside with Leo.

On the sidewalk, he angrily asked between clenched teeth, "What the fuck is Les Hommes?"

"We can check the phone book."

Some older guys, obviously over served and oversexed, wobbled out of the bar behind them. T.J. quickly put on an act of composure and feigned wide eyed innocence as he went up to them. Suddenly, he looked like the teenager no one figured he was.

"Do you guys know Les Hommes?"

The men laughed. One said in a slurred, lisping voice, "Oh, we might have been there once or twice over the years. The question is how do you know it, kiddo?"

"Is it a bar or a nightclub?"

They laughed again, as if it were an inside joke. "None of the above," the other one said, obviously as toasted as his friend. "It's a shop."

"A shop?" T.J. responded. "What kind of shop?"

"A sex shop," the first man qualified. "Magazines and books, videos, poppers and lube. Toys."

"Oh," Leo said, figuring it out.

"Cock rings, butt plugs, dildos, handcuffs—everything you've been wanting from Santa," one said.

"But were afraid to ask," finished the other. They laughed again and he added, "Plus private booths, if the spirit moves you."

"Don't get these boys all excited, now," said his partner.

"They're too young to go in there."

T.J. needed more information in case Andy was there. He kept his innocent act going. "I'll be eighteen soon," he told them. "Where is it?"

As the sloppy men put their arms around each other's waists and started to walk away, one of them turned back to him. "It's just on 80th, east of Broadway. Maybe you can get your daddy to take you for your birthday."

They staggered away and when T.J. looked at Leo, Leo was shaking his head.

"Come on," T.J. nudged. "Now it's a scavenger hunt."

"No, it's a mistake. I'm heading home. You should, too."

"No way. I'll call you later."

Leo had learned how headstrong his friend could be so rather than fight it he simply said, "Be careful," before darting across Amsterdam Avenue where some taxis were parked curbside at the Beacon Theater.

Minutes later, T.J. was walking along 80th Street on the block coming up to Broadway. There was no signage anywhere to indicate the presence of a business, respectable or otherwise. Only brownstones and other residential dwellings occupied this stretch, at least until he reached the northbound thoroughfare of Broadway. A few men came out of the shadows to step quickly up to an intercom buzzer on the side of an otherwise nondescript building. T.J. stopped and drifted back to some brownstone steps where he could discreetly observe.

The latch opened electronically and the men entered. The door shut with a thud, quickly and heavily behind them. T.J.

weighed the idea of ringing the buzzer or slipping in next time the door opened. A moment later, a man in a long overcoat, almost the comical cliché of a flasher, emerged and then strode quickly away.

T.J. sat down on the steps, deciding to give it more time and just observe. He pulled out a cigarette and lit it, his gaze fixed on the mysterious entryway.

There was no further movement for several minutes and he had just stamped out his smoke on the sidewalk when the heavy door swung open again. His stomach flipped over when he saw Andy coming out, unsteady on his feet and obviously high. Now the dilemma was whether or not to keep up the surveillance or confront him.

As Andy was about to stagger by him on his way homeward via Amsterdam Avenue, T.J. simply stood up where he was and said with sarcasm, "Yep, you're working late."

Andy was startled to see him, but not unhappy. "Hey, you!" he exclaimed with a cheerful smile, opening his arms for an embrace.

T.J. pulled back. "I know what's in there. I haven't seen you in a week, but that's where you'd rather be?'

Andy took a deep breath, too exhausted for a confrontation, and sighed heavily as he continued plodding down the block. "Oh, God, here we go."

Following beside him, T.J. vented his frustration. "I don't understand why you make excuses if there's something you'd rather do than spend time with me. Why can't you just tell me if you want to be on your own?"

"Maybe because I know how you'll react. Like this."

"I'm the bad guy because I want to spend time with you? Why shouldn't I be hurt?"

"You're not hurt, you're having a tantrum. Because you're a spoiled brat."

That stung. T.J. was unaccustomed to being criticized in such a way. They had just reached Amsterdam and began the walk to Andy's building. T.J. stepped quickly to keep up with Andy, knowing he just wanted to get home and crawl up the ladder to bed.

"Why am I a brat for thinking my boyfriend shouldn't have to go to a sex shop when he could be home with me having the real thing?"

"First of all, I didn't go there for sex. Although I could have done that if I'd wanted and there'd be nothing wrong with it. And second of all . . ." he momentarily weighed the effect his next words would have and then said them anyway, ". . . we are not boyfriends. Although you are certainly acting like a boy."

T.J. had never been in this kind of situation and it seemed almost unreal, like a scene from a play. He lacked the skills for such a conversation, so he simply responded from pure emotion. "Then what have we been doing all these months? I gave myself to you!"

Andy chuckled at the melodrama, and his dismissive tone further infuriated T.J. "You didn't give yourself to me. I won you in a bet."

He kept walking but T.J. stopped dead in his tracks, crushed and not knowing if he would burst into tears, punch

Andy in the stomach or both, but either of those options would only prove Andy's point.

By the time Andy reached his street corner, T.J. broke into a light jog to catch up with him, afraid that if he let him get out of his sight and back into his apartment, whatever relationship they still had would be finished.

"Let's sleep on it and talk about it tomorrow over brunch," T.J. suggested, trying not to sound as desperate as he was suddenly starting to feel.

"Sleep yes, talk no," Andy replied, fishing into his pocket for the keys to the front door. "You talk too much."

It felt like the hits kept coming as he followed Andy into the building and across the lobby to his apartment door.

"I care about you, Andy," he choked out before venturing, "I think I'm in love with you."

Andy opened his door and tried to muster enough energy and compassion to finish this off. "Look, you are very cute. And very talented. You came to the city to grow up. So go do that and maybe I'll see you after."

T.J. wished he'd gone for the punching option.

"Goodbye, T.J."

Swallowing hard, T.J. made a last ditch effort to get inside the apartment. "Let me pee first. I'll never make it all the way back home unless I go."

Andy acquiesced, flipped on the light by the switch just inside the door and they went in, Romeo strolling up to greet them.

Wordlessly, Andy proceeded directly to the living room

loft, tossing his jacket onto the Soloflex. He missed and it crumpled on the floor. T.J. went into the bathroom and looked at his red, flustered face in the medicine cabinet mirror. As he urinated, he could hear his own voice saying to him, "You tell him you love him and he tells you to grow up."

After flushing, he decided to leave the lid up (a habit of which his mother had broken him years before). He then opened the medicine chest and began tossing most of its contents into the toilet bowl. Toothpaste, floss, deodorant, vitamins. With particular satisfaction, he opened Andy's favorite cologne, Drakkar Noir, and emptied it all. I'll show you a tantrum, he thought.

For good measure, he finished by plunking Andy's new WaterPik toothbrush in with everything else. He gave the toilet another flush, knowing there was no way all those things would make it through the plumbing. Then, he put the lid down.

As he was about to walk out of the apartment, presumably for the last time, he could hear Andy's resounding snores already coming from the other room. Romeo was still by the door, looking up at him, lazily. It occurred to T.J. that there was nothing keeping him from just leaving the place wide open.

Sharing a sad look with the sleepy old feline, he couldn't do it.

"So long, Romeo," T.J. said, closing the door, and this chapter, behind him.

CHAPTER THREE
Happy Birthday

Objectively, T.J. knew that July 15 wouldn't have some magical effect just because it was his eighteenth birthday. Nevertheless, Andy's words still stung and he was eager to officially become an adult. The fact that it would be a Wednesday was unfortunate, and since Independence Day fell on a Saturday, he and Leo decided that would be the best time to go out for a big celebration. Not only for T.J.'s birthday but also in honor of Leo's graduation from Business School and finishing up at The Gap to start interviewing for entry level positions in the world of finance.

While most Manhattanites fled the city on summer weekends, especially holidays, to places like Fire Island or The Hamptons, they thought it would be fun to take advantage of lighter crowds and treat themselves to a night out somewhere they'd ordinarily have trouble getting a reservation. They settled on the famous Windows on the World restaurant high atop the World Trade Center's North Tower.

Donning their summer duds, T.J. in Ralph Lauren and Leo in new Abercrombie & Fitch, they emerged from the 107th floor elevator bank. They were more stunned by the clientele than the breathtaking city views—and not in a good way.

"Jesus Christ," T.J. said almost breathlessly, sounding a lot like his mother. "Who are these people?"

"Tourists," Leo stated, blankly.

Sure enough, the dining room was moderately occupied by dozens of leisure-wearing out-of-towners, talking so loud they drowned out the clatter of dishes and flatware. Many of them were snapping pictures of each other with their Kodak Instamatics and Polaroid cameras.

"Why didn't they tell us it was Amateur Night?" T.J. asked.

"I wonder where they parked the tour bus," Leo volleyed back. "Should we go somewhere else?"

"No question," answered T.J. "Let's go up to Brandy's. Hopefully Luke is working."

"This place is beautiful, though," Leo admitted.

T.J. considered a moment. "Let's save it for New Year's Eve. I bet the fireworks would be great from here."

Leo agreed and as they headed back to the elevator, he asked, "Do you think you'll still be here for New Year's?"

Trying to sound confident, he answered, "I'll find a way."

He didn't need to figure it out. The day before his birthday, his mother travelled into Manhattan to take T.J. and Leo out to lunch at Le Train Bleu, the charming French restaurant hidden behind the sixth floor housewares section of the flagship Bloomingdales store. It was her first time meeting Leo and she found him adorable. The feeling was mutual, especially since Janice Porter was so different from Leo's own mother. He told Janice she reminded him a lot of the actress who played Krystle Carrington on the new hit show, Dynasty. Like Linda Evans, she was a WASPy beauty, but she peppered her speech with posh profanities that seemed all the more charming coming from someone with her undeniable poise. She was also outwardly affectionate with her son, which Leo noticed with some envy.

They followed lunch with a short birthday shopping spree for T.J. that included a basic set of stainless steel pots and pans, even though T.J. never cooked anything that couldn't be heated on his electric hot plate. Janice contended that they were a kitchen staple he should have regardless, and she encouraged him to save money by eating at home more often. Not to leave out Leo, she surprised him at the cashier's station with a lovely set of linen napkins.

When the trio got back to T.J.'s apartment, laden with their Big Brown Bags from Bloomies, T.J. tried to ignore the wall calendar as they unpacked their purchases. He had less than a month and a half before his back-to-school deadline.

Janice checked her watch as she was stacking the new cookware into the cupboards, sending a couple roaches running for cover. "It's almost four," she said. "I'd better get going. My train is in an hour." She went into another cupboard looking for the Raid bug spray.

Now aware of the time, T.J. realized he needed to check in with his answering service before the end of the business day. Even though things were quieter during the middle of summer, it was an important habit to keep. He dialed in while Leo used his height to help Janice retrieve the Raid from its storage place on an upper shelf.

T.J. had a message and waved to them frantically. "A pen. I need a pen!"

Leo grabbed one off the table and handed it to T.J., who

asked the operator to start over with the information. He scribbled onto the calendar as she relayed the message. Janice and Leo looked on, expectantly.

After he hung up, they waited to be filled in. T.J. turned to them with a cocky smile.

"That was from Bella at Tomorrow's Promise."

"The soap opera?" Leo asked.

"From the TV acting class?" Janice inquired,

T.J. nodded affirmatively to them and continued, "She wants to know my availability for the next three months." Tapping the calendar hard with his index finger, he pointedly repeated, "Three months!"

The three of them burst into cheers and a spontaneous group hug. He had beaten the deadline. Just!

T.J. had Leo escort his mother downstairs to grab a cab to Grand Central so he could collect himself and return Bella's call. His heart beat excitedly as he waited for someone in the studio production office to transfer him to her extension. She sounded genuinely happy to hear from him and thanked him for returning her call so promptly, especially when most people seemed to be out of town for the summer. Whatever job they had in mind for him, T.J. wondered, was he their second choice because someone else was unavailable? It was a fleeting thought because, whatever it was, it had come in time and was his now.

Bella explained that the casting director—Harry—was away at the Jersey shore, so she was calling on his behalf with the offer. It was the non-contract role of Artie, a young soda jerk at an old fashioned ice cream parlor where a new storyline would play out featuring the show's teenage characters. Because the show taped a few weeks in advance, it was part of a Back to School plot with the leading characters heading off to their first semester of college. The irony was not lost on T.J.

She described the part as an Under Five, meaning that for budget purposes the writers had to restrict his lines of dialogue to five or fewer. She assured him it would be steady work, a chance for him to learn his way around the rigors of daily TV production and make an impression on "The Powers That Be," in case bigger opportunities were to arise.

He was to go in Monday to pick up his first script and have a fitting for his costume, a retro take on the traditional soda jerk with a bow tie, red and white striped apron and paper hat. She finished up the phone call by proposing he come by midday and they could grab a quick lunch together after he met the wardrobe designer, Deidre.

T.J. was shaking with excitement when he hung up the phone. He wished they'd picked up an ice cream scoop while they were at Bloomingdales. He grabbed his house keys and dashed out to go buy one and a pint of Haagen-Dazs, so he could practice his technique. He didn't consider himself a method actor, but he thought this was a skill he needed to master.

Leo convinced him to keep the celebrations going, saying they should meet at Brandy's for cocktails. Armand would be tagging along with some other friends so they could commandeer a whole corner of the bar.

After a few rounds of cocktails, handsome Luke came to the microphone and sang a beautiful rendition of Corner of the

Sky from Pippin, silencing the swooning, appreciative crowd. As he finished, he spoke softly before the applause could start and said, "I'd like to dedicate that to tonight's birthday boy, T.J. Preston."

"Birthday MAN," Armand quipped back, flourishing his empty martini glass.

"I stand corrected," Luke smiled and began the Happy Birthday song. Everyone in the bar joined in singing. When it ended, they all applauded. Leo leaned over to T.J. and asked, "Are you dying right now?"

"I didn't think he knew my name," T.J. answered, sotto voce.

Luke came over to their table and, unabashed, gave T.J. a kiss right on the lips. "Happy Birthday, man."

They weren't even sure if Luke was gay, so everyone at the table was dumbstruck. Except for Armand, who shouted across the table, "Honey, my birthday is September third!"

After ordering another round for the table, T.J. asked his best friend, "Did all that mean he's interested in me, or was he just being nice?"

"I've never seen him do that for anyone else."

"What should I do?"

"Why not go for it? You've got nothing to lose and you deserve a rebound after Andy the asshole."

T.J. knew how to flirt but he didn't think he had the nerve to ask out someone as chiseled and handsome as Luke. One more screwdriver before they called it a night would be the liquid courage he needed.

As they headed to the door, he stopped by the bar where Luke was clearing away some empty glasses and said, "Thanks again. For the song."

Luke had all the confidence T.J. lacked and brazenly winked at him. "I'm a July baby , too. It was last week. Want to return the favor?"

"You want me to sing you a song?"

"I'm off tomorrow. How about a movie?"

Gobsmacked, T.J. simply said, "I like movies."

Luke seemed to know the effect he had on people, especially after they'd been drinking. He wrote his number on a cocktail napkin.

"Call me after noon and we'll figure it out."

Eighteen is starting off very well, T.J. thought.

Even though it was a hot summer afternoon, T.J. dressed up in the new Armani shirt and pleated pants he'd gotten at Bloomingdales. It took most of the morning for him to decide what to wear and get his hair "splowed" (sprayed and blow dried) to his satisfaction. He'd managed to control himself until noon, and he had the movie listings from the newspaper spread out on the table. Superman II, Endless Love or For Your Eyes Only were their choices.

Luke chose the latter and T.J. started wondering if this was going to be an actual date or if Luke was just being nice, in a flirtatious kind of way. Maybe he was just a sexual person and acted this way with everyone, in spite of what Leo said. After all, no one ever saw him outside of Brandy's.

They sat in the darkened Cineplex on East 34th Street but T.J. could barely focus on 007's adventures. He sat waiting nervously for some kind of signal from Luke, but the only action coming from him was his wide-eyed appreciation for the action on screen. Robotically he pushed popcorn into his mouth, then wiped his salted finger tips on his jeans, chewing with his mouth open. With a side glance, T.J. noticed all this but his only thought was, What a gorgeous specimen Luke is, in spite of his manners.

When the film finally ended, after more than two hours, and the credits began to roll, Luke said, "Roger Moore's good, but I like Sean Connery better."

T.J. had no opinion about James Bond. All he could think about was tasting the salt on Luke's lips.

"Want to grab some dinner?" was all T.J. could think to say.

"There's really good Chinese takeout on my corner. We can eat at my place."

Bingo! T.J. made a note to himself—his new Calvin Klein briefs which "sit at the hip with the high cut leg" would now be his lucky underwear.

Less than an hour later, they arrived at Luke's top floor studio apartment, a four-flight walk up. It was dusk and the place was small, dark and messy with the only light coming from an overhead windowed skylight. Luke put the bag of pork fried rice, pepper steak and egg rolls on the counter. Then he picked up a matchbook and lit the candle and incense that were also on the counter.

He said nothing—he just went over and put his arms around T.J., pulling him close so their mouths could meet. T.J.

was happy to cede all control over to him and Luke seemed to sense it. He hungrily pushed his tongue inside T.J.'s mouth, going in as far as possible. T.J. had never been kissed this way. And Luke DID taste like salty popcorn.

They had their clothes off within minutes, including the lucky underwear. Their naked bodies fell onto Luke's unmade bed and he took charge of every move, alternately rolling on top of T.J. and then pulling him over and staying on his back. It was almost acrobatic—Luke obviously was a highly skilled lover. He also possessed the most enormous phallus T.J. had ever seen. It would have been intimidating if he'd not been so consumed with appreciation for every aspect of Luke's rock-hard physique. He even had the indentations from his abdominals to his crotch that Armand so charmingly would refer to as a man's "cum gutters." And T.J. realized there was no more resentment of Andy, he of the small penis and cigarette breath.

After an hour of making out, Luke finally grabbed T.J. by his mane of hair and pushed him down to his groin so he could thrust himself into T.J.'s mouth. There was no way it would all fit, but T.J. was determined to try. It would be nice to have a new boyfriend, but even if this was just a one-time event, he wasn't going to risk missing out on a moment.

T.J. had developed his own considerable talent for oral sex and it wasn't long before Luke was ready to climax, but he pulled back, stopping himself and panting slightly.

"You're good," he told T.J. with a smile.

"And you're fucking amazing," T.J. responded.

"I want to fuck you."

That wasn't what T.J. was expecting to hear. As turned on as he was, there was no hesitation—but it was something he had never done before. "You'll have to show me how," he whispered.

Wordlessly, gently and with passion, that is exactly what Luke did. T.J. laid on his back, looking up through the skylight at the black sky as this Adonis pushed deep inside him. It was intense in both pleasure and pain.

After they'd both climaxed and Luke collapsed beside T.J., he said, "The food'll be cold. Hungry?"

"Nah. I'm full." He laughed. There was an awkward silence while they both tried to think of what conversation they could possibly have. When they couldn't come up with anything, they started kissing again and went for another round.

It was almost midnight when T.J. finally put on his rumpled Armani. The candle was just about finished and the incense was now just a string of ash. Buttoning his shirt, he knew this would not be the beginning of a love affair but it would certainly be a night to remember. And it set the bar for the kind of sexual prowess he would come to expect from his lovers. He knew Prince Charming was somewhere out there in Manhattan, but he would certainly enjoy kissing frogs in the meantime.

Sore from the experience, T.J. was ready to limp down the four flights to find a cab for home. Luke was already dozing off. As tempting as it would be to climb back in bed with him and get more playtime in the middle of the night or in the morning, T.J. knew he had to go and prepare for Tomorrow's Promise.

Today was amazing, he thought as he made his way slowly down the wobbly, squeaking steps, and tomorrow will be even better. He knew he was too excited to sleep.

T.J. arrived at the Midtown East studios the next day, a full half hour earlier than his appointment, and he killed the extra time on a nearby bench in Bryant Park. He was dressed the same as his last class at the Gotham TV Academy, figuring that was the look that landed him this opportunity, so why mess with success? Five minutes before he told Bella he would arrive, he checked in with the friendly security guard who found his name on the day's Visitors List. Maybe soon, T.J. mused, it would be on a dressing room door,.

The guard directed him down a long, fluorescent-lighted corridor to the production office. His perfectly shined shoes clicked on the linoleum tiles as he walked. He almost felt like he was on a catwalk, trying to remain poised and confident for any producer who might be watching. Rounding a corner he saw a plastic sign on the heavy door indicating he had reached Production. Overhead, there was a covered light that said On Air, but it wasn't illuminated. He opened the door and stepped into an immense office crammed with desks, typewriters, filing cabinets and boxes stacked to the ceiling. There was also a beat-up old sofa and some folding chairs in front of a panel of television monitors. It looked more like someone's garage than Metro Goldwyn Mayer.

Nor was it the hive of activity he was expecting. Instead of a crowd of cast and crew, there were two lone women working at the desks, one of whom was Bella. She was using

White-Out tape on a script when T.J. walked in. She looked up from her work and smiled.

"Good timing. I'm almost finished here."

She saved her place in the script and stood up to greet him. They shook hands and she gestured to the messy room. "Welcome to the glamorous world of television!" she said cheerfully.

He laughed and thanked her, adding "It's not exactly what I imagined."

"Wait 'til you see the sets. Then you'll really be disappointed."

On the contrary, when he looked at one of the monitors, he could see the taping taking place on set. There was the matriarch of the show, Hope Stewart, in her familiar kitchen. He'd seen it what felt like a million times over the years, whenever he was at his Nana's or she was visiting. Nana never missed her stories.

"Come on—I'll introduce you to Deidre in Wardrobe and then we'll go to lunch. I'm finishing up your script now."

Bella walked T.J. to a staircase that took them up two flights to another corridor that went past a long line of small dressing rooms. Most of the doors were closed but the ones that were open showed the traditionally lighted mirrors, many with pictures taped to them, and magazines and soda cans were strewn on the tabletops. They walked past a large room that looked like a beauty salon, with several chairs and a long line of mirrors, sinks and salon-style hair dryers. A hairdresser, a cigarette dangling from her lips, was rolling a woman's hair with the biggest curlers he'd ever seen.

"Obviously, that's Hair and Makeup," Bella said as they continued.

Reaching the end of the hallway they came to another large room marked Wardrobe. It was another two-story space packed floor to ceiling with every imaginable kind of clothing and costume, one side labeled Male and the other Female. There were lots of sequins.

"Deidre, I brought you your Artie," she announced.

From in between a rack of clothing, Deidre appeared, almost as if by magic. She was a tall, attractive brunette around his mother's age and she smiled and extended a hand as she said, "Hello, jerk."

Seeing his stunned expression, she quickly clarified, "As in soda jerk! Artie's the soda jerk, right?"

They all laughed and Bella said, "I'll leave you in good hands, T.J. Can you find your way back down to Production when you're finished?"

He nodded, thinking how fun it would be to get lost and explore every nook and cranny of this magical place. Bella departed and Deidre set about getting T.J.'s measurements using the tape she kept around her neck like a feather boa.

As she knelt down to measure his inseam, he flashed back to Luke's presence in that same, intimate spot just the night before. He still hadn't called Leo with all the juicy details and couldn't wait for their catch-up that night. They would have spoken early that morning but Leo was already at his new job with the Citibank training program.

"The latest schedule has you starting Wednesday, so I'll

have everything pulled and pressed for you," Deidre told him. "It will be on a hanger in your dressing room."

"How will I know where to go?"

"When you get your call time and come in, it will be posted in Production. Extras and Under-Fives usually share the two big rooms at the end of the hall, one for the boys and one for the girls."

She stood up and retrieved the paper cap she had for "Artie" on a nearby ironing board. Plopping it on his head to test its size, she observed, "It fits. So don't go getting a big head." He liked Deidre and he liked being there.

When he rejoined Bella, she handed him a script. "Here you go, hot off the Xerox machine." It was actually still warm. She tapped on the script cover that had a scene by scene breakdown of the episode as well as a column of character names. At the bottom of the list, there was "Artie U/5 - 7am" and she pointed out, "Seven a.m. call time. You'll have a dry rehearsal in the rehearsal hall, then report to hair and makeup and hang out until it's time for dress rehearsal and taping. Just like we taught you at school."

"Can't wait," he said as she started straightening out some things on her desk in preparation to go to lunch.

Just then, Martha Feldon the actress playing Hope Stewart, came from the studio floor, through a soundproof door, and T.J. felt a bit star struck. Nana's all time favorite TV star! She had been on the show since the very first day it premiered, decades before, and she was the beloved heroine of the stalwart Stewart family. The actress was smaller in person than she appeared on

TV—almost tiny, but her diminutive size did nothing to dispel her commanding presence. She strode across the production office with authority and called out to Bella and her colleague, who was at another desk typing up a script.

"Ladies, tell the writers I am on my way," she announced without looking at them or stopping. She charged right up the steps.

Bella and the other woman, Phyllis, exchanged a knowing glance.

Phyllis picked up the phone receiver and Bella whispered to T.J., "She always changes her lines. And she's got hearing like a bat."

"That's not where the resemblance ends," Phyllis muttered.

T.J. had expected a quick lunch with Bella would be at some nearby sandwich shop but instead he found himself at a very dark steakhouse, sitting in a corner booth of red leather. It was apparent that she was a regular customer, as the ancient waiter with a clip-on bow tie greeted them briefly before escorting them back to her "usual" table. When he asked if they'd like to start with something to drink, T.J. asked for a Coca Cola and Bella told the waiter, "You know what I want." He brought her a martini with an olive, served in a dainty little glass.

Two sips later, her glass was empty and she folded her hands on the table top. "So, T.J., what do you think of the studio?" she asked enthusiastically.

"So cool," he answered, as his soda appeared. "I can't wait to see all the sets."

Before the waiter could depart, she made a point of telling him, "Chablis, please."

It was unusual for T.J. to see someone drinking at lunch, unless it was a weekend brunch situation. Bella, however, didn't seem to be anything but her usual cheerful and efficient self. She explained that she had read the upcoming story breakdowns and his Artie character would have more lines and screen time as the plot involving the young college-aged characters developed in the weeks ahead.

Delighted, he admitted, "It was always my grandmother's favorite soap opera."

"It was everybody's grandmother's favorite," she said with a chuckle. "But now, with Luke and Laura running around General Hospital and all the racy stuff on The Young and the Restless, the writers are scrambling to come up with stuff for younger audiences. Hence, the college kids."

It made sense to T.J. and he was excited to be a part of this new direction for the show.

"That's why Martha is on the warpath," she continued. "Martha Feldon, the grande dame. She's not used to being on the back burner."

They ordered club sandwiches and got to know each other a bit while Bella knocked back a second glass of wine. Although Bella was only a couple years older than T.J., she had grown up in the City with a similar private school education to his. She, however, was the love child of a prominent newspaper editor and the Puerto Rican family nanny, whom he eventually married when she insisted on going through with the pregnancy and his first wife divorced him. Bella had been ostracized by her prep school classmates because of her darker skin tones and the family scandal that faculty and parents still whispered about.

"Real life is juicier than any soap opera," she surmised. "Even if I don't have an evil twin."

"Not that you know of," he joked. "Or maybe you are the evil twin!"

She chortled and said, "More likely."

Tilting the glass to get the very last drop of Chablis, Bella said, "Damn! I wish we had time for one more but I have to get back. They're doing some screen tests this afternoon for the part of Angela Van Dyke."

T.J. had actually heard of that character, a leading player who'd been on the show since the days when he watched with his Nana. "What happened to the actress who's been playing her forever?" he asked.

"Nothing," she answered, matter of fact. "But she's a pain in the ass and her agent wants more money, so they figure if they have screen tests for a replacement, it'll scare her into submission."

Real life was juicier, indeed. T.J. was already entertained and intrigued. And while Bella might technically be a work colleague, he felt like they were already on their way to a fast friendship.

CHAPTER FOUR
The Actor's Life

T.J.'s first few days as the campus soda jerk went off without a hitch, even if the scripts didn't call for him to do anything other than say, "What'll you have?' and "Here you go." None of the characters addressed him by name, but Deidre did include a name tag pinned to his costume's lapel that read, "Artie." Now he could legitimately say he had a named part on a national television show, something about which his mother was boasting all over Connecticut. He quickly overcame his insecurity about the silly costume while all the principal actors were decked out in gorgeous fashion after Martha Feldon passed him in the corridor and commented, "Cute. I remember those."

He had been well trained at the Gotham TV Academy and knew how to hit his marks and not upstage himself, and how to avoid pulling focus from the stars of the scenes. He was always punctual and prepared, only spoke when spoken to and didn't try to engage any of the cast or crew in extracurricular conversation.

Bella was an exception and he would often linger briefly in the production office for a chat, on his way to the set or the dressing rooms. She regaled him with stories of her nighttime adventures around town, scoring drinks or drugs by flirting with men and rewarding them with sexual favors. T.J. found her impressively cosmopolitan and self confident, unworried by what anyone else thought about her liberated libido or partying ways. It didn't seem to affect her work as she daily churned out her duties of what she called script cleaning, issuing revised production schedules, arranging car services for the senior executives and coordinating casting sessions. Amazingly, she managed to do it five days a week with work hours that ranged from long to endless. An omnipresent bottle of aspirin was part of her morning coffee routine, the two or three drink lunch was normal when she didn't have to suffice with a bagel sandwich at her desk. T.J. suspected she probably called upon a bump or two of cocaine when tapings went into the evening.

He loved the routine and pace of TV production and was anxious with every script he received to see if Artie would have more to do than just scoop and serve. Bella told him to be patient as she was confident the Powers That Be would notice him and expand the role. Best of all, the first episode he had taped was set to air and he notified his parents and Leo to tune in.

"I don't think Citibank is going to let me take a day off to stay home and watch soaps," Leo said. "I guess I need to buy a VCR."

It occurred to T.J. that he should buy one himself, and begin recording his work for an ultimate demo reel for the agent hunt.

"I'll go to Macy's and get one. We can have a viewing party at my place!" He never entertained at his apartment and this was the perfect excuse to invite Leo and Bella over.

"I'll bring the vodka," Leo suggested before adding with innuendo, "It's time I meet your new best friend, Bella."

T.J. rolled his eyes at Leo's sarcasm. "You're busy building your banking empire, Mr. Moneybags. Besides, you'll love her."

His parents and friends back home had all tuned in for the live broadcast and, when T.J. saw it, he was disappointed that his background appearance was so brief and unexciting. He also thought he would benefit from getting his near-mullet trimmed to better accommodate the paper hat which seemed to be perched on top of his head. He wondered if he looked heavier on camera, as the old adage noted that "the camera adds ten pounds."

Of all T.J.'s many talents, technology was not among them so Leo helped him hook up the new VCR. He recorded his first three appearances so they could watch along with Bella, who also brought along some guy she'd met on the M104 bus coming downtown. He introduced himself as Joe, but Bella confessed later that she thinks he was just making it up to cover his tracks after their inevitable one night stand.

After several screwdrivers, Leo and Bella did indeed hit it off and by the time she staggered out with "Joe," they all agreed to get together more often. She recommended a bar and restaurant called Extra Extra, around the corner from the studio, next to the Daily News Building on 42nd Street and Second Avenue. She promised a great jukebox and bartenders that were as generous with their liquor pours as they were easy on the eyes.

"Count us in," Leo said, "Even if it means schlepping to the East Side."

Over the course of the weeks that followed, T.J. began to feel more comfortable not only on set, but backstage as well. Cast and crew members got to know him by name and would engage him in banter and water cooler conversations. Deidre's domain in the wardrobe room was usually the most fun place to start the day, having a coffee and cigarette while she was ironing or steaming costumes. The Hair & Make Up department was the place to go for gossip or a laugh: Martha never failed to offer up some sarcastic comment such as the morning she was getting her thinning hair teased and sprayed while she read a newspaper account about a hotel collapse in Missouri, killing over a hundred people and injuring dozens of others. "All those people died," she observed drily, "and not one of them was a writer."

Even sitting around on set in between takes or set ups was fun and T.J. enjoyed the camaraderie with the salty, middle-aged stage hands, camera and boom operators even more than with the main actors who seemed to always be running their lines or checking their appearances in the ever present hand mirrors and touching up with powder to erase any trace of shine. The old guys were like surrogate uncles and the stage manager, Gerry, always made copies of the daily crossword puzzle and handed them out for everyone to work on during breaks. T.J. quickly became adept at figuring out the puns and themes that made them a challenge.

It was this puzzle expertise that led Martha herself to approach him one afternoon while he was sitting on the Ice Cream Parlor set waiting for everyone else to come back from a lunch break. Bella had proposed they go to the steakhouse, but he hadn't felt like changing his costume so he just stayed put and made do with a coffee and a bag of pretzels from the vending machine.

"I hear you're the Will Shortz around here," she said to him, unexpectedly, referring to the famous puzzle writer. She held up the Xeroxed copy of the puzzle she'd gotten from Gerry. "38 Across . . . I give up. It must be a generational thing."

T.J. had his completed copy under the soda fountain counter and pulled it out. He checked it and smiled. "You sure you want me to tell you?"

"I surrender."

"It's Minnow. The shipwrecked boat on Gilligan's Island was the S.S. Minnow."

Raising up the reading glasses that hung on a chain around her neck, she focused on the paper and nodded. "Ahh, so it is."

She turned and walked away, back toward the Kitchen set where her scenes would be taped and, without looking back, said to him, "Thank you, Mr. Shortz."

Would this be a new nickname? Mr. Shortz was preferable to Jerk.

The next time he was bellied up to the bar at Extra Extra with Bella and Leo, T.J. asked her more about the venerable Martha Feldon and learned that her private life was even more colorful than her TV counterpart's. After two divorces and a less than stellar attempt at a Hollywood film career in the 1940s (Jack Warner allegedly told her she looked too much like Bette Davis, and "one Bette Davis was more than enough"), she came to New York and carved out a niche as an actress in radio dramas.

With the success of Irna Phillips' The Guiding Light, she and her soon-to-be third husband created a new serial which eventually moved to the new fangled medium of television. The fifteen-minute continuing story of ingénue Hope Stewart was an instant hit and daily staple of millions of American housewives, spawning fan magazines and generating thousands of letters a week ranging from admiration for Feldon's dramatic skills to delusions that her character was a real person in seemingly constant peril.

Martha, who had never had children, became a widow after her third husband and even tried her hand on Broadway and as a folk singer, but show business had indelibly pigeon-holed her as a soap star. As her show expanded to thirty minutes and eventually a full hour, it was a position she appreciated and protected fiercely, especially as changing tastes dictated younger and racier content. She managed to survive the transitions by adopting the matriarchal role both on screen and off, even though she was nowhere near as demure as the long-suffering character she'd been playing for nearly three decades.

"I give her a lot of credit," T.J. defended when Bella was quick to criticize the old lady. "If you think about it, she's doing what even Brando or Olivier couldn't do: keep one single character interesting every single day for all these years."

Bella polished off the olive at the bottom of her empty martini glass and winked at the bartender for a refill. "If you play your cards right," she said, "maybe Artie will still be around in thirty years."

"Do you really want to be scooping ice cream for thirty years?" Leo laughed, admiring the bartender's arms as he worked the martini shaker for Bella's next round.

"It beats folding shirts," T.J. replied.

After drinks and a bar meal of chicken wings, a lightheaded T.J. swerved his way to the bus stop on 42nd Street, having spent the last of his cash at the bar. Luckily, he still had a token in his pocket to get himself home. As he walked by the Daily News building, immortalized in the Superman films as the stand-in for Clark Kent's Daily Planet headquarters, he bumped into a statuesque and beautiful blonde he instantly recognized. Not only had he seen her on television, her face was plastered all across the city on the sides of buses and benches. It was "New York's Most Trusted Newswoman: Carolyn Lee Jessup."

They both begged the pardon of the other for the collision before stopping in mutual recognition. As if cued, they both said, "I know you."

With a chuckle, T.J. replied, "Everybody in New York knows you, but how would you know me?"

With a guilty smile she admitted, "I watch your soap during my lunch break every day. Aren't you the ice cream guy?"

It was the first time T.J. had ever been recognized from television and he suddenly felt ten feet tall. The vodka helped. He immediately thought of Andy and couldn't help hoping he'd somehow found out about T.J.'s new role.

"Yes, I am the ice cream guy," he proudly admitted. "His name is Artie."

Preparing to go on her way, Carolyn Lee said, "Well, it

was nice to meet you, Artie."

Stepping in front of her to clarify, T.J. kept on. "No, Artie is the name of the ice cream guy. On the show. I'm T.J."

"Well, T.J. you and Artie are both adorable. See you around."

"Gosh, I hope so," he said.

Pointing to the Daily News building, she explained, "This is our studio." Then pointing down the block to where T.J. worked, "And I know that yours is over there. So we're bound to bump into each other again. Literally."

"Maybe we could have lunch sometime—if you don't mind missing the show. My treat."

She told him later she admired his moxie and could tell he'd been enjoying Happy Hour. Plus, she found his earnest admiration charming.

"Only if you tell me some backstage secrets," she said with a mock tone of conspiracy.

So began another great friendship in T.J.'s life. Carolyn Lee's parents had named her for the lovely doe-eyed actress/model Carol Lynley, and she had grown up in the posh Main Line suburbs of Philadelphia before attending Columbia University and getting her degree in journalism. Her public image was initially as a scrappy investigative reporter, working her way up through newspaper articles, but her stunning, patrician looks trumped everything else. A canny news director saw her on-camera potential and started her on a successful path as one of New York's first female news anchors. She was a regular fixture in the Manhattan social scene and known as a squeaky clean teetotaler more interested in philanthropy than fashion. Still, she turned up regularly in the Liz Smith and Cindy Adams columns, usually alongside her handsome longtime boyfriend, Gary Sutton, a lawyer who worked in Mayor Koch's administration. Even though she hailed from Philly, Carolyn Lee was really as New York as it got.

The kitchen calendar indicated T.J.'s one-year anniversary of living in New York City had arrived, and he ceremoniously tossed the red pen he'd been using to mark off the days into the trash can. Even though he'd grown up accustomed to being an overachiever, he was proud of what he'd managed to pull off in the last twelve months and, though still on a tight budget, he wanted to celebrate. He came up with the idea of planning a dinner out at Marvin Gardens, a fun, casual restaurant on 82nd and Broadway. He'd ask Leo, Bella and Carolyn Lee and tell them to invite dates. The idea of it all sounded very swanky and grownup to him. But what about his own date?

He hadn't been hitting the bars as often since he started on Tomorrow's Promise. Ever since Carolyn Lee had spotted him from the small screen, he was paranoid about being recognized in a seedy bar and jeopardizing the future of Artie's character before it had barely begun. He decided to ask Luke. The worst case scenario, he thought, would be if Luke had to work at Brandy's. The best case, he'd have another passionate night beneath the skylight.

As it turned out, Luke did have to work but he suggested that T.J. come by after dinner for a last round at the piano bar and they could go back to his place afterwards. T.J. felt that was a winning compromise. Leo found a date from Uncle Charlie's, a cute flight attendant from Texas who was in town for a couple days. Bella showed up with one of the boom microphone operators from the show who happened to also know Carolyn Lee from when he'd worked on their network news crew. Her fiancé, Gary, was apparently tied up at the Mayor's office, so like T.J., she came solo.

The flight attendant couldn't keep his hands off Leo and everyone was amused by how demonstrative they were, which was pretty much out of character for Leo. Carolyn Lee and T.J. sat across from Bella, who was woozy from the time she wobbled into the restaurant. Mr. Boom Operator kept her propped up until he finally handed her a small, folded-up paper from his blazer pocket and suggested she take it into the ladies room and wake herself up. She needed no persuading and when she returned to the table a few minutes later, sniffing, she seemed back to her old self.

"Happy Anniversary, T.J.," she toasted, lifting her second martini glass. Everyone clinked glasses.

"You guys have become my New York family," he acknowledged. "I appreciate it more than I can tell you."

Carolyn Lee was the one who finally got them to wrap it up when she pulled out her wallet to throw some cash on the table. "I have to get home before Gary," she explained. "Or there will be hell to pay."

"Is he planning to run for office himself, one day?" T.J. asked.

"He wouldn't admit it, but I think that's the plan."

"Next time we want to meet him," Leo said, now almost completely conjoined with the flight attendant.

"No one sees him much outside of City Hall or Gracie Mansion," she told them. "I'm not sure I would, if we didn't live together." Seemingly eager to change the subject, she asked T.J., "What about your fellow?"

"Luke?" he responded, sharing a knowing look with Leo. "I wouldn't refer to him as my fellow."

"More like a fuck buddy," Leo clarified.

"More than a fuck buddy," T.J. retorted and then admitted, "but not much more."

Everyone laughed, kicked in some cash and T.J. hightailed it up to Brandy's, confident that his lucky underwear would once again work its magic.

After Luke finished up at Brandy's it was after two a.m. and T.J. was exhausted and relieved he didn't have to work the next day. He was in the mood not only for some physical satisfaction but also for a few drinks, but T.J. was already buzzed from his anniversary dinner. He was content to sip the one Luke poured for him. By the time they got naked and crawled into bed together it was nearly four in the morning and Luke fell immediately asleep, breathing heavily. T.J. didn't mind. It was enough just to be there beside him, drinking in his pulchritude and having the satisfaction of where he was and what he'd been able to accomplish so far in his first year away from home. And he was looking forward to a little morning delight.

They slept in until almost ten and, after some playtime between the sheets, Luke made them coffee and served T.J. in bed. It was like playing house and they enjoyed the domesticity, even though they both knew it wasn't going to lead to anything more permanent. T.J. didn't suggest carrying the day on beyond that and made his way back home, rather enjoying "the walk of shame" when he came out of Luke's apartment building at the crack of noon, then to the subway station, rumpled in his obvious afterglow.

Turning up at the studio the next day and looking forward to a full five lines of dialogue and interacting with one of the lead characters, he began to experience some discomfort midway through the day. He was itching like crazy and had to fight the increasing urge to scratch at his crotch and legs. Had Deidre changed laundry detergents? Why was his costume making him itch so intensely?

He casually mentioned it to Bella during a break in the production office, adding, "I think it's time for some new pants or something."

With a matter of fact tone, even in a whisper she advised, "You'd better check for crabs."

"For what?" he whispered back a bit too loudly, incredulous.

"Or scabies," she offered, blasé. Then, opening one of her desk drawers and rifling around for her magnifying reading glasses which she handed to him, she added, "Go in the bathroom and take a look."

T.J. was stunned but did as he was told. Once in the privacy of the men's room stall, he unzipped and opened his pants to begin the examination.

"Fuck, fuck, fuck," he said out loud as he squinted through the lenses in disbelief at the sight of the translucent little critters attached to him. He could actually see them wriggle.

He hurried back to Bella's desk in an obvious panic. She was almost maternal as she reassured him. "I'll go around the corner to the drug store and buy you some Rid. Try not to scratch. Spill some coffee on your pants at the end of the day and I'll tell Deidre you're taking them to the dry cleaners. And when you get home, you'll use the shampoo. Then you have to strip your bed and wash all your sheets and bed covers."

"How do you know all this?"

"Oh, please," she said dismissively. "It's not my first time at the rodeo! When you have a bad hangover, I have aspirin. Or a steak across the street. For this, it's Rid."

For all Luke's good looks and sexual prowess, T.J. vowed this would mean the end of future trysts with him. Wait until Leo finds out. Would he be as nonplussed as Bella?

True to Bella's word and the promise on the package, the Rid shampoo did the trick and by his next day on set, T.J. was itch free with newly dry cleaned pants. The lucky underwear had been dispensed to his building's trash incinerator.

Martha Feldon was working that same day and called to him from her Kitchen set as he was making his way over to the Ice Cream Parlor. "Hey, Mr. Shortz."

He went to join her and she gestured for him to sit down at the table where she was working on the crossword puzzle. How many times, he wondered, had his Nana watched her play scenes at this very table over the years? It made him feel very close to Martha as if she somehow represented his grandmother.

"You're good with a crossword, but how are your technical skills?" she asked.

"Not so hot," he admitted. "With a little help, I did manage to hook up my VCR, but that's about it. And I finally got rid of my answering service and got an answering machine at Radio Shack."

"I just bought myself an Acorn personal computer from IBM. It's being delivered today and I thought maybe you could help me set it up."

He was flattered she thought to ask him but he told her, "I've never used a PC before. I'm really good on an electric typewriter though."

"Let's figure it out together, shall we? I can pay you ten dollars an hour," she offered.

"Oh, no, I'd never take money from you."

"Even better. We'll barter, then. I'll trade you something if you come over and give me a hand. How about some coaching for acting? They don't give you much to do, but from what I've seen you're pretty good. Hell, those bastards don't give me much to do, either."

He couldn't believe she'd noticed his acting—and thought enough of him to make such a generous proposal.

"Now that's an offer I will happily accept, Miss Feldon."

"As long as you call me Marti, like the rest of my friends do. And I can't keep calling you Mr. Shortz. What is your name?

"T.J. Thomas John."

Writing her address and phone number on the completed crossword puzzle before sliding it to him across the table she said, "This weekend?"

T.J. was unfamiliar with the Upper Eastside neighborhood of Madison Avenue Martha had called home for several decades, so he was early for their eleven a.m. appointment on Saturday. The first chill of autumn was in the air, so he killed some time by grabbing a piping hot coffee from a corner vendor before heading over to her stately building on the corner of 69th Street. He gave his name to the elderly, uniformed doorman who seemed like he'd probably been there since the place was first erected.

"Tenth floor," he croaked to T.J., pointing to a beautifully preserved elevator across from his post in the small, understated but elegant lobby.

Similar to Dottie O'Hara's residence, the elevator landed with a metallic thunk and opened right into her living room. The entire tenth floor was spread out before him, more resembling a country farm house in Westport, Connecticut, than a Manhattan apartment. It was a homey place and a shaggy bearded collie was sitting before him, wagging its tail as if it had been awaiting his arrival. A muted buzzer sounded from somewhere below in the elevator shaft and it made another thunk as its door closed and it descended to another floor.

Martha called out, "In the kitchen!"

T.J. followed the sound of her voice, with the dog trailing dutifully behind. He discovered Martha packing a delicious looking sandwich, an apple and a can of club soda into a brown paper bag. There was a beautiful gray Persian cat watching her every move from the adjacent window sill.

"You're right on time," she said, without looking up from her task. "I, however, am running behind. Madison has been waiting for his walk all morning." The dog's tail wagged faster at the word, "walk."

She handed T.J. the bag telling him, "You take this, I'll get his leash." Following orders, he held the lunch while she retrieved a leash and her sweater from a hook on a service door on the other side of the kitchen. "First things, first."

Down in the noisy elevator they rode with Madison, who was growing more excited. Out onto 69th Street, they began the short walk west to Central Park.

"I have a friend who counts on me for lunch, at least on the weekends," she told him and he assumed they were going to a nearby apartment building. Instead, she led him into the park and a few yards from the entrance, he was surprised to see a gaunt older lady, probably around Martha's own age, surrounded by plastic bags and a small, beat-up valise, sitting against a stone wall. She wore a ragged coat, a floppy sun hat and sat regally under assorted umbrellas she had fashioned into a makeshift canopy.

"Bonjour, Claudine," Martha sang out to her "friend." Madison seized the moment to lift his leg and relieve himself against a tree. "C'est mon ami. Il a pris votre dejeuner." She indicated to T.J. to give her the bag. He did so, smiling awkwardly. He had never interacted this way with a homeless person.

"Voila!" Martha continued merrily, as if they were all in a bistro on the Left Bank of Paris. "Nous avons des choses de faire. A plus tard!"

With that, Martha started off into the park with Madison now moving at a trot. T.J. waved a farewell to Claudine and hurried after them.

"Who's your friend?"

"All I know is her name is Claudine and she's been living in the Park since last spring. She won't let me call anyone or take her to a shelter, so I just keep trying to get some weight on her until she changes her mind. Oh, sweet Jesus, will you look at that?"

He followed her gaze to what she was indicating. Before them was a maple tree, with fiery orange leaves.

"It doesn't just feel like fall," she observed. "It has arrived too early."

T.J. was perplexed. This was the woman Phyllis, the production coordinator, referred to as a bat? The same indomitable star who terrorized the Writers Room at the studio?

It wasn't long before they were back in Martha's apartment and she announced she would now make sandwiches for them to enjoy before they tackled assembling her new word processor. They sat at her long, formal dining room table while they ate, although there was nothing formal about this place. To T.J. it all felt relaxed and comfortable and Marti, as she again insisted he address her, was just as casual in her dress and demeanor.

A grandfather's clock chimed the noon hour from the adjacent living room and she commented, "If you stick around until five, I'll mix us martinis. Do you like martinis?"

"My parents do. And a good friend of mine drinks almost nothing but," T.J. said, keeping Bella's identity anonymous since they all worked together. "I've been meaning to try."

"Good, then today's the day."

The next five hours did indeed fly by. Marti not only showed him around the sprawling, bright three-bedroom apartment, she stopped to show off her eclectic collection of memorabilia, keepsakes and other assorted treasures which included an Emmy Award, framed photos of herself with famous movie stars and politicians including John F. Kennedy, and a crystal ball which "never worked."

They finally got around to unpacking and setting up the computer, a surprisingly simple, straightforward task, much to their mutual relief. T.J. thought she was wonderful company and felt badly that Dottie couldn't take a page from her book. He wondered if they had ever been acquainted. It was hard to imagine.

Once the machine was up and running, Marti walked over to a filing cabinet in the makeshift bedroom-turned-office, nearly tripping on the cat that had appeared underfoot, and pulled out a thick manuscript that was three-hole punched and in a binder. She plopped it down on the desk and explained that it was a play she had written and would appreciate him reading it and giving her feedback. As if he needed convincing, she added, "There happens to be a role in it for you, too."

"Okay," he agreed, flattered. "I'll read it and bring it back to—"

Interrupting him, she said, "It doesn't leave the apartment.

But you can read it here anytime you like, give me your notes and then we'll type it up on our new friend, here." She patted the top of the word processor as if it were a pet.

What had he gotten himself into? Whatever she was becoming—a friend, a mentor or an employer—T.J. was on board.

The clock was chiming again and Marti checked her watch. She may have been dressed in a sweatshirt and old khakis, but her timepiece was Cartier. "Five bells is quitting time. I promised you a martini."

Traveling as a pack along with the dog and cat, Marti and T.J. returned to the dining room where she gave T.J. a step-by-step lesson in the art of making her version of a perfect martini. Stirred, not shaken, Beefeaters Gin in a Vermouth-rinsed glass garnished with two plump green olives and a little splash of the water from the olive jar.

"I call it a Desert Martini, 'cause it's so dry," she said as they took their first sips. Her eyes rolled back and she sighed with dramatic ecstasy. T.J. agreed it was delicious and she remarked, "Next time, you'll make them. Now that you know how."

T.J. began spending most of his days off at Marti's apartment, not only helping her with her play but assisting with daily household duties that included Madison and Claudine (and the cat, whose name he learned was Fido). In exchange, she helped him with some of the monologue he used in auditions and suggested other material as well. Even more fun was when she gave him little lessons in home economics such as the best ways to slice a bagel, the secret to her delicious deviled eggs or how to make a perfect omelet by sliding it from the stove top and folding it over so it finished cooking on the plate. She followed that up by giving him the gift of a cast iron omelet pan with the advice, "Every bachelor should have one. You'll never go hungry as long as you have eggs in the house. You can make an omelet out of any leftovers."

Carolyn Lee and T.J. were finally able to meet for lunch and they opted for The Saloon near Lincoln Center, which had the novelty of waiters on roller skates. The floor show was better than the food or the service, but it was a festive atmosphere and not a bad option for diners content with a simple salad or burger.

As a closet soap fan, Carolyn Lee was excited to hear his stories about Martha Feldon, including her recipe for Desert Martinis and how he'd be helping her put together her famous annual Christmas party.

"How come you never drink?" he asked the beautiful anchor woman.

"I'm not known for self control. It's easier for me to abstain than to just have one or two," she explained.

"I'm like that with chocolate," he said, watching a cute waiter in tight jeans whiz by their table while somehow managing to balance a tray of glassware.

"Food is a whole other issue for me."

"How can that be? You're so svelte." Then he noticed how little of her quiche she had actually eaten, preferring just to push it around the plate with her fork.

"I exercise like a demon," she admitted. "And I know how to . . ." She made a gesture with two of her well manicured fingers going into her mouth.

"I wish I could do that," T.J. he marveled. With a wink, he added, "No gag reflex."

"When all else fails," she leaned in, whispering, "I eat Ex-Lax instead of dessert. Don't tell anyone I said that."

He made a motion to indicate zipping his lips, delighting in learning all sorts of things from his new friend.

"Gary and I have been talking more about the timing of a wedding, too. I don't even want to think about what a wedding gown will do to me."

"You got engaged?"

"Not officially, not yet. Everything with him needs to be discussed, analyzed and scheduled. It's the lawyer in him."

"You'd better get a big rock out of it. If you can keep your fingers out of your mouth long enough to put it on."

She wrinkled her nose at his sarcasm and told him, "I already have one. My Grandmother's. Gary says we shouldn't spend the extra money if we don't have to. I've got it in a safe deposit box until we decide to announce it. He wants to make sure we do it while Koch is still in office to maximize the publicity. It will be good for both of us."

"A wedding at Gracie Mansion?"

"Maybe. But I'm hoping for the Metropolitan Club."

"Ooh, fancy. I've always wanted to go there."

"But you'll get to go to Martha Feldon's Christmas Eve party. That will be fancy."

He shrugged. "I don't know. She lives very well, but she's really down to earth."

"Like her character?"

"Not as sugary sweet, but sort of. She gets a bad rap around the studio 'cause she stands up for herself."

"Being a woman in television isn't easy," she observed, taking the paper napkin from her lap and placing it over her uneaten lunch.

The next day at the studio, T.J. and Marti had lunch in her dressing room so he could help her put together the guest list for her holiday bash. She had a recipe box of index cards with names and addresses on them, as well as an old leather diary, and they cross-referenced the entries.

"We should put all these into one master list on your word processor," he told her.

"Good idea. You know, you're welcome to bring a date to the party."

He thought for a moment and asked, "Would you prefer if I brought a female date?"

"I want you to bring whoever you want, of course. I'm not uptight about that sort of thing and no one I invite would be, either." With a chuckle, she added, "Have you met Bobby? He's always there." Bobby was a flamboyant older makeup artist who worked with them and was almost exclusive to Martha whenever she was in the studio. He knew all the little tricks she preferred to disguise her facelift scars and a drooping left eyelid.

T.J. would have to enlist Leo and Bella to help him go on the prowl for a suitable date. Someone fun and handsome, of course, but classy enough to be around Martha and her circle of friends. He recognized many of the names on the index cards from "old New York," such as Arlene Francis, Joey Adams and Elaine Stritch.

A bell rang in the corridors, indicating that the lunch break was over and the afternoon taping schedule would commence. T.J. jumped up because his scenes were next and he still had to retrieve his paper hat and apron from his dressing room.

"Gotta go, I'll see you later, Marti."

"Okay, kiddo," she replied, not looking up from her task.

When he raced through the production office on his way to the set, he looked for Bella at her desk but she wasn't there. When he finished his scenes an hour later, he checked again but there was still no sign of her. In fact, the plastic cover was over her typewriter, which he'd never seen before. He walked over to Phyllis, who was practically buried under a stack of scripts.

"Is Bella off today?"

"You could say that," she answered, seemingly exasperated with her workload.

"Is she out sick?"

With a heavy sigh, Phyllis said, "You could say that, too."

T.J. didn't understand and pressed. "What's that mean?"

Stopping long enough to look up at him, she spoke with a tone that clearly indicated her irritation. "Look, she's taking a leave of absence." Seeing his bewilderment, she added, "To work some things out."

"Things? What things?"

"I know you're friends, so you'll find out soon enough." She motioned for him to lean down so she could quietly say in his ear, "Bella's parents sent her to rehab."

That night, T.J. and Leo met to discuss Bella's situation over drinks at Ted Hook's Backstage, an upscale supper club across the street from T.J.'s apartment, next door to the Martin Beck Theater. It was pricier than their usual haunts, but the occasion seemed to call for it. Even though it was the theater hour of nine p.m., the place was busy with lots of fashionable looking artsy types whom T.J. felt he should recognize, but didn't.

"I thought you were going to bring Armand," T.J. had said when Leo walked into the dark bar area where T.J. had commandeered a corner table.

"He said he isn't feeling well. Besides, you have to fill me in on what's going on with Bella."

"I don't know much. It's not like I could call her mother and ask, 'Hey, why did you stick your kid in a clinic?' Could I?"

"Do you think it's something more than drinking?"

T.J. shrugged and said, "I left a couple messages. Hopefully she'll get in touch soon."

Eagle eyed to any noteworthy guys entering the place, both of them looked up when a small group of gentlemen made their way to the bar area, enthusiastically and loudly greeted by Ted Hook, himself. These older, well-dressed men were obviously VIPs.

T.J. sunk down in his seat as he glimpsed Ross Woodhouse among them. "Oh shit! That's Velcro Head."

Leo was more struck by the man standing next to Ross and his toupee. "Look who's with him."

They both instantly recognized Benjamin Lord, the beloved father from TV's popular, long-running sitcom, Dear Old Dad. The series still repeated in syndication multiple times a day, so Lord was easily one of the most famous actors of his generation. He occasionally popped up in TV movies and guest-starring roles, but his image was indelibly etched into 1970s pop culture. He still looked the same except for graying hair and the addition of a Marlboro Man style mustache. There had always been whispers that he was a closeted homosexual and his presence at Backstage indicated the rumors were true.

"It's Dear Old Dad," Leo said, almost breathlessly, using the catch phrase from the TV show.

"Oh my God, I've loved him forever."

"He looks almost the same," Leo marveled. "Except for the mustache and hair."

"At least it's his own hair," T.J. retorted, thinking of Ross' bald pate in the back of the taxi cab.

At that precise moment, Ross noticed T.J. He smiled and gave T.J. a little wave as Ted Hook escorted their group to a table, avoiding the possibility of an awkward encounter.

The best friends continued to discuss Bella's predicament, ordering a round of cocktails and acknowledging the irony of imbibing while discussing her time in rehab. Leo also caught T.J. up on his status with the Citibank training program, explaining that he'd soon be moving to a position downtown. He'd be working as a runner for a trader on the floor of the New York Stock exchange. It had the potential to turn into a full-time position with the firm, so they toasted to that, with Leo promising it wouldn't interfere with their social exploits.

Suddenly a waiter appeared with another round of drinks for them, which they hadn't ordered.

"Compliments of the gents over there," the waiter explained, indicating Ross, Benjamin Lord and their friends.

"Thanks!" Leo said enthusiastically, grabbing for his glass.

T.J. saw the men looking their way and he raised his glass to them, mouthing the words, thank you. Considering how slimy Ross had behaved after Dottie's party, T.J. thought this was a classy move.

"That was nice of him."

"Oh, please," Leo responded. "When do we ever have to pay for more than the first two rounds? Maybe Dear Old Dad will come join us."

That didn't happen, no matter how much they tried to get Benjamin Lord to notice them. They finally decided to head out and as they made their way to the door, Ross emerged from the restroom and strode over to them, holding his hand out for T.J. to shake.

"Ross, this is my best friend, Leo," T.J. greeted him. "Leo, Ross Woodhouse."

They shook hands and exchanged pleasantries before T.J. added, "Thanks again for the drinks. Nice to see you."

Ross leaned closer to T.J., who stiffened in case a grope or wet kiss was to follow, but the director simply whispered, "My friend, Ben, is here from L.A. for the holidays. He thinks you're a dreamboat."

So Dear Old Dad noticed, after all. Feeling emboldened, if not a little cocky, T.J. asked, "Would he mind if I said hello?"

"He'd be thrilled," Ross assured him.

Leo was taking this as a cue to be on his way, but T.J. grabbed his arm and led the way over to the group. The others had circled around Benjamin, literally the center of their attention, but he looked up at T.J. and Leo with obvious appreciation.

"Hello, gentlemen," T.J. said with confidence, as if he were performing a monologue back at Saperstein's acting class. "Mr. Lord, welcome to New York City."

Leo couldn't believe what was happening.

"Well, thank you, young man," the celebrity said. "Please, call me Ben."

"If you don't have plans yet, Ben, would you like to join me for a Christmas Eve party?"

The men all seemed impressed with T.J.'s brass and expectantly looked to Ben for his reply.

Smiling with the same feeling of appreciation that T.J. was experiencing, he smoothly accepted. "I think that would be wonderful."

Ben told T.J. to call him at his hotel, the Warwick on 54th Street, and one of the other gentlemen gave his business card to Leo, so they left Ted Hook's Backstage feeling pleased with themselves. Ted said to them on their way out, "Come back again soon, fellas," so they knew they'd made a good impression all the way around.

Over the weekend, after walking along Madison over to Central Park and dropping off a sack lunch for Claudine, T.J. and Marti began decorating the twelve foot Scotch pine she'd had delivered that morning. They brought two big boxes of ornaments and a plastic bag of string lights up from the basement storage room and carefully unwrapped everything. They sipped hot apple cider as carols played on the Hi-Fi while they worked. Merrily they strategically placed each decoration according to Marti's direction. It culminated with her retrieving two new boxes of tinsel which had to be perfectly (and to T.J., agonizingly) hung, strand by strand. It was old-fashioned decor, like the trees he remembered from his early childhood in Connecticut, but worth the effort. The end result was breathtaking.

They plopped themselves on the sofa, exhausted and proud of their work. Fido was already investigating the lowest hanging ornaments, which Marti knew from experience had to be feline-proof.

Taking a cigarette from the box she kept on the coffee table, she offered one to T.J., who accepted. As she lit them, she mentioned, "I have an early present for you."

"Oh, gosh, Marti, that isn't—" he began.

She cut him off, waving to the other side of the room. "It's in the piano bench."

He loved presents, so he sprang up and moved to the bench. Lifting the lid, he uncovered the small gift, beautifully wrapped in green paper with a small red bow.

"May I open it now?"

"Yes, please. I hope you like it."

He loved it. Beneath the wrapping was a Tiffany box, in the iconic robin egg's blue, which held a sterling silver cigarette case. It had a beautiful scroll design and was engraved with his initials, "T.J.P." He pushed the little clasp to spring it open and a dozen cigarettes were stacked inside beneath the small elastic band designed to keep them in place.

"It's gorgeous. Thank you so much."

"I know everybody's quitting these days, so if you decide to do that you can keep business cards in it or something. Or you can take it back to Tiffany's and exchange it for something."

"Not a chance. And now I'll never quit smoking," he said with a little laugh. "I'll show this off at your party."

"Did you find a date yet?"

"As a matter of fact, I did," he smiled, slyly. "Do you know Benjamin Lord?"

Marti was surprised. "The TV actor? Dear Old Dad?"

T.J. nodded, lighting his cigarette and taking a drag. She did, too, and told him, "I knew him a hundred years ago in Hollywood. He's delightful. But he has a reputation which is probably well deserved. Proceed with caution."

"Maybe he'll fall hopelessly in love with me." T.J. knew it was unlikely but it was fun to imagine.

"I suspect there's a reason he's a perpetual bachelor, but then again . . . he may be at the age where he's looking to finally settle down."

Snuggling up beside Madison, who had jumped onto the sofa, T.J. optimistically said, "We'll find out in a few days." Patting the seat cushion, he added, "Right here."

"Don't kill yourself looking for love, Presh. Let it find you."

The last day at Tomorrow's Promise before the Christmas break was Friday the 23rd and Phyllis pulled T.J. aside to let him know that something had arrived for him in studio mail. Excited, he wondered if it was his first piece of fan mail, but it turned out to be a Christmas card. From Bella.

Beneath the pre-printed seasonal greeting, she had written, "T.J. Sorry for disappearing but I'm trying to get my shit together. At least they still let me smoke. It was either this or get fired, so hopefully I'll see you soon in the New Year. Love, Bella."

He was relieved to hear from her and thanked Phyllis for passing it on to him.

"One more thing," she mentioned. "Thought I'd give you a heads up because I had to type up the story breakdowns for January and going into Sweeps."

"Sweeps" was TV-speak for the all important Nielsen ratings periods of February, May and November. That was usually when the biggest, most important storylines occurred in television, particularly for soap operas, and actors were hired and fired to help create a surge in viewership.

"They're getting rid of the Ice Cream Parlor," she continued and he felt an immediate pit in his stomach. Was this the end of Artie, before he'd ever gotten out from behind the counter? "But don't worry," she quickly assured him. "They're keeping you around to go work at Finnegan's."

Finnegan's was the long-standing Irish pub set where many of the main storylines intersected. If Artie was working there, it sounded like a promotion. He brightened and ventured, "Why the change? Do you know?"

"They're writing out the college storyline, but Martha

Feldon insisted on keeping you around," she answered matter-of-factly. Then, adding with a tinge of resentment, "It helps to have friends in high places."

T.J. felt awkward and had no response. He couldn't help but think Marti's support with the writers was an even better Christmas gift than the Tiffany cigarette case.

Marti's party was the mob scene he expected, even though he'd popped over earlier in the day to assist with the arrival of the uniformed caterers she'd engaged. They had transformed the kitchen into Command Central, set up a full bar operation in the dining room and transformed a section of the entryway off the elevator as a coat-check. Fortunately the added burden of umbrellas wouldn't be necessary because the night was clear, albeit bitterly cold. His mentor obviously had this down to a science, because everything was going off without a hitch.

Even his rendezvous with Ben Lord was going smoothly. As they had briefly discussed on the phone, T.J. arrived punctually at the Warwick Hotel lobby at seven p.m. sharp. T.J. thought he looked handsome in a three-piece gray suit over which he wore a heavy black Polo winter coat and matching cashmere scarf. Mindful of his public image, there was no physical contact between Ben and T.J. until they crawled into the back of a waiting taxi and Ben pressed his thigh up against T.J.'s, even maintaining discretion with the cab driver.

T.J. followed his example and refrained from being demonstrative either in action or words. He was just thrilled to be in Ben's company and enjoyed basking in the attention commanded from passersby who recognized the aging star.

"So who's having the party?" he had asked.

"An actress friend of mine, Martha Feldon."

"The old soap star?"

It seemed to T.J. that he and Marti would have been about the same age, but he only nodded in response. "I think I went to one of her Christmas parties back in the sixties."

"Then you'll recognize the ornaments," T.J. teased. "We decorated the tree last weekend."

Once they got inside the apartment and checked their coats, Ben confirmed it. "Yes, I was definitely here before. God bless the old girl."

Again with the "old." T.J. wondered if he seriously believed he was significantly younger than Marti.

They pushed their way into the crowded room. The music—a jolly song from the Ray Conniff album—could barely be heard over the conversations, laughter and tinkling glasses. Smoke filled the air. As Madison let out a few barks from wherever he was roaming nearby, Ben swiped his finger across some wall moulding trim and mouthed to T.J., "Filthy."

What a bitchy old queen! T.J. thought.

Finding a seat on the sofa or anywhere else was out of the question, but they happily accepted glasses of champagne from a waiter who was valiantly working his way through the crowd. T.J. knew there wouldn't be a scenario like there had been at the Peter Allen Waldorf Astoria bash, but decided he'd better keep an eye on his date's behavior anyway.

"Merry Christmas, precious one!" Marti's voice sang

out as she appeared from behind some taller guests. She gave T.J. a big hug and asked, pretending she didn't know, "Who is your handsome escort?"

"As if you don't remember me, Martha," Ben gushed, dripping with charm. "Benjamin Lord," he obliged.

"Good Lord, indeed!" she exclaimed, laying it on thick and standing on her toes to give him a kiss on the cheek. "Ben, you look marvelous. Merry Christmas."

"And you're younger than springtime," he told her, not as convincingly. "It's wonderful to see you."

"Now that we're all finished lying to each other . . ." she replied, ". . . find your way to the dining room and have something to eat. We have everything but a goose!" With that, she goosed Ben's buttocks and he visibly jumped. "T.J. can show you the way."

Marti disappeared into the crowd, the hostess with the mostest.

"Pretty much exactly as I remember her," Ben commented quietly to T.J.

They found a corner between the library and the dining room where they could lean against the wall. A few party goers, including Bobby, the makeup artist, and Elaine Stritch, the Broadway and TV star, stopped by to say hello to Ben and make pleasant chit chat. Between drinks, T.J. pulled out his new cigarette case and offered a smoke to Ben, who waved it away saying, "I quit three years ago."

The champagne had given T.J. just enough confidence to bite back at Ben's snobbish behavior. "Boring."

Ben's big hand took T.J. firmly by the wrist and they locked eyes. "Well, seeing that it's Christmas Eve," he said, "I'll make an exception."

Smiling and extending the case to him, T.J. was enjoying the sexual volley.

After a long, satisfying drag on his first smoke in several years, Ben executed a perfect and impressive French inhale, then looked down into T.J.'s wide blue eyes. "We can dine and dash," he suggested,

T.J. paused to appreciate the fact that he was at a soap star's party, flirting with a TV star he'd idolized for as long as he could remember. It all added to the existing arousal of the situation.

On Christmas morning, T.J. arrived late for his breakfast with Leo in the coffee shop outside Grand Central Station. He'd had to hurry back to his apartment from the Warwick Hotel where he'd left Dear Old Dad exhausted and panting, have a quick shower and grab his suitcase and bag of presents for his folks, before getting to a quick Yuletide bite with his best friend. A light flurry of snow had just begun to fall.

"Merry Christmas, Star Fucker," Leo greeted.

"I doubt I'll be seeing him again," T.J. offered, setting down his bag and parcels and squeezing into a chair. "Not unless I'm really desperate for a fancy dinner."

"Dear Old Dad was a dear old dud?"

"Do all older guys just lay there?"

"I wouldn't know. I've never slept with anyone over thirty.

Not that I know of, anyway. Your train leaves in twenty minutes."

"Sorry I don't have more time, but I'll be back Wednesday, and the next night is New Years Eve. I made reservations at Windows on the World, so we'll give it another try."

"Just us? I'd ask Armand but he's still under the weather."

"Yeah, no more word from Bella, and Carolyn Lee has plans with her boyfriend. She's not much fun at dinner anyway since she doesn't eat or drink. My New Year's resolution is to save her for Broadway shows and shopping. That girl knows her way around Saks and Bendel's."

"I'm heading straight from here to Staten Island," Leo told him. "I'm sure my entire family is already up to their eyeballs in eggnog. I hate leaving Manhattan."

"Me, too. But 1982 is going to be our year, pally."

Pally was the nickname the two friends had adopted for each other a few months before, when Mommie Dearest had hit theaters and quickly became a cult classic, especially within the gay community. Joan Crawford, as played by Faye Dunaway, and her husband referred to each other by this pet name. It was amusing because, as Crawford said, "That's what he calls you when he can't remember your name."

"My resolution is to find a decent apartment somewhere near the Stock Exchange," Leo said. "The commute is a pain in the ass."

"Me, too. Time to check out of the Roach Motel."

A waitress appeared to take T.J.'s order but he apologized for not having time. As he stood up and clumsily gathered his belongings, Leo said, "Merry Christmas, Pally."

CHAPTER FIVE
Welcome to Finnegan's

The new year brought T.J. onto a new set, Finnegan's Pub, and it was a dramatic change for the character of Artie, just as Phyllis had promised. No more corny paper hat, bow tie, apron and name tag. Deidre brought him in for a fitting and tried out several looks suited for a young man working as a waiter. They settled on a few sweaters and slacks combinations from Ralph Lauren and T.J. was finally starting to feel like part of the soap opera family. In the first scene, one of the lead characters who had occasionally patronized the Ice Cream Parlor had a line that explained his presence at Finnegan's. "Hello, Artie. Good to see you. Table for two, please."

Most of his own dialogue was relegated to customary servile responses, but Gerry the stage manager, was giving him more background action to do. Rather than just handing out menus or wiping down the counter, Artie helped customers carry things in and out of the pub, notified them of phone calls and delivered messages. These usually resulted in ad libbed, "Thank you, Artie" lines and T.J.'s screen time increased dramatically. He was sure he would soon be lending more significant support to a storyline. He hoped it would be in scenes with Marti.

Because so many scenes played out in Finnegan's, T.J. was working at least three episodes per week, resulting in bigger paychecks. Like Leo, he decided it was time to find a new apartment.

In his desire to be closer to work, he found a small, eighth-floor one-room studio in the Churchill, a high rise apartment building on the corner of Second Avenue and 40th Street. His mother's walk-in closet was about the same size as his new unit, but being in a doorman-attended building was a luxury, and he happily bade farewell to 45th Street, Tom Kat's and Ted Hook's Backstage, carefully packing boxes with a can of Raid on hand to make sure no cockroaches tagged along. Carolyn Lee had a big station wagon she used on weekends and was happy to lend it to him so that he and Leo could execute the move on a single Saturday. As a housewarming gift, since they were no longer giving him an allowance, his parents bought him a quality sofa bed that helped him maximize the tiny space. His may have been the tiniest apartment in the Churchill, with an uninspiring view of an industrial building next door, but he loved walking through the lobby and having a uniformed doorman open the door and greet him whenever he came in or out. Nothing made him feel more like a true New Yorker.

Leo was now living on West 23rd Street, near the Chelsea Hotel, with a college friend as a roommate. There wasn't as much time for clubs and bars these days, but they still managed to get together several times a week for dinner. Inevitably they ended the night at one or the other's apartment watching The Robin Byrd Show on the cable access Channel J, which fired up every night after ten and featured often graphic, adult content. Byrd, a former porn star turned self-produced talk show hostess, had become a New York City icon for her ditzy, provocative persona as she interviewed other adult entertainers, both gay and straight, all while wearing her signature black crochet bikini. Each episode ended with everyone dancing and stripping to her novelty number, Baby Let Me Bang Your Box. It was more hilarious than titillating with its commercials for assorted phone-sex fetishes and escort services.

One night after Leo had left and Robin Byrd's show had segued into another adult offering, The Ugly George Show, T.J.'s phone rang. He was surprised and delighted to hear Bella on the other end of the line.

"I got sprung today," she announced, sounding exhausted.

"I'm so relieved to hear from you. Where are you? I've missed you!"

"I'm staying with my mother for now. That was one of the conditions."

"I want to hear everything. When can I see you?"

"We can have breakfast or lunch anytime. Dinners are out. I'm supposed to avoid triggers, the doctors tell me. No drinking, no drugs, no nightlife. Not yet, anyway."

"No more steakhouse lunches, I guess," he tried to say with levity. He wondered how Leo's hard drinking Aunt Jennie had still managed to avoid such a fate when she was nowhere near as composed and high functioning as Bella had always seemed.

Bella paused for a moment of awkward silence which she finally broke by saying, "I won't be coming back to work, T.J. They fired me."

"Can they do that?" He was stunned.

"They can and they did. Phyllis will find someone else if she hasn't already. Watching television is one of the few activities they let me do. I'm really proud to see you working in Finnegan's."

"I wouldn't be there if it weren't for you," he acknowledged, feeling sad for how it had worked out for her. "I'm just so glad you're better."

"According to them, I'm not cured. I'm 'in Recovery.' You have to catch me up on all the dirt I've missed. It's the only thought that's kept me from strangling my mom."

"Don't do that," he teased. "If they can lock you up for partying, imagine what they'll do for matricide."

Bella finally found her laughter.

After a long breakfast gossip session that spilled into lunch, T.J.'s and Bella's friendship felt almost back to normal. It was almost one when they finished off the last cigarette in T.J.'s silver case, and she announced she had to get to an Alcoholics Anonymous meeting at a nearby church. It was part of her ongoing rehabilitation regimen.

"Are there ever any cute guys at those things?" T.J. asked.

"When there are, they are usually so fucked up you wouldn't go near them with a ten-foot pole. I wonder if that's how they see me, too."

As he walked her down the block in the direction of the meeting, T.J. took her hand and reassured her. "You are beautiful. And you have more sex than anyone I know."

She looked at him with a smirk. "That was mostly thanks to booze—and coke, too. I'll probably never have sex again. If I can't go to bars and clubs, how am I going to get laid?"

T.J. considered this for a moment and came up blank but comforted her with, "Bella Black, you WILL have sex again, I have no doubt. Doesn't AA tell you to take it one day at a time?"

"I need to find a guy who'll take one for the team. I also need to find a job. Any job."

She let go of his hand and stopped walking for a moment to pull something out of her handbag. T.J. was surprised to see it was a joint. He didn't say anything as she defended herself with, "It's no different than a cigarette."

When they parted ways, T.J. stopped at the first payphone to call and check his answering machine. There was a message from his mom and one from Leo, asking him to call him back at work. He pumped another quarter into the coin slot and dialed the special number he had memorized that connected him with a phone on the floor of the New York Stock Exchange.

After several rings, someone answered and yelled "Yeah?" over the noisy voices of the finance world.

"Leo Tucci, please."

"Hang on," the nasally New York accented voice barked back.

T.J. inserted another quarter while he waited for Leo to reach the phone. He had to get one of those new calling cards and stop hoarding spare change.

Finally, Leo was able to pick up and sounded uncharacteristically anxious.

"Bad time?" T.J. asked.

"Yeah, but I wanted you to know. Armand is in the hospital. The ICU at St. Luke's."

"Jesus. What's wrong?"

"They don't know. They thought it was a flu he couldn't shake. His parents are on their way from Senegal but one of the other managers at The Gap called me after I'd left a bunch of messages for him. He's supposed to be moved into a regular room later today, so I'm going over after work. Can you meet me?"

"Sure. I can pick up some balloons or flowers or something, if you think I should."

"I'm not sure what to expect," Leo said nervously. "Apparently, it's bad."

T.J. was at a loss for words. Other than his grandparents' deaths from old age, he'd had no experience with hospitals or encountering serious health issues.

"Meet me on 59th and 10th and we can go in together. Six o'clock?"

"Sure."

Leo hung up and T.J. tried to figure out what he could bring to cheer their ailing friend.

Knowing Armand's penchant for martinis, and now having Marti's cocktail recipe under his belt, he decided to stop into the new Gourmet Garage market near Lincoln Center, on his way over to St. Luke's. There he could find both a jar of fancy martini olives and a bouquet of flowers, covering all the bases. When he passed a liquor store en route, he had the idea to pick up a pint sized bottle of Tanqueray and cleverly poured out the water from the olive jar and replaced it with gin. Gin-soaked olives would be an ideal treat to sneak in. Better than bon-bons.

Meeting Leo, who had also picked up some flowers from a bodega just outside the subway station, they tried to brace themselves for whatever awaited them inside the sterile environs of the hospital.

A receptionist at the desk staffed by overworked nurses and volunteers directed them to a fourth floor waiting area, where the mood was sad and somber. The rooms here were adjacent to the Intensive Care Unit, so it was the site of serious cases. The two friends remained silent and patient after they asked for Armand's room and were told an attendant would come to take them in.

An exasperated thirty-something Asian man in medical scrubs finally appeared. "You're here for Armand?" he asked. They nodded and he held his hand out, adding, "I'll take the flowers. He can't have them at the moment."

Obediently putting them down on the waiting room table littered with old magazines, T.J. and Leo followed him down the hallway past room after room of misery and pain, all accompanied by a soundtrack of unpleasant sounds ranging from soft whimpers and sobs to the omnipresent mechanical beeps and hums of medical equipment.

The man in scrubs stopped by an open door where two patients laid in beds separated by a curtained partition. Neither T.J. nor Leo would have recognized the person in the bed before them as their friend. Other than his long, thick eyelashes and dark black skin, now covered in sores and lesions, the emaciated figure beneath a thin sheet looked nothing like Armand. To steady himself, T.J. grabbed Leo by the arm and summoned all his acting skills to suppress his shock and fear.

Leo spoke up, tentatively, unsure if Armand could even hear him. "You up for visitors?"

"Please, no physical contact with the patient," the man in scrubs instructed them before he walked away. "Five minutes only."

They were at a complete loss for words until Armand tried to ease the awkwardness of the situation. "Thank God there are no mirrors here," he commented weakly. "I know what I must look like."

Grateful for the opening, T.J. moved closer to the bed and smiled. "Don't be ridiculous. Anything's better than the new Gap line."

"She speaks truth," Armand responded and they all laughed uncomfortably.

"What did the doctors tell you?" Leo asked.

"You know I'm a trendsetter," he said, trying to shift in bed to face them better. He winced as he moved and so did his friends as they watched him. "It's the hot new thing. The gay plague."

AIDS, acquired immunodeficiency syndrome, was a condition that was just starting to make mainstream news headlines, especially within the gay community. It also had an assortment of other medical related descriptions but, when it was discussed at all, it was referred to, as Armand had said, "the gay plague."

T.J. shivered. The thought of sex being dangerous, let

alone fatal, was something no one he knew had dared to consider. Now here it was, a few feet in front of him practically devouring a friend. Trying to offer some optimism and encouragement, he said half heartedly, "I'm sure the doctors will figure out how to make you better. You're young and healthy, after all."

"Exactly," Leo chimed in. "How many times did you work after pulling an all-nighter? You'll be okay."

They were on a roll now and T.J. kept going. "This place has an excellent reputation, too. My Dad lost a malpractice suit against them, that's how good they are. He almost never loses."

"You always wanted to meet a cute doctor," Armand responded. "Now's your chance."

Armand's ability to keep up a brave front was now beyond its limit and what started as a forced chuckle to their conversation started to cause him to well up with tears and then launch into a deep, racking cough he couldn't control.

T.J. and Leo looked around for some water but were interrupted by the return of the man who had walked them in, now adorned in latex gloves and a mask. He moved quickly to Armand and lifted his torso to a more upright position to ease his congestion. It didn't seem to help. Over the unceasing coughs, he told them, "That's enough for today, guys."

"Hang in there, Armand," T.J. said as they backed out of the room.

"Yeah, The Gap needs you. And we miss you. We'll come back soon."

As soon as they were in the corridor, the attendant managed to shut the door to the room and they slowly walked off in silence. The sound of Armand's raspy coughing added to all the other terrible noises in their ears.

When they finally reached the elevator, Leo put his arm around T.J. and said, "I need a fucking drink."

They entered the first bar they found—a smelly old beer joint called Tap a Keg. Leo ordered a double vodka with a splash of orange juice and T.J. asked for a dry martini. Perched on the wobbly bar stools, they said nothing. T.J. pulled the jar of gin-soaked olives from the Gourmet Garage bag and set them on the counter. After a moment, he took the lid off and they started eating them right there. For the first time in their friendship, they sat at a bar without making any conversation.

The next weeks passed with somber slowness. Leo told T.J. that Armand's parents had arrived from Senegal and were staying with extended family members somewhere in the outer boroughs. Non-family visitors were no longer allowed on the floor where Armand was hospitalized, as it was now designated as an AIDS floor. As sad as that was, T.J. was strangely relieved because there was so much misinformation and fear about how the disease could be spread. This same anxiety had rapidly made its way through gay circles and, while the bars and nightclubs continued to carry on in seeming denial of the problem, public awareness campaigns on the risk and spread of AIDS became more evident every day.

The newly formed Gay Men's Health Crisis was quick to take to the loud speaker with public service announcements and grassroots campaigns within the heart of the businesses most patronized by gay men. "Safe Sex is Hot Sex" and "Cum On Me, Not in Me" became catch phrases. Baskets and bowls filled with colorful condoms appeared everywhere for the taking. T.J. remembered his father giving him a box of condoms when he turned fifteen with a half-hearted attempt at a sex talk, but that was the sum total of his experience with what his dad referred to as "rubbers." As far as he knew, that box was still in a drawer somewhere in his childhood bedroom back in Connecticut.

T.J. and Leo had often joked about how they never went to any of the museums, galleries or performance arts venues the city was famous for, since they usually opted for the raucous party scene. They began to change that and now, at least occasionally, found themselves trying out the exhibits and performances at places like Lincoln Center and the Metropolitan Museum of Art. While they weren't hot beds of opportunity for meeting men, they provided good chances to socialize with Bella and Carolyn Lee, both of whom continued to avoid the temptations of the partying lifestyle.

Daily routines went on and work at Tomorrow's Promise was always a welcome distraction from the problems of the real world. Artie was kept busy at Finnegan's and always had at least four or five lines of dialogue. The writers were careful not to exceed that limit or it would have resulted in T.J. being catapulted from an Under Five to Day Player status and a significant difference in pay scale. T.J. was confident that would eventually happen and was happy just to be a regular part of the pub-set storylines.

A handsome new leading man had came on board as a love interest for the long-running character of Angela. Tall, chiseled Rick Alderson, a former minor league football player turned actor, now played Doug, who had come to town on some nefarious mission that had yet to be explained. He definitely had a universally appealing resemblance to JFK Jr. Fortunately, he spent a lot of his time at Finnegan's Pub so he hung around on that set for several hours a day. T.J. was very attracted to him, as were most people. As affable as Rick was, he seemed to keep to himself and was usually alone on the set when he wasn't working, studying his lines or reading some dog-eared old paperback book. Based in Los Angeles, he'd come to New York to accept the role and was being put up in the no-frills Beacon Hotel for the first thirteen-week cycle of his contract.

T.J. had never met a professional athlete before and tried to loiter in his proximity whenever the cameras weren't rolling. It was titillating to be around him. To T.J.'s happy surprise, Rick eventually did initiate a conversation one afternoon.

"Man, would you mind helping me run lines?" he asked T.J.

T.J. smiled and sat down across from him in one of the pub booths where he was hanging out.

"Happy to," he answered. "I'm T.J."

They shook hands with an unnecessarily firm and macho grip.

"Rick. Thanks, I appreciate it. I've never had to learn so many lines before."

"I don't have that problem," T.J. joshed. "Since they never give me more than five at a time."

"Hey, it's a gig, right?" Rick responded cheerfully.

That was about the extent of things, aside from T.J. helping him run through his scene. He didn't think Rick was going to set the world on fire with his acting abilities, but his good looks and a decent plot for his character would more than carry him through. Some shirtless scenes were surely in the cards for him, as well—even though, T.J. lamented, those wouldn't play out at Finnegan's.

T.J. had washed off his makeup and was just about to grab his fanny pack to head off to dinner with Carolyn Lee, but he decided to check his answering machine before leaving the studio. There was a message from Leo saying simply and sadly, "Just found out. Armand died this afternoon. His parents were with him. Someone from The Gap is planning a memorial. I'll keep you posted."

That weekend, Leo informed him that several of Armand's friends would be gathering at Pappardelle Ristorante, down the street from The Gap, for a remembrance dinner followed by a celebration of his life at The Works. It didn't sound like something his traditional Senegalese parents would have planned and Leo explained that they would not be in attendance. Not only had they not known Armand was homosexual, but the fact that he died of AIDS was further cause of their shame and grief. Because of strict repatriation laws, they had decided that Armand would be cremated in lieu of burial back in his native country. Everything about the situation was tragic, especially for his many friends who loved him for his outrageous sense of humor and flamboyant personality.

Even though Bella had known Armand only peripherally through T.J. and Leo, T.J. had asked her to come along. Other than vague memories of his Nana's funeral in her big Lutheran church back home, he'd had no experience with the rituals surrounding death and appreciated her support, even if it was just as a friendly escort. He'd invited Carolyn Lee too, but as usual, she already had plans with her boyfriend.

When T.J. and Bella walked in, a host directed them to the back area of the restaurant where about twenty people, including Leo, were gathered, sharing Margherita pizzas and drinking red wine. Sensitive to Bella's sobriety, T.J. asked the waiter for two club sodas. He recognized most of the mourners as employees from The Gap and Leo told him the others were also store-affiliated: regular vendors, corporate representatives or patrons.

After less than an hour of pleasantries, small talk and swapping Armand-related anecdotes, it was clear things were winding down. Standing at a corner cocktail table with T.J. and Leo, Bella whispered, "If this is a celebration of life, where's the celebrating?"

"That will be up at The Works," Leo explained. "I think we can start making our way there."

As they walked briskly north on Columbus Avenue, Bella asked for the latest office buzz from the soap set and

T.J. jumped at the opportunity to tell them both about the new actor, Rick, and the crush he had, that seemed to grow with every passing day.

"Rick Alderson? Isn't he straight?" Bella inquired.

"T.J. loves a challenge," Leo commented, dryly.

As they approached the entrance to The Works, they could already hear the loud dance music blasting from inside. Madonna's Holiday was just mixing into White Lines and Bella asked sarcastically, "Is this some kind of a test?"

T.J. took locked arms with her and assured her, "I've got you, sweetie."

Inside the bar, scores of male patrons crowded together as strobe lights pulsated. In between the flashes, one could see a giant poster of Armand plastered on the large wall opposite the bar area. It was him in all his glittery glory, smiling broadly in a dramatic pose, with his arms akimbo.

The trio pushed their way deeper inside with Leo yelling over the music, "There's more room in the back."

An inebriated man in a tank top sneered at Bella as they moved past and said loudly with disdain, "Didn't she know this would be mostly men?"

Wryly, over her shoulder, she snapped back, "Mostly?"

When they finally reached the rear bar by the pool tables, Leo offered to buy them a round. Bella asked for a Diet Coke and told T.J. not to worry about her—she wasn't coveting cocktails. Once they found a comfortable corner, drinks in hand, they were able to unwind and enjoy the revelry around them.

"Armand would have loved this," Leo admitted.

After an hour, Bella decided to leave. Once they felt less mindful of Bella's abstinence, T.J. and Leo started to really throw back the beverages. Leo asked if they were hallucinating when they spotted Carolyn Lee suddenly appear in the sea of men, trying to navigate her way through. She was decked out in a full-length, black mink coat with broad padded shoulders that would put Joan Crawford or an NFL linebacker to shame.

Shouting over the din and slurring his words, T.J. asked, "Sweetie, what are you doing here?"

"And why are you so dressed up?" Leo added, grabbing her by the arm to pull her closer to them and avoid getting splashed by a wayward beer.

"I made it to Pappardelle but they said I'd probably find you here," she explained, struggling to take off her enormous fur in the tight space they occupied. "Gary and I were at a dinner for the mayor at the Plaza. He was being an asshole, so I left."

People were starting to recognize her from television and, pretending not to notice she started looking around for a place to stash her coat.

T.J. laughed. "There's no coat check here."

She tossed it onto the unused pool table beside them as if it were a dish towel. "I'm in the mood for a drink. Which one of you boys will get me a glass of champagne?"

"There's no champagne here, either. And if there were, you wouldn't want to drink it."

"How about a white wine?" Leo suggested. She nodded and he ventured off to get it.

"I've never seen you drink before," T.J. said. "Gary must have really set you off."

"I suck up to my bosses at work all day. There's only so much more I can do with Ed Koch and his cronies. I try to fake it for Gary, but as soon as I saw a chance to escape, I got out of there."

"You missed Bella. But I'm glad you made it."

"How are you doing? How's work? I saw the show the other day but you weren't on."

"They're using me a lot more now. And there's a new heart-throb that just started. He's fucking beautiful."

T.J. continued gushing about Rick until Leo returned with Carolyn Lee's wine and another round of drinks for himself and T.J., who was by now feeling no pain.

"Is he still talking about the actor?" Leo asked.

"I'm going to ask him out, I swear I am," T.J. pledged, taking more of a gulp than a sip of his gin and tonic. "He's single. Never talks about women. He's probably just afraid to come out."

Leo rolled his eyes and then looked at Carolyn Lee, "Will you tell him he's going to embarrass himself?"

"You don't even know him," T.J. snapped through the haze of too much booze.

"You're delusional," said Leo. Then he added, pointedly, "The guy. Is. Straight!"

"I can make him want me."

"Now, now, fellas," Carolyn Lee interjected, trying to tamp down the rising alcohol-fueled tension between them. Two guys behind her had figured out who she was and were watching her intently.

"You've been around soap operas too long," Leo told T.J. dismissively. "You're turning into Alexis Carrington."

Feeling belligerent, especially with the comparison to Joan Collins' Dynasty character, T.J. hurled what was left of his drink in Leo's direction. Too drunk for proper aim, the gin, tonic and ice cubes landed mostly on his shoulder but he ducked and in doing so, knocked into Carolyn Lee. She stumbled backwards, but the men behind her helped her get back on her feet.

T.J. charged out without another word and started stalking down Columbus Avenue so quickly it was almost a jog. He was swerving and on a determined course for the Beacon Hotel where he knew Rick was staying.

Fortunately, he soon wobbled his way, out of breath, and came upon a taxi stand where there were several available cabs. Making the spontaneous but fuzzy decision to climb into one, he managed to give the driver his address before falling asleep in the back seat.

What seemed like only a moment later, but was actually the next morning, he woke up in his bed atop the bedding, the morning rays of sun pouring in blindingly. Groaning aloud from an epic hangover, he looked with shame at the line of strewn clothes that stretched from the door to the bed. He had no memory of the journey home, but was relieved to see his keys and wallet on the small dining table.

He lumbered to the bathroom and bent over the sink to take a long, hydrating drink from the faucet. Then, he plopped himself down on the toilet for much needed relief. It was at that moment he remembered how he had departed

The Works, mortified by the memory of his actions with Leo. Again, he groaned.

After swallowing two aspirin, he returned to bed and pulled down the covers he'd never bothered with the night before. He climbed back in with the telephone from the nightstand. He had to call Leo and endure the humiliation of apologizing. The digital clock radio read, "Saturday, 7:40 a.m." It might have been early for a weekend morning, but he felt so guilty about his behavior, there was no putting off making amends with his best friend.

After a few rings, Leo answered, groggy.

"Oh. my god, Pally," T.J. croaked in a raspy morning voice. "I am so, so sorry. I don't remember much, but what I do isn't good."

"Please tell me you didn't go over to his hotel."

He scratched his head and answered, "No, no I didn't. I'd remember that."

"Thank God."

"Leo, I'm really sorry. I don't know what came over me."

"You were drunk. And emotions were high because of Armand."

"That's no excuse, Pally. I'm really sorry. Please let me make it up to you."

"Oh, you will," Leo teased. With that, it was clear their moment of conflict had passed.

"Thank you. Did Carolyn Lee make it home all right?"

"Yeah. Some guys helped me get her back in her mink and into a cab."

Crisis averted. Or so T.J. thought as he hung up the phone. It rang a moment later. He assumed it was Leo calling back but it was Bella.

"You were smart to leave when you did," he told her, wishing the aspirin would kick in.

"I take it you haven't heard from Carolyn Lee this morning?" she asked with hesitation.

"No. It's not even eight o'clock."

"Go pick up a New York Post. And check out Page Six."

Page Six was the tabloid's snarky but popular gossip column that covered celebrity shenanigans among New York City's social and entertainment elite. Both a loved and feared institution, it was considered by many as a must-read.

"Oh fuck," T.J. ventured. "What is it?'

"The good news is that they're obviously not soap fans because you weren't recognized. But Carolyn Lee didn't get off so easily."

He sunk into the pillows wanting to burrow under the covers and never emerge.

"Read it to me?"

She paused for what seemed to T.J. an eternity. He heard her shuffling the paper before clearing her throat and reciting the blurb.

"Every weeknight, most New Yorkers rely on television's longtime anchor woman Carolyn Lee Jessup to bring them the important news stories from around the world, across the country and right here in the Big Apple. We have come to rely on her objectivity, professionalism and judgment. Everyday Gothamites, as well as politicians and celebrities, consider her their go-to source for reliable and accurate information. This extends to City Hall and Gracie Mansion, where her longtime beau Gary Sutton is a top legal aide to Hizzoner Ed Koch. We imagine tongues in those hallowed halls will this morning be wagging over the after-hours activities of Ms. Jessup shortly after leaving last night's dinner with power players at the Plaza Hotel."

"Oh, no. Please, no."

Bella cleared her throat and kept reading, "The glamorous broadcast journalist was spotted in an Upper West Side gay bar cavorting among a sea of homosexual men in various states of undress. She, however, was decked out in the same smart St. John knit suit she had worn to the Plaza dinner accessorized by a luxurious full-length mink coat which ended up draped across a pool table while she enjoyed a glass of wine with the boy bar patrons."

"Make it stop," T.J. moaned, wishing he could put the pillow over his head.

"It's not over yet," she warned before finishing up. "Two of her homosexual cohorts ended up in a cat fight and, while no punches were thrown, drinks were. The lovely lady would have taken a tumble had she not been propped up by some same-sex Samaritans. Also in her favor was the fact that, unlike in her work life, no news cameras were present to capture the breaking news. One wonders how Mr. Sutton, and her devoted audience, will react to her being the headline instead of reporting one."

Relieved and grateful that he hadn't been identified in the article, T.J. had never felt worse. And not because of the hangover. He went back to the bathroom and vomited.

He left several messages on Carolyn Lee's answering machine over the next few days, but never heard back from her. Fortunately, there was no further coverage in the papers but he was certain whatever damage had been done was going to cost them their friendship. If only she could forgive him as easily as Leo had, or be as judgment free as Bella. He was also worried about what it would mean for her relationship with Gary.

After the hellish weekend that began with Armand's remembrance and ended with the splash on Page Six, T.J. welcomed a new work week and promised himself he would keep trying to find a way to mend fences with Carolyn Lee. As he said to Leo, "You were worried I'd embarrass myself with Rick and it ended up being something a hundred times worse."

Heading into the studio to pick up his script and call sheet, he walked dejectedly across East 42nd Street, bundled up against the winter cold and hunched over to fight the wind blowing from the East River. Just as he neared the Daily News building, he caught sight of Carolyn Lee emerging from a town car, clad in her now-famous mink coat and wearing large Jackie O-style sunglasses, even though the day was overcast. T.J. broke into a run to catch her before she made it from the curb and into the revolving door entry.

"Please," he called. "Please wait."

She charged forward and he followed her through the revolving door and into the ornate lobby. There was a security guard inside who stepped forward upon seeing her, but she gestured to him that she didn't need his assistance. She turned to face T.J. without removing her sunglasses, her arms rigid with hands buried in the pockets of her fur.

T.J. couldn't see her eyes, but his own were damp with tears. "You have to forgive me," he implored. "Please."

She spoke quietly, measured. "Gary went ballistic. I thought he was going to . . ." She didn't finish the sentence, but she slowly, almost ominously, pulled off the glasses and T.J. half expected her to reveal a black eye. There was none.

"He screamed for hours about publicity and damage control. I told him it was only Page Six, a bit of tabloid gossip. It's not like it was The Times, but he kept saying it could derail both our careers. Our future."

"I wish I could take it all back."

"I don't," she surprised him by saying and then broke into a wide smile.

She pulled her left hand from the coat pocket and held it up in front of T.J. There on her finger was the biggest diamond ring he'd ever seen, sparkling like her smile. The one she'd mentioned inheriting from her grandmother

"He decided we should give the press something positive to report."

T.J. was stunned. One of the tears in his eyes spilled down his cheek, reflecting his simultaneous surprise and relief.

Back at Finnegan's, T.J. was starting to feel almost back to his normal self. His scenes today were mostly in support of a conversation between two of the principal actors, one of whom was Rick. The Page Six incident had more than crushed any attraction he may have felt for the leading man and the thought of even being around him conjured up the uncomfortable malaise of that terrible "morning after."

The best part of the day, T.J. knew, would be Marti entering the last scene as an episode cliffhanger and he would finally get to act on camera with his friend and mentor.

The script called for her to come into the pub, looking around for someone. T.J. was to greet her and see if he could be of service, but she would reply with a mysterious line that would leave audiences guessing until the next episode. They had briefly run through the stage blocking during the morning's dry rehearsal, so it all seemed very straightforward.

Gerry called out as the On-Air light was illuminated, "Quiet on the set! Rolling in five, four, three, two . . ."

Marti, as Hope Stewart, entered Finnegan's through the front door, scanning the room nervously for any sign of whoever she had come to see. Noticing her, Artie crossed to her from beside the bar, where he had been working.

"Hello, Mrs. Stewart. How are you this evening?"

Distracted by her visual search of the sparsely occupied pub she answered, "Fine, fine, thank you. You're not very busy tonight."

"No, not yet. May I show you to a table?"

"I'm supposed to be meeting someone. Has anyone asked for me?"

"I'm sorry, no. Would they have made a reservation? I could check the list."

"That won't be necessary. You see, I don't even know

who it is." Then, she added with dramatic apprehension, "But apparently, they know me."

Music swelled and the camera moved to a close up of Hope's anxious countenance, then—Fade to Black.

Gerry got a message through his headset from the director in the far away control room and called out, "One take wonders. That's a wrap, everybody."

The On Air light went out and the crew ended their silence and began moving cameras and set pieces in preparation for the next set up.

Marti gave T.J. a forced smile and a little pat on the arm, suggesting, "Why don't you walk me back to my dressing room?"

"Sure,' he said, following alongside her as they left the soundstage and made their way through the production office. "I wonder who Hope's looking for. Do you even know, or will they drag it out until next week?"

Marti didn't reply and T.J. instantly realized she had some important information she didn't want to share in front of other cast or crew members. They moved quickly upstairs to her dressing room where she, uncharacteristically, closed the door. He remained silent, waiting for her to explain what was happening.

Finally, she said, "Hope is looking for a geologist."

He nearly laughed. An evil ex-husband, a long lost sibling or an illegitimate child would be understandable, but a geologist? Did she mean gynecologist? Maybe it was a menopause story. She saw his perplexed expression and explained further, keeping her voice down even though the door was closed.

"The U.S. Geological Survey is sending a representative to meet with Hope, because she sits on the city council. Seismic activity has been detected in the surrounding countryside."

Trying to put it all together, he surmised, "So we're in for an earthquake? That will be interesting for Sweeps ratings."

"The writers pulled me aside this morning to give me a heads up. It's top secret."

"My lips are sealed," he reassured her. "Besides, it sounds like it could be fun."

She shook her head. "It's for ratings, all right. But not for fun. They're going to revamp the entire show. The earthquake will destroy all the existing sets and kill off most of the cast."

T.J. gulped. He may have dodged Page Six but could Artie make it out of the rubble?

"They can't kill Hope, but I'm about to get a four week vacation in the form of her extended coma. I'm not sure about anybody else, but I wanted you to be prepared."

Earthquake preparedness. T.J. thought that was something only people in California worried about.

CHAPTER SIX
After the Earthquake

Wasting no time, Gary Sutton got the positive press he wanted, in The New York Times no less. His marriage to Carolyn Lee made the wedding section, even though the proceedings were rushed along at lightning speed so that the Page Six incident was quickly eclipsed and forgotten. The bride looked ravishing, and bone thin, in a David Emanuel-inspired gown reminiscent of his creation for Princess Diana to walk down the aisle to wed Prince Charles in 1981. In addition to all the requisite information about their high profile occupations, the article included considerable attention to the "sweetheart bodice with lace trim and puffed sleeves" of the bride's attire as well as the "wired lace and flower headpiece from which a two-tier circular veil was attached." She was the Princess Grace of the moment and Gary looked appropriately dashing in an all-ivory colored tuxedo. Barbie's boyfriend Ken dressed up as Prince Charming would have paled by comparison.

The newlyweds got their wish that the service was conducted by the mayor himself, inside the hallowed halls of Gracie Mansion, and the reception that followed took place at the Metropolitan Club. A carefully considered guest list was curated not only by them, but by a wedding planner working with publicists from city hall and the news network that employed Carolyn Lee. Consequently, those in attendance were a safe mix of society stalwarts and immediate family. Friends like T.J. would have to settle for seeing the coverage on television or in New York Magazine, although Carolyn Lee promised they would soon have a big celebratory dinner party in their massive new three bedroom co-op apartment on Central Park South.

T.J. thought it was strange that, while he considered her to be one of his closest New York friends, he had yet to meet the man she married. He'd mentioned this to his mother who reacted wryly and surmised it was likely a case of "Street Angel/House Devil" and that anyone Carolyn Lee didn't feel like showing off was probably not worth meeting, anyway. That fancy new Dutton residence, Janice added for good measure, probably was an indication that she was a bird in a gilded cage. T.J. hoped not.

The Jessup/Dutton nuptials weren't the only headline of interest to T.J. and his friends. Mother Nature's wrath poised to strike the daytime TV stalwart Tomorrow's Promise had created the kind of buzz the producers had hoped for. Whether or not ratings would follow remained to be seen, but the episodes revealing Hope Stewart being warned by the mysterious geologist had aired and ominous, foreboding music seemed to now finish every scene. The fictional citizenry waited and wondered if his predictions were correct, while savvy fans and viewers at home knew the disastrous events were scheduled to play out the week of February 12.

T.J. had been notified of his final taping day, January 30. There would be no shaking and rattling, no falling beams or chandeliers. Artie would simply serve patrons at Finnegans with business as usual. Its destruction would come off camera, saving producers from extensive and expensive special effects. The writers had crafted a scenario to place all the surviving characters together in an underground nightclub where they would wait out the cataclysm only to eventually emerge and find their world in ruins.

Holding out hope that Artie would somehow crawl out of the pub debris, T.J. kept a stiff upper lip for his final day on set. At day's end, Marti invited him to her dressing room where she had a small cake for them to share, decorated with icing that read, "That's Showbiz." She also had a split of champagne for them to drink a toast.

"Any thoughts about what's next?" she asked him.

"Auditions, I guess. I need to find a job."

"The actor's life," she said sweetly, her voice tinged with nostalgia. As she poured the last drops of champagne into their glasses, she added, "I'm still going to need a hand with my play, fan mail and a million other things. Maybe now you'll let me pay you."

He clinked her glass. "Not yet, anyway."

T.J. remembered the sting of Andy telling him to "grow up." Even though he had stopped marking a calendar with red X's, he recognized that the time had come.

Leo was working his tail off, still on the floor at the Stock Exchange but now in a junior executive role with Citibank. Bella, desperate to get out from under the same roof as her mother, took a minimum wage job with New York Sports Club, which was opening up gyms all over the five boroughs of the city. Even though her receptionist position consisted mostly of checking in members and handing out towels, employment there included a free membership and, because of all its locations, as much work as Bella wanted. It helped keep her sober and independent, and her previous television production experience meant that she was vastly overqualified. There would be promotions and management opportunities whenever she wanted to pursue them, but for the time being, desk duties suited her. As for Carolyn Lee, her weekday news reading duties continued without interruption, not even taking time off for a honeymoon.

T.J. missed the structure of a soap opera schedule and decided he would try to create a regimen for himself—never sleeping past eight a.m., scheduling as many auditions or interviews as he could during business hours, and filling any gaps with acting, singing or movement classes. Evenings could still include nights out on the town with Leo and Bella when their schedules allowed, but Marti's sentimental reference to "the actor's life," helped him make sure he included the Arts in his outings. He saw plays and films and finally took advantage of the many museums and cultural events available to him. His memberships in Actors Equity and the Television Artists unions provided lots of freebies and discounted opportunities.

It was a spectacular time for Broadway and it seemed like hit shows filled every theater. Cats, La Cage aux Folles, Zorba, Rink, Baby, My One and Only, Dreamgirls, A Chorus Line, The Tap Dance Kid and Sunday in the Park with George were musical smashes. Meantime, Hurlyburly, Noises Off, Glengarry Glen Ross, Death of a Salesman, and Quilters were going strong, too. Becoming increasingly dependent on his morning coffee, T.J.

would drink two or three cups each morning while he scoured the trade papers for audition opportunities. There seemed to be plenty of spots for chorus boys, but he lacked the required dance skills. Besides, after all that time paying his dues as Artie, he no longer wanted to be relegated to the background.

An opportunity suddenly presented itself, thanks to the slightly older rising star, Matthew Broderick, who'd had a hit with the film WarGames and was now appearing on Broadway in Neil Simon's Brighton Beach Memoirs. He had previously starred alongside Harvey Fierstein and Estelle Getty in the mega hit Torch Song Trilogy and had been eventually replaced by Fisher Stevens. It had set them both on the fast track for stardom and now producers had put out a casting call to fill the role of David, that Broderick had originated. Dressed down, freshly scrubbed and shaven and forgoing hair gel to spike his hair, T.J. could still pass for a teenager so he eagerly submitted himself by taking his headshot and resume to the casting office. He dropped it off with the receptionist, walking confidently in and out of a very unglamorous office on 52nd Street.

Shortly before six p.m. someone called him to set up an audition for the very next day and, to T.J.'s delight, it wasn't just to return to the casting office. They wanted him to prepare a three-minute dramatic monologue to perform on an actual Broadway stage, directly for the producers who would be sitting in the audience. He was also told that if they like his performance, he would be asked to stay and read "sides" from the script, with a casting assistant as his scene partner. He recognized what a tremendous opportunity this would be but was even more hopeful when they told him the location: The Music Box Theater on good old West 45th Street, the site where he'd seen his very first Broadway show, Side by Side by Sondheim. He considered this a great omen.

He called Marti and asked if she would be available for a quick coaching session that evening and she happily told him to come join her for dinner and then they would work on his monologue. He had selected one from the play, Blue Denim, and she agreed it was a good choice: playing a high school student who gets his girlfriend pregnant and is confronted with the possibility of arranging her illegal abortion. They also ran through a few scenes from Torch Song Trilogy so he would be prepared in the event he got that far in the audition process.

The next afternoon he took the cross town bus back to his old neighborhood, walking past his former apartment building, the Martin Beck Theater and Tom Kat's. If all went well, he thought, maybe he would stop in at Ted Hook's Backstage for a celebratory gin and tonic. As he entered the theater lobby, a representative from the casting office greeted him, telling him to go through the stage door and to the waiting area backstage.

It was thrilling to walk through the discreet stage door adjacent to the theater and enter the behind-the-scenes world of Broadway actors. Directional signs had been taped on the walls and he could hear the murmur of others voices as he neared the backstage area. Folding chairs were lined up just stage right of the large, dramatic set for Agnes of God, which was enjoying a successful run there. The New York Times' Frank Rich described the scenery as a "curving expanse of blond wood rising from the floor to the skies." T.J. thought it looked as massive as a mountain.

A woman with a clipboard hushed the other waiting young actors then indicated for T.J. to take a seat. In a whisper, she asked for his name and then checked him off her list. There were half a dozen others ahead of him and they all appeared to be younger than he, so T.J. now had worry that he was wrong for the part of David. But, as Marti said, this was "the actor's life" and he loved being there even if he got only as far as the audition. Maybe Harvey Fierstein himself was out there in the darkness, waiting to hear the monologues, he thought. Would they have the chance to read sides together?

All the waiting actors listened intensely as each was individually called to go on stage to perform. The competition was palpable and nerve wracking. As much as T.J. didn't want to admit it to himself, they were all excellent. This wasn't the Connecticut Yankee Playhouse or the little theater downtown where he had to tell a dirty joke to land the role of Sir Duncelot. This was the big time.

So far, no one had been asked to perform anything beyond their monologues, and each received a curt but friendly, "Thank you," before being dismissed. Every time a new actor took the stage, those in wait obediently shifted down to the next chair in line. After about fifteen minutes, T.J. found himself "on deck." He tried not to pay too much attention to his predecessor, who was a dead ringer for Matthew Broderick, and focused on taking some deep breaths and remembering the intentions of his character before speaking the opening lines, just as Marti and Sarah Saperstein had taught him.

The actor on stage finished his speech and T.J. was about to stand up for his turn when he heard a voice from the other side of the stage announce, "That was great, Todd. We'd like you to read this scene, now."

A reader strode onstage from the opposite wings and handed the actor a script to quickly scan before they'd read it aloud together. T.J. was anxious, wondering if he would get the same opportunity. It was a short scene, only a page or two, lasting less than two minutes and then Todd was given the perfunctory "thank you" and T.J.'s name was called next.

He took center stage, where white tape marked the X on which he should stand. An overhead light shone down on him and he indulged in a moment to gaze out at the beautiful theater he had only ever experienced from the audience. Over a thousand seats, mostly hidden in darkness, were now empty but soon would be filled by an audience clamoring to see Agnes of God.

"Whenever you're ready, T.J.," someone called from one of the middle rows.

He launched into his monologue, earnestly and with emotion. The butterflies in his stomach reminded him that nervousness is only a sign of caring . . . a positive. He smoothly delivered his lines without a stumble and remembered all the right notes Marti wanted him to hit. He even managed to get his voice to tremble at the precise moment she wanted him to exhibit the character's fear. He finished, pleased with his performance and waited expectantly, unmoving, in case they would ask him for more.

"Thank you."

That was it. He managed to smile and nod his head in acknowledgement, then turned and walked off stage. Maybe there would be a surprise callback, but this seemed to indicate that his shot at Torch Song Trilogy was, for now, over.

He walked back out the stage door onto 45th Street, his eyes squinting to adjust to the bright sunlight after being inside the darkened theater. He paused briefly to indulge in the fantasy that he was a working Broadway actor, just emerging from a performance as he did eight times a week. An ambulance and a fire engine shattered the reverie as they suddenly blasted down the block, jarring him back to reality. He began to walk through noisy, dirty Times Square to make his way home.

He picked up a couple of pizza slices for his dinner and then came around the corner to his building where the doorman alerted him that a package had arrived for him. The doorman retrieved it from a storage closet while T.J. juggled the pizza box and checked his mailbox. A couple of bills and a circular from Bed, Bath & Beyond were all that was waiting for him.

"Here you go," the doorman said, carefully setting the small package atop the pizza box for T.J. to carry. It was smaller than a shoebox, wrapped in plain brown paper with a post office box return address from somewhere in Long Island City. He had no idea what it could be.

Once inside his apartment, he set everything else down and tore open the wrapping paper. Lifting the lid, he pulled aside the white tissue paper surrounding its contents. The first thing he found was a Xeroxed photograph of Armand, the same image that had been poster-sized at The Works on the night of his remembrance party. He turned it over but nothing was written on the back.

Digging underneath the remaining tissue, he found a little plastic bottle with a curly white ribbon tied around its neck. It looked like a mini shampoo bottle from a hotel bathroom. But it wasn't filled with shampoo. He held it up closer to get a better look at its contents.

He gasped at the realization. Ashes. It was a bottle of cremated remains.

As if he suddenly handling a snake, he dropped it back into the box and went immediately to the phone to call Leo who, fortunately, picked up before the answering machine.

"Hello?"

"Did you get your mail yet?" T.J. asked, incredulous.

"I was just about to call you," Leo answered, affirmatively.

"Who sent them? Is that what Armand actually wanted? Who's in Long Island City?"

"That's where his parents were staying with cousins, I think."

"What the hell are we supposed to do with it? I don't want that sitting around on a shelf for me to see every day."

Leo was quiet for a moment and then said, "After I finish work tomorrow, meet me at The Gap."

As requested, T.J. arrived outside The Gap on Columbus Avenue at six p.m. the next evening. Regardless of what time Punxsutawney Phil the Groundhog had predicted back in February, spring was definitely arriving in New York. T.J. wore his heavy black pea coat and gloves to fight off the damp chill that had blown in that morning. While he waited for Leo, he looked into the store window, not recognizing any of the employees who now worked there. Folding was obviously still mandatory criteria, he noticed, eyeing the tables and shelves that were uniformly packed with merchandise.

Just as he had felt nostalgic the day before on 45th Street, now he was remembering all the time he had spent here on Columbus Avenue, especially the half-mile stretch between Andy's apartment and The Works. Would he always feel like there were ghosts in this neighborhood? Some of Armand's pulverized bones were contained in the bottle now in his coat pocket, but where was his spirit? Maybe it was, at least in part, here at The Gap or swirling around the dancing patrons of the bar.

A light, cold drizzle began to fall and T.J. ducked under the awning of the gourmet cheese shop next door to The Gap. He was growing impatient just before his friend scurried up the block, ducking his head in a vain attempt to keep dry. Leo came up beside him and said, "I didn't think I'd need an umbrella."

"Let's get this over with and go to Ernie's for dinner." Ernie's was a popular Italian restaurant known for its enormous bowls of pasta. It seated three hundred patrons and was almost always at full capacity.

"Okay, but we have to be discreet," Leo cautioned. "I don't think it's legal to scatter human remains on the streets of Manhattan."

"Let's open the bottles and when we walk past the store, just pour them out onto the sidewalk."

"The sidewalk? Not the curb?"

"Does it matter?" asked T.J., exasperated, as he pulled the bottle from his pocket. Having difficulty unscrewing the top with his gloves on, he fumbled to take them off and dropped the bottle onto the wet pavement.

Leo chuckled. "Good thing it's plastic."

T.J. retrieved the bottle and was able to unscrew the cap. Leo did the same. It was starting to rain steadily and they both shivered.

Leading the way, Leo walked at a brisk clip past The Gap, trying to look nonchalant as he inverted the open bottle and gave it a couple shakes. The gray dust inside disappeared in a little puff and he kept going to the end of the block, where he waited for T.J. under a bodega canopy. He motioned for him to follow.

T.J. started to stroll in his direction and tried to shake his bottle as Leo had, but nothing was coming out. He shook it harder, but the remains would not dislodge. He squinted to look at what was stopping it. A bone fragment? After another few fruitless shakes, he gave it a good thwack as if he were trying to put ketchup on a hamburger. One big clump spewed out into a pile on the sidewalk at his feet.

"Oh, for God's sake!"

T.J. hurried to join Leo so they could hightail it to Ernie's and left the last bit of Armand to eventually dissolve and be washed away down Columbus Avenue.

By the end of the week, there was still no feedback from his Torch Song Trilogy audition, so T.J. answered an ad in Backstage looking for singers to join an established troupe that toured around New York City area nursing homes, entertaining residents on weekday afternoons. He was hired on the spot, without even having to audition. The pay was decent, lunch was included (chicken or fish, and T.J. quickly learned to stick with the chicken) and the musicians and singers were more talented than he had expected, given the venues. That was one of the perks of New York City: there was never a shortage of talented artists looking for opportunities to strut their stuff.

He found the shows to be fun and he liked the old folks who, in spite of their often sad health circumstances, always seemed to appreciate the energy and attention of the young performers. The show consisted of simple standards from the Great American Songbook and a few specialty numbers specifically catered to the geriatric generation. It was as much fun to learn silly songs like How Ya Gonna Keep 'Em Down on the Farm and Take Your Girlie to the Movies as it was to sing classics like Younger Than Springtime and Autumn Leaves.

For most of the show, he was paired with a gifted young soprano, appropriately named Melody. Despite her angelic appearance and dulcet tones, she had a ribald sense of humor and naughty streak. They enjoyed mischief backstage, trying to make each other break character or improvising some comic bit to crack themselves up. Once, during the set up for her to sing I'm Gonna Wash That Man Right Out of My Hair, T.J. was supposed to playfully swat her backside with a small hand towel, which she would then grab from him and use as a prop during the song. However, he happened to hit her peach-colored leotard's wraparound skirt in the process and it fell to the floor, causing her to look as if she were suddenly standing buck-naked on the small stage area. Seizing the moment, he grabbed the skirt and quickly left her alone onstage with only the towel to provide some modesty while she sang. It was the most enthusiastic attention she'd ever received from the old men in the audience.

It felt good to play opposite this pretty young woman and often it seemed as if there might be a romantic spark between them, especially when singing a duet like The Best Thing For You Would Be Me or even Making Whoopee. This prompted a few stolen kisses backstage or in their makeshift dressing rooms and when T.J. mentioned this to Leo, his friend was not amused. Just as he'd sternly admonished T.J. about actor Rick's heterosexuality, he was quick to advise him against flirting with danger by possibly leading her on.

"T.J., you are gay. Gay!"

Still, the combination of intimacy and normalcy he felt when he was with Melody was intoxicating for T.J., especially since he had no man in his life.

By the time he got home from these matinees, sometimes as far out in the boroughs as Mott Haven in the Bronx, T.J. was usually happy just to sprawl out on his sofa bed and watch The Powers of Matthew Star, Dynasty or Dallas, occasionally joined by Leo or Bella.

He hardly ever saw Carolyn Lee or Marti, unless it was on television, but they did spend lots of time catching up over the phone. Carolyn Lee revealed that she and Gary had been discussing the possibility of starting a family while Marti was lamenting that, while the fictional earthquake that had rattled the soap opera world provided a momentary uptick in ratings, things had slumped back down. Tension and frustration were running high behind the scenes there. Marti asked if he had any interest in coming back to put his fledgling computer skills to use in the production office as Phyllis was struggling with everyone she had hired after Bella. T.J. wasn't ready to forfeit his dreams of stardom for a career behind the camera, especially since he was making money singing every day for grateful, if not captive, crowds.

Channel J usually provided some temporary sexual distraction for T.J. before bedtime, but he was missing the "chase and capture" adventures of his club outings with Leo. It was still happening at places like Danceteria and The Pyramid Club but the AIDS epidemic was ravaging their community with such speed and cruelty that most guys preferred to gather in smaller groups just for dinners, movies and house parties. Every time T.J. got the itch to splow his hair and squeeze into some tight "pleather" pants, he reminded himself of how it ended for poor Armand. An infestation of crabs from Luke was bad enough, but T.J. didn't consider death worth the risk of a hot sexual encounter. He never missed the way things were with Andy, but he absolutely missed the feeling of having a boyfriend.

The foursome of friends were finally able to coordinate a dinner date for a Saturday night before everyone would disperse for the Memorial Holiday weekend. Carolyn Lee and Gary would be spending it in Naples, Florida, Leo was heading to the Hamptons with a new beau he had met at Citibank and T.J. was off to Connecticut for a joint Mothers and Fathers Day visit with his parents. Bella was the only one staying in the City, covering shifts for vacationing staff at New York Sports Clubs.

Carolyn Lee, always wanting to stick close to home on Central Park South in case her husband summoned her, suggested the popular Ru'elles and persisted until everyone agreed and she made the reservation. Decorated all in burgundy with large white, Corinthian columns and twin stairways around its octagonal bar which led to an exclusive balcony, it was a place to see and be seen. T.J. and Leo were looking forward to an opportunity to cruise some cute waiters and busboys. Bella brought everyone two-week, all-access guest passes to the New York Sports Club.

"I'll definitely give it a try," T.J. said, gratefully accepting. Ever since the earthquake, I can tell I've put on weight. No matter how much I smoke!"

Midway through the meal, one of the hostesses came by the table with a message for Carolyn Lee. Her husband had rung and wanted her to call him back. She excused herself and went to a payphone.

Bella couldn't help but comment as soon as she was out of ear shot, "God, she's like Pavlov's dog. He rings the bell and she goes running."

Looking at the measly serving of grilled chicken salad Carolyn Lee had been poking at with her fork, Leo added, "At least her food won't get cold."

T.J. felt compelled to defend her. "Aw, give her a break. She's trying to be healthy so they can start a family." Lowering his voice and leaning in to them, he also said, "I think she's having trouble getting pregnant."

Bella came back with, "Of course she'd have trouble getting pregnant. Her husband's busy fucking every girl under thirty at City Hall."

They looked at her, surprised, and she explained, "His shenanigans are pretty much an open secret in city government circles."

"The front desks at New York Sports Clubs are better than Page Six," Leo observed, between bites of his dinner.

The waiter appeared and refilled their water glasses. "Can I get anyone another round of drinks?" he asked.

Simultaneously T.J. and Leo said, "Yes."

"I'll have a glass of your house Chardonnay," Bella piped up, stunning them into silence. As the waiter left to fill their orders, she looked at them defensively and said, "I'm allowed to have a glass of wine with my dinner, guys."

They didn't have to pursue the subject since Carolyn Lee returned to the table with a forced cheerfulness. "Gary just got home from a day trip to D.C.," she told them. "He was wondering what time I'd be home."

"Is he scared to be home alone?" Bella asked sarcastically.

Giving herself a miniscule serving of chicken salad, Carolyn Lee responded cheerfully, "Well, a baby isn't going to make itself. Two to tango, and all that."

T.J. avoided making eye contact with Bella, whom he knew would be looking his way after that remark. He changed the subject to ask Leo about the new guy he was seeing and if they'd be together long enough for them all to meet him.

"Yeah, because we haven't even met Gary, yet," Bella added, to T.J.'s annoyance.

Leo told them about Don, the banker he'd met through work, a handsome Greek executive type, whom he said was not so straight laced when they were between the sheets. He had a home in East Hampton and, if things continued to work out, they could all be hanging out there in the upcoming summer months.

Dinner segued into dessert, which consisted of cappuccinos for the ladies and the guys had sambucas and shared a piece of Caramel Apple Pie.

"I'll try out the Sports Club as soon as I get back from Memorial Day," T.J. promised Bella, finishing off his final bite of pie. She was conspicuously eyeing their liqueurs and Leo finally extended the glass in her direction.

"Do you want a sip?"

Without saying anything, T.J.'s reaction was apparent and everyone, especially Bella, noticed.

"Are you going to become the Booze Police, now?" she asked him.

T.J. defended himself. "Hey, I never thought you had a problem in the first place."

Before Bella could decide whether or not she was going to take Leo up on the offer, a tall and generically good-looking man came to their table, his eyes wide and hair disheveled. They immediately recognized him although he looked very little like his usual well-groomed and composed self.

"Gary!" Carolyn Lee exclaimed, trying to sound as if the surprise was a happy one.

"You're just in time for dessert," Bella said, "Or an after-dinner drink."

Ever the gentleman, T.J. began to stand and offer a handshake but was halted by Gary's hyper focus on his wife.

"You should be home by now, Lee," he barked at her. "How long do you expect me to sit there waiting for you? I can't keep calling the restaurant."

Carolyn Lee was doing her best to ad lib her way through the awkward encounter.

"Honey, I've told you all about my friends. Now you finally get to meet them."

"I didn't come here to meet your friends from the gay bar. Or have dessert. Let's go. Now."

Her friends watched her intently, trying to communicate their support amidst this unpleasant scene. The patrons at the next table were also observing and whispering amongst themselves.

"Gosh, it is later than I realized," she stammered, without checking her watch. She hurriedly pulled out her purse while he stood over her.

While she rifled for her wallet he moved away, saying, "I'll wait for you outside."

He hustled down the steps from the balcony dining area and disappeared to the lower level. Carolyn Lee, face flushed, took some cash and tossed it on the table, rising from her seat. "Sorry, guys. I've got to run. This was fun."

Bella dryly said, "Yes. So fun."

Too ashamed for further eye contact, Carolyn Lee kept her gaze down and quickly fled. As soon as they saw her descending the staircase, they looked at each other in disbelief.

Leo finally broke the silence with, "What the fuck was that?"

T.J. remembered one of his mother's favorite sayings, "You never get a second chance to make a first impression."

Bella took the sambuca snifter from Leo.

"I think I will try a sip, thanks."

One glass of wine and a single sip of sambuca was somehow enough to make Bella visibly woozy and, once they paid the bill, it was obvious she'd need help getting down the stairs and into a cab. Even though she resisted their assistance, T.J. and Leo walked on either side of her as they slowly made their way out to the street.

Leo hailed a cab as T.J. propped her up.

"You okay, doll?"

She murmured an unintelligible response. Leo opened the car door for her and as she stepped off the curb to climb into the back seat, they winced as they saw and heard her smack her forehead into the doorframe. She was feeling no pain and kept climbing in, almost as if she were getting into bed.

Knowing she'd probably be fast asleep by the time they drove away, T.J. decided to tell the driver her address and gave him a twenty dollar bill to pay for the ride in advance.

After watching them drive out of sight, Leo said to him, "Those girls are a mess."

CHAPTER SEVEN
Cruise Control

T.J.'s parents were there to pick him up from the train station just in time to head directly to the Country Club for dinner, their Friday night ritual. He had grown up knowing all the staff, the waiters, valet parking attendants, tennis instructors and caddies. Sitting down in the comfortably rustic country-style dining room, after greeting several other longtime early-bird diners, he had no need to look at the menu. He knew it by heart.

His parents ordered a carafe of Pinot Grigio to share and T.J. asked for a dry martini with an extra olive.

"When did you start drinking martinis?" his father asked.

"When I met Marti Feldon. She showed me how to mix the perfect one," he said, pulling out his cigarette case to have a smoke while they waited to order.

Janice, who seemed to always have a remark for any occasion or on any subject, said, "One martini makes you relaxed. Two makes you mean."

"And after three, you don't remember anything anyway," T.J. joked. She laughed and held out her hand for him to offer her a cigarette, too. The senior Porter instinctively pulled out his lighter and ignited it for her. It was a ritual they'd played out several times a day for as long as T.J. could remember.

T.J. offered one to his father, but he waved it away saying, "Trying to cut down. Doctor's orders."

"Tell us all about the new show, honey," Janice enthused. "I think it's awful that they killed you off the soap opera. I've told everyone to stop watching."

Old friends and acquaintances stopped by their table, interrupting their reunion. They all wanted to know how T.J.'s life in showbiz was going in the big city. They had watched him grow up performing, and they expected big things from him. Being on a soap had some credibility but most of them were asking when he'd be "getting a big Broadway break." By the third or fourth time he went cheerfully through the spiel, he was wishing he and his parents had stayed home for dinner.

He did like the Club's crab cake appetizer, though, and the Chicken Marsala was an old reliable. A waitress placed it before him just as he lit another cigarette, so he snubbed off the head of it and placed it carefully in the ashtray for later. His mother noticed and scoffed, reaching across the table to pick it up by the filter and smash it out.

"Be rich," she admonished.

"I stopped getting an allowance a while ago, remember?" he teased. "And a pack costs more than a buck, now."

"We'll get you a carton," Thomas Sr. said, cutting into the steak he'd just been served to ensure it was cooked properly. Medium well, as always.

T.J. went on to tell them about the musical touring show and how much he enjoyed singing with Melody, as well as all the new musical material he was learning.

"You should bring the show up to Connecticut," his mother suggested. "You could perform it here at the Club."

Looking around the dining room, T.J. admitted, "It's almost the same age as our usual audience."

Both his parents laughed, always amused by their clever son. Over the course of their meal they continued catching up on family and neighborhood gossip. Since Janice and T.J. both claimed they were trying to lose a few pounds, only Thomas had the customary chocolate mousse dessert.

The feeling of going back to his childhood home was always a comforting and comfortable experience. He would see the American flag flying high over the hedges as they turned the corner onto their street. Their long driveway led up a gently sloping hill to their house. He walked through the heavy front door, which was a vibrant red with a big brass hunting fox door knocker in the center, near the top. Other than the fresh flowers in the foyer, nothing ever seemed to change. T.J. set his valise in its usual spot at the bottom of the stairs and they automatically headed for the kitchen where Janice would make a pot of decaf coffee.

"How about a few hands of Hearts," Thomas suggested as he took a pile of mail over to the card table and sat down to skim through it.

"Sure," T.J. responded, joining his dad. On the wall behind the game table was an assortment of framed photos of T.J. as a performer, taken over the course of his young life. Everything from his school plays and productions with the Connecticut Yankee Players to some snapshots taken on set of Tomorrow's Promise—and his most current eight-by-ten headshot. It wasn't exactly a shrine, but it was clear the Porters cherished their only child and were proud of his talents and burgeoning accomplishments. Without ever discussing it, or even necessarily thinking about it, it was the security in their love and support that allowed T.J. to have the outgoing personality that won him so much admiration and friendship.

It was then that he realized how much he had missed them and the sweet familiarity of everything he had known his entire life. Only a little more than an hour's train ride away from Manhattan, but an entirely other world.

Later that night, as he lay in his childhood bed in the room still decorated with posters and mementoes reflecting early triumphs as well as future aspirations, he listened to what he realized was an absence of sound. Aside from the steady rhythm of the crickets outside in the yard, there was total silence. He was surprised by how much he missed the sirens, honking horns and the rumble of buses on asphalt.

Still, he slept well and later than usual. When he opened the closet the next morning, he found his entire old wardrobe right where'd left it. After putting on an old sweat suit adorned with his high school logo, the Chiefs, he went downstairs where he could hear his mother puttering around in the kitchen.

"Good morning," he called to her cheerfully.

"Not for much longer," she answered with a nod to the wall clock that showed it was after eleven. She was busily making her famous potato salad, and the counter top was covered with spices, bowls and a big cutting board. Raw steaks were on a platter by the stove and a brown paper bag was stuffed with ears of corn waiting to be shucked, traditionally T.J.'s job.

As he helped himself to a cup of coffee he asked if anyone else would be coming over for their afternoon barbecue.

"Nope, it's just us. Unless there's someone you want to invite?"

"Nah. I haven't really stayed in touch with anybody. Besides, this is our Mothers and Fathers Day combo."

She smiled sweetly at her darling boy, grateful. "I was hoping you'd say that. But you know you're always welcome to bring up some of your City friends. I really like Leo."

"He's the best."

"And what about the new girl you're singing with, Melanie?"

"Melody. She's cute, but it's just a work thing."

"I met your father when I was working at his law firm," she said, eyes twinkling. "Food for thought."

Talking about women in a romantic context made him feel like he was lying. Even if it was only by omission. But was this the right time and place to discuss the sexual excitements he had discovered after moving away from home? He'd always been able to tell his parents anything. Especially his mother. His dad even referred to them often as "Apple" and "Tree."

"I don't think of her that way," he managed to say, wishing he hadn't left his cigarettes upstairs.

Putting her attention back on mixing the potato salad, Janice only said, "It's a big city. Working in television and on stage. There must be beautiful young ladies everywhere."

"Yes. I'm just not interested . . ." He watched her closely as he ventured on, with her own words, ". . . in young ladies."

She paused her stirring but didn't look up. The awkward pause seemed to T.J. to last hours before she simply said, "You're still so young. Plenty of time."

He instinctively put his hand on her arm and softly said, "Mom, do you know what I'm trying to tell you?"

Now she cast her eyes, the identical blue as his own, up to face him. They were quickly beginning to brim with tears and she said almost breathlessly, "Yes, son. And I love you no matter what."

T.J. felt like this was a big, special moment for him. For them. He knew how close his relationship with his parents was, especially as an only child who'd been encouraged, supported and praised his entire life. Leo had repeatedly told him how taboo the subject of sexuality was in his conservative Italian Catholic home on Staten Island. It wasn't like that for T.J. The Porters were special.

He leaned in to embrace Janice, but she turned her body away and resumed stirring her salad, reaching with her other hand for some celery salt to add. Surprised, he simply stared at her as she said, "Let's not talk about this with your father."

His mother's reaction rattled T.J. and he wanted to press her further. In fact, he could think of nothing else throughout the remainder of the day as they went through all the familiar motions of making a holiday meal . . . shucking the corn and helping Janice set the table on their screened-in back porch while Thomas dutifully manned the grill, the sounds of Sinatra and Steve & Eydie coming from the portable boom box.

"Let's not talk about this with your father," echoed in his head. In his nearly twenty-one years, there had never been anything off limits in discussions with his family. T.J.'s precocious nature, combined with being an only child and constantly surrounded by adults, had made him a miniature grown-up. Even to himself. He'd never gotten in trouble for being disrespectful or disobedient because he never was. Now, suddenly, he was supposed to censor himself?

He couldn't decide if he was hurt or incensed. Perhaps he should be both. He wondered if, in a single moment, he had become an embarrassment.

The hours that followed, right up until the steaks were served and they sat down for their afternoon feast, left T.J. unsettled. Janice continued on as though nothing had occurred between them and, of course, Thomas was oblivious and unfazed. He talked about some legal cases from his office and the Soviet Union boycott of the upcoming Summer Olympics ("Good riddance"). There was some discussion of a Bermuda holiday later in the year before hurricane season, but T.J. wasn't really absorbing any of it.

After dinner, and what seemed like a protracted amount of time to clean up, Thomas announced that they should play a few more hands of Hearts before it was time for Airwolf, the military drama series on television. This had become their Saturday night alternative to The Love Boat, which everyone agreed has lost its charm.

At one point, his father mentioned to T.J., "It seems like you're smoking an awful lot. Maybe you should think about cutting back, son."

T.J. felt like he'd been biting his tongue all day and overreacted to the remark with misguided frustration, "You're the one who bought me my first pack of cigarettes, remember? Or was that the condoms?"

Taken aback by his tone, Janice said nothing but Thomas chuckled and recalled, "That's right. You were always complaining about how much our smoking annoyed you."

T.J. filled out the story for him. "So you tossed me a pack and said, 'Here, now it won't bother you.'"

He chuckled again. "Well, I was right, wasn't I?"

"Yes, it was swell. I was the only fifteen-year-old in school who didn't have to sneak around."

His mother chimed in, trying for a lighter mood, "We didn't know then everything we know now. I guess we should all cut down or quit."

If he didn't have to sneak around for cigarettes when he was fifteen, T.J. thought, why should he have to censor himself as an adult? Or was sexuality like smoking and one should not subject people to the subject who don't care for it? No Smoking areas were becoming more popular in places like malls and restaurants. Was a "No Gay" zone simply a way of being considerate?

After Airwolf the crime drama, Mickey Spillane's Mike Hammer, began and T.J. saw his opportunity to break away from the frustration of the day. God, how he missed New York. He longed to be in a dark nightclub, surrounded by horny, handsome men.

"I'm going to head upstairs," he told them, dutifully kissing his mom on the cheek. "I may take the train back tomorrow instead of Monday since we have two shows Tuesday."

"Awww," she lamented. "I was planning to bake tomorrow. Maybe if I start early, I can send you back with some goodies."

He smiled sweetly at her. She had always excelled at expressing her affection with food.

"Good night, son," Thomas said as T.J. walked to the doorway that led from the family room out to the foyer.

"Good night," he called back. He stopped and turned to look at them so contentedly sitting on their overstuffed sofa, nestled in between magazines and pillows and illuminated by the bluish glow of the TV screen and a single table lamp.

He took a pause that was just as much to summon courage as it was for dramatic effect then said, "And I'm pretty sure I'm gay."

His mother smiled at him and his dad remained silent, staring at the TV screen. T.J. went up to bed.

Never in his life had he felt awkward around his parents but that had changed in a single day. He'd never once felt that they had any kind of social hangups. They had always shared everything, or so he thought, so how could this be a surprise? Besides, they're the parents. They should have figured it out a long time ago. And if it was such a shock, then what might he not know about them?

He also felt guilty about how he'd dropped the gay bomb on them and then fled the scene. Only sleeping in fits and starts, T.J. climbed out of bed shortly after sunrise, stalled for time by taking a long shower, and finally went downstairs just before eight. The house was quiet, but there was a pot of hot coffee on the counter, his favorite mug and a pitcher of milk beside it.

After pouring himself a cup, he wandered through the kitchen and dining room and spotted his mother outside doing one of her weekend tasks, refilling the bird feeders with seed. It was a spectacular spring day and he thought how beautiful and healthy she looked out there amongst the azaleas and rhododendrons, lifting the big, heavy bags. She may have carried herself like a society lady, but she was equally at ease working in the yard or vegetable garden.

"Need a hand?" he offered, almost as a white flag.

"No, thanks, I'm almost done," she called back, cheerily.

"Where's Dad?"

"It's so lovely out, he got up early and went to play golf. He should be back in time to take you to the train station. If not, I can."

"Mom," he began, at a loss.

She stopped her task and walked over to him, wiping some perspiration from her forehead.

"Honey, I understand."

"Does he?"

She shrugged. "We didn't discuss it. It's not what anyone wants for their child."

He quickly came back with, "But I'm not sad about it. Why should you be?"

Her eyes started to moisten and she spoke with a trepidation he'd never heard from her before.

"You are our sunshine. There's nothing we wouldn't do to make your life easier. I'm just afraid that this . . . that being homosexual . . . will make your life harder."

"It won't. It doesn't!"

She touched the side of his face with her hand, looking at him lovingly as her eyes continued to fill until the tears spilled out. It gutted him to see her in pain.

"Please be careful while you figure things out, okay?"

"I promise," he said as they came together for a long, strong hug.

Thomas did return just in time to get him to the station for his train back to the city. T.J. wondered if the timing had been intentional to avoid having a conversation, but now they were faced with the fifteen-minute car ride.

To T.J.'s relief, they mainly discussed the changes that were coming to the Club's golf course, the rising travel costs for their annual vacation and Janice's high school reunion they were trying to worm their way out of attending. Pulling up outside the depot, T.J. jumped out of the car and pulled his valise out of the backseat. It looked like he was making a clean getaway.

"Thanks for the ride, Dad. I'll talk to you soon. Love you."

"Love you, son. Just do me a favor, huh?"

T.J. steeled himself for whatever was coming next as his father fixed him with his most serious, lawyerly gaze.

"Get the fuck back in the closet."

His father drove away, leaving T.J. stunned and standing alone, feeling like, after his pronouncement the night before, he'd probably deserved that.

T.J. wanted to call Leo but there was no time to use the pay phone before the train pulled in. Besides, his friend was out on a beach or in a pool somewhere in the Hamptons. This was something he would have to come to grips with all on his own.

Back in Manhattan, he walked the few short blocks from Grand Central to his apartment where he dropped his luggage. He sat down on the sofa bed and lit a cigarette. He had come this far, coming out to his parents. There was no turning back. He wanted comfort and he wanted it in a man's arms.

For a mere nanosecond, he considered calling Andy. Luke. He wished Ben weren't in Los Angeles.

This week's Village Voice lay on the table and he started thumbing through it from the back cover where the classified and personal ads proliferated. Everyone read them for amusement or titillation but T.J.'s eye was caught by a quarter page advertisement for Uncle Charlie's Memorial Day Weekend celebration of Fleet Week, a new local tradition honoring the U.S. Navy, Marine Corps and Coast Guard. There would be military demonstrations, ceremonies and ship tours. But the real attraction for most New Yorkers, gay and straight, was the presence of thousands of visiting sailors roaming the streets looking for fun and adventure.

On The Town was one of his favorite movie musicals: the story of three sailors on a twenty-four hour leave in New York City. As he showered and dressed for a night out at Uncle Charlie's, he couldn't help but hum the film's most memorable song, New York, New York (It's a Wonderful Town).

T.J. decided this was the night to break in some new clothes he'd purchased through the International Male catalogue. He chose the lightweight electric blue aviator jacket "with plenty of zippers to keep things handy" over a boat-neck T shirt, tight dark blue jeans and high top sneakers. He blow dried his hair as high as he could then locked it in place with some Dippity-do gel. No preppy country club style if he was going to find a randy sailor looking for a city boy. Tonight, he was emulating Matt Dillon, Rob Lowe and George Michael. He wished he had a pierced ear.

Riding the Number 6 train downtown to Union Square, T.J. was on the lookout. He had seen a few sailors on the 42nd Street platform wearing their dress whites but the three on the train car wore the casual uniforms just like in On The Town. None of them were particularly good looking, nor probably even gay, but he tried to catch the eye of any one of them nonetheless. A goofy looking guy sitting across from him noticed T.J.'s efforts and smiled coyly but he was too distracted to respond.

Walking westward to Uncle Charlie's, there didn't seem to be any sailors milling around Greenwich Village. He wondered if maybe the idea of gay sailors was just a fantasy. There were a few guys, and even a drag queen, wearing sailors' caps but that and some colorful Fleet Week '84! Hey, Sailor! posters were the extent of anything nautical he observed.

Entering the bar, he immediately noticed how much quieter it seemed, unlike usual standards, and the clientele appeared to be largely tourists. He supposed, like Leo and Carolyn Lee, most Gothamites were out of town for the holiday weekend.

Determined not to waste the evening he took advantage of an open barstool, ordered a beer and started cruising the room for anyone interesting.

Opposite him, leaning against a railing, was a conservatively dressed black man standing alone with a drink in his hand. In a plain gray suit with a white shirt and a wide paisley tie, he looked more like he belonged in a Park Avenue office building than a Village bar. They made eye contact and, embarrassed, T.J. looked away. After another sip of beer, he cast his glance back and the man was still looking at him, now with a grin. T.J. smiled back but didn't further engage.

By the time T.J. finished the beer and was about to decide where else he might wander in search of an elusive gay sailor, the man had walked over to stand beside him.

"How about I get the next round?" he asked.

T.J. was surprised, pleasantly. The man was even nicer looking up close.

"Sure, thanks. Thanks very much."

"I'm Terry," he said, motioning to the bartender.

"T.J. Nice to meet you."

They made small talk, chatting easily. Terry was a real estate agent who lived in Brooklyn and had been in the neighborhood with a colleague to see a brownstone property that would soon be coming on the market.

"Any plans for the holiday tomorrow?" he asked.

"Not yet," T.J. told him. "Most of my friends are out of town."

Flashing a broad smile, Terry proposed, "How would you like to come out to Brooklyn?"

T.J. appreciated how forthright he was, while still managing to be charming. He relished the thought of picking up a random guy just hours after being told to "get the fuck back in the closet." He also couldn't help but wonder about the stereotype of black men being especially well endowed and wanted to find out.

"How do we get there?" T.J. asked flirtatiously, rather than answering the question.

Terry leaned in close and said softly in his ear, "It's a quick trip on the 2 train, but I think you're worth a taxi."

T.J. could identify his cologne as Drakkar Noir, one of his favorites.

"Safe sex only?" T.J. ventured as Terry remained close to him.

"Of course," he whispered before bestowing a gentle kiss on T.J.'s ear, arousing him further.

When T.J. woke up the next morning, his first thought wasn't about the incident with his parents, nor how Terry had disproven the cliché about size. He had to figure out how to get home from wherever the heck in Brooklyn he was. Terry was a nice enough guy and served the purpose of being last night's "port in a storm," but now all T.J. wanted was to get back to his own apartment and connect with his friends.

He scrambled to dress and slip out before Terry awoke, but got caught just as the socks were going on.

"Want me to make coffee?" Terry asked, still groggy.

"No, no, that's okay. Thanks for everything."

Terry rolled over. There were no further pleasantries or pretensions of planning a second rendezvous. T.J. slipped on his shoes and let himself out to find his way to a subway station in the quiet morning light of the Memorial Day holiday.

Once at home and showered, T.J. lit a cigarette and managed to catch Bella by telephone as she was about to head off to a shift at the New York Sports Club on Second Avenue, not far away. She would have a dinner break at six, so he told her he would swing by and they could spend the hour together.

The fitness craze had really gripped America and chains of health clubs, private aerobics dance studios and gymnasiums had sprung up everywhere. The New York Sports Clubs ("NYSC") had particularly proliferated and seemed to have opened in every neighborhood in the City. T.J. had never thought much about it since he had enjoyed plenty of tennis and swimming while growing up and, since moving to Manhattan, walked miles and miles a day. Sure, it would be nice to be more muscular but padded shoulders and baggy pants were the fashion style and none of the guys who'd seen him naked had ever complained. Even so, walking into the shiny, new club filled with mirrors, bright neon lighting and an assortment of hard bodied men and women made him feel as though he should drop a few pesky pounds and firm himself up.

Especially now, in the Era of AIDS, the gym culture was becoming a healthy alternative to club-hopping. It wasn't just a place to stay fit, it was an entire social scene. Family Fitness, New York Health & Racquet Club, Bally's, 24 Hour Fitness and Gold's were just some of the many options from which people could choose. Fitness classes were especially popular, with all day/every day options ranging from Calisthenics and Stretching to Jazzercise and High Impact Aerobics. Movie star Jane Fonda had helped kick off the trend with her popular Home Video Workout, and good instructors were sought after and well paid. Fanatical students, including everyone from serious athletes to lonely housewives, lined up an hour before a class to secure a coveted spot. The Aerobics Studio was a fitness melting pot.

Bella showed him around the main floor of the club before they went to the coffee shop next door for a bite to eat. She reminded him about the guest pass anytime he wanted to try it out. As soon as they sat down in a booth, any thoughts of athletics evaporated and they both ordered tuna melts.

T.J. poured out the story of coming out to his parents and their unpleasant, uncharacteristic reactions. She listened patiently before weighing in and counseled, "Give it time. It's a lot for them to get used to, especially 'cause you're the only kid. And a son."

"Are you saying they would have taken it better if I were a lesbian?" he retorted.

"You're Junior," she reminded him. "No matter how cool they may be with gay stuff, parents have expectations. Obviously theirs started the day they named you."

"I hate the thought of disappointing them," he admitted, "but I also hate that it disappoints them at all. It shouldn't."

"You'll show them that. Just by being the same wonderful, sweet, funny person you've always been."

He was grateful for her insight and support. They had just enough time for a quick smoke before paying the bill and getting

Bella back to work by the end of her break. She gave him one last bit of advice as they reached the NYSC entrance.

"If my parents can handle all my shit, your parents can handle this. They'll come around."

He was skeptical. "Leo said he could never tell his family or they'd cut him off."

"Play along for now and don't throw it in their faces. The fact is, now they know. They'll always know. When the time is right to be open about it, you'll all just sense it."

"Bel, you're a smart one," he said and gave her a kiss on the cheek.

"At least when I'm sober," she joked.

He opened the door for her as a tall, lean fair-skinned guy with reddish hair and a ripped, hairless body was coming out. In his late twenties, he looked like a model right out of the International Male catalogue. He carried a bright red gym bag over one shoulder and was wearing a turquoise tank top and his black Lycra shorts seemed painted onto his muscular legs. He gave T.J. an admiring glance, and then looked at Bella.

"Good night, Bella," he said as he walked away.

"See you later, Steve."

As soon as he was out of earshot, T.J. asked, "Okay, who is Steve?"

"One of the most popular aerobics teachers in the city. He goes from one club to the other and must teach thirty classes a week."

"Gay?"

She gave him an "of course" look and went inside as T.J. said, "I'm going to take you up on that guest pass."

After unsuccessfully trying to convince Leo to join him for an aerobics class, T.J. used the guest pass to check out the schedule at the Second Avenue location where he'd met Bella and, more interestingly, Steve. He didn't want to show up in one of Steve's classes until he'd tried out some others and felt more confident about being able to execute the rhythmic moves and choreography. He'd never excelled in any of the serious dance classes he'd attended, but hopefully this would be easier.

It was, indeed, easier than formal dance. And thanks to the music, a lot more fun. Hit Me With Your Best Shot, Eye of the Tiger and Walking on Sunshine were among the many popular remixes teacher Pam had on her cassette tapes and T.J. quickly felt he was mastering the moves and pivots required to move from the line in the back of the room to the front. He couldn't remember ever sweating so much.

After a few days, he was ready to try Steve's Happy Hour class and got Bella to let him know the inside scoop on how to secure a spot. He hustled right from the Nursing Home Du Jour to the Sign-In sheet at the Group Fitness Desk.

When it was time for the six p.m. class, T.J. was among the two dozen people who filed in clamoring for their preferred positions near a water fountain, the mirror or, most likely, in close proximity to Steve. T.J., clad in a black spandex cropped T shirt, mid-length gray Lycra shorts and a brand-new, blindingly white pair of Reeboks, hustled up to the front line. Bella had clued him in that Steve liked to move around a lot while he taught, so

T.J. wasn't too worried as long he managed to catch his eye. He noticed that he wasn't the only participant who'd put thought into their appearance: all the ladies seemed to have their hair and makeup done and none of the men were in ratty T-shirts like the ones worn by the guys in the weight room.

Steve strutted in with the same red gym bag he always carried. T.J. admired his punctuality, his confident stride and especially his physique. He was graceful but manly and carried himself in a statuesque manner that T.J. found very attractive.

"Okay, people, who's ready to move and groove?" Steve called out with unbridled enthusiasm and surprising volume.

"We are!" many of the regulars shouted in response, along with some random hooting and cheering.

Steve noticed immediately that T.J. hadn't said anything, so he looked him right in the eyes.

"I asked . . . who's ready to move and groove?"

"I am," T.J. replied but obviously not loud enough for Steve, so he added louder, "We are!"

Steve hit Play on the tape deck and Kool & the Gang's Celebration blasted from the speakers. After an aggressive march in place, a quick stretch, a few grapevines to the left and right, Steve & His Gang were off and running. At designated moments in time with the song, he'd cheer, "Celebrate!" and the class audibly responded. T.J. managed to keep up for most of it and it reminded him of being in the chorus of a musical, backing up the leading man, who was in this case, Steve.

After the forty-five minute workout came to an end and they had completed a cool down and stretch, the students began to disband. Most of them took time to thank Steve or make small talk before they left the studio. T.J. wanted to stall for time, so took the opportunity to retie his sneakers. Steve, soaked with sweat, was mopping himself with a towel before packing his music cassettes into his bag.

Noticing T.J. lingering behind, he asked, "Are you a new member?"

"I'm thinking of joining. Bella's my friend."

"She's fun."

Walking over to T.J. and extending his hand for a firm shake, he said, "I'm Steve. But I guess you know."

How doe someone so sweaty still look so handsome, T.J. wondered.

"T.J. Porter."

"You did great, T.J. Keep coming back and you'll be teaching before you know it."

"Yeah, right."

Steve gave him a crooked, sexy smile before going back to packing his bag and adding, "Seriously. Come back."

"Thanks. I will."

As he walked out of the room, T.J. realized he hadn't retied his left shoe and the laces flopped on the floor as he moved. He didn't want to spoil his exit, so he kept going and went straight to the Membership Office to sign up for their latest special One Year Deal.

Not only did T.J. become a fixture in Steve's class in the weeks that followed, he dropped nearly ten pounds he wasn't expecting to lose. He mastered most of the moves, knew when to sing out "Celebrate!" and was always in the front line, near the center. T.J. didn't want to seem like just another groupie, but Steve always encouraged him to stay after class for some conversation. Ultimately Steve suggested they go for coffee.

Strolling over to the coffee shop next door, they took their discussions beyond gym talk and got to know each other a bit. Steve seemed impressed by T.J.'s television and stage experience, especially as he was an aspiring Broadway actor from the midwest with a few regional theater and national tour credits under his belt. Like Andy, he was thirty, but that was where the resemblance ended. Steve was a "star" in the gym, but out in the real world he was bookish and soft spoken.

Whenever he didn't have another class to teach, Steve would simply ask, "Coffee?" and off they would go. It became so routine that the restaurant's cashier would greet them like regulars, which they were quickly becoming. Blessedly busy with his daytime singing and his evenings at the NYSC, T.J. was uncharacteristically patient with the pace at which they were moving the friendship, romance, or whatever it was.

He hadn't spoken to his parents other than quick, perfunctory phone chats with his mother. There was no mention of their Memorial Day conflict, both of them dutifully pretending that everything was exactly as it had ever been. They would make some idle chat and that was that.

The week before his birthday, he was surprised to find a manila envelope in his mailbox with their Connecticut address on the return label. He took a seat in the lobby to open it, his curiosity too piqued to wait. Inside was an oversize card that had a large, multicolored "21" on the front with "Happy Birthday" embossed over the numerals. In the card was a smaller, business sized envelope on which was written in his mother's handwriting, "For your birthday."

He hoped it was a check, but instead it was two tickets, paper clipped to a note card with his father's monogram, TJP. The tickets were for two passengers aboard the SS Bermuda Star, sailing from NYC in late July to Hamilton, Bermuda. On the note card, he saw his father's recognizable penmanship.

"T.J., for your birthday and our family holiday, we would like to treat you and the lady of your choice to join us in Bermuda. Love, Dad."

He shook his head in disbelief, murmuring, "The lady of my choice?"

It would have been a fantastic gift if he could bring Leo. He and Janice had hit it off great and the idea of running around a luxury liner together, cruising men while cruising the sea, sounded like an incredibly fun way to turn twenty-one. T.J.'s flair for the theatrical almost made him tear the tickets in half, but he recalled Bella's words of advice: "Play along for now and don't throw it in their faces."

Bella. She would be the lady of his choice.

CHAPTER EIGHT
International Male

"Mom, Dad, this is Bella."

"We have heard so much about you, Bella," Janice gushed, giving her an embrace. "T.J. told us how helpful you were with the soap opera."

"You're so beautiful, you should be on camera, yourself," Thomas added, laying it on thick.

T.J. and Bella had arrived on the SS Bermuda Star two hours later than his parents, who had already settled in their stateroom. T.J. figured it would be easier than spending all that additional time with them as they filed through the boarding process, so while the porters took T.J.'s and Bella's luggage to their cabin, they found Janice and Thomas on the Promenade Deck as arranged. They were on deck chairs enjoying iced coffees while awaiting departure.

"I've heard a lot about you, too," Bella told them, on her best behavior. "I'm a big fan of your son."

"Wonderful, wonderful," Thomas responded, his voice reflexively lowering an octave in the company of an attractive young lady. He gestured for them to sit down in the chairs alongside them.

"Not only your namesake, but almost as handsome as his dad," Bella added for good measure. She could lay it on thick, too.

It had taken no arm-twisting to convince Bella to come along for the trip. She'd never been on a cruise before, nor visited Bermuda. Those were bonus incentives to helping T.J. navigate through the tricky task of placating his parents until they came around to his homosexuality.

"The cuisine on board is supposed to be incredible and they feed you day and night," Janice enthused.

"T.J. can afford it . . . he's been working out at the gym every day," Bella told them.

"I noticed right away. Honey, you look wonderful," his mother said to T.J. as she gave him a squeeze of inspection. "Don't lose too much weight."

T.J. felt confident and cute. He and Steve had recently started a discreet affair, swapping out post-class coffees for trips to T.J.'s bed. The only people who knew about it were his inner sanctum of Leo, Bella and Carolyn Lee. It was casual, sexy, fun and a great motivator to keep up with his workouts: being naked alongside someone with a body as impressive as Steve's called for commitment.

Steve's major drawback for T.J. was that he had a live-in partner: a man with whom he'd been involved for nearly five years. Steve explained to T.J. that they had "an open relationship" and gave each other permission for extracurricular play with others, as long as they didn't bring it home and kept it discreet. As disappointing as it was that a commitment with Steve would never be in the cards, T.J. immensely enjoyed having a "friend with benefits" that was as good looking, sexually voracious and mutually attracted as he.

The ship's horn suddenly blew loudly and the engines accelerated, startlingly. They were about to set sail. A waiter was passing by with a tray of assorted drinks: champagne, orange juice or sparkling water. Janice started to wave him away, but T.J. quickly grabbed a champagne and Bella followed suit.

"I'm off the wagon for the duration of this holiday," she said to him, aside. He believed she could handle it and toasted her. They drained their glasses just as the horn sounded again and passengers lining the rails began to cheer and wave.

Once out of New York Harbor and into the open sea bound for Bermuda, the two couples left the Promenade Deck and strolled back to their cabins to unpack and prepare for their first night at sea. The plan was to meet for their eight p.m. seating in the Main Dining Room.

In their small cabin, with only a small porthole through which to see the vast ocean surrounding them, T.J. asked Bella what she thought of his parents.

"They're gorgeous. And so are their manners," she told them. "You're lucky to have parents who are still together . . . and who so obviously adore you."

With some skepticism, he mused, "As long as I'm with a beautiful woman. Do you think they'd have the same manners if I'd brought Steve?"

Sitting on one of the twin beds she had claimed as her own, she began digging through her purse and teased, "Are you saying you'd rather be here with your aerobics instructor?"

A voice suddenly boomed out of the ship's PA system, along with the high-pitched whistle of whatever microphone the person was using. It surprised them and they looked around for the speaker.

"Welcome aboard the SS Bermuda Star, ladies and gentlemen. This is Andrew, your Cruise Director. My office, along with that of the Purser, is located on the Main Deck forward on the starboard side. Do not hesitate to call or come by if we may be of assistance. This is to let you know that in exactly one hour, we will be having a mandatory lifeboat drill which all passengers must attend."

"I wonder if Andrew is cute," T.J. said.

"Your lifejackets can be found in your cabin closet along with a diagram directing you to your designated lifeboat station. This will take approximately twenty minutes, after which a cocktail hour will be held in the Upper Deck's Dolphin Lounge. You're invited to come for Bermudian Rum Punches before the six and eight p.m. dinner seatings."

"Rum Punch!" Bella repeated, appreciatively.

"We wish you a Bon Voyage. The ship's whistle will blast in exactly forty-five minutes to signal you to move to your lifeboat station for the drill. I look forward to meeting you soon. Ciao for now."

"Ciao for now?" Bella laughed.

"Ciao, Andrew," T.J. directed to the speaker. "I look forward to meeting you soon, too!"

Bella pulled a small plastic film canister out of her purse and T.J. assumed she was readying to snap some photos during the lifeboat drill. Instead, she popped off its circular cap and pulled out a joint. T.J. was surprised. He, himself, wasn't a marijuana fan.

“Got a light?” she asked.

As he fished his lighter out of his pocket and handed it to her, she added, “If I’m going off the wagon, I’m going all the way off.”

After the perfunctory lifeboat drill and two rounds of Rum Punches, T.J. and Bella found themselves back in the cabin, dressing for dinner. There had been no sign of Andrew, but a shipboard Daily Bulletin had been slipped under the door and they were greatly amused as they scanned the social opportunities offered.

A Meet and Greet in the Safari Room, a piano bar in the Observatory Lounge and a passenger talent show in the Star Showroom were among the night’s highlights.

Bella suggested, “You should definitely enter the talent show. Guaranteed winner.”

“Let’s see how dinner goes with my folks. I suspect we’ll end up at the piano bar. It’s not like I can meet and greet any guys with them around.”

“If you sneak off to someone’s cabin, my lips are sealed.”

Tonight’s Dress Code was listed as “Summer Casual,” so T.J. put on a Blue Oxford shirt and khakis while Bella opted for a pretty striped midi dress with a V neck and high waist. She loosened her thick dark brown hair so it fell down past her shoulders.

Entering the main Dining Room, they drank in the sumptuous decor and tried to scan the room for any sign of T.J.’s parents. Almost every table was filled and the passengers were boisterously buzzing with the excitement of the first night at sea. The tinkling piano music was all but drowned out by voices and the clatter of dishware.

"Welcome aboard," a somewhat familiar voice said to them over the ambient sounds of the room. They looked up at an extremely tall man in a white uniform with a name tag that said, "Andrew, Cruise Director." He had enormous green eyes that looked down on them from high atop his six-foot-seven frame.

"Your names, please?"

"Porter. We're meeting my parents," T.J. told him, instinctively moving his body weight onto his toes to gain a bit of height.

Scanning his clipboard, Andrew located their table assignment and told an attentive steward standing beside him, "Please show the Porters to Table 21."

Bella still had just enough of a buzz that she couldn't resist hanging back to tell Andrew, "FYI, I'm not a Porter. I'm just the Plus One. He's single."

Once seated at a large round table with a lovely ocean view, alongside the senior Porters and a middle aged couple from somewhere in Pennsylvania, Bella immediately flagged down their waiter to request another Rum Punch.

"Apologies, madam. We are serving a selection of beer, wine and soft drinks. The list is on the back of your menu."

"I thought on a cruise you were supposed to be able to have anything you want," she said, disappointed, and turned her menu around in search of the beverage list. T.J. immediately noticed that his mother wasn't impressed and quickly helped Bella out with the menu.

As they all made "getting acquainted" small talk, Bella's equilibrium continued to deteriorate with every sip. Eventually her speech became slurred and T.J. tried to help compensate and distract by carrying on an energetic conversation about the soap opera world and how much he was looking forward to showing Bella around Bermuda, since she had never been and it was a longtime favorite holiday destination for his family. The couple from Pennsylvania was either oblivious to her altered state, or too polite to show they noticed. Thomas and Janice were not as discreet.

This went on through dinner and when the bus boys finally came to clear their main course dishes, Bella looked up at one and cooed, "I'd like another Trout Almondine, please." She was serious.

T.J. covered for her with a forced laugh and "She's kidding, of course. That was great, thank you."

Bella protested, "Isn't it supposed to be All You Can Eat?"

Thomas, who was seated to her left, diplomatically suggested, "You want to have room for dessert, don't you?"

"Kahluha and coffee!" she exclaimed.

Janice made her distaste obvious to all by chiming in with forced cheer, "Coffee sounds like a splendid idea."

T.J. slid his chair away from the table and took Bella's arm. "Actually, I think we'll head back to the cabin for a while. It's Bella's first cruise and I think she's feeling kinda seasick."

"Honey, you'll get used to it in another day or two," the Pennsylvanian lady advised. "It always takes me that long to find my sea legs. Would you like a Dramamine?"

Bella enthusiastically answered, "Yes!" as T.J. simultaneously replied, "No!"

By now he had her up out of her seat and he told them, "We'll catch up with you later. Enjoy dessert."

"The French call it mal de mer, but I call it agony!" the Pennsylvania lady told her table mates, now finally coming out of her shell.

Andrew was still towering over the host's podium as they wobbled out of the Dining Room. Obviously already smitten with T.J. he said, "Check your Bulletin for tonight's activities. I'll be kicking off the Talent Show in the Star Lounge at nine. Then I'll be in the Observatory Lounge after that."

In spite of her denials that she was neither tired nor inebriated, Bella was obviously both and within two minutes of T.J. getting her to kick off her shoes and plop onto the bed, she had passed out. There was a blanket folded at the foot of the bed, which he draped over her before pulling the black-out drapery across the porthole so she would remain undisturbed until she'd slept it off. He sat on the edge of his bed, looking at her and wondering how she had managed to so quickly and thoroughly become wasted. Maybe it was something in the pot she had smoked, or maybe the time in rehab had diminished her tolerance. Whichever it was, it had certainly been a buzz kill for him. Had he miscalculated by not inviting Melody as his date?

Since it was still early, he decided to explore the ship while she slept it off. The Talent Show was a hard pass, because he suspected that if his parents were there, they would badger him to perform a song. Since he'd had no luck finding a sailor to fool around with during Fleet Week, perhaps this cruise would be his chance to experience some action with an able-bodied seaman.

He brushed his teeth, gave himself a freshening spritz of cologne and headed up a few decks to the Observatory Lounge. If all else failed, he could count on Andrew showing up eventually for some fun flirtation.

As with most cruises he'd experienced, the passengers were an older crowd. The Observation Deck, however, was stunning and the starry night sky over the tranquil Atlantic waters made for a bucolic view. He leaned against a railing for several minutes, drinking it all in. Further aft, he noticed a younger couple probably not much older than he. Newlyweds, perhaps. They were in a romantic embrace, looking out over the ocean and nuzzling between kisses. T.J. wished he had someone to nuzzle in such a romantic setting. There had to be someone out there who would prove to be his Mr. Right.

"Hello, there, Mister," a voice said to him, startling him from his thoughts. He turned to see Sky-High Andrew had walked up behind him.

If not Mr. Right, maybe Mr. Right Now.

T.J. parked himself in the Observatory Lounge for the next hour and a half, while Andrew admirably performed his Cruise Director duties, stopping by T.J.'s table frequently to check on him and make conversation. He may not have been an officer, but with his colossal size clad in a crisp white uniform, Andrew definitely cut an impressive nautical figure.

According to Andrew, he was twenty-nine years old and had been with the cruise company for three years, recently promoted to his current position. He was based in Miami, but spent most of his time at sea and was frequently in New York City as a port of call for the SS Bermuda Star. He came from a large southern family, where all of them grew up tall but none of them grew up gay, so he'd opted for a career where he could not only travel but be free to be true to himself. He struck T.J. as very earnest and sensible. He also displayed an outgoing personality when interacting publicly with the passengers, and he was funny and charming. Height aside, they seemed to be very much alike.

Once his work was finally over for the night, Andrew bid farewell to the assembled passengers, wishing them a restful night's sleep before their next fun-filled day at sea tomorrow. He made one last trip to T.J.'s table to invite him down to his cabin below decks, C-125, where passengers were not permitted but if he were to take the elevator to C, make an immediate right and proceed down the passageway, Andrew would be sure to leave the door open.

Only needing a moment to consider, T.J. told him, "I'll see you in ten minutes."

Making his way down to C Deck felt like a thrilling act of subterfuge, although there was no labyrinth of passageways nor obstacles to overcome. It really was as simple as Andrew had said, and he arrived at C-125 completely undetected. He couldn't help but think how fun it would have been to have Leo accompany him on this floating Uncle Charlies while poor Bella was out like a light, fully clothed, in their darkened little stateroom.

Andrew turned out to be a surprisingly enthusiastic and generous lover. In fact, T.J. had never been with anyone so thoroughly dedicated to providing him with pleasure. He wondered if that was just Andrew's personality or some other level of customer service he had yet to experience! Regardless, it was great fun to kick back and feel so consummately desired by someone. Andrew earned bonus points for being an excellent kisser.

T.J. slipped back to his own cabin sometime around three a.m. and he didn't have to worry about being quiet, as Bella was still out cold and breathing heavily. He had a quick rinse in the cramped little shower before pulling on some sweat pants and climbing under the covers. It had been an exhausting day and he, too, was soon sleeping soundly.

T.J. and Bella woke up at eight a.m., sharp, to the sound of the ship's horn reverberating throughout the vessel and Andrew's cheerful voice bursting over the PA. In the utter blackness of the darkened room, it was as if their eyes were still closed and all they could hear was the omnipresent greeting blaring around them, and to every other passenger aboard.

"Good morning, seafaring friends of the SS Bermuda Star!" Andrew sounded even more chipper than before, if that was possible. "Welcome to your first full day at sea where the forecast is for calm waters, a cool seventy-two degrees and mostly sunny skies. Of course, our skies are always sunny on board regardless of the weather! You will find the Daily Bulletin under your door outlining all the activities offered throughout the ship. From shuffleboard to a Scrabble tournament, there is something for everyone. Even if you just prefer to sun bathe poolside."

In the darkness, Bella moaned. "For Christ's sake, how do we turn him off?"

There was certainly no turning him off just a few hours ago, T.J. thought.

"We hope you'll take the opportunity today to get to know your fellow shipmates, and let me remind you that all of our staff remain at your disposal if we can be of any service while you're on board with us, or need help in planning your excursions while in Bermuda. It's been called The Isle of Devils, but I think that's just because you'll have a devil of a good time!"

Bella fumbled in the dark for the nightstand light and managed to flip it on just as Andrew finished his announcement.

"Finally, an extra special Good Morning to passenger T.J. Porter and his family. We are so excited to have you on our voyage."

On hearing this, Bella, slumped. Badly hung over, she looked green as she cast her gaze at T.J. "What did you do?"

He rolled over and pulled the covers over his face, still half asleep but awake enough to be mortified by what he'd just heard. "That's what happens when you pass out and leave me alone!"

Skipping the ordeal of a breakfast buffet with his parents and the Pennsylvanians, T.J. ordered a large pot of coffee and an assorted basket of pastries be delivered to them. Bella nursed her hangover and he persuaded her to manage some dry toast while he regaled her with the story of his encounter with Andrew.

"How are you going to explain the special greeting?" she asked, following her toast with two aspirin tablets.

"If it comes up, I can say he's a soap opera fan."

"I've got to get my stomach under control," Bella told him. "I feel so queasy."

"Okay," said T.J. "Let's follow the advice in the brochure—to combat motion nausea, find a high point on the ship."

They made it to the uppermost deck, accessible by elevator, and then climbed two sets of stairs to a small balcony set with four deck chairs. It required all of Bella's fortitude to plod slowly upward, all the while swearing she was going back on the wagon, effective immediately.

Once settled comfortably in their hidden perch, T.J. surmised, "This is a good place to lay low until you've recovered enough for us to face my parents."

"I'm so sorry if I embarrassed you," she said sincerely, pulling the brim of her sun hat down to shade her eyes. Even with sunglasses on, the light burned brightly.

"I think I need to hide out from Andrew, too."

"Awww, he likes you, that's all," she teased. "Besides, if you avoid him, he'll just worry that you've gone overboard and call out the Coast Guard."

"Maybe then I'd meet an actual sailor."

From somewhere, a wave perpendicular to the ship caused it to roll noticeably. It was just enough that they had to steady themselves and it had a particularly bad effect on Bella's already delicate condition. "Oh, crap!" she exclaimed softly, "I'm about to un-swallow everything I've eaten for the last two days!" She leapt up and grabbed onto the rail surrounding the open deck.

Whatever was left in her stomach came out and landed on the deck below where, mercifully, no one was standing. She held her position for a long moment in case there was a second explosion from within. When there was none, she turned to T.J. with a forlorn expression and said, "Shoot me now."

"Next time, aim for the ocean. I bet you'll feel better now that it's out of your system," he said reassuringly.

She did, indeed, soon feel better and transformed into her old self. "Don't worry," she said. "I've learned my lesson, and believe me—I have the willpower to abstain from alcohol for the rest of the cruise." In fact, she became so charming that T.J.'s parents forgot their first impression of her, and they all dined together for both lunch and dinner.

There was no discussion of Andrew's intercom salutation to T.J. and when they encountered him in the Dining Room, he remained the consummate professional, greeting T.J. as he would any other passenger and not letting on that anything had happened between them. T.J., however, could clearly see the desire on his face and wondered if his parents noticed it as well. If they did, they made no comment.

Dinner was followed by Casino Night in the ship's discotheque, but as the Porters entered, T.J. caught sight of Andrew costumed as a Blackjack dealer, complete with visor, vest and armbands. Having spent more than enough time in Artie's silly soda jerk attire, T.J. wanted to get out of there altogether. He suggested they should instead go to the Game Room for several hands of Hearts, and there they spent the evening before calling it a night. They would arrive in Bermuda the next day.

By the time they pulled into the port of Hamilton and docked, it was nearly noon. T.J.'s parents were among the first passengers to disembark. Thomas had arranged to meet some colleagues in nearby Tucker's Point for a round of golf and Janice was excited to hit some of her favorite shops, including Trimingham's, Archie Brown's and Frangipani. "Why don't you and Bella rent some mopeds and explore some of beaches," she suggested. "There's Horseshoe Bay and Jobson's Cove."

T.J. and Bella packed their beach bags for the day and headed for the gangway. Most of the overzealous tourists had already left and were milling around all the popular spots on Front Street, so they were able to enjoy a leisurely stroll. Before they could exit from the terminal, Bermudian authorities asked to inspect their totes. It was a common practice, so T.J. handed over the large blue and white Ralph Lauren canvas bag he'd borrowed from his mom. Bella was more reluctant to give up her brand-new one from L.L. Bean.

"It's just beach stuff," she said defensively. The previously friendly looking official dropped his smile and held out his hand, silently commanding her to hand him the bag. "And feminine products," she added. "If that's how you get your kicks, fine."

T.J. watched him rifle through its contents which did in fact include a box of tampons in addition to sunscreen, lipstick, a pack of cigarettes and lighter, some magazines and her camera. But he was horrified when the inspector pulled out a film canister, identical to the one in which she had stashed her marijuana blunts. Bermuda has a strict zero tolerance for drugs and T.J. suddenly panicked at the thought that he had never warned her.

The inspector popped off the lid from the small container to see there was film inside.

"Please don't expose my film," Bella told him sternly. "I'm planning to get a lot of beach shots."

He dropped it back into the bag and returned it to Bella with a cursory, "Have a Bermudaful day."

As they stepped up their pace and moved away and out onto the street, T.J. whispered to her, "Thank God there was film in there."

"Of course. I have six rolls. Only one has the doobies in it."

He breathed a sigh of relief. Yet again, as his dad would say, he had walked between the raindrops.

"Let's swing in to one of the souvenir shops before the beach," T.J. suggested. "I want to pick up a few goodies to take home to Leo and Carolyn Lee." He hadn't decided if Steve merited a gift.

A store called Hidden Gems had a wide selection of Bermuda-themed merchandise so T.J. knew they could quickly accomplish the mission, but there was an unforeseen delay in the form of a debonair sales clerk. He looked to be in his mid twenties, and seemed almost rakish in his "rig." Local formal wear for men consisted of a dark blue blazer, crisp white shirt with pastel pink tie, and traditional Bermuda shorts and knee socks. T.J. and Bella were both struck by his looks, made even more handsome outfitted as he was with his unkempt mop of sun-bleached hair. He had a lovely tan, narrow brown eyes framed by laugh lines, and a jaunty air as he offered to be of service. His colleague, a middle-aged black woman in a colorful flowered caftan dress, remained behind the counter.

T.J. jumped at the opportunity, even more besotted when he heard the unique Bermudian accent coming from the fellow, who introduced himself as Peter. The dance had begun.

After a moment, Bella said, "Hey—I feel like a third wheel. I'm gonna go to the nearest beach." When she asked Peter for directions, he walked her over to the window and pointed. "Black Bay Beach," he said. "A twenty-minute walk or a short bus ride."

Not wanting to be disloyal, T.J. offered to go with her. "Nah . . . that's okay," she told him. He could tell she knew there was chemistry happening between him and Peter. "I'll be fine," she assured him. "Anyway, I want to do some exploring on my own." She gave him a quick kiss on the cheek and headed down Front Street, leaving him and Peter to pick out his purchases. He got a bottle of locally made Royall Lyme cologne for Leo and, for Carolyn Lee, a china candy dish hand-painted with the ubiquitous Hibiscus flower.

After Peter carefully wrapped them up in tissue paper and placed them in a gift bag, he suggested to T.J., "Now that you've taken care of your shopping, and since I've deprived you of your friend's company, you must let me make it up to you with a glass of wine."

Charmed and turned on, T.J. asked, "Do you serve those here in the store?"

"No, but it's my store so I can leave whenever I want. Maudie will look after things here, won't you, dear?"

Maudie answered him with a nod that indicated this was nothing out of the ordinary at Hidden Gems.

As they emerged from the store into the bright sunshine, T.J. asked Peter, "So where do you have in mind?"

Breaking into a brisk walk with T.J. scurrying to follow, Peter answered, "I'm parked right up here."

It was exciting to climb into his tiny car, with the steering wheel on the right side, and navigate the winding back roads out of Hamilton. They took a scenic local route off the beaten path, right alongside the turquoise coastline, with little pastel-colored houses dotting the landscape. T.J. drank in the breathtaking view as he felt Peter's hand come to rest on his thigh. Without speaking, they could feel a mutual arousal intensifying.

It was thrilling, yet T.J. still felt the need to make some sort of conversation. Peter seemed like a classy guy and he didn't want to come off like some kind of slutty American tourist.

"Did you grow up in Bermuda?"

"Born and raised. Is this your first visit?"

"Gosh, no. My parents and I have been coming here for vacations as long as I can remember."

"Are they back at the hotel?"

"We came by ship this time."

"Who's the woman you were with?"

"A good friend from home. My parents are hoping to turn me away from the dark side," he said with dramatic effect.

"It's good to be discreet," Peter told him, in a more serious tone. "Homosexuality is still illegal here."

"You're kidding."

"A blow job could get you ten years in prison."

After a thoughtful pause, T.J. asked, "Giving or receiving?"

They pulled into the driveway of a little archetypical Bermudian house, low and square with a white, stepped roof and faded yellow walls. It was charming and framed by bright purple bougainvillea and lots of Bermudiana, the purple and yellow iris that is also their national flower.

Following Peter quietly into the house, careful not to draw any attention from neighbors or passing cars, T.J. felt an extra rush of excitement knowing that their encounter was considered illicit. He had always been such a "good boy," so this was especially stimulating.

The small two-bedroom house had low ceilings but was impressively, elegantly appointed like a miniature English country home. Bermuda was an English colony, and the decor reeked of old money. With no further talking, Peter led T.J. into his bedroom, which was dominated by a king-sized four poster bed, lush with white linens and draped with sheer white curtains. A large French door opened onto a small, enclosed yard with a miniature table and two chairs. Tall hedges, as high as the house, afforded complete privacy.

Peter switched on the stereo, which sat on a side table, and instrumental jazz music filled the room. Then he turned on the overhead ceiling fan, immediately cooling the room and causing the curtains to billow in its breeze. T.J. could smell the fragrant flora in the yard and he felt like he was in the most romantic setting he had ever seen.

After taking off his blazer and tossing it over the only chair in the room, a handsome, old fashioned wingback with matching footstool, Peter took T.J. in his arms and kissed him passionately. They were both filled with anticipation at discovering what was underneath their clothing, but there was no rush. Each piece came off slowly, in between kisses. It was not the kind of heated passion T.J. had primarily experienced. Instead, it was slow, sensual and deliberate.

When they were both finally undressed, Peter guided him onto the bed. It felt like they were floating in a sea of pillows, with the sheets cool against their skin as their bodies melded together.

Any time either of them came close to climaxing, the other would instinctively pull back, passionately prolonging the experience. Just as their lovemaking was reaching a crescendo, the skies outside turned a menacing, dark gray color and the air crackled with electricity. In perfect harmony with their consummation, lightning flashed and thunder roared while the heavens opened to a pounding downpour.

The curtains blew tempestuously and mist from the rain sprayed in on them as they finally exploded simultaneously. They collapsed, still entwined in each other's arms, their skin damp with a mixture of sweat and rainwater. Both of them were out of breath and spent. T.J. felt lightheaded, as if he might pass out. He'd read enough to know that the French expression for what he felt was called la petite mort—the little death—a colloquialism for an orgasm so intense you momentarily lose consciousness.

They laid there until the deluge eased up and turned to a trickle. That's when Peter asked him if he'd like a glass of wine or a cigarette.

"I'd love both," T.J. replied, reluctant to move from this idyllic position.

Remaining naked, Peter pointed to a Wedgwood china box and matches on the nightstand, before walking out of the bedroom to get their wine. T.J. propped himself up and lifted the lid from the box, helping himself to one of the unfiltered cigarettes inside. It was strong and made him cough as soon as he lit it.

"I hope white Burgundy is okay?"

Indifferent, T.J. just answered, "Perfect." The scene outside the window was breathtaking, and he dreaded the idea of having to go back to the ship. He thought of Bella and hoped she hadn't gotten caught in the downpour.

Peter returned with their glasses and they clinked with a mutual, "Cheers." After only a few sips, Peter wrapped an arm around T.J.'s shoulder and they nestled closer. Soon they were making love again.

The thought of leaving this love nest and returning to the SS Bermuda Star was a sweet torture, and they delayed it as long as possible. Peter lit some candles and drew a warm bath in the big claw foot bathtub in the adjacent bathroom. They got in together, and in addition to getting clean, they kissed passionately until the water turned cold.

The rain had stopped completely and it was well past sundown when Peter dropped T.J. back at the dock. They exchanged numbers, in case either would visit the other's city of residence, but T.J. assumed this was probably the last time they would see each other.

"Thanks again," T.J. called to him from the sidewalk, his bag of souvenirs in hand.

Peter gave him a cheeky wink, said "Bon Voyage." Then he sped away.

Languidly T.J. made his way back to his cabin, still swooning from the experience. When he opened the door, Bella was sitting up in bed reading a magazine. He was surprised to see her there.

"I thought you'd be out on the town or in one of the ship's clubs," he said.

"I had dinner with your folks then decided to come back and wait for you here. Catch me up. How were his hidden gems?"

"Veritable crown jewels," he quipped. "What did you tell my parents?"

"I said I wanted to do some exploring on my own so we split up. They were very sweet."

"Atta girl."

"They want us all to have breakfast at the Waterloo House in the morning, before we set sail home. Is it nice?"

"That's the guest house where we usually stay. You'll love it. Very British."

"And what about your new Bermudian friend? I don't suppose he can join us?'

"I think not," he said, sitting beside her on her bed. "Did you know that being gay is actually illegal here?"

"Between my weed and your seed, it looks like we dodged a bullet in good old Bermuda."

They also managed to dodge Andrew for most of the next day before the ship pulled up anchor and began its return voyage to New York. He did, however, stop by their table at dinner ostensibly to see how everyone had enjoyed their time in Bermuda. T.J. assured him, "It was my best visit yet."

On the final night of their journey, the Porters made a last ditch effort at cultivating some sort of romantic connection between T.J. and Bella, suggesting they have a private dinner in one of the shipboard eateries. They jumped at the opportunity to escape parental scrutiny and opted for a meal in the Safari Room which had been re-imagined for the evening with a Mexican Fiesta theme, complete with a Mariachi band. It was renamed Casa Bermudez to honor the explorer Juan de Bermudez, credited with discovering the archipelago in 1505. No one bothered to point out that he was actually a Spaniard who died in Cuba.

T.J. and Bella were seated at a round table in the center of the room, close to all the adjacent tables and similarly decorated with Mexican flag tablecloths, an assortment of candles and piñatas hanging overhead. Three other passengers joined them: a forty-something married couple from Long Island and a vivacious redheaded widow from San Antonio—Julie—who was picking through the basket of chips on the table alongside a bowl of salsa.

In her twangy Southern drawl, Julie observed, "I'm from San Antone, so I know Mexican and this ain't it."

A waiter presented a tray of shot glasses and asked if anyone cared for some tequila.

"Now that's more like it," Julie enthused, reaching to take two glasses for herself. The married couple took theirs and sipped them cautiously, as if they were filled with rocket fuel.

T.J. took his and looked at Bella, who considered for only a moment before reaching for one.

"What the fuck," she said. "It's our last night. Down the hatch."

She had two more before the waiter brought a pitcher of Margaritas for the group. The Mariachi band was strolling the room, squeezing themselves in between tables as the tequila was taking effect on everyone seated. Julie had stopped caring about the chips and was howling along to La Bamba. Waiters weaved in and out with smoking skillets of sizzling chicken and beef fajitas, their spicy aromas filling the air.

T.J. was feeling no pain and looked across the table at Bella, who was also glassy eyed, but smiling broadly with another empty shot glass beside her Margarita. Slouched, she had leaned her chair back on its rear legs. As the band segued into the ever-popular Tequila, by The Champs, T.J. noticed that the aroma of fajitas had changed to a more acrid one that was not at all pleasant.

He wrinkled his nose and suddenly saw flames shooting up from behind Bella. Her hair was on fire! No one seemed to notice, not even Bella, who continued to smile and sway to the music as it came up to the part where everyone shouted, "Tequila!" T.J. squinted in disbelief, thinking he had to be hallucinating from all the booze.

But no—small orange flames were shooting up from her smoking head! He sprang into action and started smacking the side of her head with his napkin. Still the band played on, while Julie and the couple from Long Island stared in stunned disbelief at what they were witnessing at their own table.

Bella, thoroughly confused, screamed—not from pain but from this strange and unexpected assault. T.J. seemed to be making no progress against the licks of fire when, seemingly out of nowhere, an entire pitcher of ice water doused it out. She continued to scream in shock and terror.

T.J. looked up, instantly shocked into sobriety, and saw Andrew standing before them, holding the now empty water pitcher.

Andrew picked up a candle from the table directly behind Bella and showed them. "Here's the culprit." When Bella leaned back in her chair, her hair had touched the flame.

At a loss for words, T.J. just stared at him.

Soaked, smoldering and with half her hair gone, Bella said, "Well—let's look on the bright side. I've been meaning to get a haircut."

The next day at the Arrivals Terminal in New York, the Porters collected their bags and hugged T.J. goodbye before the shuttle took them to the parking lot where they could retrieve their car. They hugged Bella, too, and exchanged pleasantries without asking why she had chosen to wear a headscarf on a perfectly mild and windless day.

Thomas had only a brief moment before they departed to pull his son aside and tell him, "Bella is obviously a fun time, son, but she's not the right girl for you. Let's keep looking, shall we?"

T.J. didn't answer. All he could think was, thank God he was home.

Wasting no time in working off his holiday calories, T.J. went immediately to the gym the next morning for two back-to-back aerobics classes. He had a few more days before he started back with the matinee concerts so he was looking forward to catching up with Leo and Carolyn Lee and regaling them with tales of their Bermuda cruise misadventures. Since Bella hadn't been hurt in the Margarita incident, they found it hilarious.

When he finally did see Steve for a workout in the gym (and then between the sheets), Steve told him about a job offer he had received while T.J. was away: a three month stint teaching aerobics at a high-end health spa in Tuscany, Italy. In addition to all-paid travel expenses, the offer included free room and board, a car at his disposal and seven hundred fifty U.S. dollars a week—in cash.

"Wow, that sounds amazing," T.J. reacted to the news. "I've always wanted to go to Italy. Tuscany is supposed to be amazing."

"It's a great opportunity. Which is why I'm telling you about it," Steve began to explain. "I'm not taking the job. But I think you should."

"Me? I'm not an instructor."

"Not yet, but it's easy to get your certification. You'd be a natural and I can help you."

T.J. rolled on top of him and gave him a soft kiss on the mouth. "You'd do that for me?"

"Of course. Someone should take advantage of the chance. And from Tuscany it's easy to get to Rome, Bologna or Venice."

"So if it's so great, why don't you want the job?"

"I don't want to teach aerobics all my life. I'm an actor."

"I'm an actor, too," he reminded Steve.

"Yes, but you're younger. And single. Nothing's holding you back."

It was an uncomfortable reminder that the man with whom he was lying naked was committed to someone else. He had a point—nothing was holding T.J. back. And Steve might not even miss him in his aerobics class or in his bed.

"One more stamp for my passport, then."

CHAPTER NINE
Bodies in Motion Stay in Motion

Plans to ring in 1985 with friends were scuttled when T.J. came down with the flu shortly after Christmas. He was convinced he'd picked it up on the Metro North train back from Connecticut. He spent New Year's Eve in bed with a quart of Hot & Sour Soup he'd had delivered from the nearby Chinese place, Ivory Chopsticks. The temperature outside was above normal (and so was his), but the gray skies and drizzle made it feel wintery, nonetheless. He was content to stay in and catch up with everyone through phone calls, in between replenishing his supplies of Kleenex, lozenges and soup.

He and Marti had a long conversation about the state of Tomorrow's Promise. She admitted there were lots of rumors about the show's cancellation and replacement by a cheaper-to-produce game show or an all-talk format like The Phil Donahue Show. Not only did she hate the prospect of so many people being unemployed by such a decision, she wasn't sure that, after more than three decades of playing one single, highly identifiable character, she would ever work again. He bucked up her spirits by assuring her that any other show would be eager to hire her.

Carolyn Lee was experiencing similar whispers at her TV job, where a younger twenty-something field journalist was getting more and more air time as a fill-in anchor. Carolyn Lee had been reporting in an ongoing series on advances in in vitro fertilization. It was a relatively new procedure that had shown clinical success and something she was considering for herself and Gary. Having sex with Gary had become a chore, centered only on the goal of getting pregnant, and the more she thought about it, she told T.J., the idea of making a baby in a laboratory instead of a bedroom had its appeal.

Bella was plodding along at New York Sports Club and occasionally attending AA meetings, although her heart wasn't in it. She truly believed she could drink and party recreationally. The fact that she had been promoted to manage one of the most popular Upper West Side facilities seemed to prove to her that she was able to function well. Even so, she and T.J. didn't run around together nearly as much as they used to.

The flu had struck T.J. at a convenient time as it pertained to his training plan with Steve, who was away for the holidays with his boyfriend. Once he returned, they would help him achieve his IDEA certification so he could become an instructor and hopefully take the spa position in Tuscany. IDEA stood for International Dance-Exercise Association and was rapidly becoming the most respected organization for aerobics professionals.

As for Leo, he had been diligently performing his duties at Citibank and charming his way up the corporate ladder to score a position as a Portfolio Operations Assistant. His focus on that cost him his relationship with Don the lawyer. He told T.J. they had decided before Christmas to take a break and see other people since Leo wasn't able to (or interested in) giving him the time he demanded.

"Separating before Christmas was a bad idea," T.J. observed. "You cost yourself a good present."

Leo wasn't bothered in the least. In fact, his work colleague, Mike, had recently come out as gay and proposed going out on a date. Taking his Aunt Jenny's charming advice, "Don't shit where you eat," he passed on the offer but thought Mike could be a potential match for T.J. Knowing his best friend would certainly be game for a set-up, he told Mike who suggested they go on a "double blind date." Mike would bring along a friend for Leo and Mike and T.J. would hopefully hit it off.

T.J. thought this was a brilliant plan and pumped Leo for as much information about Mike as he could provide. Like Leo, he was a Citibank junior executive and, according to Leo's description, T.J.'s type. That had evolved into meaning more masculine and "straight acting" than classically or mainstream handsome. Ever optimistic, T.J. also started musing on what it would mean if both couples were compatible. Like the Ricardos and Mertzes or the Flintstones and Rubbles, the four of them could live happily ever after, seeing Broadway shows together, taking holiday trips or making happy homes next door to each other. It was a fantasy of heterosexual normalcy that would perhaps be wholesome enough to please society . . . and even his parents. Maybe he could even be a parent, himself, one day. Fifty years from now, T.J. only half-joked, when they would all retire to Florida together, they would reminisce how it all began back in 1985 with a double blind date!

Leo had learned that when T.J. fixated on an idea, there was no stopping him. That's why he was more amused than judgmental, and even encouraged his friend. The Tuscan Aerobics plan was another of T.J.'s schemes of which Leo was skeptical, but it was definitely more interesting than the dry analytics of day-to-day investments and banking duties. One of the many things they had in common was having not yet learned how to be alone but not lonely. They craved constant stimulation.

Fully recovered from the flu, T.J. was back on his feet by the following week and eager to get things underway. On his way over to the NYSC where Steve was teaching, he passed a newsstand and noticed the new issue of Backstage on sale. He felt guilty for not having put any time in on his acting pursuits since he left the musical matinee show before Christmas. That had been nice steady employment and he learned a massive amount of new vocal material, but his heart wasn't in it. The producers kindly left the door open to him returning anytime he needed the work, so he reasoned that now was time to focus on fitness. He would gain not only a new money-making skill, he would be able to parlay it into a once-in-a-lifetime travel opportunity. From there, who knows? Added incentives were keeping slim and hopefully getting some extracurricular time with Steve.

The certification process was more complicated than T.J. had imagined—it included what seemed like volumes of work-books on kinesiology, anatomy, cardiovascular health and first aid. In many ways, it was like being back in high school, cramming for exams. He'd really assumed it would be like an audition after acquiring some fun credentials in choreography and music mixing. Steve cajoled him into making it fun and routinely quizzed him, which T.J. especially enjoyed when they were alone in bed together. Test Prep with benefits.

The certification test was set for February 14, on a Thursday. It would include a one-hour written portion, an interview, and then a group exercise class during which T.J. would have a turn to lead everyone in a routine of his own. He was surprised to find himself as nervous about it as if he was back on a Broadway stage trying out for a play. As he prepared, he emulated Steve—not only in his moves and instructing style, but also in attire, opting to don a brand new black lycra singlet over which he threw a red cotton NYSC T shirt. To this he matched a red head band, and his new Reebok sneakers had red laces.

He also set a date night with Leo, Mike and the as-yet unknown Charles, for February 16. T.J. was putting almost as much work into planning that as he was with the IDEA certification, consulting with Leo over what to wear and what they should do for the evening. He thought it was a good omen that it was Valentine's Day weekend without actually being on the day, which would be way too much pressure for all of them.

T.J., ever the diligent student, sailed through all the sections of his certification process. While scoring a sufficient seventy-five percent on the written test, he was given a 9/10 on his Instructor's performance and, not surprisingly, a perfect score in the interview. He could now call himself a professional fitness instructor and, to show his appreciation, he treated Steve to dinner the next night. Steve presented him with a letter of recommendation and the contact and hiring information for the Fitness Director at Spa Vitale.

After their meal, T.J. paid the bill. Steve told him he assumed they would be going back to the Churchill for an unclothed celebration but T.J. deferred, saying he was exhausted. The truth was, he was now more interested in the mysterious Mike than he was in Steve. As nice and as sexy as Steve was, his partnered status had diminished T.J.'s interest. What was the point, especially if an available bachelor was on the horizon?

T.J.'s natural inclination to look on the bright, hopeful side of situations had been nurtured not only by his parents' support and encouragement but bolstered by the fact that successes had always come easily to him. His mother used to say that luck was a more important quality than any other: "You can't buy it. You either have it or you don't." His more pragmatic father countered that with, "The problem with optimists is that they get disappointed too often. A pessimist is happily surprised."

After an hour long phone call, T.J. and Leo settled on a plan to seduce their blind dates. They would start with a pre-movie drink at Marvin Gardens on Broadway, next door to the Cineplex. They would give the guys the choice of which movie they wanted to see: A Nightmare on Elm Street, The Breakfast Club or The Flamingo Kid. Something for everyone. After that, they'd taxi down to the Supreme Macaroni Company on Ninth Avenue, a casual, almost hidden Italian eatery that became famous when Billy Joel featured a photo of it on the back cover for his hit album, The Stranger.

T.J. and Leo got there first, and Marvin Gardens was bustling as usual. They had coordinated their outfits to be casual, but on trend, with T.J. in a crisp new pastel lavender shirt and jeans over which he wore his blue International Male jacket and Leo in a more conservative sweater and high-waisted, pleated slacks with the cuffs rolled up above the ankles to show off his new Docksiders. He'd blown his last paycheck on a Merino wool bomber jacket, of which T.J. was immediately jealous. They could have been the kid brothers of Crockett and Tubbs from Miami Vice.

Mike and Charles shoved their way into the crowded bar area just as Leo was about to order. "Not so fast, buddy," Mike called out in a thick New York accent.

T.J. and Leo immediately scrutinized their blind dates. T.J. liked what he saw. Mike may have been around their same age, but he looked older because of his receding hairline and surprisingly unkempt appearance, as if he had come directly from a softball game. In fact, everything about him looked straight, which was a turn on for T.J. Charles was a plain and slender brunette, well dressed and groomed but otherwise nondescript. The kind of guy who could easily fade into the background.

"Two Sam Adams," Mike shouted out over the bar sounds. Leo signaled that he'd received the order and communicated it to the bartender.

Introductions coincided with the arrival of their drinks and it was obvious that both sets of friends had been briefed in advance, so each pair stood in the appropriate positions to chat with their dates. Charles was too soft spoken to be heard in the noisy bar environment but Mike was loud enough for all of them and launched into a recounting of their subway trip there in blusterous detail.

"Some assholes on the train were playing their fucking ghetto shit on boom boxes and asking for money the whole way up here. If we'd hadda go two more stops with them, I swear I woulda fucking unleashed on them."

T.J. thought that his straight-acting bravado might be a defense mechanism, because this wasn't the first impression he'd hoped for.

Mike carried on. "They wanna raise the fare to a buck and I'm like, fugeddaboutit. I mean, what the fuck?"

"Well, it's faster than the bus," T.J. said, trying to come up with a suitable response.

"Drink up, guys," Leo advised. "The movie starts in five minutes."

Somehow, in the midst of his subway rant, Mike had already managed to chug down his entire beer. Charles meekly offered, "The first fifteen minutes are always trailers, anyway."

Their film choice, Nightmare on Elm Street, was sold out, so they opted for The Breakfast Club. On their way into the theater, Mike paused by the concession stand and announced, "I'm gonna grab a dog. Anybody else want one?" He looked at T.J.

"No, thanks," T.J. replied. "I'll wait for dinner."

By the time Mike got his hot dog and added on all the extra condiments, in addition to a box of popcorn, the only seats they could find together in the darkened theater were in the second row from the front. Leo sat between Charles and T.J., with Mike on the end. The pungent aroma of the hot dog with extra sauerkraut, onions and mustard enveloped them. There was also a subtle hint of a buttery chemical scent emanating from the popcorn.

Leo and Charles were pulled quickly into the film with its amusing teen angst and excellent soundtrack, while Mike was more focused on his gastronomic purchases from the concessions counter. T.J. pretended to be looking at the screen, but his peripheral vision was fascinated by the systematic ingestion of food he was witnessing. Mike pushed the hot dog, bun and toppings into his mouth, inch by inch. Each bite was never quite able to make his lips meet for full mouth closure. Simple Minds' Don't You Forget About Me couldn't override the sounds of slurping, chewing and swallowing that seemed to harmonize. When the last of the frankfurter finally disappeared into Mike's orifice, T.J. hoped there would be a reprieve—but almost immediately the popcorn portion of the performance began: kernels going in a handful at a time followed by finger licking to make sure every bit of salt on his hands was ingested. T.J. forced his eyes back to Molly Ringwald and Judd Nelson, hoping to settle his queasy stomach.

Alas, that became impossible. When Mike reached the bottom of the box with only a few unpopped "grannies" remaining, he let out a belch that did not go unnoticed by the people directly behind them.

Then he leaned across T.J. to ask them all in a loud whisper, "I'm going for a Coke. Anybody want one?" No one did.

He lumbered out of his seat to the audible chagrin of other audience members and headed off to the soda fountain.

In the flickering light from the projector, Leo looked over at T.J. with a silent inquiry. "What do you think so far?"

Whispering into his ear so that Charles couldn't hear, T.J. told Leo, "Are farts next? He's an animal!"

Leo grinned slyly. "Maybe that's not a bad thing."

Mike came back before T.J. could respond and not surprisingly, two hours later when the elderly Sicilian waiter at Supreme Macaroni asked for the dinner orders, Mike opted for only a cup of Minestrone soup citing the fact that he was "not all that hungry." T.J. and Leo exchanged a look.

They also carried the conversation throughout the meal. Mike and Charles didn't seem to contribute much, other than a few comments about The Breakfast Club.

Between slurps of soup, Mike commented, "Emilio Estevez is smoking hot. I'd take him over his brother, Charlie Sheen."

"Or you could take them both," Charles suggested, trying to sound witty. Mike thought that was hysterical and laughed so broadly that T.J. could see the tonsils in the back of his open mouth.

Before the plates were even cleared from the table, Mike suddenly stood up from the table. He pulled out his wallet and threw a wrinkled twenty-dollar bill on the table.

"I got an early start tomorrow. You guys have a good night. Leo, I'll see you Monday. Chuckie, I'll call you later."

That was it. Nothing to T.J. specifically, and then Mike was gone.

Leo looked at his watch. "It's not really that late. Why don't we go over to Mama's and get one for the road?"

Don't Tell Mama was a nearby piano bar. T.J. wasn't sure why his friend would want to carry on this fiasco of an evening unless he had some kind of interest in Charles that T.J. hadn't detected. If Charles were a color, T.J. thought, it would be beige.

His personality was as nondescript as his looks.

They split the remainder of the dinner bill and strolled over to Don't Tell Mama, happy to find there were three available barstools for them. Most of the patrons were crammed into tables along the walls of the long, rectangular room at the end of which was the grand piano where a rotating roster of regular pianists banged out requested show tunes. They had arrived right in the middle of a Rodgers and Hammerstein medley.

Drawing anything out of Charles was laborious and T.J. didn't even try but Leo gamely asked, "How long have you and Mike been friends?" He already knew from Mike that they'd gone to college together, but he was doing his best to give this guy a shot.

"A long time," was all Charles could come up with, obviously distracted by one of the bartenders, a decent looking guy with more than decent looking biceps.

They both noticed Charles' lack of attention and T.J. simply said, "I don't think we'll be having a double wedding, Pally."

The pianist launched into Cockeyed Optimist from South Pacific and T.J. couldn't help but sing along to the lyric, "But I'm stuck like a dope, with a thing called hope." For him, it seemed to spring eternal. Maybe his Mister Right would be waiting for him in Tuscany.

***

From the time his Alitalia flight touched down in Rome, T.J. sensed that this would not be the paradisiacal opportunity he and Steve had imagined it would be. The sparsely detailed instructions Spa Vitale had mailed him included five hundred dollars in traveler's checks and his round-trip plane ticket. Armed with only his pocket-sized Berlitz Italian for Travelers, he wondered why he'd spent all those years in school learning French when he almost never had an opportunity to use it. Dragging around his suitcase filled with aerobics gear and cassette tapes, he managed to find a taxi to Roma Termini where he was able to quickly board a train to Florence for a scenic three-and-a-half hour ride.

T.J. had been cutting back on his smoking as he worked on his fitness studies, but the stress of this trip, especially without any pertinent language skills, had him immediately back in the habit. Luckily, it seemed like everyone in Italy was a smoker, indoors and out. Several cappuccinos and cigarettes later, he disembarked in Firenze and searched for the connecting local train that would carry him another ninety minutes to Chianciano Terme, his final destination. He had barely slept since his journey began and he was ready to stretch out in a bed for some much needed rest and recovery.

Killing time in a little trattoria a short walk from the train station, T.J. people-watched while he enjoyed a panino and a big bottle of sparkling water which, according to the label, was sourced from the very town where he was heading. Chianciano was known as one of Europe's premiere thermal spa destinations and T.J. was excited by its proximity to medieval cities like Montepulciano, where he planned to partake of the famous wines, and also to Perugia, famous for its chocolates. Everywhere he looked was rustic and reminiscent of a BBC film or The Godfather, and T.J. felt fortunate that a casual pickup with a guy at the gym had somehow led to this unexpected work and travel experience.

Stepping onto the deserted platform at Chianciano just as a light rain began to fall, T.J. wondered if his luck had already run out. There was no one to meet him, as he had expected, nor was there a soul in sight to ask for assistance. "Where do I find the toilet, please" and "May I have a cappuccino, please" were about the sum total of his Italian skills, so he ducked inside the tiny depot and was relieved to find a solitary person working at a small counter, partitioned by a smudged plastic screen. It was a rail thin elderly gentleman with an ink black toupee, two sizes too large, perched atop his head.

Pulling along the suitcase, which now seemed to weigh a ton, T.J. approached the man and exhaustedly yammered in a mixture of English and elementary Italian.

"Excuse me . . . Mi scusi, signor . . . Dove prendo un taxi . . ."

Was the old man deaf or was his Italian that horrible? He seemed to comprehend nothing T.J. said.

T.J. tried again, "Ho bisogno un taxi. Sono americano."

The man nodded. "Sei americano, assolutamente." T.J. wasn't sure what he meant, but it was a start.

As if playing a round of charades, T.J. pantomimed driving a car. "Taxi? Automobile?"

"Si, si. Dove stai andando?"

"Dove." T.J. recognized the word for "where."

"Spa Vitale!" He fumbled in his pocket for the instruction sheet which was printed on the Spa Vitale letterhead.

"Si, Conosco le terme."

Patting himself on the chest to indicating himself, he added, "Posso guidarti."

T.J. didn't understand, so the old man revealed his rudimentary English skills and said, "I drive. My car. To Spa Vitale."

"Your car! No, there should be someone to pick me up. But I can pay for a taxi." He again began to act out giving money to a driver.

The man pulled down a shade over the partition which said "Chiuso" and disappeared. T.J., not ordinarily one to panic, suddenly felt abandoned in this strange place. What was he to do now—so far away from civilization and without a working knowledge of the language?

Nightfall was coming soon and the light rain had turned steadier. Maybe he was destined to spend the night on the solitary bench of this little station house.

As all these thoughts were racing through his tired, worried mind, the little old man emerged through a door on the side of the room, still pulling on his overcoat. He had an umbrella in his hand. He motioned to T.J. to follow him.

Had this been the plan all along, that the station attendant would take him to Spa Vitale? Or was it just another coincidental development? Either way, it took T.J. no time at all to consider following the man's directions. Although he'd been warned from his earliest childhood, "Don't accept rides from strangers," this was no time to be over cautious. Besides, he joked to himself, how many strange men had he followed over the last few years?

Stuffing his suitcase and backpack into the man's rusty old Renault, T.J. climbed into the passenger seat and fruitlessly searched for a seat belt, and then he anxiously clung to the seat as his savior turned the ignition key and the engine sputtered and eventually roared to life. The solitary wiper squeaked as it struggled to keep the windshield clear while they made the nail-biting twenty-five minute trip in silence along the narrow, dark and winding roads.

Nestled into the side of a hill was an expansive villa, difficult to see at night in the rain, but there was an illuminated sign that clearly read, Spa Vitale, so T.J. was relieved he would not be some serial killer's victim this night.

"Grazie, grazie, molto grazie," he gushed as he took his belongings from the back seat. He dug into his pockets for some lire and offered it to the man who waved him away. T.J. was insistent that he take something. "Per favore!"

"No, no," the man said, finally showing a smile for the first time. "Benvenuti a Chianciano."

To avoid getting drenched, T.J. moved as quickly as he could from the car to the Spa entrance, a large glass door dimly lit by a single bulb in an overhead fixture. As the Renault putt-putted away into the rainy night, T.J. pulled on the door handle and discovered it was locked. Of course it was!

He banged as loudly as his knuckles would allow. He had no idea what time it was, nor did he care. He needed a shower and a bed.

Noticing a sign over a doorbell or buzzer that read, Suona la Campana, he began pressing it repeatedly. His heart raced nervously as he waited, until he finally saw someone inside, walking briskly in his direction. It was a tall young man in a white Spa Vitale bathrobe and slippers. Even in his fatigued state, T.J. could instantly evaluate him: decent looking, well built and younger than he appeared, with that unfortunately thin hair.

"Buonosera, buonasera," he said apologetically, unlocking and opening the door.

"I'm T.J. Porter. The new aerobics instructor . . ."

Instantly understanding, the man motioned T.J. inside and grabbed his bag while taking care not to let his bathrobe open up.

"T.J., yes—I'm Mitchell, the Fitness Director. We weren't expecting you until tomorrow. Please come in out of the rain."

An American—what a relief! T.J. thought. "Well, my plane ticket was for today," he said. "It's been a long trip just to get here from Rome." Then, not wanting to sound difficult, he added, "But I made it."

"How did you get from the station?"

"I've always relied on the kindness of strangers," T.J. joked, quoting a line from A Streetcar Named Desire.

"You and Blanche DuBois," Mitchell quipped back. The reference, T.J. thought, indicated that Mitchell was probably gay. "You must be exhausted. Your room is already made up, so let me get you settled."

"Grazie, Mitchell, grazie."

Falling into a coma-like sleep, T.J. crashed for the next twelve hours and woke up only when he heard a gentle rapping at his door. It was Mitchell, carrying a tray with a pot of coffee, a small bowl of berries, a basket of biscuits and some jam.

After making some small talk, Mitchell explained to him

that he had been working at Spa Vitale for the last six months, hired from his hometown in San Diego to help Italian socialite Patrizia Agnelli open her establishment after converting the family villa into its current spa incarnation. They employed an international staff of chefs, beauticians, masseurs and fitness experts to offer their wealthy European clientele a variety of programs to jumpstart healthier lifestyles. Mitchell explained that they were currently in a slow season, so there would be plenty of time for T.J. to get acclimated to the job as well as enjoy some of the local Tuscan tourist attractions.

It seemed obvious to T.J. that Mitchell, a popular instructor from the sunny West Coast who had jumped at the chance for a European work experience, was new to this world as well. What wasn't clear was whether or not he was interested in keeping this new relationship with T.J. strictly professional or somewhat friendlier. It would certainly not be romantic, T.J. knew, as there was no physical attraction between them.

"Slow season" was an understatement as there was not a single client currently staying at the Spa. Mitchell said the next group of six would be arriving in a few days, so he showed T.J. around the grounds, including a sitting room, game room, full gym, aerobics studio, indoor pool and what he called a wellness wing with facilities for beauty treatments. The expansive dining room overlooked the bucolic Tuscan hillsides, bursting with mature Cypress trees everywhere. Certain staff members, like T.J. and Mitchell, were required to be present for the healthful meals with the patrons.

Mitchell explained that those who paid to visit Spa Vitale

were kept on a very strict low-calorie diet since they are promised significant weight loss by the time they check out. Consequently, the hard working staff would require more sustenance than provided at mealtimes in the dining room, so they were expected to attend a staff meal an hour prior to the public one. There they could fill up on pastas, antipasto, soups and other traditional Italian fare. The caveat, Mitchell made sure to impress on T.J., was that they were not to let the customers know they'd already eaten. T.J. wasn't crazy about the idea of deception, but maybe it was simply a case of smoke and mirrors. After all, as Marti said, "That's Showbiz."

Just outside the spa facility were adjacent mineral baths and hiking trails that led to and through scenic vineyards and olive gardens, all bordered by ancient stone walls.

Mitchell told T.J. that most clients would be older than fifty and tremendously out of shape by American standards, so he should customize his classes accordingly. Aqua aerobics were sought after, as well as calisthenics and stretching that could be executed while seated. "We call it Sit 'n' Fit," he said. It didn't sound to T.J. like he'd be getting to call out "Who's ready to move and groove?" to this bunch, especially if they were being systematically starved.

The ability to speak Italian was not a prerequisite, according to Mitchell. The European guests found American "experts" to be exotic merely by their nationality and the ability to count to eight in Italian along with a few descriptive words like piccolo (small), grande (large), lentamente (slowly) and velocemente (quickly) would serve him well.

In the Wellness wing, he met a pretty Dutch girl, Sara, an aesthetician, and a freckle-faced blonde from Canada named Sally, whose expertise was all kinds of massage therapy. At least he was finding other people who spoke English. He realized how much he relied on long, gossipy conversations with his friends back in New York and what a struggle it would be not to share the minutiae of his daily adventures.

The tour ended in a grand hall next to the dining room that more resembled a hunting lodge than an Italian villa. A massive fireplace, heavy leather furniture and shelves brimming with art pieces and sculptures featuring various expressions of the human physique filled the room but the dominant feature was a gigantic portrait that seemed to watch you no matter where you were positioned. It was an almost impressionistic rendering in pastel colors of a beautiful woman with golden hair and a wide, toothy smile.

"Let me guess," T.J. said to Mitchell as they entered the room and "She" came into view.

"Patrizia Agenelli. La Signora Capo," Mitchell responded quietly.

T.J. would soon learn that was Italian for "the boss lady."

Sara offered to drive the employee station wagon into Montepulciano that evening for dinner and T.J. was eager to explore before the return of the boss lady and the onset of his work duties. Sally went along and they were good-natured tour guides, pointing out the most popular attractions from the Piazza Grande in the center of the hilltop town.

The weather was balmy and mild and they enjoyed walking along the cobblestone streets admiring the local shops and churches, especially the Sanctuary of Madonna di San Biagio. Eventually they ended up in a cozy corner table of Ristorante Osteria del Conte, sharing a bottle of the region's famous, delicious red wine and a few items off the menu including a mushroom ravioli and salmon with penne. T.J. was surprised at how much smaller the portions were by American standards.

Sara was a lesbian who had come to Spa Vitale from her native Amsterdam in hopes of building up her resume as an aesthetician so she could work in the USA. Money had always been scarce for her so she was very grateful to have landed her position here. Sally had been working as a masseuse for a large hotel chain and wanted a change from the corporate experience, so had taken the position at Spa Vitale only a few weeks earlier.

"So what's the dirt on Signora Agnelli?" T.J. asked, filling their glasses to hopefully help loosen their lips. "And Mitchell?"

They looked at each other, obviously weighing how they would respond.

After a moment, Sara offered, "She is from one of the oldest and wealthiest families in Europe. A famous and beautiful socialite when she was young."

". . . A thousand years ago," Sally chimed in.

"She blows in whenever guests arrive and puts on a big show and then blows out again."

"It's definitely nicer when she blows out."

"Maybe I can charm her," T.J. suggested. "Does she like Americans?"

Sara shrugged. "I think she likes anyone who has money or will give her money."

"As for Mitchell," Sally continued, "he is nice but he's scared to death of her. Most of the staff is."

T.J. knew how to lay it on thick. And older ladies, especially, always liked his wholesome looks and Yankee manners, so he wasn't too worried about La Signora Capo.

Watching everyone who worked at Spa Vitale, from the bellhops to the busboys, snap to attention for her Friday arrival reminded him of the TV commercials for Leona Helmsley's luxury hotels. A frenzy of last minute activity and preparation always caused the entire property to buzz. Gardeners were trimming, clipping and sweeping while housekeepers vacuumed, polished and dusted.

"Is there anything I can do?" T.J. asked Mitchell after the staff breakfast.

"Just be dressed in your workout gear and ready to demonstrate your workouts if she asks," he answered, audibly and visibly on edge.

"Will she want a private class?"

"Oh, no. La Signora never actually exercises herself, even though she's always dressed in designer sweat suits. The most she will do is join a group hike for a few kilometers with the guests."

T.J. reckoned their buildup of her domineering personality was exaggerated. After all, he had expected Marti to be a diva and she was one of the warmest and most down-to-earth people he knew.

Friday at eleven a.m. precisely, as scheduled, the gravel driveway leading up to the Spa entrance crackled under the weight of the long sedan with tinted windows carrying the boss lady. T.J. was looking out the front windows in anticipation, along with most of the employees at the ready. He thought the vehicle looked more like a boat than an automobile. It came to a stop right at the door where the old man from the train station had left him a few nights earlier. The Concierge opened the front door as the lobby staff lined up to be inspected.

Mitchell motioned T.J. to come over and stand beside him in the line. He liked that he was fourth in line behind the Concierge, Manager and Mitchell. It was better billing than he'd ever gotten on the soap opera!

A uniformed driver emerged from the car and walked around to the opposite passenger door to open it. He stood tall, eyes forward, with almost military formality.

From somewhere in the backseat, Patrizia Agnelli emerged and T.J. was mesmerized by the sight of her. She looked absolutely nothing like the portrait of her younger self and was as tiny as a grade-schooler even though she radiated the vitality that was her Spa's namesake. Whatever hair she had was hidden beneath a turquoise silk turban, and her expensive crème-colored sweat suit was emblazoned with the Spa Vitale's "V" logo, sewn with gold thread. She squinted at the bright sun overhead. T.J. was surprised she could move her eyes at all, given that her face looked so tightly pulled she was rendered devoid of expression. She appeared to be in fine physical shape, slender and ample breasted, but had the obvious beginnings of a dowager's hump.

As she swept into the lobby, a chorus of "Buongiorno, Signora," seemed to come from everywhere.

"Buongiorno, amici miei," she said in a soft, raspy voice. She sounded like a longtime smoker.

T.J. expected to see her do the double cheek air kisses for which Italians were famous, but her only greetings were head nods as she walked the receiving line. No handshakes, either. Maybe she was a germaphobe, he thought.

When her eyes caught a glimpse of T.J., whom she didn't recognize, she came to a halt in front of Mitchell.

"Signora Agnelli, our new aerobics instructor from America," said Mitchell. "T.J. Porter."

T.J. instinctively made a dutiful half-bow and said, "Hello, Signora."

"From where in Amereeeca?" she asked, interested.

"New York City, Signora," T.J. responded, proudly.

Her tightly stretched lips barely managed a smile, but her voice indicated obvious pleasure when she said, "Aaah, New York Ceeetee. Il migliore!"

One of the housekeepers handed her a glass of mineral water which she took and drank all in one gulp before handing back the empty glass. Then she continued walking toward the sitting room, and the Concierge and Mitchell dutifully followed.

Nothing further was required of T.J. that afternoon, so he and Sally decided to swap services. He would give her an aerobics workout in the gym and then she would give him a massage. He also spent a couple of hours in his room writing postcards to his friends and family back in the States. Mitchell had told him the staff would be briefed at dinner about the roster of guests who would be arriving the next day and the services they would be expected to provide for them.

As everyone gathered in the kitchen to feast on spaghetti and sautéed escarole with white beans, the Concierge and Mitchell explained that their six guests would be two wealthy Italian married couples in their fifties and two middle aged sisters from Monaco. The marrieds were all looking to achieve weight loss and the sisters were more in search of pampering. It sounded like there would be plenty to keep the staff busy.

Signora Agnelli emerged from her private office off the lobby with each arrival, greeting them grandly as if she was the Queen welcoming some foreign dignitaries. She wore her signature sweat suit but today had added an Hermes head scarf over her hair.

It would turn out, however, that exercise was of little interest to any of them. They each tried a bit of T.J.'s workouts, but none completed a full class. Fatigued or bored, they simply petered out and wandered off to soak in the pool or mineral baths and stroll the hiking trails. No alcohol was available to them, but they were permitted to smoke outdoors in a patio area. Sara and Sally had much the lion's share of responsibility since it seemed like all of them were interested in booking massages, facials, pedicures and aromatherapy treatments.

The sister duo did try one of T.J.'s Tonificante a Piscina (Toning at the Pool) classes, an improvised calisthenics workout using elastic resistance bands, but when a band loosened from beneath one of the sister's feet and snapped the other one in the calf, they were both so instantly flummoxed that they threw the bands at T.J., barked some words he didn't understand, and then stormed off. He had never witnessed such a tantrum from adults. At least when Dottie O'Hara behaved badly, it could be blamed on the alcohol.

Two days of steady rain did nothing to help the spirits of the guests who were beginning to feel the effects of cabin fever in addition to hunger pains. Since no outdoor activities could occur, La Signora was trying to encourage them to take greater advantage of the spa and fitness services but their 500 to 700 daily calorie intake left them lethargic and irritable. T.J. wondered if he should sneak them some bread and cheeses from the staff meals, but knew the wrath he would face if they hadn't achieved their promised weight loss on the final weigh-in day.

Finishing his first week of service, T.J. asked Mitchell about collecting his first payment. Mitchell reacted with a surprising eye roll and a heavy, derisive sigh.

"Is there a problem?" T.J. asked, trying not to be offended. He was generally uncomfortable discussing money, but couldn't understand why his weekly pay should be cause for Mitchell to act so put upon.

Waving him away, he said, "No, no. We are just short on cash right now. Can I give it to you in lire?"

"As long as the amount is correct, sure," T.J. agreed.

"I'll bring it to you at the staff meal, this evening."

Irritated at having to ask for the pay he had rightfully earned, T.J. decided to splurge on a long distance call to Leo and catch each other up on things. New York was six hours behind Italy, so he got him right before he was heading to work.

T.J. painted a vivid picture of his first week in Tuscany, making Leo laugh out loud, especially about the snooty sisters. Leo had been at Brandy's the night before and had some gossip on Luke. He had landed a touring production of West Side Story, playing Tony, the male lead, and had knocked up the actress playing Maria while they were somewhere between Minneapolis and Mankato. He really would fuck anybody, Leo joked and T.J. hoped she didn't get a case of crabs in addition to a fertilized egg. Word was, they were not planning to go through with the pregnancy.

Leo also revealed that, after his and Leo's disappointing double blind date, he gave in to Don's requests to give their relationship a second chance. They'd had dinner together at a new Tex-Mex restaurant near T.J.'s apartment, El Rio Grande, and had loved it. The Mystery of Edwin Drood had recently opened on Broadway and Don got them Orchestra seats for the following week. "So far, so good," Leo surmised.

Hearing his friend's voice and talking about things back in New York was soothing for T.J., and he left his room, heading downstairs for dinner with renewed enthusiasm. He decided to stop by the Wellness wing and see if Sara or Sally wanted to accompany him.

He could hear screaming before he even opened the door. Ordinarily this was the quietest place on the property with the only sounds coming from small water fountains and piped-in New Age music to create a sense of serenity.

"Ragazza stupida! Stupida!" the gruff voice yelled repeatedly.

The door swung open and T.J. jumped out of the way as Sally, one of the sisters from Monaco, burst through, red-faced and clad in a white terrycloth spa robe. She stormed past him and disappeared down the corridor. She had pushed the door with such force that it remained open and he could see inside to the reception area.

"Incompetente! Inutile e stupida!"

There was Signora Agnelli berating Sara for some infraction. She was gesticulating wildly as she screamed at Sara, who meekly kept her eyes cast downward without any attempt at defending herself. It was apparent there was no arguing with the Boss lady.

"Non sarai pagato!" Agnelli screamed, stabbing the air with her index finger.

T.J. didn't know what her words meant, but Sara must have because she finally spoke up with a sad plea.

"Scusami, Signora. Per favore. It wasn't my fault."

Her arm already in the air, Signora Agnelli swung it, open handed at Sara, striking her square in the face with a loud slap and screaming, "Leccafighe!" T.J. couldn't translate that but he would have been disgusted at the vulgar, derogatory Italian slur for lesbian.

Sara absorbed the blow and reflexively reached for her face as T.J. gasped and yelled out, "Stop it!"

Both women looked up at T.J., surprised to see him standing there. Sara blushed, embarrassed, and La Signora spun around to look at him with her tight, expressionless face. Venom flared in her eyes as she walked right up to him and, even though she had to raise her chin to meet his gaze, she spoke with utmost authority and in perfect English.

"Do not tell me what to do, leeeetle boy."

With that, she gave him a hard shove and walked past him and in the direction of the neurotic Monegasque. T.J. couldn't believe she had been physical with him. Even as a child, he had never been spanked or in a school yard confrontation. Jaw dropped, he moved over to Sara.

"Are you okay?"

"You shouldn't have said anything. Now you'll be on her shit list, too."

"What happened?"

"I was giving that bitch client a mustache wax. She wouldn't sit still and when I pulled the strip off it took some of the skin off her lip."

"That's no reason to call you names and hit you."

"She gets physical with us all the time. She's like a five year old." Rubbing her face, she added, "It doesn't really hurt. She's pretty weak. It's better than a kick in the shin."

T.J. was incredulous. "Does everyone know this? Mitchell?"

Sara got up and started her afternoon duties, switching off the lights and fountain as if nothing at all had happened. "Of course. This isn't America, T.J."

No, he thought. It certainly wasn't.

T.J. arrived for the staff meal, deflated and upset. He

wanted to talk to Mitchell about what he'd just witnessed, but if it was true that he "was as scared of Signora Angelli as the rest of the staff," what was the point?

When Mitchell walked in, he exchanged a nervous look with T.J. and asked, "Do you have a minute to speak?"

"Absolutely," T.J. said, pleased, as they moved together to the far end of the room.

They stood with their backs to the dining area and Mitchell started off in hushed tones, saying, "Signora just told me what happened in the Wellness wing."

"I'm glad," T.J. replied, not lowering his volume a decibel. "Did she also tell you how she was screaming at Sara before she hauled off and hit her in the face?"

Mitchell was trying to maintain composure but was clearly uncomfortable with the conversation.

"That's between Signora and Sara, T.J. We can't get involved with anything outside of our fitness positions."

"So you're okay with the fact that she pushed me, as well? She probably didn't mention that."

"She pushed you?" he asked, rhetorically. "She's a ninety-pound old lady."

T.J. looked at Mitchell and shook his head. The expression on his face said, "You are pathetic." He didn't need words.

"Just stick to your duties and let other employees stick to theirs," Mitchell advised, trying to diffuse and placate.

"Will do," T.J. said blankly and then asked, "May I have my money, please?"

Mitchell handed him the envelope he'd been carrying and

T.J., unabashed, opened it to count his pay, even though he had no idea what a lire was worth.

"It's all there," Mitchell noted with a hint of attitude. "Less the exchange rate."

"Grazie, Mitchell."

The rainy weather finally cleared up overnight, just in time for the guests to have their weigh-in and final breakfast. Signora Agnelli was decked out in an emerald green silk caftan and matching turban when she appeared to thank them and bid them farewell. Afterwards, three taxis arrived simultaneously to transport them to connecting transportation home. The same sedan with tinted windows that had previously delivered La Signora was also parked in front of the Spa, its driver leaning against the back fender having a smoke. After the clients' departure, she would be heading to her home in Livorno.

By early afternoon, Spa Vitale was quiet again with only the staff in residence. At three p.m., another taxi pulled in but this one was for T.J., who had his bag packed. He had said nothing to anyone, not even goodbye. He couldn't wait to get his long journey underway.

Finally arriving in Rome's da Vinci Airport shortly before eight that evening, he made his way to the Alitalia counter and presented the open-ended round trip ticket he'd received when he landed the "dream" job. He requested a seat, any seat, on the next flight to New York City. The agent checked schedules and availability, entering the ticket information into her word processor. With a concerned look she told him, "Mi scusi, signore. This ticket has been canceled."

Dismayed but not surprised, T.J. pulled out the envelope Mitchell had given him the evening before.

"I'll buy a ticket, please."

He had just enough cash to pay for a middle seat in the back of the plane in the smoking section. The perfect opportunity to restart his smoking habit.

Since the flight wouldn't be departing until early the next morning, T.J. decided to have an airport meal and make himself as comfortable as possible in one of the waiting areas, and perhaps get a little sleep before the arduous nine-and-a-half hour flight ahead of him.

T.J. had one more thing to take care of before saying, "Arrivederci Roma." He went to a pay phone and pumped in enough coins to get through to Spa Vitali. He asked to speak with Mitchell and, a few lire later, the Fitness Director was finally on the line. "This is Mitchell." He announced brusquely,

"It's T.J."

"That was very unprofessional behavior, T.J. I'm afraid I won't be able to give you a recommendation."

T.J. laughed. "Likewise, Mitchell. But what I can do is have my father reach out to Spa Vitale's lawyer for reimbursement of my air fare. He's a very well known lawyer in the States. Thomas Porter. Feel free to look him up."

"You'd go to all that trouble for a couple hundred bucks?"

"We don't have to go to any trouble if you just send me the money. Otherwise, I would be delighted to contact The New York Times Travel section and tell them exactly what kind of business La Signora Capo is running."

There was a long silent pause before Mitchell hung up and the line was disconnected.

Three days later, as T.J. was just getting over his jet lag, a FedEx envelope arrived with a cashier's check for five hundred dollars.

CHAPTER TEN

That's a Wrap

"You got out of there just in time," Bella commented after hearing T.J.'s Spa Vitale story, with which he regaled her over a pre-movie coffee shop meal. "Can you imagine if you'd been stuck there the entire three months?"

"I admit I'm rather proud of the way I handled it," he said, pulling out his cigarette case and offering her a smoke, which she accepted. "Plus, now I know how to teach an aerobics class in Italian."

Bella laughed, "A skill that is sure to come in handy. And you never even met a hot Italiano?"

"If I ever go back to Italy, I will steer very clear of the countryside. I'm sure all the sexy guys are in Rome, Venice or Milan. I'm an avowed city boy from now on."

"So what's the plan? Singing for seniors?"

"That feels like a step backward," he admitted. "I'd rather hit the pavements and find a real show or some TV work."

"Even if Artie had survived the earthquake, I don't think there would be a future at Tomorrow's Promise. Phyllis told me the ratings are worse than ever."

"Poor Marti. She told me their morale is pretty low."

"I bet. There just isn't much television work here anymore. It's all in Los Angeles these days. You know if they canceled The Edge of Night, things are bad. Saturday Night Live and The Cosby Show are about all that's left."

Lighting his own cigarette, he observed, "I don't see myself fitting in on either of them."

"Oh, come on," she teased, "you'd be perfect as the long lost, gay Cosby love child!"

"I've got to come up with something soon. For all my pursuits of Mister Right, I never seem to meet guys with money. Leo has all that luck."

"He's back with Don, right?"

T.J. nodded. "I guess they're a good match. He's nice looking and makes a great living, but Leo has all the personality."

Bella checked her watch. "We'd better get to the movie."

As they fished out cash to pay the bill, T.J. said, "I'm excited to see this one. John Travolta looks sexy as hell."

"What more could you want after everything you went through in Italy? An entire movie about aerobics!"

They were about to see the Travolta film Perfect, costarring Jamie Lee Curtis, set in the sexy, sweaty world of the athletic club culture. Based on a series of Rolling Stone articles exploring the world of "gyms as the new singles bars of the '80s," everyone was talking about the films' strong sexual content, catchy soundtrack and dazzling aerobics dance sequences.

"Anytime you want to pick up work, I'm happy to set you up at the Sports Club. They're always looking for good instructors."

As they rose from the table to head to the cinema, T.J. told her, "I may not have a letter of recommendation from Spa Vitale, but Steve can certainly vouch for my skills."

Amused by the double entendre, she cooed, "Oh, I know he can!"

He threw his arm around her shoulder as they walked out of the coffee shop. "You're always so good to me, Bel."

"You're like the kid brother I never had. Or wanted."

The movie was campy fun and it certainly made the gym scene look like the place to be, especially for anyone good looking and under thirty-five. Of course, seeing Travolta with Jamie Lee Curtis and Marilu Henner gyrating in their leotards and skimpy short-shorts was an entertaining way to spend two hours.

It also provided the last little nudge T.J. needed to convince him to accept Bella's offer to meet with NYSC's corporate Group Exercise Executive, a no-nonsense, serious woman closing in on forty. Nonnie was barely five feet tall and weighed less than a hundred pounds soaking wet. She had short cropped hair, bleached platinum, and was built like Peter Pan on steroids. T.J. had never seen a woman with such a hard body.

Nonnie taught only two classes a week, but they were serious events held in the flagship club's large aerobics studio, by reservation only. The fifty available spots always sold out quickly and had a long waiting list. As the final phase of his job interview, T.J. had to attend one so she could judge his fitness skill level.

Blasting tunes from Power Station, the Eurythmics and even a bit of Aretha Franklin, Nonnie's class was the best show in town. It was also the toughest workout he'd ever had and he was completely surprised by what a pocket rocket she was. He not only came out of the hour-long, high impact extravaganza physically exhausted, but incredibly, simultaneously energized. Was this the "runner's high" people talked about? It was a terrific feeling.

After she said goodbye to her devoted groupies, Nonnie called T.J. over to the stereo where, still dripping with perspiration, she was packing up her mixtapes.

"So when can you start?" she asked him.

Still flushed from the intense workout, he smiled and told her, "How about tomorrow?"

"I have several classes I need subbed, so we'll start with those and get you on the permanent schedule next week. Let's go back to my office and look at the calendar."

He knew then that if he could somehow marry his own personality with Nonnie's skill and Steve's sex appeal, he could be a top instructor. Here he had been spending the last five years looking for his own show—perhaps he would finally find it at the New York Sports Club.

Nonnie set him up with several classes in need of coverage for instructors who were out sick or on vacation, so he'd get an opportunity to try out a variety of different classes at several different club locations (Stretch, Low Impact Groove, High Impact, Calisthenics, Bands and Buns, and Only Abs to name a few). He already had an eclectic assortment of music mixes he'd put together with Steve in preparation for Italy, but he wanted to step up his wardrobe, so he planned an immediate outing to Modell's and Paragon Sporting Goods stores.

Carolyn Lee would be downtown lunching with her agent, not far from Paragon, so she told T.J. she'd meet him and help him pick out some items. Before she had poured herself into the in vitro project, she had been a self-confessed "gym bunny" and knew exactly where Paragon kept the best stock hidden for savvy, regular customers.

"Our doctor thinks it's only a matter of time before I get pregnant," she explained as they rifled through racks of neon-colored tank tops. "It would make such a difference for Gary and me."

She almost never discussed Gary in any meaningful way, so this information piqued T.J.'s interest.

"How so?"

"He is so wrapped up with himself and his career that it's like our marriage is only an afterthought. Unless he needs me on his arm for something."

"And a baby would change that?"

"It sure would. Then we wouldn't just be a couple, we'd be a family. Couples come and go, but families are forever. Mayor Koch doesn't understand that. He's a lifelong bachelor with no kids."

"Koch has to be gay, come on. Everybody thinks so."

"Don't tell that to Bess Myerson." Myerson was a local political celebrity and Koch's frequent companion, and she had the distinction of being the first, and only, Jewish Miss America.

"Forgive me for saying so, honey, but I just don't think your husband's very nice to you," T.J. ventured.

She looked at him, exhausted from having to constantly

defend Gary. After a moment, she said with considerable sadness, "I think a baby would change that, too."

He gave her a hug, right there between Training Gear and New Arrivals. For someone who appeared to have it all, Carolyn Lee was struggling.

"Well, if your doctor says it's okay, then you have to come and try one of my classes."

"Totally," she said enthusiastically, having adopted the popular new Valley Girl lingo. "And I may have a lot of time on my hands. I think the writing is on the wall at work."

"You're an icon. Why would they ever get rid of you?"

Spotting a hot pink sports bra, she grabbed it and used it to illustrate her explanation. "Because in television, especially for women over thirty, there is always a newer, brighter model just waiting to step in and take over."

"You're barely over thirty. You're also gorgeous and popular. Most importantly, you're too good at what you do to be replaced."

"Au contraire, my friend. They can have someone younger and less expensive in my chair in time for tonight's broadcast. And, unlike me, she'll probably let the boss cop a feel. Or more!"

"There's a casting couch in the news business?" he asked, surprised.

"Sweetie, there's a casting couch in every business," she answered, putting the bra back on its rack. "That's why I'm meeting my agent. To discuss an exit strategy. I'd rather quit than be fired."

T.J. thought wistfully of Marti and how she must be feeling at her age, after all the decades with her soap opera that was now in jeopardy. There was no way she would ever quit.

Emerging from Paragon into a bright and bustling stretch of Broadway, Carolyn Lee put on her sunglasses and looked around for her agent, Alan, who was supposed to be meeting her on the corner so they could walk together to lunch in Union Square. T.J. juggled his two bags of clothing purchases while he fished his knockoff Ray-Bans out of his fanny pack.

"Thanks for tagging along," he told her. "I got some good stuff."

"Yes, you totally did. I'm glad it worked out."

They heard a deep voice call out, "Hey, good looking," and looked down the block to see Alan waving happily at Carolyn Lee, walking briskly in their direction. She waved back.

"Let me introduce you before you head off," she said to T.J.

But as Alan approached, only a few yards away from them, his smile suddenly left his face as his eyes widened and he collapsed in a heap, face down, right in the middle of the sidewalk.

"Alan!" Carolyn Lee screamed out, assuming he'd tripped. They ran quickly to his side and turned him over. His nose was bloody and his eyes glazed.

T.J. immediately dropped his bags and began the CPR techniques he'd learned during his aerobics certification program. He barked at Carolyn Lee to loosen Alan's tie and collar as he performed chest compressions.

As she did so, she yelled to passersby, "Somebody call an ambulance, please."

Help arrived a short time later, but it was no use. The paramedics believed, and it was later confirmed, that Alan had died before he'd even hit the ground. After his body was loaded into an ambulance, the busy New York City street immediately reverted to its usual state as if nothing unusual had happened.

Carolyn Lee was shell-shocked and T.J. offered to escort her back home.

Wiping her tears, she told him, "It's awful to say, but I hope Gary isn't there."

"As we just learned," he said, "You're only an aneurysm or heart attack away from being a widow. Then we can go out and find a guy who deserves you."

She didn't want to smile, but she did.

***

"I'm going for an HIV test."

A shiver ran down T.J.'s spine when he heard Leo so bluntly say those words during their morning phone call.

"How come? Do you think you were exposed?" he asked nervously. It was the unfortunate new normal of paranoia about every casual sex partner, unexpected rash or night-sweating incident.

"No," Leo explained, "but Don and I decided we want to be exclusive and think it's a good idea for both of us to be tested. Do you want to come with me?"

Carousing in nightclubs and partying in restaurants was what the two friends did best, but after the sad and scary experience of visiting Armand as he was dying of AIDS, T.J.

didn't know if he was brave enough to confront the reality of being tested, himself. Even if he was with Leo.

"It's a simple blood test and the GMHC offers it free and anonymously," Leo continued. Confidentiality was an important factor since such a stigma was attached to the disease, especially for gay men. It was that prejudice as well as governmental inaction against "the plague" that had resulted in the formation of the Gay Men's Health Crisis in 1982. Playwright Larry Kramer, who was getting rave reviews for his Off Broadway AIDS drama, The Normal Heart, was one of its original founders and the organization. He quickly achieved respect for its care and concern for the gay and bisexual communities being ravaged by the disease.

Although he'd gone to Sunday school and been confirmed in the Episcopal Church when he was fifteen, T.J. didn't often think about God or remember to pray but he thought this would be a good time to start. If he could be spared testing positive for the virus, he told himself, he would find a church to attend, say his prayers regularly and never have unprotected sex again. Even as it flashed through his mind, he knew he was lying to himself so he said to Leo, "When do you want to go?"

Hearing the terror in his friend's voice, Leo calmly suggested, "I'll leave work early tomorrow and we can go in the afternoon and then have dinner at Cafe Lux. My treat."

Cafe Luxembourg was one of T.J.'s favorite places on the Upper West Side, with its lively bistro atmosphere, handsomely polished nickel bar and an abundance of good looking professional guys eager to buy cocktails and flirt with each other.

"Pally, if it takes a blood test to get a free meal at Cafe Lux, I'm in," T.J. said with a tentative chuckle.

A few days later, when both their test results came back as negative, they celebrated at Chita Rivera's newly opened restaurant in Times Square. Don, having also been tested separately, joined them and they took a corner table where they could see famous faces like Regis Philbin, Ann Reinking and New York Mets star Keith Hernandez as they came and went past the hostess station, where Chita's lookalike sister, Lola, greeted them.

T.J. arrived fresh from teaching a class and was still clad in an oversized hood sweatshirt and black parachute pants over his Lycra shorts. No sooner had the waiter uncorked the first bottle of Stag's Leap than he asked Don as his "best friend-in law" to introduce him to any eligible bachelors he might know.

Don and Leo, although physically similar in size and build, were a classic example of opposites attract. Everything that was warm and fun about Leo seemed nonexistent in Don, who was a soft spoken corporate lawyer, which was just as well. When he did express an opinion, it was usually in a haughty manner.

After T.J. made his case, Don replied with a hint of derision. "Most of my colleagues are Suits. Your special personality would probably be lost on them."

Leo and T.J. glanced at each other, recognizing it as a dig, but they let it go as the waiter filled their glasses and placed the wine bottle in a nearby ice bucket.

Holding his glass up in a toast, Leo said, "When being negative is a good thing."

"Thank God," T.J. toasted, reminding himself to try and keep up with his prayers now that they had seemed to help manifest the test results he'd wanted. If Rock Hudson, one of the world's most famous, handsome and manly men, could succumb to AIDS, anyone was vulnerable.

Rock Hudson wasn't the only notable death that autumn. Leo and his family had to say goodbye to his Aunt Jenny, when her liver finally gave out after one too many of her special see-through screwdrivers.

T.J. accompanied his bestie out to Staten Island for the open casket mourning service at the Scarpaci Funeral Home. The deceased was laid out in a peach-colored dress with a dainty ruffled collar, and her hair was so neatly coiffed it almost looked like a wig. Neither of them had ever seen her dressed or styled that way in life, so it was like looking at a stranger.

"She would hate this," Leo whispered, referring to the reverent and somber atmosphere.

Looking around the parlor, T.J. saw the Tucci family all silently sitting in rows, clad head to toe in shades of black, gray and navy blue with most of the hat-fitted women sniffling and dabbing their eyes with tissues. Toward the back, a more rag-tag collection of Jenny's friends was gathered, hands folded and looking uncomfortable. Leo identified them as her barfly friends.

"I never understood the open casket thing," T.J. confessed.

"It's gross," Leo agreed. "As if she'd want to spend eternity in that dress."

Leo's mother appeared to be the only woman who wasn't displaying or feigning grief. They could hear her commenting to another relative, "We knew this is how she'd end up. Out of six siblings, booze has already killed three of them. Don't tell me it's not genetic."

Leo's dad was Jenny's older brother and simply sat, dry-eyed, and stared at his sister in the coffin. A riot of flowers with satin ribbons that bore messages like "Sympathy," "Rest in Peace" and "Always in Our Hearts" were festooned all around it. A line of people waited patiently for their turn to gaze upon her blotched and bloated face one final time before the lid was closed and everyone headed to Our Lady of Perpetual Help, three blocks away.

When Leo rose from his chair to take his turn in line, he nudged T.J. "Come with me," he said. Solemnly they shuffled through the line and took their places to say their farewells. T.J. felt Leo's father intently watching their every move.

Leo dutifully made the sign of the cross then whispered to T.J., "The family will hang back for a few more minutes before we head to the church. I'll meet you outside."

T.J. nodded and went out to the street where a balmy Indian summer day greeted the mourners. He was certain Leo must have a cute Italian cousin somewhere in attendance, but had yet to spot one.

As the funeral director appeared from an adjacent room to usher the family out, Leo's dad approached him and said to him between clenched teeth, "This is how you honor your Aunt? By bringing a fanook to her funeral" That was the derogatory Italian slang for "homosexual."

"That fanook is my best friend, Dad," Leo said without wanting to get into a debate on sexuality, especially at that moment in that place. "And he and Aunt Jenny really liked each other."

"Drinking buddies, eh?" his father retorted disdainfully. Leo bit his lip, even though he wanted to tell his father he was certain Aunt Jenny had been gay herself.

After the funeral mass, T.J. and Leo took a checkered cab back into Manhattan and headed directly for Chita's to start knocking back screwdrivers in Jenny's honor. They splurged for the Stoli and, after the first sips, they winced.

Frank, the attentive bartender, asked them, "Too strong?"

T.J. pushed the glass back across the bar and said, "Take this back and put some vodka in it!"

"Lotsa ice and just a splash of OJ," Leo instructed. Then they both added simultaneously as Jenny always had, "For color!"

***

T.J. was hustling to get to the 34th Street New York Sports Club for his regular Friday lunchtime class, a forty-five minute high-intensity workout for people with limited time off from work during the day. Coming from teaching a ten a.m. class uptown, via a subway delayed by signal problems, he arrived just in time. This was where Bella was working, and they usually took a coffee break together when T.J. was finished.

He didn't see her at the front desk when he dashed through, and there was still no sign of her when he returned afterwards. He asked the young man handing out towels and locker keys if he'd seen her.

"She never came in today," was his answer. "You're T.J., right?"

"Yes."

"Nonnie left this for you," he said, handing him an envelope which T.J. pocketed.

There were plenty of banal possibilities to explain Bella's absence, but T.J. was concerned. When he got home, he ignored the messages waiting for him on his answering machine and immediately dialed Bella's number. When her machine picked up, he disconnected and decided to try the number he had for her from when she was living with her mother.

Mrs. Black answered after only a single ring. Her voice was thin and she sounded tired. There was a definite trace of her Puerto Rican accent. T.J. identified himself and said he was concerned when he hadn't seen Bella at work.

"Oh, T.J., I'm glad you called," she told him, recognizing him as one of Bella's close friends. "I'm afraid our girl is in trouble again."

"What kind of trouble? Can I help?"

"I wish you could, dear. It's up to the doctors, now."

"Doctors? Where is she?"

"I went over to her apartment last night with groceries, and she was passed out. There was also one of those glass things for smoking marijuana next to her."

"Mrs. Black, where is she now?"

"I've done all I can do. I'm at the end of my rope with her," she prattled on, her voice cracking. "I called Hazelden. They came and took her around midnight."

Hazelden was a well known rehabilitation center and part of the Betty Ford Foundation, with residential and outpatient programs at several locations around the country. It had a reputation for being outrageously expensive, usually effective and a haven for celebrity addicts like Liza Minnelli, Eric Clapton and Natalie Cole. Rehab and AA meetings were one thing, but being admitted to Hazelden meant things were serious.

"Here in New York?" he inquired, impatiently.

"Yes—and I have no idea how we're going to afford it. My ex–husband is just going to have to pay for it. God knows, I can't."

"Can she have visitors?"

"Oh, no. Not even me. She has a long road ahead of her, T.J. They told me her detox will take at least a week."

He felt badly for Mrs. Black, but his heart broke for Bella. How unfair it was for her to be so disabled by the things everybody else seemed to be able to enjoy—if not in moderation, then with recreational tolerance. There was also a twinge of guilt knowing he'd gone along with her occasional social usage of those substances.

Bella's mother agreed to keep him updated with any developments and he made sure she wrote down his telephone number. After he hung up, he said a little prayer for his friend, asking God not to let her end up like Aunt Jennie.

He sat down on the edge of his sofa bed and kicked off his sneakers. Realizing he had stashed the envelope from Nonnie in his gym bag, he retrieved it and opened it. It was a memo to a dozen of her best, most popular instructors and T.J. was pleased to be included among them.

It was an invitation to participate in a new fitness certification program by an industry-famous, Atlanta-based aerobics competitor named Gin Miller. Only a select group of elite instructors from across the country would spend a weekend retreat at her gym in Georgia, being personally coached and authorized by Miller to become her first squadron of Step Reebok Workout teachers. To T.J., this was the aerobics equivalent of being nominated for a Tony Award. He couldn't wait to RSVP.

Noticing the light blinking on his answering machine, he hit play. After a friendly "checking in" message from his mother came Marti's familiar voice.

"Hello, Presh. It's me. The news is going to be announced tomorrow morning but the network actually had the decency to give me a heads up. It's official. They're canceling us. After thirty years, I got my two-week's notice. That's showbiz. Love ya."

A world without Tomorrow's Promise? It was one of those reliable comforts of his youth; always there if he was too sick to go to school, on snow days, or during visits to his grandmother's. Then it became his first TV job, and it changed the course of his life, rescuing him from tedious academia. It would be a bittersweet loss for him, other cast and crew members and generations of fans. But for Marti, it was personal.

Her no-nonsense attitude surprised and impressed him. "The writing was on the wall," she had said. And "No job lasts forever." She never ceased to teach him life lessons, simply by example.

T.J. had to fly to Atlanta with Nonnie and some other selected instructors on the day Marti taped her final episode. She was heavy on his mind until he arrived at the Convention Center where aerobics junkies from around the country had assembled to study under Gin Miller. There was a massive registration and meet-and-greet before they would climb aboard the shuttle buses to check in to the nearby hotel. Too bad, he thought, that the gathering was serving bottled water and the tasty new Power-Bar snacks instead of cocktails and hors d'oeuvres. The place was crawling with great looking instructors, and to T.J. it was like a sports-oriented smorgasbord. How he wished Leo was there to help him sample the wares.

Along with Nonnie and the other NYSC instructors in attendance, T.J. dined that night in the hotel restaurant. They were more excited to be learning all about the Step craze than he was. T.J. considered the whole concept gimmicky, and a likely flash in the pan. After all, how entertaining or challenging could it be to step up and down on a plastic platform for sixty minutes?

He found out the next day. It could be as simple and straightforward as he had assumed or as choreographed and complicated as the instructor devised. Either way, the workout became very strenuous very quickly, especially if using multiple "risers" to increase the height of the step. In addition to being more difficult than he imagined, it was more fun. He also had the bonus of working directly next to a buff little blond guy from nearby Alpharetta, Georgia. His name, T.J. soon learned, was Maximus. T.J. assumed it had to be a concocted moniker, but he didn't care. Maximus was adorable and actually had Leo Tucci written all over him, with a bubble butt in the back and an obviously ample package in the front. T.J., an unabashed crotch watcher, christened him (in his mind) Phallus Maximus. After spending the day sweating together, T.J. invited Maximus back to his hotel room for a shower, and then they spent the night sweating together in his bed.

T.J. and his NYSC colleagues flew home from their weekend as newly certified Step Reebok Instructors, and he was anxious to introduce classes to their clientele as soon as possible. He and Maximus made some vague promises about staying in touch, which neither one of them believed they actually would—but they'd had a fun night in Hot-lanta, as the tourists would say.

This new fitness skill resulted in T.J. getting his schedule upped to a whopping twenty–two classes a week, which equated to a full-time job and generated a very respectable paycheck twice a month. He got into the best shape of his life and found that it actually made him more energetic. He also learned how to teach a class without actually having to execute all the movements one hundred percent, conserving his strength to maintain the busy schedule and even taking on additional classes and occasional private clients, as well. Nonnie was so pleased with his performance and popularity that she bumped up his pay scale to as high as the corporate office would allow, with occasional bonuses for special event classes and holidays. There was usually a long waiting list for those.

Since his classes were like mini shows, they also satisfied his desire to perform. Broadway actors got to do only eight shows a week, and he was knocking out at least twenty! His father had made a derisive comment about "my son, the aerobics star," but there was no arguing with the success he was enjoying in his new line of work.

Carolyn Lee, too, was happier than she had been in a while and excitedly announced to T.J. (and the rest of New York City, courtesy of Liz Smith's column in the New York Daily News) that she was finally pregnant. Along with that, she decided to reveal that she would be leaving her longtime TV anchor position to concentrate on delivering and raising a healthy baby. The timing worked out well for her personally and professionally since, as she said, "Gary is happy I'll be staying home."

Sure he is, T.J. thought. He'll be able to control her better if she's stuck at home.

Of course, he didn't say that to her, even though she was well aware of his opinion about her husband. Instead, T.J. volunteered to help her plan and pick out items for the nursery she was creating in their apartment.

Meanwhile, Tomorrow's Promise recorded its final show, which was now scheduled to air the Friday before Christmas. That struck T.J. as somehow cruel—it would be the first year in three decades that Marti and her fans would be deprived of a special holiday-themed episode. She invited him to come over and watch the broadcast with her and a few other friends. Ever the bon vivant, she told him to wear black because the theme would be "Irish wake."

She was true to her word. When the elevator opened into her vestibule, there was a huge funeral wreath on an easel with a black ribbon emblazoned comically with "R.I.P." Madison bounded in to greet him with his ever-wagging tail. Being there felt as warm and familiar as going home.

He was delighted to walk into the kitchen and find Deidre, Gerry and Marti's makeup artist, Bobby, there as well. As directed, everyone was dressed in black. They were still exchanging greetings when Marti swept in from the dining room, looking resplendent in a sequined black dress, the fanciest outfit T.J. had ever seen her wear. She was clutching a large bottle of Jameson's whiskey and called out, "Irish Coffees for everybody!"

Once everyone had their drink in hand, Marti led them into the living room where the television set was already on and the familiar theme song to the show began to play for the final time. Everyone took a seat and T.J. found a spot on the floor next to Madison, right at Marti's feet. He caught a glimpse of her watching herself on screen and wondered what emotions she was feeling.

The episode itself was nothing out of the ordinary and played out almost as if it were any other day. Most of the characters were new additions brought on after the earthquake storyline. Other than Marti's character, Hope, the only other two T.J. recognized were "David" and "Angela." After twenty minutes, Marti said aloud, "This is it," and finished off her spiked coffee.

David and Angela were commiserating over a painful separation, deciding to give their marriage another try, thanks to the sage counsel of the wise and reliable Hope.

David: Hope, how can we ever thank you?

Hope: Seeing you two together is all the thanks I could want. (Hope rises from the table and crosses to the door).

Angela: See you tomorrow?

Hope: I promise. (Hope exits. Fade to Black).

With that, Tomorrow's Promise rolled their closing credits and came to a quiet end. The little group assembled in Marti's living room remained silent as a commercial announced, "Premiering Monday at this time, join us for an exciting new game show, Fortune or Folly!"

Everyone started to boo and hiss until Marti used the remote control to power off the television. Her eyes were moist as she addressed Gerry and asked him, "Will you do the honors, sir?"

The burly, usually brusque stage manager, his voice trembling, tried to replicate his traditional end-of-day call to the cast and crew, "And . . . that's a wrap!"

CHAPTER ELEVEN
Hello, Hamptons

The summer of 1987 was one of Manhattan's hottest on record, kicking off with ninety-seven degrees on Memorial Day weekend, with the temperatures rarely taking a break, even at night. With the concrete canyons of skyscrapers exacerbating the humidity, air quality and heat, the word, oppressive, was not an exaggeration.

Bella was once again out of rehab and back to work at NYSC. She kept to herself most of the time, except at the gym, and she spent her evenings avoiding the party lifestyle, becoming addicted instead to renting VHS movies from Blockbuster.

Carolyn Lee rarely left the air-conditioned confines of her apartment unless it was to take new baby Jaclyn to the pediatrician, accompanied by full-time nanny, Therese. Therese was an overweight but devoted forty-something emigre from South America. Neither attractive nor able to speak much English, she was the perfect fit for a married woman like Carolyn Lee, who was insecure about her husband's wandering eye and uncomfortable when they were alone together. That wasn't often as, since Jaclyn's birth, Gary spent even less time at home. Carolyn Lee didn't know what he was up to and she didn't care. Content in her Central Park South gilded cage, she doted on her good–natured little daughter.

Since Jaclyn's arrival allowed T.J. to enjoy playing "uncle," he stopped by several times a week, usually between aerobics classes, to hang out with Carolyn Lee while Therese tended to the more rigorous baby duties like diapers and bath time. His friend finally seemed to have the life she wanted, even if her marriage was pretty much in name only. It always made T.J. pledge to himself that when (not if) he met "the One," theirs would be a true love story.

Leo was thriving at Citibank and fielding offers from corporate headhunters who were trying to lure him into the world of private investment banking. He and Don were living together in a decent-sized apartment in a spectacular building on Park Avenue South, and they spent nearly every weekend at Don's East Hampton place, unless they were jetting off to a party in Provincetown or Key West. T.J. rarely tagged along on those jaunts, less interested in the promiscuous lifestyle that continued to permeate the gay community, but he did enjoy the Hamptons scene when invited. Leo was always generous with accommodations and Don seemed to begrudgingly accept his boyfriend's best friend and family's frequent presence. T.J. and Bella agreed that it was better to be single than saddled with a husband or boyfriend who brought less joy than aggravation to the relationship, as seemed to be the case with Don . . . and certainly with Gary. "Alone but not lonely," T.J.'s mother sometimes reminded him. He often wondered if she secretly meant, "Better single than with another man."

In an already sweltering mid-June, one of T.J.'s regular students at the Upper East Side branch of NYSC, tarried after class to ask him if he was interested in escaping the city for the rest of the summer. She was a wealthy fifty-five-year-old divorcee named Ginny who did little other than shop, exercise and turn a blind eye to her teenage children's drug use. She was in fabulous shape and looked half her age, and she split her time between her condo on East 79th Street and a sprawling Hamptons home she referred to as, "the beach house." She informed him that the local gym there, Hamp-Fit, was looking for seasonal staff to teach classes. The couple who owned it were friends of hers and she'd told them about T.J.'s high-energy, vivacious style. It was also an asset that he was a proficient Step instructor and incorporated so much fun and choreography to those classes (including a campy new trend called Vogue dancing). Voguing originated in Harlem and quickly evolved in the mainstream, and it was becoming increasingly popular in the clubs. If he wanted a weekend job there, she could arrange it. All he would have to do is take the Jitney bus out on Friday afternoons, teach a few classes Saturdays and Sundays, and then Jitney back at his leisure. Ginny had more bedrooms than she could possibly use and told him he was welcome to crash at her place.

It took T.J. just a moment to consider before he accepted the offer. Even if it ended up like another Spa Vitale situation, it was only for the weekends and it was a chance to escape the summer sauna of Manhattan. He was excited about the opportunity. A bonus would be spending time with Leo and taking advantage of the local beach scene in the increasingly gay enclave of East

Hampton. The Swamp, a hot Hamptons club, was known as a dump compared to the chic, upscale party palaces in Manhattan but it attracted everyone in the gay community with its casual, laid-back atmosphere. Of course, it was the perfect place to practice and perfect Vogue moves and routines. It wasn't surprising to run into celebrities like Mick and Bianca Jagger, who sweated and danced inside the unpretentious, poorly ventilated dance hall. Nor was it surprising to run into entwined bodies in the parking lot, moving in time to the disco music inside until just before dawn.

Ginny's gigantic property on Egypt Lane overlooked the Maidstone Country Club golf course and featured all the traditional exterior design elements popular there, such as a gabled roof, sun-bleached wooden shingles, lantern-style lights and ox-eye windows. Even having grown up in the upscale suburbs of Connecticut, T.J. was impressed by the palatial homes there. She rewarded him with his suite on the ground floor, with its own entrance near the garage and pool house. The only downside he could see when she gave him the tour was his room's proximity to a small reading room that housed cages filled with half a dozen of her absentee son's pet ferrets. They made constant noises that ranged from hissing when agitated to a clucking sound when content. It seemed like they were in constant motion and T.J. could hear them even with the doors closed. Fortunately, the housekeeper took care of them—that would have been a deal breaker for T.J. He had zero desire to snuggle up with ferrets like he would with Madison, Marti's sweet dog.

Hamp-Fit was an airy, modern, fully equipped gym right off Main Street frequented by the town's creme-de-la-crème: uber-wealthy Manhattanites keeping up appearances when not melting back in the concrete jungle. The ones who didn't come out by private plane or car rode the Jitney bus alongside their nannies and housekeepers, and T.J. happily straddled those two worlds—at least on the commute. He never knew if the cute guy across the aisle was a wealthy young broker or a struggling pool boy, but he knew he'd figure it out when they inevitably ran into each other at The Swamp (and all to the soundtrack of the popular hit film of the summer, Dirty Dancing).

His classes were an instant hit, not only because they were challenging and fun, but more because he was "fresh meat" in town: a handsome new face that social climbing Hamptonites wanted to befriend to determine whether or not he should be admitted into their social cliques. Once an eagle-eyed housewife recognized him from Tomorrow's Promise, word got around and everyone clamored for his attention, in and out of class. He loved every moment of it.

Ginny seemed strangely territorial with their friendship, since she was the one who had introduced him to the scene and was hosting him. It was immediately apparent to T.J. that it would be bad form to bring any romantic partners back to her place so, more often than not, he got back to his room in the mornings after his trysts with a variety of sexy admirers. He drew the line at group sex, too uncomfortable with the memory of the scene with Andy in the basement of the Candle Bar. It was shaping up to be a terrific summer, he thought, and all set to Madonna music, which seemed to be everywhere.

Another bonus was getting to spend time with Leo. They often took the Jitney together and hung out at someone's pool party or on Two Mile Hollow Beach where older guys waited in the parking lot to have a car-quickie with willing young prospects. Don had hired a local girl named Lucy to do his housekeeping and cooking on the weekends, and generous Leo made sure T.J. was always invited to any dinner parties he and Don threw.

For one of those parties, T.J. asked if he could bring Ginny along. He was feeling guilty for not spending more time with her. Between teaching classes at Hamp-Fit, carousing with Leo and picking up Cute Guy Du Jour at The Swamp, he only saw her for morning coffee in her kitchen. It was an intimate affair by Hamptons standards, with Lucy serving just twelve guests, along with one of her muscled young "cater-waiters" (hired more for their looks than their hospitality skills). Cocaine was passed around with the canapés and Ginny overindulged in both, which made her so talkative everyone tried their best to avoid her. T.J., of course, noticed. Feeling some kind of responsibility for her, he asked Leo if he could spare everyone by taking her on a tour of the house.

Don interjected, "Just not our bedroom, please. We didn't have time to tidy up in there."

T.J. and Ginny wandered away from all the activity on the first floor and made their way upstairs to inspect a guest room and another bedroom that had been converted into Don's satellite office. The rooms were connected by a Jack and Jill bathroom decorated with whimsical, nautical-themed wallpaper featuring whales and dolphins.

"This is adorable," Ginny observed, running her perfectly manicured hand over the paper, the effects of cocaine making her focus in on the illustrated marine life, her face just inches from the wall.

"Everything's perfect," T.J. added, wandering to the hallway to admire some Warhol-esque artwork hanging there.

"I recognize it," she commented, breezing past him. "It's from a gallery in Sag Harbor."

She grabbed the door handle to the main bedroom before T.J. could stop her. In a loud whisper, he urged, "Ginny, don't go in there!"

Too late—she was already in the middle of the room, which was hardly as untidy as Don had claimed it to be. A large four–poster bed, sheets unmade, dominated the room across from a large fireplace and a wingback armchair with a tee shirt crumpled on the cushion. A large ceiling fan turned slowly overhead.

T.J. motioned her to come out of the room but she shook her head.

"I love a good master bath," she said, disappearing around a corner. T.J. stepped in to follow her, scolding, "Ginny, come out of there."

The next thing he heard was her nasal voice saying in a long, drawn out way, "Ohhhh my Gawwwwd . . ."

Moving quietly but quickly, he joined her in the large, mirrored bathroom, which multiplied their reflections so there were dozens of them staring in wide-eyed amazement at what was resting on the counter of the tiled double-sink vanity. It was a bright red, double-headed dildo, and well over a foot long.

"How does that even work?" Ginny asked, tilting her head to study it.

"Who would want to find out?" T.J. replied, grabbing her by the arm and pulling her out of the room. Together they scurried out and he closed the bedroom door behind them. They paused, once they were back in the hallway, to collect themselves.

"Poor Leo," she remarked.

Reflexively, T.J. said, "Leo? Poor Don!"

With cocaine-enhanced gravity and seriousness, Ginny took T.J. by the shoulders and looked at him squarely as she uttered, "It had two heads."

They suppressed the desire to laugh out loud and quietly padded their way back downstairs. T.J. knew he would get to the bottom (or top) of this the next time he got Leo alone.

Some of the famous faces he saw in town included Billy Joel, Steven Spielberg, smoldering Alec Baldwin and his gorgeous wife Kim Basinger, and Broadway notables like Jerry Orbach, Joel Grey and Elaine Stritch. One, however, was a regular client at Hamp-Fit and it was always a thrill for T.J. to see her in person. Judy Gillette was a beloved icon with a musical and dance career that had spanned more than three decades. Although never really famous outside the theatrical community, she had done some TV and film work and, now in her late sixties, was remarkably fit and feisty. Unlike Dottie O'Hara, Judy Gillette was known for being genuinely sweet and generous. She still sported the jet black bob that was as much her trademark as her provocatively arched back that accentuated her perky posterior, even in the lavender terry-cloth sweat suit she always wore.

Judy never took T.J.'s frenetic, loud and boisterous classes, but she would watch them with intent fascination as she waited in the back of the aerobics studio to attend the Stretching and Flexibility session that followed. He was keenly aware she was watching him, so he couldn't help but show off for her, kicking or jumping a little higher than usual and adding some extra flair to simple club moves like the Running Man and Melbourne Shuffle.

Finally, in mid-August, she approached him between classes while his students filed out and the people coming in for the Stretch class staked out their places with their floor mats and towels.

In her unmistakable Kewpie-doll voice, she said, "Excuse me. Do you have a second?"

Honored to be speaking with her, he enthusiastically answered, "Of course, Miss Gillette," and instantly wished he'd played it cooler.

"Please, call me Judy. You're T.J., right?"

"Yes, ma'am."

Putting a hand on his arm, smiling, she teased him, "Now I just told you to call me Judy, didn't I?" She seemed charmed that he recognized her.

"Sorry. Judy."

"Do you live in the city, T.J.?"

"Yes—midtown East. I usually take the Jitney back on Sunday nights or Monday mornings."

"I was wondering if, after Labor Day when I get home, you could maybe give me some private training. Your class looks like so much fun. I don't have the endurance for it, but I'd love to learn some of the choreography."

T.J. was gob smacked. Tony winner Judy Gillette who had danced with the likes of Tommy Tune, Bob Fosse and Michael Bennett wanted to learn some steps from him? He was too surprised to respond so she added, "Of course, I'll pay you for your time."

Deciding it wasn't too late to tamp down the adulation, he composed himself sufficiently to say, "That would be fun. I'd be happy to do that."

"Great!" she squeaked. "I'll leave my number with the girl at the front desk. Call me after Labor Day and we'll set it up. I'm on the Upper West Side."

Some New Age, synthesized music started to play over the sound system and it was time for the next class to begin so Judy wiggled her fingers at him in a "Toodleloo" and went to claim her spot. T.J. was excited to prepare their lessons. He would definitely be dragging Leo out to the clubs to gather and rehearse new moves.

True to her word, Judy had left him her telephone number with the Hamp-Fit receptionist and T.J. looked forward to visiting her apartment. He wondered if it was near Dottie's. He also wondered what Judy thought of Dottie. Surely they had to be acquainted.

When he met Leo later that day at Georgica Beach, he told him about the celebrity encounter.

"That's amazing, Pally," Leo told him. "She might help you get a Broadway show, after all. Who knows what doors aerobics will open?"

"I should have slept with Steve sooner," T.J. joked. "I'm dying to see her place."

"Don wants to start looking at bigger apartments up there."

"How much more room does he need?"

"It would be for both of us. We want to buy something together."

While Don wasn't T.J.'s favorite person in the world, he was happy for his best friend and gave him a big hug. "That's totally awesome, Pally. Well done, you."

"Things are going well for us, so I figured why not. And with the state of the stock market, it's really a good time to buy."

With mock seriousness, T.J. asked, "So the question remains . . . will the double-headed dildo survive the move?"

Leo's eyes widened and his mouth fell open.

T.J. nodded and confessed, "Sorry, I snooped."

Chuckling, Leo explained, "One of Don's friends bought it at Les Hommes and gave it to us as a gag gift."

"Well, it made me gag," T.J. quipped.

Firing back, Leo said, "And you don't even have a gag reflex!"

They dissolved into a fit of mutual laughter.

***

Summer wrapped up with great fanfare as Hamptonites prepared to close the season with the usual rounds of events and parties that culminated with Ginny's annual clambake for a few dozen people. She suggested T.J. invite Leo and Don. She rented long tables for the backyard and had them elegantly set with vases filled with hydrangeas in alternating colors: pink, white and blue. Their blooming season had passed, but her florist somehow managed to harvest them, regardless. Money could make anything possible, especially in the Hamptons. Individual lanterns were strategically placed along the tall hedges to create a dramatic, beachy ambiance.

Shrimp cocktail appetizers seamlessly segued to North Shore Littleneck clams and mussels before the main event: Atlantic Hardshell Lobster with sweet melted butter and fresh, local corn on the cob. The nearby Wolffer Estate Vineyards supplied all the wines and when the dozen cases were delivered, T.J. thought there was no way they would polish it all off. But by the time they completed the entertaining ritual of making S'mores over the fire pit and closed the evening, there was nary a bottle of Rose, Chardonnay or Pinot Grigio left.

It was a festive farewell to the ferrets and to summer and, for T.J., a successful send off before getting back to Manhattan and resuming his busy teaching schedule with the added highlight of a new celebrity client.

Judy Gillette's apartment was on 87th Street and stately Riverside Drive, across from the impressive Soldiers and Sailors Monument where neighborhood kids would skateboard and rollerblade while their grandparents spent hours on benches, gossiping and dozing. It was a beautiful stretch of the Upper West Side, nicknamed "Heaven on the Hudson," because it bordered the mighty river to the West and seemed somehow less untamed and safer than Central Park, to the East.

Her building was an unpretentious apartment complex sandwiched between much grander structures, without a doorman and only a simple intercom and an entry buzzer. He arrived promptly for their four p.m. appointment, clad in one of his spiffiest new aerobic outfits and carrying his gym bag. He'd brought along some of his latest cassette mix tapes that included high energy songs from Whitney Houston, Duran Duran and Rick Astley but still weren't too fast, in case she tired quickly. He had become expert at determining the right beats per minute to adjust music for various fitness levels. He did not want to see himself splashed across the front page of the New York Post as "The Man Who Killed Beloved Broadway Legend, Judy Gillette!"

Once he was buzzed in and entered the modest, sterile–looking lobby he heard her distinctive voice calling to him from the stairwell. "The elevator's busted so come up the stairs. Apartment 2C!"

Sure enough, a handwritten Out-of-Order sign was taped to the door of the single elevator, so he sprinted up the stairs to find her standing in the doorway of her apartment, smiling. She was clad in her signature lavender sweat suit and merrily welcomed him.

"Sorry about the elevator. They keep saying the repairman is coming but, so far, nothing! The steps are murder on my bad hip."

T.J. had never noticed her with any infirmity, but assumed that all the wear and tear she would have endured over her many years of dancing would have slowed her down. He'd also made a point of looking up her age and was impressed by how fit she was for sixty-nine.

"You're a real inspiration," he told her. "You never seemed to miss a weekend at Hamp-Fit."

"I can't do what I used to do," she admitted. "The mind is willing, but the body doesn't always cooperate. But I'm a New Yorker so I still pretty much walk everywhere and take a dance class when I work up the nerve."

He couldn't imagine an icon like her being intimidated by anything but he knew all too well the insecurities of being in a New York City dance class alongside professional young chorines at the top of their games.

"Can I get you anything to drink, sweetie? Juice or soda?" she asked maternally.

"No, I'm good, thank you," he answered, opening his bag to pull out his music.

"Maybe after, then. By then it will be after five o'clock and we can enjoy something stronger."

Judy was definitely more like Marti than she was like Dottie. He knew they were going to get along well.

The apartment was as unremarkable as the exterior of the building, rather generic and lacking any of the personal memorabilia that reflected her long and prestigious career. There were no posters or Tony awards in sight and, other than one wall of the large living room mirrored with a ballet barre, there was no indication that this was the home of a great star of the Broadway stage.

Within an hour, Judy was doing both the Running Man and the Melbourne Shuffle, albeit with more shuffling than running. Her talent might have been professionally dormant but all the skills were just beneath the terry cloth, and they popped right out. She had a laser–focus attention span and an innate sense of mimicry and was easily able to follow T.J.'s tutelage.

"By George, I think I've got it!" she said and giggled like a schoolgirl, paraphrasing Professor Higgins' famous line from My Fair Lady.

"You sure as heck do!"

She especially liked the songs from Madonna's Who's That Girl soundtrack, and by the time the wall clock said five p.m., she was winded and plopped herself down on the sofa.

"Judy, you're fantastic."

"Thanks, kid, but it takes me a lot longer to recover than in the old days," she admitted putting her feet up on the ottoman. "And I have to stretch and stretch afterwards. Never my favorite thing."

"Me, either."

"I've tried to get into Yoga, but it's so darned boring to me."

"And hot!" T.J. added, having had his own experiences with it at NYSC.

She held out her hand for him to help her up, saying, "Come on . . . it's Wine O'Clock."

"Twist my arm."

"I have a Louis Latour Chablis that will knock your socks off."

She led him into the adjacent kitchen and, for the first time, he could see how her gait compensated for a sore hip. She could tell he noticed and joked, "I was in Sardi's last week and Max, the manager, saw how I was walking and asked me if I was okay. You know what I told him?"

"What?"

"Too much sex!"

That struck them both as hysterical, especially as it was so out of character for someone with such a wholesome reputation.

Still laughing T.J. asked, "Did he believe you?"

"I assume so," she quipped, "After all, I'm an award winning actress!"

They kept laughing for another hour as she shared more delightful stories from the wonderful world T.J. had been dreaming to enter his entire life.

Judy engaged T.J. for three more private training sessions at her apartment, over the next two weeks. The elevator was eventually fixed but her lavender attire always remained the same. T.J. wondered if she washed it every day or simply had multiple versions of the same outfit.

She also showed him some simple dance steps she thought he could master and incorporate into his classes including tourner, glisser and elancer. In turn, he helped her learn other trendy moves he'd picked up at the clubs and on TV shows like American Bandstand and Soul Train. These included The Robot and The Egyptian, inspired by the Bangles' hit song. Neither of them could figure out Michael Jackson's Moonwalk but had a memorable, laugh-filled afternoon valiantly trying. Her goal, she had decided, was to choreograph an entire routine made up of these "modern" movements and perform it for the Broadway League's annual fundraiser at Lincoln Center. T.J. flushed with pride at the thought of it: a far cry from Sit and Fit at Spa Vitale.

"There's just one more thing I want to try first," she told him.

"What's that?"

"I want to take one of your classes at New York Sports Club. Whichever one is the most popular."

Suddenly petrified, T.J. worried that his Friday night Ultra Impact Groove workout would be far too taxing for Judy, but he couldn't risk modifying it for the fifty gym members who always reserved spaces for the highly coveted class. He warned her that, even though he could get her a guest pass to the club, she would have to sign a standard liability waiver. "It will be an intense seventy-five-minute cardio blast," he finished.

Sounding as if she were wise-cracking a line from one of her stage triumphs, she coquettishly told him, "Bring it on, buster!"

T.J. had told his mother all about his new friendship with Judy and she teased him that she was going to get a complex after all the friendships he'd forged with women old enough to be his mother. With pointed sarcasm to remind her that he was keeping his sexuality under wraps for her and his dad, he merely said, "What can I say, Mom? I'm a real lady's man."

Janice wanted to see her son in action and asked if she could come down to the city and discreetly observe the class from somewhere nearby. When or where else could she see him perform a starring role with Judy Gillette as his backup? Thanks to Bella, he arranged for his mother to sit with her at the Membership desk which overlooked the huge glass-encased aerobics studio.

Judy arrived precisely ten minutes before the class was to start and T.J. was nervously waiting for her at Reception to have her sign the guest waiver and class attendance sheet, fully reserved with fifty spots. She sauntered confidently in, toes out like the great dancer she was, a dance bag slung over one shoulder and sporting her usual lavender sweat suit. If her hip was sore she displayed no sign of it. What a pro, he thought.

As all the Ultra Impact Groovers lined up outside the studio, waiting for T.J. to open the doors, Judy positioned herself at a nearby stationary cycle and started a series of stretches. T.J., Bella and Janice, watching from their spot across the gym floor, were impressed. Her flexibility, as she effortlessly put one leg up on the bike's handlebars and leaned over for a seemingly impossible stretch, was remarkable. She repeated the move on the other side and then stiffened her long legs, knees locked, and touched her toes several time as easily as if she was made of rubber.

"She's amazing," Janice remarked. "I hope I can do that when I'm her age."

"I wish I could do that now," Bella added.

Then, Judy pulled the sweatshirt over her head, managing not to disturb a single jet black hair in the process. Next, she stepped out of the sweatpants and revealed herself standing there in the traditional dancer's attire: a black leotard and tights. The only person in the entire building without sneakers on her feet, she wore black leather Capezio jazz shoes. Her face may have shown the years, but from the neck down Judy was as shapely and lithe as she ever was. T.J. couldn't believe what she had been hiding under her sweats.

Now limbered up and ready to get going, Judy casually leaned against the bicycle, propping her elbows on the handlebars, crossing her feet to accentuate her curvy calves, and shifted her weight onto one hip, presumably her good one. In the process, her splendid bottom stuck out to one side. She was the spitting image of her provocative twenty-something self when she was the toast of the Broadway stage.

Bella gave T.J. a nudge. "It's show time."

Judy hadn't wanted any special treatment or acknowledgment, eager to see if she could prove her fitness capacity to herself without T.J. extending favoritism, so he pretended to ignore her and just entered the room to begin class as he normally would. The young clientele seemed not to recognize Judy so they, too, scurried in to claim and set up their spots. Displaying her dancer mentality and modesty, Judy stuck to the back line.

As the first song, Belinda Carlisle's Heaven is a Place on Earth, blasted, the class got underway. Bella and Janice moved from their places behind the desk to walk over to the windows of the studio and get a closer look.

T.J. was in his element, his outgoing personality on full display while he cued the students and expertly flew through the moves. In the back, after a tentative start, Judy was keeping up and adding a certain jazzy flair to the choreography. All the usual groupies were swept up in the music and the adrenaline rush and were hooting and cheering as the routine progressed.

"He's really very good, isn't he?" Janice asked Bella, impressed by what her son was doing.

"He's the best," Bella admitted. "People love him."

Gym protocol dictated that once you had your spot in an aerobics class, that was where you were fixed, but Judy's theatrical mentality meant that, as she mastered more and more of the steps, she would inch her way further up toward the front line of the class. T.J. noticed, but didn't mind. She was a legend and, as far as he was concerned, she could do whatever she wanted. As long as she didn't drop dead of a heart attack or break a hip, he was fine with it.

About twenty minutes into the class, however, Judy started to show fatigue and drifted back to the rear of the room. As T.J. introduced some speedy new movements to an accelerated remix of the Pet Shop Boys hit, You Were Always On My Mind, she stopped moving altogether, carefully watching the footwork of those around her, studying them to try and catch on to the steps. Ordinarily, an instructor would tell a student to keep moving, even if it was simply to march in place, but he wasn't about to give orders to Judy Gillette.

She finished the class with some modified versions of the movements she couldn't quite master, but by the time they went through the cool down and final stretch, everyone was satisfied with another great class from T.J. Afterwards, she immediately put her sweatshirt back on. T.J. hurried over to congratulate her.

"Judy, you did great." Then, lowering his voice, asked, "How's the hip?"

"Oh, I feel great," she answered gleefully. "It was so much fun. I'll probably pay for it in the morning, but for now . . . wonderful! Do you think I'm ready for the Broadway League?"

"I have no doubt," he said, laughing before they shared a big, sweaty embrace.

Being one of those rare, determined troupers who could manifest her own destiny, Judy called a few days later with some news. She asked T.J. to be her guest for her appearance on New York City's most popular local television program, The Morning Show, hosted by Regis Philbin and Kathie Lee Gifford. She had been asked to go on to promote the League fundraising gala coming up at Christmastime and was planning to show off her new aerobics-inspired dance skills.

Having found a disco remix of the classic Broadway number, If My Friends Could See Me Now, from Sweet Charity, she had conceived her own routine made up of classic moves intermingled with most of the new ones T.J. had taught her. She ran through it a few times with him and he had no notes to give: it was perfect and she was amazing. Not only did she execute every moment with precision and style, she had that unique razzamatazz star quality that made a critic once refer to her as lightning in a bottle. She still had it in abundance and looked amazing in her leotard!

Thrilled to accompany Judy to the Columbus Avenue studio where Regis and Kathie Lee's show was broadcast, T.J. helped her get settled in her dressing room and then a production assistant escorted him to his place in the audience. It was a cheerful atmosphere and he recognized Fred Savage, the little boy from the TV series The Wonder Years, who was also a guest that morning. Being back on a set made him nostalgic for Tomorrow's Promise and he hoped Marti would be tuning in to see Judy's performance. He had alerted all of his inner circle, as well as students and staff from NYSC.

Watching Regis Philbin host the live hour-long show was fascinating for T.J. "Reege" possessed a sophisticated ability to simultaneously banter with his cohost, his guests, the live studio audience and the audience watching from home, all while navigating the cues on the teleprompter and whatever voices were in his earpiece coming from the control room. To so adeptly handle the requisite technical skills in addition to his on screen performance was impressive.

Judy's segment was toward the end of the show and when she was reverently and warmly introduced by Regis, she strode out from the wings in complete command, as if she owned the stage. She looked like a million dollars in a sequined version of her black leotard ensemble and even had some silver glitter sprayed into her hair. T.J. applauded enthusiastically, as did everyone in the audience, regardless of being prompted by the stage manager. She hopped up on a stool alongside the hosts and promoted the fine work of the Broadway League and how excited she was to be participating in their annual holiday fundraiser.

"That's why I wanted to come see you today and give you a sneak peek."

"We can't wait," Regis practically shouted. "Maybe some shimmies and Fosse jazz hands for us?"

"Maybe some. But it's a mix of old and new. I've been learning from my wonderful aerobics instructor, T.J. Porter."

T.J. was surprised and flattered, and he blushed when she pointed at him in the audience, adding, "He's sitting right there so I hope I don't mess up."

The audience laughed and one of the big cameras spun around to zoom in on T.J., who gave a little wave and then a thumbs-up to Judy.

"Ladies and Gentleman, from the Broadway stage to ours . . . Miss Judy Gillette!" Regis announced as he and Kathie Lee stepped off to the side. The music began and Judy seemed to fly off the stool, taking center stage to absolutely nail her two-minute performance. If it had been an Olympics competition, T.J. thought, she'd have scored a perfect ten.

The applause was thunderous and Judy basked in the adoration as it continued right into the commercial break.

The brief but impactful appearance on The Morning Show worked more magic than just being a plug for the Broadway League. By the following week, Judy had received an offer to go to Los Angeles and dance her way through a series of national television commercials for IBM personal computers, and an old agent she'd forgotten even existed reached out to her with a movie audition request from Ron Howard. An unexpected career resuscitation was underway for her and she was grateful to T.J. for the part he played in making it happen. As a thank you, she invited him to lunch at Tavern on the Green.

As they both dove into big Cobb salads, Judy told him all about the ad campaign and a new commercial agent she would be meeting while in Los Angeles. It was scheduled to be a two-week trip, but if she managed to land the part in the Ron Howard film it would be extended.

"Have you ever thought about moving to Hollywood?" she asked, taking him by surprise.

"No, not really. My ambitions have always been for Broadway and the theater," he told her. "I loved being on the soap opera, though."

"You never talk about classes or auditions, so I wasn't sure what your long-term goals are."

If it had been one of his parents saying that, he would have fired back defensively but with Judy, he simply felt embarrassed. "I guess I got sidetracked with the whole aerobics thing."

"You're very good at it," she assured him. "But with that face and your personality, you could and should be doing so much more."

A bit crestfallen, he didn't know what to say.

"Look, honey," she continued, putting her hand on his across the table in a loving gesture, "I am all for being open to surprises, but nothing beats having a plan."

She reached into her purse and pulled out an envelope. She slid it across the table to him.

"When you figure out what that plan is, I want you to use this to help you execute it."

He lifted the flap on the envelope and peeked inside to see a check made out to him for twenty-five hundred dollars. His pride wounded, his first instinct was to refuse it and she immediately recognized how he was feeling.

Cutting him off before he could protest, she explained, "IBM is going to be paying me handsomely, so you have to take it."

"Was this part of your plan?" he asked quietly.

"I knew I had to find something to keep myself professionally relevant. And when I saw you at Hamp-Fit, I came up with the idea." Tapping her index finger on the tablecloth to accentuate her point, she told him, "You earned that. Put it to good use, T.J."

She was right. He hadn't skipped college and moved to Manhattan to become the most popular aerobics instructor at the New York Sports Club.

CHAPTER TWELVE
Next Stop: Hollywood!

At the end of July, 1988, Thomas Porter would be celebrating his sixtieth birthday with family and friends at their country club and as much as T.J. enjoyed his parents, he was dreading having to face all the cousins, neighbors, colleagues and friends. Not only would there be endless questions about the state of his acting pursuits, which had been almost entirely sidelined by his fitness career, but there would be the constant bobbing and weaving over the inquisitions about his love life.

"How are the ladies treating you?"

"So who's your girlfriend these days?"

"Why didn't you bring home a date, T.J.?"

"You must be quite the lady killer. How many are you juggling?"

"Are the women in New York as wild as I hear?"

That sort of thing.

He was complaining about it to Leo, who had finally come out to his own family and suffered through their tears and rage. They cooled considerably when he and Don bought a larger Hamptons house together and invited them all out for a weekend, complete with round-trip car service from Staten Island.

"Continuing to avoid the subject with your folks is a weird courtesy," he told T.J. "Being gay is who you are and it's their problem to handle, not yours."

"I know you're right but they're already disappointed that I'm not on Broadway or starring in a movie. They can't brag about their only child, the queer aerobics instructor. The Richard Simmons comparisons alone would kill them."

"It doesn't have to be some momentous public declaration. Just stop hiding who you are. Besides, anyone important to you has probably already figured it out by now, anyway."

"You think so?"

Leo pointed to the Punk leather spiked wristband T.J. was wearing and answered, "I know so."

"Touché." T.J. chuckled. "Maybe when I meet the right guy, like you did."

Leo shrugged, "You'll find yours, Pally."

T.J. had become a dating machine but had yet to find a special someone. Of course, he was also having tons of sex because he never resisted any opportunity to jump in bed with a willing partner, hoping it might somehow develop into a more romantic relationship. It never did, but if Prince Charming was out there somewhere, he was sure as hell going to enjoy kissing the frogs in the meantime. Bella had taught him to make sure he always tipped the overnight doorman at his apartment building, who witnessed all the comings and goings of T.J.'s many visitors. It was, as she called it, "hush money."

The most recent trio of trysts had all begun with promise and ended disappointingly as sexual duds. Greg, the good looking young med student T.J. had met in Macy's Department Store where he had been working part time as an Elf in Santa Land, made love like a jack rabbit and it always seemed to be over as soon as it began. What was most frustrating was that Greg somehow seemed to think the sex was great.

Erik, the thirty-something tee-totaling Jewish writer from New York Magazine, was nice looking, well spoken and what his Nana would call a natty dresser but unfortunately, he would get overly aroused before their clothes even came off. Sheepish and embarrassed, he would try to hide the damp spots on his slacks with, "Pretty suave, eh?"

T.J. had high hopes (literally) for Dave, who towered over everyone at six-foot-eight, inching out Andrew, the cruise director, for the height record. A happy-go-lucky manager at a hair salon in SoHo, Dave also possessed an anaconda-like phallus that matched his enormous stature. Alas, for all its length and girth, it was forever flaccid, leaving T.J. too frustrated to settle for a sexless or platonic relationship.

Just before he left to catch the train to Connecticut, Marti telephoned with some happy news. The National Academy of Television Arts and Sciences was going to award her an Honorary Emmy for her contributions to the medium of television.

"It's the TV equivalent of a gold watch for a lifetime of service," she joked.

"Marti, that's totally awesome. Don't downplay it. Congratulations!"

"They're flying me out to Hollywood for the Emmy Awards. Wanna be my Plus One?"

"Hell, yeah!" excited, he accepted. "I'm heading out to my parents for the weekend. Can I call you Monday and get all the details?"

"Of course, Presh. I think it will be a good opportunity for both of us."

T.J. couldn't help but think this would make conversations at his dad's birthday festivities a whole lot easier to navigate.

The elder Porter's sixtieth celebrations were held on an overcast but blessedly temperate summer Saturday. Eighteen holes of golf for those who wanted to play were followed by special "Transfusion" cocktails in the clubhouse. These were a colorful blend of vodka, ginger ale and Concord grape and lime juices served over crushed ice. T.J. skipped the golf, but arrived with his mother in time for the first batch of beverages, and he noticed how tame they tasted. He'd obviously grown quite accustomed to a stronger pour.

As soon as he and Janice joined the golfers everyone, predictably, began buzzing around him with questions about his life in Manhattan, both personal and professional. Thanks to Marti, he was armed with the distracting development that he would be heading to the Golden State with beloved TV star Martha Feldon, to escort her to the Emmy Awards.

Of course, this prompted a new angle of interest from the local admirers he'd known his entire life.

"Hollywood! Do you think you'll see any movie stars?"

"Martha Feldon is still alive?"

"You must like older women, eh?"

"Do you think you'll move to L.A.?"

"Maybe you'll be discovered!"

"When are you going to get your Emmy, T.J.?"

"Still no Broadway shows in New York?"

T.J. took one of his parents' Louis Vuitton suitcases home from his visit to use for his trip to the West Coast. He consulted with both Marti and Judy about what he should pack. He would rent a simple black tuxedo when he arrived. Judy encouraged him to include plenty of headshots and resumes in case he could arrange meetings with industry professionals. She followed through with a referral to her commercial agent at the famed William Morris Agency in Beverly Hills and arranged an introduction. When he called Nonnie to sub out his NYSC classes while he'd be away, she urged him to pick up a few Guest Instructor spots at their sister club, Sports Connection, in West Hollywood. It was turning into a real business trip, to his happy surprise.

Marti arranged to cover the cost of their rooms at the Roosevelt Hotel, right across from the famous Mann's Chinese Theater on the Hollywood Walk of Fame. They would be able to see the iconic Hollywood sign on the nearby hillside, even if it was hard to discern through the yellowish haze of smog that hung over the skyline, lower than the omnipresent palm trees.

Using the money he'd saved from Judy's thank-you check, T.J. paid for their rental car, a white Pontiac Grand Prix. It felt strange to be behind the wheel of an automobile again; other than a few trips to the supermarket or country club with his parents, he hadn't really driven since he'd moved to New York City. He was initially daunted by the maze of LA freeways, but traffic moved so slowly there was plenty of time to figure things out. It was evident, however, that he hadn't made a flashy choice with the Pontiac when it seemed like every other vehicle on the road was a Lamborghini, Mercedes, Porsche or Ferrari. He even saw his first

Aston Martin and Bentley while crawling along the 405 Freeway from the airport to the hotel.

Marti marveled at the crush of humanity all around them and had to comment, "It sure is different than when I first came here in the forties."

"You miss New York already?"

"Presh, you're about to find out that, in our business, Hollywood is a necessary evil."

"How long did you live here before you moved to New York?"

Calculating, she answered, "It took me a year to get a contract with Warner Brothers in 1946. Moved to MGM in '48. After landing only some bit parts, I finally packed up and left in 1951. We started the soap not long after I got back to the city." Gazing out at the arid, brown hillsides overlooking the sprawling, mishmash of architecture that comprised the City of Angels, she replied, "Six years. You do less time for Murder."

They laughed together as they inched along the freeway, The Escape Club's hit song, Wild Wild West, was playing on the radio as if to welcome them.

It was after dark by the time they settled in at their hotel and opted for room service burgers in Marti's room. The next day, someone from the TV Academy would be taking her for an afternoon of "beautification," with a wardrobe fitting for her Emmys outfit and a trip to the salon for a manicure, hair cut and color touch up. "I'll be damned if I'll let them make me look like Baby Jane Hudson," she had told T.J., ominously.

He would take the rental car and find his way into Beverly Hills for a morning meeting with Judy's agent, after tamping down his mullet mane of hair and dressing conservatively to match the Yuppie look in his headshot. After that, he would drive on to teach his 12:30 Guest Class. He was anxious to check out the L.A. gym scene and see if it lived up to the glamorized version he vividly remembered from the movie, Perfect. He had stashed a few different clothing options in his gym bag, assuming the attire Travolta sported in the film was probably not an accurate portrayal of what guys actually wore.

Navigating his way down Santa Monica Boulevard to the William Morris Agency was tricky, and T.J. quickly discovered that making a left turn in Los Angeles was only slightly less complicated than advanced trigonometry. Add the ordeal of parallel parking on the restricted side streets of Beverly Hills and it was a miracle that he made it to his appointment on time, self conscious about the perspiration starting to show through his clothes. Even at ten a.m., it was an intensely hot and sunny eighty-five degrees.

The agent, a fit middle-aged man named Murray, wore a tight sharkskin suit and had an almost orange skin tone T.J. assumed was the result of a tanning bed or some kind of makeup. He was cordial enough, but the conversation struck T.J. as perfunctory, sticking mostly to their mutual acquaintance, Judy Gillette. Murray seemed mildly impressed that T.J. was in town with Martha Feldon for the Emmy Awards, even if he had to dig into his memory banks to recall her connection to the industry.

After approximately ten minutes, a phone call came in for Murray that provided him the excuse to wrap up their meeting with a vague promise to T.J. that they should stay in touch if T.J. ever relocated to Los Angeles. Even as they shook hands and said their farewells, T.J. wondered how long his headshot would remain on Murray's desk before it got chucked into the waste basket, which was already stuffed with others.

Making a series of right turns in the Pontiac, T.J. managed to get himself back onto Santa Monica Boulevard and off to the Sports Connection, famously nicknamed, "the Sports Erection," because of the notoriety of its attractive clientele and the reputed sexual shenanigans that went on in the locker and steam rooms.

T.J. wound his way down the underground parking structure of the club and parked on the D level, where it was even hotter. Anxious for the cool comfort of air conditioning, he got into the elevator, deflated that he would be unable to cut an impressive figure upon entering. Sweat was coming out of every pore and his shirt was soaked through.

He tried to reassure himself that, not only was he the Guest Star, but this was no different than a Broadway audition or walking into a popular nightclub: an entrance, was an entrance. He stiffened his spine, raised his chin and strutted into the reception area across from the parking elevator. Loud dance music was playing as metallic sounds coming from weight machines reverberated everywhere. The place was bathed in shades of pink and turquoise blue, thanks to the ubiquitous neon lights and, even at barely noon, the place was mobbed with "beautiful people."

The nice thing about the New York fitness world was that it was welcoming to athletes of all skill levels, as well as different shapes and sizes. It was, after all, a city known as a melting pot, but it was immediately obvious that things were different in Tinseltown. Every man and woman in sight was model-gorgeous, impeccably coiffed and decked out as if they were on some kind of gymnasium cat walk. No one appeared to be older than thirty.

T.J.'s jaunty posture quickly collapsed in on itself and he felt like he was schlepping toward the reception desk. He had always been one of the best-looking guys in any room he entered, but this was an entirely new level of pulchritude. He tried not to let his insecurity show as he introduced himself to the pretty young woman working at the front desk.

Looking and speaking like the stereotypical Valley Girl, she welcomed T.J. to the Sports Connection and gave him a towel and a locker key before pointing out where the aerobics studio was located. She boosted his ego significantly when she informed him that his class was already fully booked in advance, as people were eager to see what kind of style he would be bringing from Manhattan.

The men's locker room was predictably cruise'y and T.J. managed to hide himself at a corner locker and avoid eye contact with all the buff, blond beefcake loitering around, scantily clad and looking for trouble. As game for adventure as he usually was, T.J. was not about to get sidetracked by one of these he-men. At least not until after he taught his class.

He entered the large, brightly lit, mirrored studio and was impressed with its proscenium stage set up for the instructor. Scores of smiling faces, mostly female, were already taking their spaces and spontaneously gave T.J. a cheer when he entered the room, instantly lifting his spirits and confidence. As soon as he popped his tape into the cassette player and the first bars of Paula Abdul's Straight Up came through the speakers, he was off and running.

It was a tremendous success and T.J.'s music, moves and personality all came together to provide an energetic and entertaining hour-long workout. At the end of class, after the final stretch, he let them know he'd be back in a couple days for one more guest class before returning to New York. That prompted a round of applause. He hung back for several minutes to meet and greet his students, many of whom were British flight attendants staying at the hotel next door for their L.A. layovers.

He was on such a high during the ride back to the hotel, he hardly noticed the bumper to bumper traffic. With the time difference to the East Coast, he doubted he would be able to reach Leo or Bella, so he called Carolyn Lee to share his experiences so far.

She answered so quickly T.J. almost didn't hear the ring. She spoke in a whisper, her mouth obviously close against the receiver, and she sounded shaken.

"Sweetie, it's T.J. Are you okay?"

"Thank God, it's you," she said breathlessly. "I've locked myself in the nursery with Jaclyn."

"What's happening?"

"Gary's on a rampage. He came home drunk and pissed off about something, then started throwing things."

"Oh, for fuck's sake! Call 911."

"It would be all over the papers by morning. Or worse, on TV. It's been quiet out there the last ten minutes. I think he must have passed out or left."

"Where's Therese?"

"She went home at five."

"You cannot live this way," he stated, unsure of what else he could say to support her.

"To tell you the truth, I prefer sleeping in here anyway. I do, most nights. There's a day bed and I can be with the baby."

God, he thought, if people only knew that this high-profile Manhattan "Power Couple" were living a Jekyll and Hyde existence. As his mother would derisively comment about such husbands, "Street angel, house devil."

"Don't worry about me," she said unconvincingly. "Tell me about Los Angeles."

They chatted for a long while and it comforted both of them.

***

Sunday's 40th Annual Emmy Awards show was held at the Pasadena Convention Center. The weather remained hot and humid but unexpected fog and drizzle had rolled into the area, so giant plastic tarps were erected around the venue, baking the assembled media scrum and attendees in a sticky, terrarium-like atmosphere. Traffic around town was especially congested as Angelenos, even on a weekend, seemed to be challenged by driving in wet weather. The Academy had sent a town car to collect Marti and T.J., who made a dynamic duo in their formal attire. Marti looked every inch a star in her black and burgundy brocade jacket over a simple black pantsuit. Elegant diamond earrings with a matching bracelet added some glitz, as well as a charming little silk flower clipped into her freshly reddened hair. T.J. kept himself simple in the classic Calvin Klein tuxedo he'd rented with a red bow tie as the only splash of color, which ended up complimenting Marti's color choices. Even with the humidity, he was having a good hair day with his locks blow dried high. He could have passed for the brother of the actor John Stamos, whose sitcom, Full House, was a new TV hit.

Arriving to the red carpet earlier than most of the A-Listers, T.J. was still a bit star struck by all the faces he recognized from the small screen. Cast members from shows like Family Ties, Night Court, LA Law and Cheers were milling around, chatting with journalists and posing for photographers. While they may not have possessed the same glamour as younger celebrities, T.J. thought that just seeing Hume Cronyn and Jessica Tandy, who were also Broadway legends, made the entire trip worthwhile.

Their seats were midway, left of center, toward the back of the Convention Center arena. It was arranged that, when it was time for Marti to receive her award, she would be ushered backstage during a commercial break so she could enter from there. T.J. would remain in the audience with a "seat-filler" momentarily taking Marti's place.

When her big moment came, Marti kept her speech short and heartfelt, knowing that most people watching probably had no idea who she was or had long forgotten her.

"What I appreciate is that this is an Achievement award," she said with all the humility of her long-running soap character, Hope. "It's often easier to recognize shortcomings in others before seeing them in ourselves. In an industry such as ours, with such high standards and a fickle nature, achievement is only possible through tenacity and the ability to . . . if at first you don't succeed, try, try again. Thank you for acknowledging my efforts."

For her "lifetime achievements and contributions in the medium of daytime television," Marti received a rousing round of applause, making T.J. feel truly proud and happy for their close friendship. He clapped so hard that it stung his hands. Even when Bea Arthur won Outstanding Actress in a Comedy Series for The Golden Girls, it seemed like an anticlimax.

The following day, their last in Los Angeles before the Red-Eye flight back to New York, Marti was going to treat herself to an afternoon in the hotel spa while T.J. returned to the Sports Connection for one more guest class. It would be one of his unique Step Aerobics power workouts that combined the bench moves with dance.

After another dynamic cardiovascular performance, T.J. lingered behind to meet and greet the admiring students after they disassembled and stored their step platforms.

"That was great. Where did you find those music mixes?"

"You should do a seminar for our instructors. We need classes like yours!"

"Do you have to go back? You should move to LA."

A cluster of three fit young women stood off to the side and waited for him to finish greeting everyone else before approaching. One with dark curly hair and—certainly by Hollywood standards—very pale skin, spoke first. She had a British accent and a broad, winning smile.

"I'm Elaine and these are my friends, Pam and Carly."

"Nice to meet you. Are you all from the U.K.?"

"Yes. The girls are air hostesses with British Airways. Their hotel is down the road."

"I fly back to New York tonight," he told them. "I teach at the New York Sports Club if you ever get to town."

Elaine put down her gym bag and started fishing through it for her wallet as she explained, "I'm a correspondent for the national breakfast show back in the U.K. We don't have any classes like yours and I thought it might make an interesting segment for us, if you'd be interested."

She retrieved a business card from her wallet and handed it to him. Delighted, he answered, "I would definitely be interested. Thank you, Elaine." The card identified her as "Elaine Worth, Presenter/Producer, Breakfast News."

Elaine moved past him with a little beckoning of her hand, dropping her voice in a secretive fashion. "May I have a word?"

He followed her to the side of the room.

"I'm good friends with many of the fitness and dance studio owners in London,"she began.

"I'm not surprised. You're in great shape and you kept up with all the choreography."

"I could arrange for you to do some guest classes as you've done here, but there might be a bigger story that would benefit both of us."

"A story? How big?"

"Massive," she whispered in reply. "You could say, positively royal."

Winging their way home on the overnight flight to JFK, T.J. recounted to Marti what few details he had so far. In addition to being a producer and on-air personality for the British morning show, Elaine Worth was a fitness fan who was well connected to sports venues there, including the exclusive private gym used by Diana, Princess of Wales. The beloved Diana was known for her affinity for exercise and dance and Elaine, after seeing T.J. in action, was confident she could convince her royal connections to have him give Her Highness private instruction with his signature style.

Marti was impressed. "My goodness, Judy Gillette is one thing—but Princess Di!"

"I know!"

"I hope you said yes."

"Of course I said yes. That crazy plastic step is opening doors for me my singing and acting never did."

"You never know where opportunity lies. If I hadn't failed in movies and taken a chance on that new-fangled thing called a soap opera, I'd probably still be back in Podunk, Oklahoma."

"And if you hadn't invited me to join you for this trip, this wouldn't have happened. So, thank you, thank you." He reached over the seat divider and gave her a hug.

Patting him as they embraced she said, "You're welcome. But we make our own luck, Presh."

CHAPTER THIRTEEN

A Workout to (Princess) Di For

To welcome 1989, the four friends gathered for their traditional New Year's Eve dinner at Windows on the World at six p.m., earlier than usual. It was because of the two "guest stars."

"Do we get to order the Early Bird Special?" Bella asked, dryly.

"Seriously," Leo agreed. "When did we go from being the Denver Carringtons to the Golden Girls?"

Carolyn Lee handed the baby over to Therese so she could grab her glass of Prosecco, excited to indulge in a rare cocktail. "Sorry, guys, it's my fault. I didn't want to leave Jac-lyn tonight."

Taking a sip of his martini, T.J. stated, "She's the only person under twenty-one in the whole place. Might as well start 'em, early."

Jaclyn started to gurgle and fuss and Bella couldn't help releasing a heavy, irritated sigh. Children and pets had never held any charm for her.

"I'll take her," Therese offered, standing up to take the restless child for a walk away from the adults.

"Thank you, Therese," Carolyn Lee said, truly grateful.

As soon as they'd stepped away, Bella asked, "Is the plan to ring in the European New Year tonight?"

Trying to keep the peace, T.J. jumped in, "Oh, it's fine. Being so early we got a great table and we can finish dinner here and then go watch the fireworks from Leo's new rooftop."

In addition to the Hamptons house, Leo and Don had purchased their co-op on Central Park West, taking full advantage of their ample combined incomes now that Leo had been promoted to hedge fund manager at a small, but profitable investment firm.

Leaning in to emphasize the delicacy of her situation, Carolyn Lee explained, "The truth is, I want to avoid Gary as long as possible. He'll be with Mayor Koch until God knows what hour and in God knows what condition."

T.J. knew she was still sleeping on the nursery daybed, most nights. "Have you considered finally getting your own place?" he asked. "You don't have to get a divorce, but wouldn't an informal separation be a big improvement?"

Finishing off her drink, she answered, "Not gonna happen, at least until Koch leaves office. With any luck that will be in the New Year. I don't think he can win another primary."

"Then what would happen to Gary?" Leo asked.

She shrugged as if to say who cares, then held up her empty glass to signal the waiter for a refill. "Maybe then I'll go back to the bedroom."

The others were surprised by her candor. Carolyn Lee wasn't one to share too much personal information. After she received more Prosecco, she added, "For now, I'm averaging about one rage fuck a month."

After a moment of stunned silence from everyone, Bella offered, "Honey, a rage fuck isn't something couples do. There's another name for that."

Carolyn Lee waved her off and asked, brightly, "What did everyone get for Christmas?"

Changing the subject seemed like a good idea, so Leo went first.

"Everything was home-related. Towels, sheets, appliances, cookware—"

"If only you could get legally married," T.J. said, "then you could have a registry."

"Not worth it," Carolyn Lee interjected. "You can buy your own toaster."

Bella decided to go next and keep the temperature down.

"My parents teamed up and bought me a long weekend at Hazelden. We're calling it a tune up. I leave next Thursday."

"You got a trip to Rehab? For Christmas?" T.J. asked in amazement.

"It's officially classified as a Retreat. Meditation classes, campfires and hikes along a wooded tranquility trail. That sort of thing."

"How bucolic," Carolyn Lee observed with sarcasm.

"Five-star all the way. Without the cocktails."

"Abstinence in style," Leo piped in.

"Who said anything about abstinence? I did one last summer and got pegged by a gorgeous Israeli recovering from a cocaine overdose. The guys are always hot and horny as hell since they can't use any substances."

"I'd love a good pounding on a wooded tranquility trail," Leo admitted.

"Except for the tick bites," Bella warned.

"What about you, T.J.?" Carolyn Lee asked. "Was Santa good to you?"

Eyeballing the jumbo shrimp cocktail that had just been placed before him, he nodded and told them, "After I borrowed their Louis Vuitton suitcase for my L.A. trip, they bought me my own set."

"Nice!" Leo enthused.

"Maybe you can lend me one for my retreat?" asked Bella.

"Anything for you, sweetie."

It hit T.J. that he'd been privileged enough to always receive thoughtful and extravagant gifts for all occasions from his loving parents, yet for all their affluence and affection the two things they couldn't give him were the two things he craved the most: acceptance of his sexual orientation and a career. In those areas, he was forging his own way.

As if reading T.J.'s mind, which Leo often seemed to do, he inquired, "Any news on Princess Diana's Step Class?"

T.J. took a big bite of shrimp, slathered with the tangy cocktail sauce, and answered, "The last I heard from the producer in London was that Her Royal Highness will be coming to New York in February and someone will be vetting me then."

"Oh, how exciting!" Carolyn Lee nearly squealed with zeal. "I love her so much. I read that it will be the first trip she's making without Prince Charles."

"He is such a pill," Bella weighed in. "I bet she can't wait."

The twenty-seven-year-old Diana was the most famous and glamorous woman in the world and even the most jaded city slickers were excited about the prospect of having her in Manhattan, if only for a three-day visit. As one admirer had told the local press, "If they don't want her in England, we'd love to have her here." Everyone was clamoring to snag tickets for her charity event and gala reception at the Brooklyn Academy of Music. But, even at two thousand dollars per ticket, it had already sold out.

"I wonder what the vetting criteria will be," Carolyn Lee mused.

"I bet there will be a urine test involved," said Bella. "No drugs for at least a week before."

Therese returned to the table, having worked her magic: Jaclyn was fast asleep in her arms, in spite of the noisy clamor of the room as more diners arrived to begin their countdown festivities. As the nanny took her seat beside Carolyn Lee, T.J. raised his nearly empty martini glass to salute his friends.

"To the family we have created for ourselves," he toasted. "And the traditions we continue together."

He had no way of knowing this celebration would be their penultimate New Year's Eve together.

***

It did not seem possible that Diana's star could shine any brighter, but her solo trip to Manhattan in February of 1989 seemed to seal her position in the celebrity stratosphere, eclipsing any other member of the royal family, let alone movie or music star. Hitting all the right notes, and looking impossibly glamorous while doing so, she pulled at the heartstrings of the most cynical and skeptical when she visited Harlem Hospital to meet AIDS patients, even greeting them with affectionate handshakes and embraces. Also on her itinerary was the Henry Street Settlement where she interacted closely with women who had experienced homelessness and domestic violence.

The usually catty and critical New York tabloids were similarly smitten and her love affair with the Big Apple was splashed on the cover of every paper and magazine, and led every newscast for the days before and after her arrival. Commemorative T shirts, hats, buttons and Union Jack flags were hawked on street corners and Diana Fever gripped the City.

A few hours before the Princess' flight had touched down at JFK, T.J. received the call from Elaine he had been anticipating for months. She informed him that, while Diana's packed schedule did not allow for any recreational or fitness breaks, one of her secretaries wanted to meet briefly with T.J. at the Carlyle Hotel for an informal conversation about what would be expected of him if the London visit and Step Training instruction were to eventuate.

Like an expectant parent waiting to rush to the delivery room, T.J. was packed and prepped for the moment to come and he agreed to meet Mister Giles Morton outside the Carlyle's sophisticated piano bar, Bemelman's, at three in the afternoon. He thanked Elaine profusely and she told him she hoped it would all work out. Regardless, whenever he could make it to London, she would be happy to arrange for him to teach some guest classes and treat him to a meal somewhere fun.

It took longer for T.J. to get to the Upper East Side hotel than the meeting itself, which lasted about five minutes. Giles Morton could have played the British butler in any Agatha Christie play, T.J. thought, when he met thc gray-haired and gaunt gentleman at three p.m. precisely.

"Miss Worth had stellar things to say about your gymnastic prowess," he told T.J. "So as long as you are willing to sign confidentiality and liability forms, we can arrange the details for your visit once we finish this trip."

"Sure," he quickly responded, realizing how over eager he sounded. He took a quick breath and affected a calmer demeanor. "I mean, certainly."

"We will also arrange for you to receive a document outlining all the requisite protocol you are expected to follow."

"Certainly," he repeated. He couldn't help but add, "I'm a quick study."

"I presume your passport is valid?"

"Yes, sir."

Mr. Morton extended his hand for a stiff handshake, signing off with, "You will be hearing from our office soon. Good afternoon, Mr. Porter."

"Good afternoon, Mr. Morton. Please give my best to the Princess."

Derisively, Morton sniffed, paused a moment and then said, "Yes," before turning and walking out of the room.

T.J. used the days that followed to tinker with his classes, experimenting with some new moves and music while refining others, trying to tailor something special for Her Majesty.

Meanwhile, Diana continued to wow the adoring American crowds and finished up her visit with a splashy appearance at the Academy of Music event. She shone like a beacon in the sea of black-tied attendees when she emerged from her limousine in an ivory sequined gown by Victor Edelstein. Afterwards, she showed no signs of fatigue as she was whisked to a seated dinner for eight hundred fifty guests at the Winter Garden. Mayor Koch was, unsurprisingly, in attendance but Gary was not on the Guest List.

A fortnight after her departure, Diana was still on T.J.'s mind as an opportunity he did not want to let slip by. He got Elaine an expensive thank-you card from Papyrus and mailed it off in appreciation for introducing him to Giles Morton, and in it casually inquired if he had passed muster during their brief interview at the Carlyle. Patience never being one of his strengths, he continued to check his answering machine several times a day in case he received a message from "across the pond."

Finally, in early March, her call came when he happened to be home between finishing classes and meeting Leo and Don for dinner at Chef Charlie Palmer's new Aureole, a well reviewed and unpretentious eatery on East 61st Street. Her elegant accent came over the line as crystal clear as if they were in the same room.

"T.J., it's Elaine here. Sorry for taking so long to get back to you. And thank you for the lovely card."

"No problem," he said, trying to sound blasé.

"Always busy and I'm heading back to LA in the morning. I wish it were New York, instead. I could use one of your brilliant workouts."

"Next time," he cajoled, then couldn't help but inquire, "Any word from Highgrove House?" He was referring to the royal residence that Diana and her husband famously called home.

"Yes, well, it's good news and bad news, I'm afraid."

T.J. always hated when those two types of news were lumped together. It seemed like the "bad" always eclipsed the "good," so it didn't matter in which order they were served up. In fact, the good news was usually some kind of consolation prize.

As if tossing a coin, he suggested, "How about the bad news, first?"

"The bad news is that the Palace won't approve having you privately instruct the Princess, even though when it was presented to her, she was very keen..."

They'd told Diana about him? And she wanted to work with him? This greatly heartened T.J.

"However," Elaine continued, "her own personal trainer at the private facility where they exercise was very enthusiastic about you coming to offer some training to her staff. I can also arrange for you to conduct some guest classes at the top studios in London. Fitness First and Pineapple are really popular."

It was disappointing, but not bad news, after all. Especially when Elaine gave him further information.

"I've told our producers here that, if you are in London, I'd like to do a week-long series on the morning show where you demonstrate some user-friendly exercise routines that the viewers can do at home. We would, of course, pay for your hotel and airfare. And all the gyms would pay you individually for whatever classes you teach."

And there was the good news! Getting paid for a week on their national morning program, further exposure in the international fitness world and private time to schmooze with Diana's personal fitness staff all sounded like tremendous opportunities.

Without hesitation, T.J. told her, "I'm in. Let's work out details."

"Great. Leave it with me to sort out the dates and itinerary and I'll get back to you after my L.A. trip in a week or two. Sound good?"

"Sounds great!"

This development really gave Thomas and Janice Porter bragging rights at their country club. After beginning with Dottie O'Hara, then Martha Feldon and on to Judy Gillette, now they could name-drop that the Princess of Wales was only a single degree of separation from their cherished son. To hear them boast, one could almost believe these affiliations were even romantic in nature.

Of course, no one was immune to Diana's magical star power and T.J.'s upcoming trip to London only served to increase his popularity and profile within the New York Sports Club and among his own friends. Don was warmer than usual and even Gary, according to Carolyn Lee, had mentioned that they "all had to get together for dinner" upon T.J.'s return from his royal assignment. T.J. was in no rush to put that in his Filofax planner.

What she had neglected to mention, though, is that Gary's late night conjugal "raids" were becoming more frequent and he was starting to develop a desire for forced intimacy with his wife. Like her previous eating disorder, prior to leaving her TV news position, Carolyn Lee was becoming an expert on keeping her private struggles under wraps, even if that now meant covering up marks and bruises and taking occasional painkillers to dull the subsequent discomfort.

The night before T.J.'s departure, Leo came over to help supervise his packing. It was mid-May, the perfect season to visit London, and Leo wanted to help make sure his Pally would be looking his best for the television cameras, aerobics students and any royalty he might encounter. He also brought along a bottle of Stag's Leap chardonnay and a large meatball pizza, contending that it would be T.J.'s last chance to indulge in junk food for a while. He also gave him a stern warning against being seen smoking since "those British tabloids make Page Six look like the New Testament."

T.J. considered himself a disciplined individual, but he had never worked as hard as he would from the moment he touched down at Heathrow Airport. "Hitting the ground running" was literal, as he was met by a baby-faced production assistant named Aidan, whom Elaine had charged with shepherding T.J. around to his appointed duties. They practically jogged out of the airport to a waiting car that whisked them as fast as traffic would allow to the massive News Breakfast television studio. It was more like a university campus than the rag-tag TV facility he had known in Manhattan. T.J. looked around in wonderment as Aidan escorted him to a changing room where he was to don his fitness attire and pre-record some promotional spots for the appearances coming up in the week ahead.

Aidan was an adorable pretty boy, tall and thin, with fair skin and apple red cheeks. T.J. doubted he had ever had use for a razor.

"Is there somewhere I can get a shower first?" T.J. asked as Aidan hoisted one of the Louis Vuitton bags onto a side table.

"No time, mate," was the reply.

Before he knew it, T.J. was standing in front of a green screen joined by some other staffers who circled around him. A Reebok Step was placed before him with three tiers of risers. He glanced up to an overhead monitor and could see himself as the camera saw him, but instead of the green background, a flashy, animated image of a health club was being projected.

"Just read off the Auto-Cue, mate," Aidan instructed. "There are five spots in all, one for each day next week."

This was a very different style of television from what he'd known at Tomorrow's Promise, but T.J. was game for anything. After an unseen voice called "Monday teaser. Action!" he did the first spot in two takes.

"Great, T.J." the voice said, then, "Tuesday teaser. Action!"

Looking at the teleprompter, he saw the next line and perfectly executed his delivery with enthusiasm and confident professionalism. "I'm T.J. Porter and I'll make Tuesday your Good News Day."

And so it went until he reached Friday, nailing all the rest in quick, one-take succession.

"Cut and Wrap!"

"He's a one-take wonder," he heard someone say.

Aidan guided T.J. by the arm and led him hurriedly back to the changing room where they retrieved his bags and returned to the car waiting for them outside, which whisked them to the Cumberland Hotel, where he would be staying. He tried to use the half-hour ride to catch some of the city sights speeding by, but Aidan was briefing him on his schedule. The weekend would be spent guest-teaching the classes arranged by Elaine and on Monday, a car would retrieve him from the hotel for his first on-air appearance and in the afternoon, he would be taken to the Princess' fitness facility to conduct a Master Class in Step for the staff.

The Cumberland was an aging but lovely hotel, just off Hyde Park and the Marble Arch. The room was very basic, with a full sized bed, small closet and single nightstand with three drawers. T.J. was desperate for a shower and, as soon as Aidan left his side, he luxuriated in one for fifteen minutes before he heard a hard knock on his door. It suddenly occurred to him how famished he felt. Other than a bad meal on the flight, he hadn't eaten anything since Leo's meatball pizza.

Turning off the shower and stepping out of the old fashioned tub, he called out "Just a minute," then grabbed a scratchy cotton hotel robe and threw it on.

He opened the door to see a breathtaking young man in the Cumberland housekeeping uniform, smiling as he held a large stack of fresh towels.

Speaking with a thick Italian accent, the curly haired, olive skinned beauty apologetically said, "We did not get the chance to bring fresh towels, sir." He held them out and T.J. was instantly intoxicated by his green eyes and charming, crooked smile.

"Thank you," he managed to reply and as he extended his hands to take the linens, he was so besotted he didn't realize his robe was wide open.

The young man noticed, though, and smiled even more broadly as he blushed. It was obvious to him that this hotel guest was not only exposed, but aroused.

"Anytime I may be of service, sir . . ."

At that exact moment, with his hands full, T.J. swung away to toss the towels on the bed and tie up his robe.

"Sorry about that," he said, although not really too sorry.

"No worries," the housekeeper assured him. He stepped across the threshold to the room and asked, "Would you like me to turn down the bed?"

Bewitched by this sexy Florentine who had walked into his room, T.J. turned back to face him. Even though the robe was now tied, his rigidity was blatantly obvious and the two men moved together into a wordless embrace. Moments later, the robe and the housekeeper's uniform were on the floor and their bodies were tangled together on the bed. T.J. never got his name, but he was impressed by the Cumberland's excellent service, so far.

Exhilarated by the anonymous encounter that kicked off his stay, T.J. jumped into his class assignments with energy and enthusiasm, much to the delight of his British students. He finished the classes by telling them all to tune in to the Morning News program for his daily fitness reports the following week. Elaine showed up to participate in the Saturday Step class and made sure word got around that T.J. would be at Princess Diana's gym and that this had been a preview of what she could expect to be learning, herself.

As she predicted, planting that tidbit of information resulted in a blurb in the next morning's widely read Sunday Daily Mirror. "U.S. fitness guru T.J. Porter is visiting London to help the Princess keep her trim and toned figure thanks to his very latest, high energy exercise trends from the sunny shores of Hollywood. He will also be appearing on Morning News live all week, giving us a reason to wake up early." T.J. was delighted when Elaine showed him the paper, even if they had mistaken one American city for the other.

"The Brits love anything with the word Hollywood in it," she explained.

T.J. loved being on the set of the morning program and received the VIP treatment from the moment Aidan walked him in at 5:45, directly to the Makeup Room. It seemed as if everyone had seen the newspaper item and treated him like a visiting celebrity. It couldn't have been further from the invisibility he often felt when being an Under Five character on the soap.

The show hosts were an over-the-top duo who seemed like Saturday Night Live caricatures. "Trudy and Dicko" welcomed T.J. warmly and with exaggerated, fanatical admiration, seeming to hang on his every word about the health benefits of the Step workouts and how he parlayed his own career in American television into one that led him practically to the steps of Kensington Palace.

It took no time at all for him to find his groove on live television, comfortably conversing with ease and humor and making sure to drop lots of celebrity names—Jane Fonda, John Travolta and even Judy Gillette—instinctively realizing that Elaine was right: the audience ate up anything showbiz related.

When it came time to demonstrate a Step routine, he did it with more razzle-dazzle than NYSC's Steve, Pam and Nonnie, combined. To the throbbing pulse of the new hit Technotronic song Pump Up the Jam, his moves looked muscular but fluid, dance-like but uncomplicated. Trudy and Dicko were milking it for all the comic relief they could, trying to emulate the moves from the sidelines and even the nearby Weather Woman and Sportscaster got into the action. They were all having so much fun hamming it up that the director couldn't wrap them, opting instead just to fade to the commercial break.

The music came to a halt, so T.J. did, too and they realized it was time to reposition for the upcoming post-commercial spots. Everyone was effusive in their praise for T.J.'s lively jolt of fun and exuberance.

"We can't wait to see what you have for us tomorrow," Dicko said, giving him a chummy slap on the back.

"Welcome to the show, darling," added Trudy as she hurried back to the anchor desk for a quick touch up.

Aidan seemed to magically appear beside T.J. to hurry him off the set as some stage hands rushed in to dismantle the Step bench.

"What do we do tomorrow?" T.J. asked Aidan as they moved quickly across the soundstage.

"Don't worry about that now. We have to get to the Harbour Club."

The Chelsea Harbour Club was Princess Diana's favorite workout facility with luxury amenities and multiple dance fitness studios in addition to tennis courts, a pool and spa. She had gone so far as to sue the gym she had previously frequented after discovering that someone had been photographing her there and selling the pictures to the tabloids. Not surprisingly, when T.J. arrived with Aidan, they went through a thorough security check, including a pat down, before they could enter. Still in his Lycra shorts, T.J. wondered what they thought he could possibly be hiding. Maybe the guard just wanted a cheap thrill. T.J. was so enthralled by the whole experience that he didn't mind.

A club manager took them to the cafe where they could wait and enjoy some yogurt or juice before the training session. T.J. was too nervous to have anything, other than some sparkling water. Was Diana on her way now? It occurred to him that nowhere in any of the protocol documents he'd been given was there any mention of formalities such as bowing, or how to address her. Could they shake hands? What if she started doing a particular move incorrectly or, God forbid, unsafely? Would he be permitted to correct her?

Eventually, a fresh faced and very fit young South African woman named Jen arrived to introduce herself as Diana's personal trainer. She explained that Diana would be unable to join them today, but she herself would be taking T.J.'s class along with the rest of the Harbour Club aerobics staff. Later, she would meet the Princess at Kensington Gardens to demonstrate some of what she'd learned.

T.J. was momentarily disappointed until he saw a cluster of photographers and reporters being led through by the manager.

Jen indicated them and told T.J., "Some very curious members of the press would like to observe as well. Everyone's interested in the Princess' new workout. Do you mind?"

T.J. beamed. "Not at all."

The Master Class went off without a hitch and by the time it was all over, including some interviews with several members of the press, T.J. was exhausted. He also realized he hadn't eaten all day. No wonder he was lightheaded.

Out of nowhere, the amazing Aidan handed him a cheese sandwich wrapped in cellophane, and a bag of crisps. He was also holding on to some bottled water. "You can eat these in the car."

It was back to the Cumberland in advance of another early start the next day and so it would go for the remainder of the week. Every morning, the show had him appearing live from a different location demonstrating a particular exercise and every afternoon, he was instructing a Master Class and giving interviews. He quickly became adept at giving pithy sound bites and celebrity name-dropping ("Heather Locklear's buttocks are literally sculpted by these exercises." And, "Jean-Claude Van Damme's cardiovascular strength doesn't come from a weight machine.").

The producers had him all over London, interacting with fans of the show. He reinvented the Sit & Fit routine from Spa Vitale when he visited a nursing home filled with pensioners. In an East End market stall, he engaged the Cockney codgers in some squats and lunges. Balancing a Step on a floating stage in the Thames River was a challenge, but he played it off to great comic effect. By the time the week ended, T.J. had been liberally peppered throughout all the daily papers and interviewed on several radio stations. Princess Diana had helped him immeasurably, without their ever meeting.

One paper had nicknamed him "Our American Step-Brother" and other outlets ran with it, too. Even at the end of Friday's show, as the hosts were signing off, Dicko improvised, "I hate to have to say goodbye," to which Trudy added, "Don't let our American Step-Brother go home!"

Friday night, Elaine treated T.J. to dinner at the famous and exclusive Groucho Club, a notorious private refuge for media and arts professionals. It was bustling, cramped and very bohemian. This was the first chance, T.J. thought, he'd had to catch his breath all week and he would be flying back home on Sunday morning.

"I can't thank you enough for this week, T.J. You were bloody brilliant. Everybody loved you."

Grateful to finally have a martini in his hands, he took a sip of his beloved Beefeater gin and said, "I should be thanking you. All these wonderful opportunities. And it was fun."

"I'm sorry it didn't work out with the Princess, but I was assured that she now loves Step aerobics."

"Maybe next time, she can give me a class."

"I'm sure there will be a next time. All of the Clubs would love to have you back, anytime."

"That would be fun. I really enjoyed doing the morning show, most of all." He thought of Regis Philbin hosting his show back in New York, and the masterful way he multitasked to utilize all his various skills and talents.

"I wanted to ask you about that," she began, leaning in to make sure she could be heard over the ambient noise and clamor of their surroundings. "Everyone loved you. Even Trudy and Dicko, which is no easy feat."

He laughed. "They were good sports."

"I'm going to talk to our executive producer next week. If I can convince him to give you a regular spot, even if it's just weekly, would you be interested? Paid, of course."

T.J. downed the last of his cocktail and decided not to try and play it cool. "Abso-bloody-lutely!"

"Leave it with me and I'll see what I can do."

A waiter appeared to scoop up T.J.'s empty glass and did a double take upon seeing him.

"You're the American Step-Brother, aren't you?" he asked.

"I guess I am," he answered, surprised and flattered.

"Next round is on me."

T.J. thanked him and then noticed an attractive older gentleman across the room, sitting at the bar, looking at him with recognition and a not-so-subtle appreciation. He was heavy set but sturdy in an expensive-looking, tailored pinstripe suit and sporting a neatly trimmed dark gray mustache and beard.

Elaine immediately noticed the two of them eyeing each other and reached across the table to touch T.J.'s hand and get his attention.

"Oops, you caught me," he said. "Maybe he knows me, too. Or just wants to get to know me."

"Probably both. That's Rodney Dean, the Publishing magnate. And notorious Lothario."

"And strangely sexy."

"He lives in Edinburgh but stays here whenever he's in London. There isn't a mammal with a pulse he wouldn't sleep with."

T.J. gave her a sly grin. "My resting heart rate is forty beats per minute."

Midway through their meal of beer-battered haddock with mushy peas and hand-cut chips, the admiring waiter returned to ask them, "The gentleman at the bar asked if he could send you both a round of drinks."

T.J. and Elaine looked across to the bar, where Rodney Dean was sipping on a cocktail and still keeping an eye on them. He smiled and gave them a nod in greeting.

"I'm fine, thank you," said Elaine.

Gin-fueled, T.J. kept his eyes fixed on Rodney but said to the waiter, "I'll have a Beefeater and Tonic, thank you. And please tell Mr. Dean, I'd like to return the favor after dinner if he's still at the bar."

"Yes, sir."

Elaine was impressed. "Your star is obviously on the rise, Mr. Porter."

The rest of the evening was pretty much a blur to T.J., when he woke up in the morning beside Rodney in his room upstairs at the Groucho. After rising so early every day that week, it was no surprise that his eyes flew open as soon as the first rays of sun poked between the curtains of the small, attic-like room.

He remembered hugging Elaine goodbye after dinner and telling her he would grab a taxi back to the hotel. Then he joined

Rodney at the bar for a nightcap and the last thing he recalled was a seemingly endless set of narrow, steep stairs to climb up to the room. Both men were still wearing their underwear, so T.J. knew nothing more had happened than some necking or heavy petting before they passed out.

Looking at Rodney sound asleep, his heavy, hirsute frame moving up and down with his breath, T.J. thought about how much more attractive he had been in the dark light of the bar, dressed in his Savile Row. It was time to make a quick escape and slip quietly out.

But as soon as he threw on his shirt and started to pull on his pants, T.J. heard Rodney murmuring from the bed in his thick Scottish brogue, "It's Saturday, lad. Surely you don't have to be on the telly this morning?"

T.J. looked at the teddy bear-ish man entwined in the sheets and smiled. "It's my last day in London. I want to take advantage of it."

"As you should, by all means. So why don't you let me take you to lunch?"

"I wanted to hit the British Museum and the National Portrait Gallery. Do you know someplace near there?"

"I am suggesting something that isn't in your Yankee Guide Book. I'm taking the eleven a.m. train to Buckinghamshire. A gathering of authors at Lee Radziwill's old estate. I'll make sure you're safely back by sunset."

"What if I'm not well read enough to keep up my end of the conversation with a room full of esteemed writers?"

Lasciviously looking him up and down, Rodney responded, "Dear boy, keeping up your end is all you need to do."

T.J. had just enough time to grab a cab back to the Cumberland for a quick shower and change of clothes before meeting Rodney's car at Marble Arch. He had no idea what could be in store for him on this last day in London, but the chauffeur-driven Mercedes was certainly a step up from bumping across 42nd Street on the M104 bus. As they drove the hour out of the city into the lush English countryside, Rodney explained that they could, in addition to some of the authors he represented, expect to meet local Members of Parliament, a few lords and ladies and other local gentry. Having witnessed T.J.'s penchant for celebrity jargon, he also threw in that he "wouldn't be a bit surprised if Jackie Collins or Princess Margaret turned up." Rodney had cleaned up well and looked dapper again in a blue blazer and a perfectly tied silk ascot with a tiny pearl pin.

The car turned onto a long, tree-lined road, which T.J. realized was a private entry to the massive estate. A huge house was set on the sprawling grounds. It looked every inch the quintessential English countryside manse, right out of a Merchant-Ivory film like A Room with A View or Maurice. As they proceeded toward the main residence, they passed by smaller, storybook-looking cottages and a stable with horses roaming in the adjacent paddock and fields. He could see a quaint gazebo set out near a large greenhouse and a grove (or was it an orchard?) of apple trees. He knew Rodney could tell he was awed by what he was seeing and T.J. admitted, "And I thought where I grew up was nice!"

Several other cars were already parked in the circular drive at the front of the house—a Citroen, a Ferrari, a Porsche and some other models T.J. didn't recognize. As the Mercedes ground to a halt on the gravel, he noticed a lavish sculpture garden off to the side of the house, with very tall pieces of iron art dotting the landscape.

T.J., for all the attention lavished on him during the week, was feeling like a fish out of water. No Connecticut country club could have prepared him for this. He followed a step behind Rodney, deferring to his obvious ease in this environment. It was a role Rodney relished and coveted: the older, experienced man taking a paternal, dominant position with the younger, impressionable "boy."

When they entered, it was like stepping into a palace albeit one that was in need of refreshing. The massive, ornate interior harkened to a grander time but still served to dazzle visitors. Soaring ceilings, massive paintings, huge chandeliers and a grand staircase leading up to the five bedrooms surrounded them as a uniformed butler ushered them in.

"Good afternoon, gentlemen," he said with a deep bow. "Allow me to show you to the dining hall where the other guests are gathered."

T.J. continued to stay a step behind Rodney as they obliged the waiter who also looked like he, too, belonged in a Merchant-Ivory film.

Taking in the incredible furnishings that included giant vases and urns, a grand piano and sumptuous sofas and rugs, T.J.'s jaw dropped when he noticed an actual suit of armor standing in a corner. Was there a sliding panel behind the bookcase? They soon found themselves in a dark, castle-like room with a long table around which sat a dozen or more guests. An enormous, unused fireplace dominated one entire wall of the room and had lighted candles in its hearth instead of burning wood. T.J. had an immediate image of the cast of Camelot singing The Lusty Month of May.

"Rodney!" everyone cheerily greeted him. Their voices echoed in unison throughout the massive chambers.

As Rodney went around hugging and shaking hands, T.J. respectfully stood back, taking in their faces. These were not physically beautiful people like those he'd encountered in Los Angeles, but they were strangely more impressive because of their exaggerated characters. They reminded him of the famous engraving illustrations from Charles Dickens' A Christmas Carol. Some tall, some short . . . plump or rail-thin. Two of the men had shoulder length hair while others were bald. There was a woman who was dressed like a man and another person whose gender was impossible to decipher.

"Rodney, who is your young companion today?" one asked loudly, upon spotting T.J.

"Friends, may I introduce you to my new American friend, T.J.? Although I don't know what that stands for!"

"Terribly Juvenile?" suggested someone, generating laughter.

"I know him!" squealed a middle aged lady with a red, page boy haircut, a large, powdered décolletage and some kind of Eastern European accent. "The American Step-Brother!" She wasted no time trotting over to T.J. and taking him by the arm. "You must come and sit next to me."

All at once everyone seemed to freeze in place and become silent as their hostess jettisoned herself into the Hall with all the fanfare of Dolly Levi or the Unsinkable Molly Brown, no orchestra required. She was a petite woman whose age was a mystery because she was buried under so much makeup and half-hidden beneath a silver wig that spilled synthetic curls down over her shoulders. She wore a diaphanous caftan dress accessorized with strands of pearls around her neck and wrists.

"Bienvenue! Bienvenue! Is everyone here and accounted for?" She warbled like a bird.

T.J. was eventually introduced to Lady Hollis, who commanded the luncheon from her perch at the table's head. He learned that she was the widow of a titled lord and had written several successful soft-core romance novels for Rodney's publishing house, back in the 1970s. Several rounds of some lethal cocktails in tiny pony glasses were passed to the assembled guests but, after a sip, T.J. merely pretended to drink his. Not only did he dislike the taste, he was still trying to shake off the fuzziness of the night before. With this assembled cast of characters, he also thought he needed to stay sharp.

It was at least an hour before any food appeared, since the unfortunate old butler was the only person serving. As hungry as he was, it looked like T.J. would continue to fake his way through the dining experience as none of the offerings appealed to him in the least. Cold Pea and Basil Soup was followed by Goose Confit Salad and Pork Pie. The others ate like condemned prisoners having a last meal (with sloppy table manners to match, he noted).

At some point between bites of food, the genderless person pulled out a small case from their breast pocket. T.J. was hoping it would be a cigarette . . . he had been abstaining the entire trip.

To his disappointment, it was filled with marijuana joints and the scent of cannabis soon wafted over the table.

Then Lady Hollis produced a small porcelain container which resembled a music box, but inside was a big mound of cocaine. T.J. saw her move her gnarled hand to her place setting where, at the farthest position on the right side, was a minuscule sterling silver spoon. She used it to scoop a tiny amount of the white powder, which she then lifted to sniff into her nostril. He looked down at his own place setting and, sure enough, he had the same spoon, too.

As everyone proceeded to get drunk as well as stoned or high, T.J. excused himself to go to the bathroom. He looked at himself in the mirror of the powder room and wondered how he'd ended up there when all he really wanted to do was go to the British Museum and National Portrait Gallery and their gift shops to purchase some souvenirs. If he could just manage to hang in for a couple more hours, he would be on his way back to the Cumberland Hotel to pack for the flight home. Maybe he could call down for fresh towels and the cute Italian housekeeper would deliver them along with a jolly good send off.

T.J. wasn't prepared for what was waiting for him when he returned to the Dining Hall. In the few minutes he had stepped away to use the lavatory, people had begun disrobing and one couple was even reclining across their corner of the table, tongues pressing into each other's mouths as the remnants of lunch were pushed to the side.

Lady Hollis' caftan was down over her wrinkled shoulders and the long strands of pearls around her neck were the only thing covering her sagging breasts. She was hungrily scooping more cocaine onto her spoon and furiously licking her lips and teeth.

In a drug-induced altered state of his own, his ascot askew, Rodney held out a hand to T.J. "Come sit down with me, my yummy Yankee."

The woman with the page boy fixed her eyes on T.J. and struggled to get out of her seat to approach him. "No, I want the American Step-Brother!"

T.J. couldn't find any words, probably for the first time in his life. This looked like a case of "fight or flight," so he made a half-hearted "excuse me" gesture and hurriedly backed out of the room. He heard Rodney call out his name as he left the room.

Even though it was still early in the afternoon, the mansion was a dark and foreboding place and T.J. moved quickly down one of the large corridors in search of some light and fresh air. Every room he passed looked more and more like a haunted house now that he knew what was going on in the Dining Hall.

Again, he heard Rodney call out his name, so T.J. stepped up his pace and nearly jogged along the halls until he found a set of French doors that led out to a veranda along the western side of the ground floor.

He gulped the air as if he'd been drowning, so relieved to be out of there. Not knowing where he should go or how to handle this predicament he'd walked right into, he tried to imagine, "What would Leo do?" For that matter, what would Jackie Collins or Princess Margaret do?

Wandering the length of the open-air porch, he came to the sculpture garden and kept on walking. As he trod through the soft earth, Rodney managed to catch up with him, out of breath.

"T.J., don't embarrass me. Come back inside."

All he could think to say was, "I'm sorry Rodney. This scene isn't really for me."

"Why are Americans so uptight? You're all a bunch of bloody Pilgrims."

With a chuckle, T.J. said, "I am the last person you could call a prude."

"Then stop acting like one."

Even stranded in some snob's sculpture garden in the middle the countryside of a foreign country, T.J. would not tolerate anyone talking down to him. He'd found a way out of Chianciano and he could find a way out of there. I'll show you what a Pilgrim I am, he thought.

"I'm going back to my hotel. If your car won't take me, he can drop me at a train station."

"Take it," Rodney said, disgusted with him. "I'll stay the weekend. If you hurry, you can make it to a Museum before closing time."

Rodney turned and began walking back toward the house.

Once finally on the highway back into London's central business district, T.J. noticed a sign for the turnoff route to Heathrow Airport and he could hardly wait for the next morning when he would be there for his flight home. In these years of chasing after "the One," he was starting to think it was a fruitless pursuit.

Maybe it was Manhattan that was the love of his life.

CHAPTER FOURTEEN
Countdown to New Year

The Museum Cafe was a lovely spot for lunch on a June weekday. With kids out of school and city folks starting to evacuate for their summer holiday, the only patrons were locals and assorted tourists and retirees who were between tours of the Museum of Natural History, across the street. Leo was, of course, busy at work but T.J. was able to meet Carolyn Lee and Bella (who only agreed to join if Jaclyn was occupied elsewhere with the nanny) and catch them up on all the stories from his trip to London.

"It all sounds very promising to me," Carolyn Lee noted, sipping her Prosecco, which had become her midday custom. "Even without training Princess Di. I bet she'll ask for you the next time you go back."

A waiter brought Bella the glass of white wine she had ordered. "I'm back to Moderation as a way of life," she told them. "Don't judge."

Unusually, it was T.J. who was sticking to coffee, only. He had a phone call scheduled with Elaine for later that afternoon and wanted to be clear headed.

"Enough about me," he said, prompting Carolyn Lee. "While Therese has Jaclyn at the playground, let's hear about what's going on at home with Gary."

"Yeah, what's his latest problem?" Bella asked.

"He's still breathing," Carolyn Lee snapped back. They laughed at her developing acerbic wit.

"With the primary coming up in September," she continued, "he hasn't been home much and when he is, he usually goes right to bed. As long as he knows I'm somewhere in the house, he pretty much leaves me alone."

"Control freak," T.J. muttered.

"How's it looking for Mayor Koch? After twelve years, can he hold on?"

"I think it's going to be a tight race with David Dinkins. Neck and neck."

"You think New York City is ready for a black mayor?"

"Frankly, I think it's overdue," Carolyn Lee observed. "Things are changing everywhere."

"And then what is Gary going to do with himself? Follow Koch?"

"He'll probably go into private practice. Maybe even run for office, himself." Lowering her voice so as not to be overheard, even though there were no other people near enough to hear, she added, "But I'm planning to leave him after the election in November."

"I'll drink to that!" Bella said, perking up.

"That's an excellent plan," T.J. agreed.

He checked his watch and realized he needed to head home for his scheduled call with Elaine. Maybe Carolyn Lee was right and the familiar routine of their lives was ready for change.

T.J. made it home a few minutes late for the designated 2:30 p.m. call time, due to a traffic jam on the FDR Drive because of the day game the Mets were playing at Shea Stadium. His answering machine showed no missed calls, so he wasn't worried. By the time he brushed his teeth to wash away the taste of his Tandoori Chicken Salad lunch, it was closing in on three o'clock when Elaine rang. She apologized for her tardiness but had been out on a news assignment.

"Our EP finally got back to me with a verdict about our using you on the show."

"Is this another Good News/Bad News scenario?" T.J. asked, sort of teasing.

"That depends on how you look at it."

Uh oh, he thought.

She continued, "After the first of the year, we're expanding to add an extra hour to the show every day so, consequently, we'll need to add a lot of new content. We'll debut a new set, a new theme song. It'll be a big splash."

"That sounds like good news to me. So what's the bad?"

"The executive producer would love to add you to our ensemble of Presenters starting in mid-January. Twice a week, Tuesdays and Thursdays—live, funny fitness segments. Live, via Sattelite"

His heart began to beat faster and he said, "Again, good news."

"I pushed for a daily spot, but he and the Line Producer only agreed to twice a week for starters. I'm confident you can prove yourself and they'll bump you up."

"I'm waiting for a but, Elaine."

"You've witnessed how important celebrity stuff is to them. They keep assuming you're in Los Angeles and I have to remind them you're in New York."

"What's the difference where I am? I'm the American Step-Brother."

"They have the Hollywood thing in their heads now. They want palm trees and beaches in the background—"

"We'll get a green screen!"

"We can also book celebrities to come work out with you, so it wouldn't just be exercise tips. You'd start doing interviews, as well. I'm thinking that will evolve into red carpets, press junkets, that sort of thing."

It was an incredible opportunity, T.J. realized. He had been expecting something great to come out of his London adventure, but never dreamed he would have to relocate. Scrambling to offer options for her to consider, he suggested, "What if we start out here in New York and see what happens if it takes off?"

She paused a moment before she laid it out for him. "I'm afraid it has to be Los Angeles or nothing. They told me to find someone else for the job if you don't want it."

Now he took a pause and she added with an encouraging tone, "It wouldn't start until after the first of the year, so you'd have plenty of time to make the necessary arrangements."

What the hell, he thought. He hadn't hesitated to go to Italy or London for a work assignment. He took a deep breath and told her, "Hollywood, here I come."

***

This was the first summer of his life that T.J. wasn't interested in celebrating his birthday. He was too preoccupied with the bottomless To-Do List for moving all the way across the country for God knows how long. And the equally daunting prospect of leaving behind the friends and family who meant everything to him. Could he be "alone, but not lonely?"

He wasn't sure if he was relieved or disappointed that his parents didn't fight him at all when he informed them of his decision. He expected their ultimate support, of course, but assumed they would push a little harder to keep him physically closer to them. As a birthday gift, they offered to give him Janice's three-year-old Ford Taurus to use in LA, where no one can manage without an automobile. She wanted a new car anyway and T.J. could opt to either have it shipped to the West Coast or make a road trip.

When he broke the news to Leo over a long dinner at Ivory Chopsticks for just the two of them, his best friend suggested they make one more adventure together. Leo would take a few vacation days and they'd pack up the Taurus and do the whole Route 66 trek across country. After reaching L.A. and having a couple of days' rest, Leo would fly back to New York. As usual, he made it sound fun: they would take turns driving and flirt their way through each new state they entered. "Cruising while cruising." He wagered the corn-fed hunks in the midwestern states would be a refreshing change of pace from their usual fare of city slickers.

Because they got to their Chinese haunt before the end of Happy Hour, they were entitled to the "All You Can Drink Wine" offer. They downed two large carafes and left the Chow Mein and egg rolls largely untouched. By the time they'd swallowed the last drop, Leo's optimistic outlook about their separation significantly dimmed.

"Pally," he told T.J., "I don't want you to go."

Emotions heightened with all the cheap wine, T.J. felt almost as if he could cry. It was like being back in Saperstein's acting class and working himself up before launching into a dramatic monologue.

"We're always going to be best friends. My moving to California won't change that. You and Don will have a great place to visit. Especially during the winters."

"Don't say 'winters,' plural. You don't have to stay that long. Maybe a year will be enough."

"Maybe. It will depend on what happens with my career. Leo, that's what I've been chasing ever since I met you at The Gap, all those years ago."

"I know. And you deserve that."

"Well, chasing a career and the Love of My Life, whoever that is."

"You deserve that, too. I'm just selfish, I guess. I'm going to miss you."

The diminutive Chinese server came over to the obviously upset young men and brought them a fresh carafe of the ghastly white wine, also offering a sympathetic expression of concern. She assumed they were a gay couple having some kind of boyfriend crisis. People had often mistaken them for boyfriends, which never ceased to baffle them when they felt like blood brothers.

Leo took the carafe from her, tears in his eyes, and said, "Thank you" before breaking into a happy/sad laugh.

"You know what I'll miss?" T.J. asked, holding out his glass for a refill. "Channel J and the Robin Byrd Show!"

In unison, they quoted one of their favorite tawdry lines from her raunchy collection of pornography advertisers, "Lance her with your spam javelin!"

***

T.J. and Marti were enjoying her spread of homemade chicken salad sandwiches and kosher dill pickles, along with a pitcher of iced tea. Madison was curled up under the table, at T.J.'s feet while Fido the cat was hiding in plain sight, perched on a high shelf alongside Marti's Emmy Award.

"It sounds like you're getting everything organized. Are you still planning to work with Judy Gillette's commercial agent?" she asked.

"If he'll take me on," T.J. answered between bites. "I'll reach out to him once I'm settled."

"And where will you be living?"

"Someplace called Hancock Park, which is supposedly halfway between downtown L.A. and Beverly Hills. One of my dad's partners has a son with an apartment there and he's looking to sublet it for a couple months. That will give me time to find my own place."

"I remember Hancock Park. It's near Paramount Studios. I think Mae West had an apartment nearby for many years. They say she haunts it now."

"I'll be sure to look for her."

She pushed the pickles at him, encouraging him to take one. "Cheer up, Presh. This isn't the end. It's the beginning! Probably the start of something pretty wonderful."

He didn't want a pickle and, as delicious as it was, he didn't want the rest of his sandwich, either. Instead, he reached for a cigarette from the porcelain cup Marti kept on the table beside a matching lighter.

"I'd better smoke while I can. Nobody lights up in LA unless they're on a diet."

"You're going to teach your classes and get to be on TV twice a week. It's going to be great. No more subways or taxis. Anytime you want to go for a hike in the canyons or a swim at the beach, you can just jump in your car. Year round!"

"I like subways and taxis. I feel like I'll be cheating on New York."

She reached over to touch his arm. "New York isn't going anywhere, T.J. Any time you want to come back, it will always be here, waiting for you." Squeezing his arm affectionately, she added, "And so will we."

***

Time accelerated as summer turned into fall and T.J. began to pack up, sell off or give away the contents of his apartment in between his class schedule and getting new headshots for Hollywood. Everywhere he went in Manhattan filled him with sentimentality, as he harkened back to his times with Andy, Luke and many of the others whose names he couldn't remember. Acting and dance studios, theaters, nightclubs, parks and restaurants were like set pieces for all the characters who had been in and out of his life since the day he drove his U-Haul into the city.

One drizzly late afternoon, he even went out of his way to walk past the playground where he'd met the circus performer for his initial gay encounter. T.J. wondered if he had survived the AIDS crisis. Was Ross' toupee still stuck to his head? Would he ever be able to hear a John Lennon song without thinking of the night the singer died and he'd been flying in the little private plane over the Hudson River? As the drizzle turned to a rain shower he remembered the homeless lady in Central Park from the first visit to Marti's apartment. Was she still safely tucked under her canopy of umbrellas? It was as if there were ghosts on every corner.

He knew there would be many new memories to make once he was living in Los Angeles, but he wished now that he'd paid more attention to life in New York. If only he had kept a journal. There was no way he would be able to remember everything. Every man, every party, every Aunt Jennie screwdriver.

Ed Koch lost to David Dinkins in his mayoral reelection bid and T.J. checked in immediately with Carolyn Lee to see how the tidal shift in city politics would affect her household. When he phoned her the morning after the election, he wasn't prepared for her news: she was pregnant again. Without any test tubes or hormones, a loveless act of intercourse was going to give little Jaclyn a baby brother or sister.

T.J. nervously asked if she intended to go through with the pregnancy.

"Of course I am!" she told him. He couldn't tell if she was feigning indignation at the suggestion.

"And what about Gary? Do you still plan to move out?"

"T.J., I can't do that now. With a second child and no job."

"You don't need his money."

It was clear she didn't want to have to defend herself and she turned on her most authoritative "anchorwoman voice" to inform him, "I moved back into the bedroom, so we'll see what happens. He seems very excited and is hoping for a boy this time."

"You're kidding yourself if you think he's going to change just because you're having another baby."

"Not working for the mayor will be the change he needs," she countered, trying to convince herself more than T.J. "He can finally be his own man."

He was happy to drop the subject. He'd been hearing nothing but unhappy stories about Gary as long as he'd known her and was fed up with trying to talk sense into her. In a way, marriage was for Carolyn Lee what drugs and alcohol were to Bella. Just a different form of self destruction for which there was no Rehab.

So what was his addiction? Promiscuity disguising as a hopeless pursuit of true love? He'd even once considered pursuing a threesome with a gay couple he'd met at NYSC in case one of them could fall in love with him. Leo had said, "I'd recommend against a Three Way. Someone always gets left out."

Since their weepy meal at Ivory Chopsticks, he and Leo had barely seen each other. His friend had used the excuse of his new hedge fund position as taking up all his time, but they both knew it was the discomfort of their impending separation that was the true reason. T.J. tried not to worry about it too much. He knew they would have the whole road trip to California to work things out before the "new normal."

Even Bella wasn't around. With the approach of her milestone thirtieth birthday, she and her family decided another "retreat" was in order and this time, instead of Hazelden, she tried out a new facility in upstate New York. Her in-and-out status at NYSC had finally meant the end of her job there and she was now surviving on unemployment insurance benefits and an allowance from her father.

T.J. would spend Christmas week with his parents and was prepared for all the emotional goodbyes, although Janice was already planning a "Spring Fling" visit to California to check out his new digs, and then follow it up with a Palm Springs excursion. He'd then drive the Taurus back into the City on the 31st and he had paid a prorated week's rent for January, so he could remain in his apartment until heading to L.A. with Leo on the third day of 1990.

It was with a mixed sense of excitement and apprehension that he approached their traditional New Year's Eve dinner at Windows on the World, wondering if it would be the last time they gathered as a foursome.

EPILOGUE
Fireworks Explosion

"Change will be good for all of us," Carolyn Lee suddenly sang out, offering up her club soda in a toast. "But thank God for all the blessings of the Eighties."

"Or we wouldn't all be sitting here right now," Leo added.

"Holy fuck, how did we survive?" asked Bella without irony.

T.J. knew the answer. "It's like my dad always tells me—we have been dancing between the raindrops."

"Are you really changing your name to Thomas?" Carolyn Lee asked.

"I'm not changing it. That's my name. I'm just going to start using it. A new chapter."

"I like it," Bella declared.

Leo warned, "Don't get too cocky, Mr. Television Star."

"That goes double for you, Mr. Moneybags."

The waiter brought their check and, as everyone fished for their wallets to chip in, T.J. waved them away and handed over his credit card.

"Tonight is on me, friends."

"Don't be stupid," Leo told him as Carolyn Lee said, "T.J., no. I mean—Thomas—no!"

Bella added, "You did demolish an entire lobster. I'm okay with it."

Her caustic humor always made him smile. He couldn't imagine finding friends like this again.

"You girls save your money. Leo can make it up to me on the road."

"Everyone says the chicken fried steak in Texas is out of this world," Leo stated.

Carolyn Lee chimed in, "I hear the red chili pork burritos in Albuquerque are a guilty pleasure. Especially with an over-easy egg on top."

The mere mention of that dish made T.J.'s stomach flip and his lobster dinner, on top of all the screwdrivers and wine, flopped.

"On that note," he began to change the subject, ". . . are we continuing on?"

"The old gal is going to turn into a pumpkin early tonight," Carolyn Lee told him.

"Same for this not-as-old gal," Bella added.

"Pally?" T.J. asked Leo.

"I'm going to head home to watch the ball drop with Don. But I'll see you bright and early Wednesday morning to hit the road."

He saw the women starting to well up with tears at the thought of saying goodbye. Bella's lower lip was quivering. Reacting quickly, T.J. stood up, giving Leo a pat on the shoulder as he did.

"Let me be the one to make the Irish Exit tonight," T.J. told them. "Let's just say 'See you later,' like we always do."

He gave Bella and Carolyn Lee kisses on their cheeks, telling them, "I'll call you tomorrow." He added, "Just like I always do."

The waiter returned, having run his credit card. T.J. hurriedly added a tip, signed it and then stepped quickly away, without looking back at them. His stomach still felt sour and he assumed the emotion of the moment added to his queasiness.

Just before he reached the edge of the dining room, where the elevator bank would carry him down one hundred seven stories to the lobby, he chastised himself for his cowardice. He turned and looked back at the trio he'd left at the table, realizing he had been their common denominator, and that it was unlikely they would be getting together without him. It could truly be his last look.

With his most booming aerobic-enthused baritone voice, he bellowed over the hum of the crowded room, "I love you people!"

They looked over to see him and waved, everyone smiling.

T.J. lingered only long enough to wave back, then turned and entered the first elevator that opened, along with three inebriated young women wearing Happy New Year buttons and 1990 hats. A recording of Guy Lombardo's Auld Lang Syne was playing on a repeating loop inside the car.

The door slid closed and he pressed Main Floor. As they descended, his stomach started making audible sounds. That was followed by cramping. His fellow passengers giggled at first but as the color drained from T.J.'s face and his body began to emit more than mere sound, they recoiled into the corner, horrified.

But no more horrified than T.J. He may have always managed to "dance between the raindrops," but on this final night of the 1980s, he was about to get soaked.

****

To Be Continued.

Coming Soon:

Dancing Between the Raindrops:

The L.A. Years

AUTHOR'S NOTE

Most of the events recounted in these pages are true, although conveniently condensed, consolidated or rearranged for story-telling purposes. The characters, too, are largely true to life although names have been changed (to protect the innocent as well as the not-so innocent) and multiple folks combined for clarity. I actually had to omit a lot of the crazier incidents if only because you would never believe I survived them. I still can't believe it myself.

What I have tried to do is capture the essence of a decade in New York as I experienced it. It was a time and place when I was young and adventurous, surrounded by treasured friends and parents who supported and adored me. Mother and Dad may be gone now, but most of those friends are still with me and my "chosen family" has made this continue to be a wonderful, exciting life. This book is only Part One. Wait until you hear about the 1990s in Hollywood!

Nelson Aspen

ACKNOWLEDGMENTS

I owe a debt of gratitude to my editor, Charlene Keel, and publisher, Myron Hyman, for their interest and enthusiasm for another book from me.

As always, my husband Jonny offered me unwavering support, objectivity and patience throughout the writing process. Working in our magnificent Harlem home office was a beautiful experience.

To all the loyal, longtime friends, especially those amalgamated into the characters in these pages, thank you for always standing by me and making the decades since I first came to New York so fun, fulfilling and meaningful. I am rich in friends, as you have probably gathered if you've managed to read this far. Thank you Glenn and Marcia. Thank you, Marie, for the two most important words of advice as I set out to write: "Full Disclosure."

Cover portrait of Nelson painted by MacDonald Eaton (1929-2013) in 1988. Nelson was a young actor working on the daytime serial "One Life to Live," where Eaton was Production Designer. Eaton was a distinguished painter and professor whose stage and set designs were featured on iconic programs like "The Ed Sullivan Show" and "American Bandstand," now archived at the New York Public Library in addition to his writings on metaphysics and politics.

Thank you, New York City.

Printed in Great Britain
by Amazon

46705905R00208